Magic Artinia

Cover art by Anthony Grigorovitch, 2011

Magic Artinia © 2011 Alesya Grigorovitch

ISBN: 978-0-9837647-0-0

theinvisibleforest.com

Contents

Chapter 01: A Distanceless Distance

Have you ever been fascinated by the idea of a parallel world existing somewhere out there in the great universe? A world with life as animated and complex as the life on our own humble planet? When you realize that it is nowhere near the scope of your mind's power to accurately visualize the entire universe, so vast and varied is it, and that if you tried to imagine the area occupied by our planet in relation to the rest of the universe, the space you allot our feeble race would be so grossly disproportionate that, were your vision true, we may as well get up and play croquet with the planets and the sun, you just begin to comprehend the unfathomable distances there are, far beyond our solar system, our galaxy, even the hundred closest galaxies to our own, and a vast amount of room is suddenly available for that enticing possibility. When you understand that there are tangible places in this universe so far away from our little corner that the distance between them and us is best understood by our minds as infinite, a dim light shines awareness on the fact that there *is* space for all of the wild imaginings you've construed in your lifetime to exist.

From childhood, we instinctively long to believe in those alternate worlds we spend hours a day dreaming up to entertain our imagination; we give everything we wish had happened here on Earth a distant home. We don't know where it exists – not here, surely – but somewhere. Somewhere out there in the wide space available to existence, but to us on Earth accessible only through our thoughts.

In that space we hide our heaven, and a million light years from there lies our hell. We find a lonely place for every one of our worlds, a million little corners for each of our planets to sit in isolation and believe that it alone is living. And we all spend some portion of our lives wishing that instead of just thinking about our fantasy worlds, we should be part of them, leave this world behind and escape into one of our paradises, whether it be a jungle-like wilderness inhabited by fantastic beasts and high-adventure death-traps, a feudal world of labyrinthine castles and exotic customs, kings, wizards, villains, and mystical creatures, moved not by money but by magic, or a futuristic society that has realized our craziest technological schemes to overcome the limitations of physics.

Dream all you want, believe in whatever worlds you want to, because for the duration of your life you're stuck on this one lonesome planet with this one hard reality you see before your eyes. Your worlds may be real, there is certainly space for them to exist, but for the amount of distance between here and there that you can bridge in your lifetime, you may as well face the fact that the closest you're ever going to get to your little escape is in your mind; and if you devote your time on Earth to *that*, to daydreaming and wishing for a different life, a different world, a great adventure where you can play hero, well then not only will you be no closer to actually doing that, but you will fail at the life you have here, and maybe even enter a mental facility.

How far away these possibilities are no one can truly know, and it is irrelevant to try and measure. Only two things are certain. First: all hope of wormholes aside, the distance for us to reach them and them us is unbridgeable, even in our minds. And second: there is so much space out there that, despite our best technology, eludes us, that we can't say for certain what does and doesn't exist. In reality, we don't know if those fantasy worlds exist, and therefore, there is a chance that they do. And if we know that the worlds of our wildest fantasies might be real, then we inevitably come to the question, what about a world that's just like ours? Not of perfection, not with magic, not with any desirable changes, but with people like us, who think like we do, react like we do, make mistakes in the hard reality they face and spend their time dreaming of a better place. A world whose society has started out and gone on to develop in like fashion with ours; whose society has, after so many constant trials, followed just our course and miraculously come to the very same ends that we have currently come to here. Somewhere a part of you yearns to know that such a world exists. You crave to affirm that a parallel world is real so that, in a way, you can affirm that all of this here is real, too. That way you can say, "See? Somewhere else, without our influence, the same exact thing has sprung up! This really is how all of history was supposed to happen."

But, again, you will never see it. All you are left to do is meander about in your endless doubt and discover without affirmation and assurance what "real" is here.

Nonetheless –

2

There is in fact such a world out there, much like our own, only it is so far away that it would take millions of light years just to say how many millions of light years away it is. It is best not to try and think about how far away that is. Just, take my word for it. It exists, somewhere, and they're out there wondering about us as well.

By the way, I titled this "Chapter 1" because I knew that if I called it "Introduction," you would deem it inconsequential to the story and in your impatience skip over it. It's okay, I do the same thing, especially when I set out to read a book where some critic has written a twenty-page "Introduction" before the actual story so that they can see "with an introduction by (insert name here)" on the book's cover, or when the seventh edition of a book comes out and its author, if still alive, feels the need to reminisce about how much time has passed since he wrote the original, and writes a twenty-page "Introduction" about the life wisdom he has accumulated since then.

This is not, however, the first chapter; it is the "Introduction".

Chapter 02: Artinia

Like I said, way out there in the universe exists a world very similar to ours. It's about the same size as the Earth, covered with vegetation, huge oceans, and people, and is part of its own solar system comprised of itself and four other planets. Its sun is slightly smaller than our own, and the planet is therefore in closer proximity to it so that the temperature on its surface may remain ideal for sustaining life.

Their sun is only about a billion years away from becoming a red giant, but that's okay because, like on our planet, the apocalypse will happen first.

As for the society on this planet, its fundamental aspects are not so different from our own, either. They have T.V.s, and computers, and video games, and shopping malls, alcohol, burgers, guns, jet planes, minivans, the internet, brothels, tabloid magazines and politicians, sweat pants, religion, vacuum cleaners, townhouses, colored pencils, highways, and all of that.

Only there are a few key differences.

First, every person on that planet possesses a superpower, but it is only to our feeble earth-bound minds that it is a superpower. To them there is nothing that super about it, and it is called a token. Everyone is born with a token and retains it throughout life. It cannot be changed, lost, a person cannot have two tokens or even more; it is as much a part of one's make-up as eye color, but it does not pertain to any genetic factor.

The presence of the token is but a humdrum fact that elicits no feelings of awe or shock, a familiar part of the collective of impressions forming the backdrop mosaic of gray against which these people's monotonous days are set, much like homeless drug addicts in American cities.

A token can be anything – any ability that inexplicably defies the standards of science and provides for its bearer a way of experiencing the world unique from anyone else. Thus, there is no "normal" mode of experience. All people are born into a state as prevents them from viewing the world objectively, apart from their token.

No one knows how many different tokens there are, or if there is a limit – some are quite common, and you will meet hundreds of people in your lifetime with such a token. Conversely, there are those rare ones which you will only encounter once in your life. And then, there are those very special few that are so spectacularly out there, the kind of shocking manifestation that appears maybe once in two decades, they render you senseless and leave you to spend days wondering how nature could be so cruel, generous, and funny all at once.

Bottom line: everyone has one, whatever it may be.

A second major difference is that on this planet, diseases plague not the body, but primarily the mind. Just like on Earth, one must get diagnosed and receive the proper treatment, but rather than interfering with the physical processes, the pills, patches, and syrups doled out in excess affect the mental ones.

Physical diseases do exist, but are often seen as an unnerving anomaly; although in recent times they have admittedly become more prevalent....

The third noteworthy difference is that there is only one religion on this planet. All peoples and nations abide by the same sacred text. However, this religion is divided into many sects that are in opposition to each other.

Some countries abide by one sect, while other countries follow another; some countries allow all sects; and some have a majority of one sect with minorities of other sects.

One final curious detail must not escape our analysis: while we may never in any way shape or form have contact with this planet, because the people there have all of the capabilities of thought that we do, an interesting phenomenon sometimes occurs that neither side is aware of. And that is the transfer of thoughts between our worlds, as if there exists a mental wormhole between our planets that transcends space and time. For instance, if a certain idea occurs to an earthling and then happens to be utterly thrown out of its head, it can be "caught," so to speak, by someone on that planet. This transfer of thought is the one thin link between our parallel worlds, and even so, very few thoughts make it to that level. It is by sheer luck, in fact, that this link exists at all; for if our races were not of the same exact make and sophistication, such a transfer would be impossible.

As said, other than the few enumerated discrepancies, this world is really very similar to ours. And though they are infinitely and forever divided from us, their lives and their experiences, as you will see, are not all that different from our own....

***

"...Our top story this morning: five prostitutes were found dead last night outside a downtown convenience store on Wickery Drive. I'm Candace Avery."

"And I'm Paul Fort."

"Welcome to today's edition of Morning Artinia." The characteristic tune hummed through the kitchen.

"Oh, Milly, turn that trash off."

"It's not trash, mom, it's the news."

"The news?" Mrs. Hallan said, her back to the television. "I heard 'dead prostitutes'; I thought it was that new show."

"The O.D.?"

"I don't know, Milly, I don't keep up," Mrs. Hallan returned absently, her focus on slicing potatoes. Milly turned her attention back to the T.V.

"...found at two thirty in the morning with a gun."

"Not only that, Paul, but the one shot through the stomach was still bleeding when they arrived. Police say the shooter had to be no more than twenty miles away...."

"I want you to put a jacket on before you go," Milly's mother suddenly snapped back as she placed a large omelet on the kitchen table.

"But I'm wearing long sleeves!" the girl stood up and threw her arms out for emphasis.

Mrs. Hallan took one look at her skirt. "Who's letting you go out like that?!"

"What's wrong with it?"

"What's *wrong* with it? Not a thing, it would make a perfectly good headband! You look just like those dead girls on T.V.!" she gestured to where Candace and Paul were still babbling. "If your father hadn't left for work already, oh ho, he'd have something to say about – *this*!" she looked at Milly's exposed thighs in disgust.

John came downstairs, straightening his tie, just in time to glance at the television and catch Candace Avery and Paul Fort shaking their heads, muttering, "Mmh... tragedy, tragedy.... Anyway, here's Keith with the weather."

"Hey, Paul, hey, Candace, beautiful morning, sixty-five degrees right now, it's supposed to get up to seventy-three with some partial cloud cover. No rain today!" Paul, Candace, and Keith all chuckled.

"Thanks, Keith, we've had enough of that all weekend. Good to start a fresh week on a high note...."

"...You are *not* leaving the house like that unless those are flesh-colored leggings!" Mrs. Hallan now turned to her son, who had been ignoring their dispute. "John, tell your sister she looks ridiculous," she implored.

"Milly, that skirt is slutty," said John without looking up from buttering his toast.

Milly's face became a small explosion of anger. "It's no different from what everyone else is wearing! What is your problem? Why can't you just – !?"

"Why can't you just be normal!?" John mimicked in a high pitched voice.

"I can't believe you I always stick up for you and you never stick up for me –!"

"Yip yip yip yip yip yip yip – !"

"Five minutes! Go change!" Mrs. Hallan cut across. Milly trampled upstairs, her round face pouting.

"At least I'm not still living with my parents after college!" she yelled from the stairs.

"Milly!" her mother exclaimed. "John, you know you can stay here as long as you like," Mrs. Hallan immediately turned to console her son, who was pouring coffee into his thermos.

"Mom, it's only temporary. As soon as I find a place I'm moving out," John said.

"Take as long as you need, we don't mind, we're your parents," she insisted.

John cast a last glance at the T.V., in time to catch sight of a very familiar face. The young man's head bore a wide smile drawing all attention to its set of shining white teeth and took up the entire screen, the top of the slightly unruly, chocolate brown hair scraping the edge and the deep teal eyes looking dead center. At the bottom across the muscular neck "Borneo Grimgae" blared in blue letters.

"That boy again?" John's mother remarked. "He's been all over the news. What did he do this time?"

"Survive another near-death episode."

"A-*what*?! What happened?" John's mother gasped, instantly hooked by this piece of gossip. "Is he okay?"

"Yes, he's – it's on the news! Right now!" John gestured to the television.

"Oh, poor boy!" Mrs. Hallan glanced over and back at John. "Invite him over for dinner tonight. Tell him your mother wants to see him alive!" she called as John wrenched himself away from her and ran down the front steps.

If there was one thing John liked about a big city like Vandorn it was the many distractions it offered. One could never remain focused too long, and John's annoyance passed like the fleeting nymph it was, absorbed by the noises (very loud, and very many of them, all discordant), and the smells (gasoline and cigarette smoke), and the thick covering of gray clouds (of cigarette smoke). Every morning, within five minutes of speed-walking in a general downtown direction, whatever course of action had started at home fell off of him and became forgotten. A new John began to operate on the streets that took him to his high office, one who was free to enjoy the comforts of a city morning –

"Argh! You! I'm an old man, I need help – please!" a rough hand seized John's arm out of nowhere. John shook it loose with some effort and walked on a little faster. But the beggar was persistent.

"Young man – you can help an old, dying man on the street. Spare some change! I have no money, no food!"

John turned around. "Slagin, you know I never carry change!"

"Please – you look like a nice young man," the bum balled his dirty hands together and shook them in front of John's face emphatically, his rags wobbling.

"I don't have any more money than I had last Friday*! And stop pretending you don't know me!"

"Ah – I am losing my memory! I am dying!" Slagin fell back as John hurried away.

The rest of his path to the metro was unimpeded. After an uneventful twenty minute ride, John made his regular detour down Mundo Street to a little shop called Schmidtstein's Bagels for his second cup of coffee.

"Ah, John!" came the greeting of an old man sweeping as he entered.

"Morning, Mr. Schmidtstein. I'm in desperate need of some coffee, I almost fell asleep on the train."

"Oh..." Mr. Schmidtstein shook his head, "that not good place to fall asleep."

"Tell me about it. How's your morning so far?"

"Not good," the old man sighed. "You are only my first customer today!"

"What? Oh, right, the prostitutes were only two streets down," John realized.

"They scare away everyone!"

"Don't worry about it. By lunch no one will care anymore," John consoled.

Mr. Schmidstein grumbled to himself as he prepared John's usual. Meanwhile John got out his wallet; as soon as it touched air the cash zoomed into Mr. Schmidtein's palm with some kind of invisible force.

"I always thought that was a pretty useful token," John took a crack at small talk. The old man forced a brief grin as he handed John back a couple twenty dollar bills.

*They use our weekday system. Or do we use theirs? Something to ponder....

"Alright, well, I'll see you later. Try and have a good day," John tried to inject cheer, but Mr. Schmidtstein had gone back to looking surly.

10

The top of his building came into view as he crossed the street, towering over the others like a fat bully on a playground. But his straight path to it was blocked at the next intersection, where a throng of people screaming and desperately clawing at something in the center had congealed. It was made up mostly of middle-aged housewives and young women, with a few men in the mix.

They blocked the whole street. There was no way around them. Preparing himself mentally and physically, John spotted a narrow gap between two giggling college girls and a madly jumping plump woman and dove in. He pushed elbows out of his way until he reached the middle, where he found none other than Borneo Grimgae, the boy he had seen on T.V. not even an hour ago. Borneo looked innocently perplexed as he turned this way and that to address bits of paper and skin flying at him from all directions, and his hair was being mussed by a fat-fingered hand with long shiny nails that reached over several heads to dig into it. John punched his shoulder and tapped his watch; Borneo nodded fervently and hastily signed the last post-it note before thrusting it into the hands of its owner. John then grabbed Borneo's arm firmly and pummeled them forward, barely squeezing through the wall of bodies before the security guards swarmed in.

Borneo straightened his clothes and took a deep breath.

"Crazy morning, I tell you," he said to John. "I was just walking to work when this lady spots me and screams 'Borneo!!!' and then next thing I know five women rush over to me, and what am I going to do? I wanted to be nice so I stopped to say 'hello', and then before I know it I'm in the middle of that mosh pit you saw right there!"

John shook his head. "A life of fame," he said.

"Scary, isn't it?" Borneo smiled.

"I wouldn't know," shrugged John as they walked away from the throng the guards were still holding back. "At least Bethesda wasn't there. We'd never be able to get away then."

"I dunno," Borneo said slyly. "She's not all that smitten with me. She seems to be going for a certain someone else," he winked. John rolled his eyes.

"A little too young for me," he said.

"Age is just a number," Borneo responded lightly, casually sticking out his arm for a guy passing the other way so that they could perform a complicated high-five handshake thing mid walk.

"Fine then. A little too insane for me."

Borneo chuckled.

"My mother's inviting you over for dinner tonight, by the way. She wants to hear all about your heroic escapade."

"Hasn't she been watching the news?" Borneo asked, surprised that John's mother wasn't more aware.

"She doesn't watch the news, only daytime soap operas."

"Rape, murder, adultery, crime – the news has got all of that, John."

"I know, but it bores her. I guess soap operas just have a more coherent storyline. And they last longer, too," John mused, "because in the real world the drama has to end at some point, usually with sudden death – "

"Except in my case," Borneo cut in smilingly.

"– but they can keep a soap opera going as long as they like."

"Psh!" went Borneo in skepticism. "I doubt it! She sleeps with *him*, he cheats on *her*, she's a *lesbian* – same thing over and over."

"Then they just take one episode, throw in an unexpected love triangle, and there you go, another hook."

"It gets old," Borneo said dismissively. "They're only switching up names, not coming up with new ideas. But with the news, you never know what's coming next."

"The news is one depressing story after another; you *always* know what's coming next! But on a soap opera you never know when the wife will finally get the forbidden fruit and have the affair everyone's been waiting for. They use the buildup to string people along," John said.

"Let's save the psychology rant for Mr. Daltuhn," Borneo said warily.

"Yeah right," said John mordantly, doubtful that he would ever get to deliver this rant. "Mr. Daltuhn finds breathing a waste of time."

"Well you gotta try. If you make yourself known, he might find something more useful for you. You could really move up."

"Borneo, I'm not like you. I'm not the guy that deals in the foreground."

"You don't have to be like me, John. No offense, but I don't think you *can* be like me. No one can. All you have to do is push yourself a little. You're too content."

John raised his eyebrows. "*Too content?*"

"Yes! You need to *want* more!"

John shrugged his shoulders. "What more is there to want?"

Borneo stared at his friend disbelievingly, then shook his head at the ground pityingly.

"Besides," John said much later, when they were in front of the NKOZ building, "how was this morning's report for unpredictability? Five dead prostitutes?"

"That is true," Borneo conceded. "They shouldn't even bother reporting such common events. What do they expect from downtown Vandorn? Now if they found a prostitute who saved herself from her attacker because she happened to be able to conceal weapons inside her flesh, that'd be marginally more interesting."

"I've never heard of that token," John said.

"Oh, yeah, there was this one guy, long ago, but I can't remember his name...."

They got into an elevator with several other professionally dressed men and women.

"Well, here comes another day," John said flatly, pushing the number thirty button.

"Look on the bright side, soon it'll be summer and you can get away for a while," Borneo said.

"I can't. I took my vacation two months into the new year," said John. Borneo cringed.

"Sorry, buddy."

John just shrugged.

They stepped onto their floor, over the whole of which Mr. Daltuhn presided. While the majority worked in the sea of cubicles that sprawled most of it, John and Borneo were privileged enough to work right in Mr. Daltuhn's own elaborate apartment of offices (something John took great comfort in), none of which could be entered by outside employees without his express permission. There was his personal office, which *really* couldn't be entered except with his express permission; there was the file room; there was the office where all of the employees directly under his wing worked, which was quite large and accommodating, with fine hardwood tables and all manner of cushioned swivel chairs; there was the break room, which was small but contained comfortable chairs and a television (this was John's favorite room); and then there was the meeting room, where they were briefed every morning. It was to this last room that Borneo and John were now rushing, for it was eight forty and the meeting started at nine, which meant that it had started at eight thirty.

Borneo opened the door and he and John sat down at the long mahogany table, where Nelson and Luke, their two other coworkers, were already sitting, Nelson rigid and noiseless in his seat, Luke bouncing a rubber ball on the table like a child.

"Where's Daltuhn?" John asked them.

Nelson acted like he hadn't heard anything. Luke looked up and spoke. "He went to the *john*. Get it??" he cracked up gleefully.

That very moment, Mr. Daltuhn strolled briskly inside and greeted them all with: "There he is! How's my superstar?" and gave Borneo a fatherly slap on the back. Borneo seemed aware of the increased silence and said sheepishly, "A little ruffled, but otherwise okay."

"Good! 'Cause you'll be keeping busy today, I can tell you that."

"Great, sir!"

Mr. Daltuhn internally approved of something no one else could perceive. He paused for a moment with an assured smile.

"Alright, sit down!" he snapped. "As you all know, things have been going extremely well for us this season. Borneo, your appearance on last week's season finale of *Artinia's Got Tokens* was a phenomenon: the show's never gotten higher ratings. But it's time to look ahead. Now, there's a big fan base for all those new reality shows, but I don't see how we're going to get you on one of them without making you an actor, which you're not, and that would ruin your image. So scrap that. I think what we need to do is capitalize on these competition-like shows. The new season of *Artinian Artist* starts in July*, and if we could talk to the producers and get you an

*They, too, use the Gregorian calendar

appearance – well, that's my goal. Maybe even get you a spot as one of the judges. But for that we need to build you up among the general populace, make them feel like you're a real 'love-my-fans'

14

kind of guy. So since we've got several months until the next big show goes live, that's what you're going to be working on. Got it?"

"Yes, sir," Borneo nodded.

"Good! Then today you, Borneo, will go do an autograph signing at the Oakridge Place."

"But, that's a nursing home!" Borneo exclaimed. "They don't even know who I am!"

"They're old people, Borneo, all they do is watch the news," John interrupted.

"Hallan!" Mr. Daltuhn barked, then turned back to Borneo. "Now, some people think it necessary to concentrate on one sector of the audience to maximize effect, which is sometimes very true; but in your case, what we want is for you to appeal to as wide a variety of people as possible. You see, the good thing about you is that you're versatile so we can use you for multiple purposes, milk you for all you're worth," he explained.

Borneo nodded in understanding. "Wait... the Oakridge Place... isn't that the one where all the celebrities send their parents?" Borneo asked.

"Now you're getting it!" Mr. Daltuhn exclaimed. "Luke, take the camera crew and go with him. Stay for lunch. In fact, treat them!" Mr. Daltuhn ordered.

"Arright," said Luke without looking up from the table. He and Borneo got up and left.

Mr. Daltuhn now rounded on the rest. "Nelson, you go down to the Statistics Department and get last week's information. You can work on that for me. Oh, and see if they have the projections for next month done yet. They should!"

"Al-alright, Mr. Daltuhn," Nelson stammered, getting out of his seat and exiting as fast as possible. It was now just Mr. Daltuhn and John.

"Okay, Hallan. You know that cabinet of miscellaneous reports I dug up on Friday?"

"Yes."

"I need that filed. Can't find a damn thing in it. Oh, and look up a February twenty-first file from this year, it should be somewhere in there," Mr. Daltuhn said.

"Alrighty then," John said dully; Mr. Daltuhn made no notice of the very audible sigh that followed as he left.

John took a stroll to the break room to refill his coffee cup, passing by Mr. Daltuhn's secretary sitting in front of his closed door, straightening with her veiny, manicured hands the brass name plate that said "Nancy-Beth Travers".

"... I *know*, a shame, her only son!... I don't know either, she was such an intelligent lady!.... The father? Ah – he was a lawyer, made *excellent* money – oh, could you hold on, dear? Someone's calling.... Edmund Daltuhn's office, hello?... Yes... twelve o'clock?... Alright, I'll tell him, hun, buh-bye.... Carrie, you there?...."

Monday morning and half the Cracks were already gone; John hated to see how irritable everyone would be by Friday when they most wanted one and had run out of their weekly supply.

John reentered the office and shut the door, getting to work. He periodically glanced out of his window; from there he could see the tops of most of the other buildings in the city. Few rivaled the NKOZ building in size, but that was because NKOZ was fast becoming one of the biggest networks in Artinia. Their new thirty-five story headquarters in downtown Vandorn, the epicenter and capital of their great country, was the surest marker of their success. And it was largely through the efforts of Mr. Daltuhn. Endowed with assertiveness, people skills, and a willingness to sacrifice personal relationships for his job, he was in charge of a relentless crusade to raise their ratings ever higher. That was, in fact, what the entire thirtieth floor was devoted to. Under Mr. Daltuhn's executive command the network had placed an enormous team of statisticians who collected information on viewing patterns from every possible angle. And Mr. Daltuhn had woven many of his own, less official teams across the network, whose primary goal was to convince the managers of the other floors to act more in accordance with Mr. Daltuhn's wishes.

As for Mr. Daltuhn himself, he analyzed reports, he made important phone calls, he hosted and attended elite dinners in the network's name and complained about the tedium of altering suit after suit. But he was remarkably good at his job, and in a year's time had taken NKOZ from mediocrity to stardom. He possessed great understanding of both the subtle workings of business and of the T.V.-watching habits ingrained in his available audience, and presented that useful knowledge to the rest of the Executive Board during their monthly meetings held in the penthouse with windowed walls perfect for overlooking the city. And on the side, he conducted interviews. Mr. Daltuhn was such an intimidating man that the network had put him in charge of weeding out bad possible T.V. personalities from the pool of hopefuls off the streets for all the new reality series they had launched in the past two years calling for average people to be their stars.

Therein came John. For as hard and dry an economist as he was, Mr. Daltuhn was hopelessly defect in understanding the psychology of the person. Knowing that this was indispensable to his duties, Mr. Daltuhn sought someone to fill that void. And one day by the hand of fate, while visiting his own daughter at Vandorn University, he met senior-college-student John, all set to enter his first year of graduate school with ambitions of becoming a psychologist-doctor like millions of other Artinian students. Mr. Daltuhn liked him immediately for possessing three qualities that he found irresistibly appealing: a) he was both educated in and understood psychology, b) his main hobbies were reading nonfiction and watching T.V., which meant that he contained a storehouse of random useless knowledge and was very up-to-date on current events, and c) he was young and unprofessional, and could therefore be paid a laughably small sum of money. But the clincher was John's uncertainty about his own future, which Mr. Daltuhn had sniffed out like a hound. Being who he was, it had been easy for him to convince John to abandon his medically-related plans and work for him. And so, two years ago, at the age of twenty-two, John had become Mr. Daltuhn's personal assistant. He spent more time with him than any other employee. John's job consisted of sitting in on Mr. Daltuhn's interviews while Mr. Daltuhn himself did the dirty work, recording them, and analyzing with Mr. Daltuhn the person's nature and quirks and the likely outcomes of hiring him or her, thereby assisting him in making cuts and other critical decisions. When he wasn't busy doing that, John wandered around the building running errands, or, when he could, watched T.V. in the break room. But as right now there was no one to interview and nothing for him to do, John's workdays consisted of – you guessed it – filing.

It was this that angered him most. When they were still climbing the corporate ladder from second-rate stagnation, his job was interesting and enjoyable; but now as they orbited around Borneo, Borneo, and Borneo in quest of their zenith – there was nothing for him to do!

John had doubts, in the back of his mind, about the safety of putting all their marbles into one basket. But Mr. Daltuhn seemed unable to stop himself; the current swept up even a mighty warrior like him. John tried to give voice to that lingering fear, that uncomfortable feeling that someday a bomb would go off and shatter their brittle base – but Mr. Daltuhn had stopped listening to him at some point – at the point precisely when NKOZ began its great, rapid rise, one year ago on another of Mr. Daltuhn's chance encounters, this time with Borneo Grimgae.

Mr. Daltuhn was walking to work one ordinary morning when he heard a sudden, terrible commotion behind him. He turned around and saw to his near heart-attack-instigating shock a tremendous stampede of zoo animals rampaging down the street, bowling toward him. He later learned that the reason behind this was a woman whose token had been the ability to talk to animals, who had decided to set them free into the streets that very morning. People all around him were screaming and dodging out of the way to avoid being trampled to death, but Mr. Daltuhn had frozen. He stared at the horde, on the very brink of being run over by a large quadruped and thinking mildly about death, when a young man, just an average college youth in a hoodie and jeans, ran across the street and pushed Mr. Daltuhn out of the way: Mr. Daltuhn fell to the ground as the animals ran past in a deafening roar of two-ton legs and splintering, smashing street benches. Once they were gone and a fragile silence had settled, he lifted his head, overwhelmed with shock. His eyes fell on a scattered pile of debris in the middle of the road: lying underneath it was a lifeless human body, one of its hands poking out from under the splintered wood below a cloud of slowly settling dust. Mr. Daltuhn moaned; this complete stranger had given up his own life to save him! Tears welled up in his eyes, something that hadn't happened in decades.

"Poor fool!" an old man nearby shook his head as the stunned people formed a crowd around them.

Then the pile of debris moved! The hand started pushing planks of wood away and the boy emerged, sitting up, looking around bemusedly at a hundred gawking faces.

"It's a miracle!" a lady yelled. Mr. Daltuhn's heart leapt with joy.

"I swear he wasn't breathing for five minutes!" yelled another.

"This is some sort of bizarro – this is like aliens! It's unreal!"

"It's the work of Pat!" a fanatic pointed his finger.

Emotions began winding out of hand; any second the crowd would move in on the boy, and really kill him. They fought each other to reach him, each spewing out an opinion, forgetting that he was probably seriously injured. But right as the danger level peaked, a tall, thin man with glasses, neatly combed hair, and a fountain pen poking out of his breast pocket emerged from the raging storm.

"I'm a professional scientist," he assured everyone as he moved to the center, and they all seemed to breathe easier.

"Hmm..." he said every so often as he circled the boy, who watched him curiously. Nobody in the circle talked or moved as they watched him, transfixed. The professional scientist stopped walking and started doing complex mathematical calculations in his head, once in a while uttering "seven-fifteenths pi squared" and "definite integral from zero to one-half of one-third x cubed."

Finally, he lifted his head, looked gravely at the onlookers, and proclaimed: "this boy should be dead." Everyone gasped. The scientist nodded, and continued:

"According to my calculations, the pressure created by the mass and speed of the animal far surpassed the maximum resistance of the human body, and, in effect, there was less than a zero percent chance of survival. Given, too, the condition of the bruises on this boy, we know that his token could not possibly be of the 'repellant' variety." And here the professional scientist paused and turned to the boy, and asked, "What is, in fact, your token, young man?"

The boy looked up at him and blushed, and said in a small voice, "Actually, sir, I'm not sure." Everyone gasped again. Even the professional scientist was taken aback.

"You're *not sure*? How can that be!" he exclaimed.

"Well, I've got a possibility, but I don't know – " the boy's awkward mumbles were overshadowed by a cry of –

"Maybe it's immortality!"

All heads turned toward its source, and the biggest explosion of voices yet ensued.

"That's impossible!"

"You idiot!"

"*Who's* to say what's impossible?!"

"The *Boble*!"

"Well how else do you explain him still being alive?"

"It was a miracle, duh! Or a fluke."

"Well," and even though the professional scientist spoke in a quiet voice everyone instantly stopped talking again, "I do not presume my deductions superior to any of yours, but scientific evidence points to this boy indeed being immortal."

And so from that day on, Borneo was the boy with the Immortal Token. The story made it into every magazine, every news station, was talked about by everyone.

Mr. Daltuhn, he did not care whether the kid really was immortal; he knew what the once-in-a-lifetime opportunity looked like, and this was, unmistakably, it. When he thanked the youth for saving his life, he said to him, "Looks like you're going to be pretty famous now, huh?"

"I guess," he chuckled.

"What's your name, son?"

"Borneo. Borneo Grimgae."

"How would you like to come work for me?"

"What kind of – ?"

"I want you to be the new face of NKOZ."

"The network!?"

"That's right."

So Borneo became the network's new official spokesperson, and Mr. Daltuhn's beloved treasure sent from above. A mass of controversy surrounded Borneo, for the whole world knew that immortality was the one token no one could possess. So it was written in the canon. Many religious leaders vehemently argued against it, crying that only Bob Himself possessed immortality and that equalizing a mortal with Him uprooted all they'd known for thousands of years! Even Borneo was skeptical at first (although that changed quickly).

Then several daring college students voiced the most controversial thought of all: "maybe what we've known for five thousand years isn't true?" Alongside them stood several other professional scientists who confirmed that there was simply no other explanation for why Borneo was still alive, and after several stormy months of heated debate and a flurry of interviews for Borneo (a time during which John was all but invisible at NKOZ) Borneo's status as 'immortal' became accepted among the masses who so desperately wanted the exciting, magical version of events to be true. And, as with all things, the fantasy eventually won.

One can imagine what all this meant for NKOZ: ratings went through the roof of their brand new thirty-five story building. But even after the controversy subsided and Borneo officially became the only immortal boy to ever have lived (however ironic), the publicity surrounding him did not cease one bit; Borneo appeared on billboards, in magazines, did interviews on popular morning shows, was used for commercials. He soon became a permanent part of Artinian public life. And that was just what Mr. Daltuhn had wanted.

To John, it seemed the true miracle here was that the one person of millions who saved Mr. Daltuhn happened to be the most charming, charismatic individual to ever cross his eyes. Borneo was universally popular, perhaps the most well-liked person in the country. He was a smooth talker and a hero, too. More of a local hero, but – well, Mr. Daltuhn was changing that. It was by his skill that Borneo appealed not only to young girls, old girls, and gays as the casually sexy non-model-like youth, but now to parents and kids (as a responsible, caring citizen who visited elementary schools across the country this past winter to teach their children about the dangers of illegal eating), to businessmen (as a likeable man with a serious side, who modeled designer suits), and, Mr. Daltuhn's latest tag, the old (as a nice-young-man).

Things had been going particularly well the past two months as Mr. Daltuhn had scored Borneo invites to several chic and exclusive parties that were attended by members of Vandorn's elite high society (producers, movie stars, and their plastic surgeons), but they were simply enveloped in gold two weeks ago when, miraculously, Borneo had *another* near escape from death and proved his immortality a second time:

He and Mr. Daltuhn were touring in the southwest and stopped to visit the Great Granber Falls, the tallest and most treacherous waterfall in Artinia, lined with sharp boulders at the bottom for anyone desiring to meet a painfully bloody death. As it happened, there was such a person there: they were standing on the bridge crossing the river just before the edge of the falls when a man next to Borneo, whom no one had noticed before, shouted, "... Bob, I'm a failure! Why do I need to live!?" and jumped over the edge. As everyone on the bridge screamed in shock, including Mr. Daltuhn, who was especially shocked since he'd just been regaling that man with tales of his early success and how he'd dated an international model when he was his age, and inadvertently knocked Borneo over the edge as well.

"Thank Bob, Borneo is saving him!!" Mr. Daltuhn then cried in his booming voice.

Reacting, Borneo caught the man in midair and somehow flipped himself over onto his back so that he was on the bottom as they plummeted the hundred and sixty feet together, hitting the water on the back of Borneo's lifejacket. Everyone on the bridge was instantly sure they were both dead, however immortal Borneo was. And out of nowhere a tiny head bobbed up out of the calm river below, and just behind it another one, and it was Borneo, dragging the man to safety, both of them very much alive and the suicidal man in tears of joy or agony – no one knew – as Borneo paddled for both their bodies, his life jacket mercilessly torn into strips. And with that undeniably brave act, Borneo's status as hero became national, and Mr. Daltuhn lost himself happily in euphoria.

John personally did not want Borneo's fame or publicity – all he wanted was to escape the boredom that came with it, at least for him: there was no need for new faces and the stream of interviews had ceased to flow. And he couldn't blame Borneo; in spite of his cockiness, which John knew he would be no more resistant to if he were in Borneo's place, Borneo was an overall good guy, and he and John had become friends quickly. The only thing that amused John was the reaction he often got when he told people that he himself worked as Mr. Daltuhn's personal assistant at NKOZ; that is to say, they were impressed, unduly in John's opinion, because all he was doing these days was going through files. He had sometimes tried to convince Mr. Daltuhn to let him go with Borneo on one of his promotional events around the city:

"Um, Mr. Daltuhn, since you don't have any interviews – or, well, anything – scheduled for today, maybe I could go with Borneo to Vandorn University. I'd keep records of everything, and I think it would provide him with a really useful tool for that interview with Morgan Prince he has next week; it would look great if he could actually quote some of his fans, don't you think?" (John had planned this for several days).

"No."

"Mr. Daltuhn, I have nothing to do! I'll be drumming my fingers on my desk all day!"

Mr. Daltuhn paused in whatever he was reading and looked thoughtful.

"That's a point, Hallan. Tell you what, wait here a second." And he ran out, leaving John with a bubble of hope.

A minute later he came back carrying a big box.

"Completely forgot. I've got a whole stack of files from last month that need to be sorted. That should keep you busy for today." He put the box into John's hands. "Problem solved!" he patted John on the back and smiled, sitting down and getting back to work.

John recalled it all bitterly. He sighed. He checked his phone and saw that it was already two fifteen. He went into the break room and turned on the T.V., to C-Span – nothing. He tried C-Span 2 – nothing there either. He tried C-Span 3 – C-Span 4 –

"Hallan! You were late this morning," Mr. Daltuhn entered the break room.

"I had to help Borneo; they mobbed him in the street," John said without turning around.

"Hmph. Well, you gave me a good idea this morning so I'm not going to press it."

This news surprised John. "What good idea did I give you?"

"Soap operas – "

"– definitely shouldn't be part of our programming."

"No! We could get Borneo on soap operas as a guest star."

"I think we've already got the middle-aged women group hooked," said John.

"I've been making phone calls all day," he ignored John's last comment.

"It wouldn't do anything, I'm telling you, just make a lot of middle-aged women really happy. Like my mother. Actually, her birthday's coming up this fall, maybe we *could* invest there, give her a birthday present."

But too late – he had already planted the seeds of doubt into Mr. Daltuhn's mind.

"We'll talk it over later," Mr. Daltuhn mumbled.

Just then, Borneo and Luke walked in.

"What are you two doing here? I told you to treat the oldies to lunch," Mr. Daltuhn barked.

"We did," said Borneo, "but right after we ate they fell asleep, and the caretaker ladies told us we could go home."

Mr. Daltuhn's face swelled. "You idiots! You were supposed to stay! Don't you know it's good manners!?" he yelled so loudly that there was suddenly a noticeable drop in the background volume of their entire floor.

Borneo and Luke looked guiltily at each other.

"Didn't it occur to you flaming dimwits that when they wake up – which a good ninety percent of them will! – if they don't see you there they'll forget anyone ever came to visit them!? *And that's the better outcome!* You dolts, that makes the entire trip *worthless!*" he shouted.

"You! Did you get the projections for June?" Mr. Daltuhn rounded on Nelson as he walked in.

"They – they didn't have them done yet, sir," Nelson stammered in surprise.

"Lazy asses! Who's in charge over there?"

"It's Ho-horatio Sanchez's department."

"Sanchez! Damned Pat, I'll never see them!" his fist hit the wall and he walked out.

Nelson stared after him, shaking slightly with nerves.

Borneo sighed with relief, rubbing the back of his neck. "What's eating him today?"

"Dunno," said John.

"Pass me a Diet Crack."

John reached into the fridge and got out a can. "You know that stuff's bad for you," he said.

"What, it's not like I drink them more than allowed," Borneo defended.

"You guys actually only drink one a week?" Luke sneered.

"Um, it's the law," said John.

"So? It's not like they'll catch you, not if you're careful."

"Maybe. But more than one of those a week, they really mess you up."

24

"Yeah, those things last," said Borneo.

"I had, like, three this weekend, and I'm fine!" Luke declared.

"Whoa," Borneo's eyes widened as he popped his can.

"I mean, it's not like I drink them every day. I'm not an addict. Just, like, socially, you know? Like if my buddies come over and we're watching the game–"

"Yeah, yeah," Borneo nodded.

"– we'll open up a six-pack. It's just casual."

"Yeah, that's alright," Borneo said in reasonable tones. Luke smiled. Then he took a Crack out of the fridge, popped it open, and he and Borneo went outside to have a social drink. John took out a sandwich and sat alone at the table. A few minutes later Mr. Daltuhn walked back in.

"Dumbass boys," he said to John. "Next time you go with them."

"You're not really mad at Borneo, are you?" John asked.

"Nah, this wasn't that important. He's got charisma and courage and all, but the kid's a dummy! I want to discuss my new idea with you tomorrow, by the way."

John felt a little ray of hope shine through his chest.

When he got back to filing and staring out his window with a little more immunity to the boredom, his thoughts meandered to what Borneo had said earlier that morning, that John didn't want. That certainly wasn't true! He wanted things, many things. But what? Not this, that was for sure. He didn't want to be filing papers every day for the rest of his life, doing something he didn't care a dime about. He didn't *mind* it, I mean, for the money it was bearable. But the sense of fulfillment, the feeling that *this is what I'm supposed to be doing*, or whatever modern-day gurus talked about – it wasn't there. What *would* he do, though, if not this? As to that he had no clue. He wanted *something*, he just didn't know what that something looked like.

But Borneo was wrong; he wasn't *too content* – he was just bored! He imagined Borneo laughing at that when there was fame, money, girls, cars, status, all to chase. But none of that gave John a thrill. Attracting girls? It was rare to find someone he truly connected with. And he wasn't concerned with his public image, so that took care of fame. He'd gladly stick to his uncomplicated life – but that had become stagnant. Go to work, go to the bar, drink a beer, watch T.V.

.... John was so bored, his food tasted bland. He knew it was *him*, and not his life, and he wished for that spark – but nothing seemed to bring it. These days everything whirled past him as if he were skimming water with his hand. Again he saw Borneo not comprehending "boredom with life" when there were so many exciting things to do!

"The world is like a boundless forest teeming with wonders to find!" he would say.

And John would reply, "I've searched the whole forest... and inside the forest I've found only the forest."

Chapter 03: Paint Me a Complete Picture

"Hahahahaha!"

"That was a clever one, son!" John's father patted him on the back.

"Thank you, sir," said Borneo. Mrs. Hallan was still wiping tears of laughter from her eyes.

"Oh, Borneo, if you weren't saving the world, you could be famous doing stand-up!" she exclaimed. Borneo blushed.

"Aw, Mrs. Hallan, I'm not saving the world, just the occasional suicidal man," he grinned.

"Ohoho!" Mrs. Hallan welled up a fresh wave of chuckles.

It was not Monday night; Borneo had been so charming and witty that he had gotten himself invited to dinner again the next day. It was now Tuesday night.

"It smells like the chicken is almost ready!" Mr. Hallan exclaimed, sniffing the air.

"I'll go check," said Mrs. Hallan, and she got up to go to the kitchen. "John, where's your sister? Would you get her down here?" she asked while on her way.

"Sure," said John from the living room couch, where he'd been absentmindedly watching a Kimi Kool commercial.

Kimi Kool was a twelve inch plastic doll made for small girls, the most popular toy on the market. Faithfully, they came out with a new one every month: princess Kimi Kool, prom queen Kimi Kool, teacher, scientist, doctor, jungle adventurer, and vacation Kimi Kool all already existed; Kimi Kool had the most exciting life. After three years of different personas it was hard not to recycle ideas.

"...Deluxe Beach Time Kimi Kool! " a voice-over exclaimed, the backdrop for a brightly colored beach scene: a blonde-haired and blue-eyed girl lay on a pink towel, chatting with another blonde girl who lay next to her; but this second girl was not as important because she had green eyes instead of blue ones. Both wore bikinis.

"Don't you just love the beach, Kali?" asked the blue-eyed girl with a smile, her long, wavy hair spread around her like a golden cape.

"I sure do, Kimi Kool!" answered Kali, smiling cutely as her curly hair bobbed around her head.

"Check out my cool heart tattoo tan!" exclaimed Kimi Kool. She turned onto her stomach and the scene zoomed in on her bikini bottom. A little heart was cut out of the fabric on one but-cheek.

"Wow! That's sexy!" exclaimed Kali.

"You have one, too!" said Kimi Kool. They showed Kali's star-shaped cut-out in her green bikini bottom.

As Kimi Kool and BFF Kali laughed joyously, two tan, shirtless cartoon male dolls appeared before them.

"Hey, girls," they said with wide smiles.

"Hey, boys," Kimi Kool said back maturely.

All four of them ran into the ocean together, splashing each other. Kimi Kool sat atop the slightly better-looking one's shoulders and Kali sat atop his friend.

While beach themed music continued to play, real-life Kimi Kool and Kali dolls appeared in disembodied hands, each clad in its Beach Time bikini.

"Deluxe Beach Time Kimi Kool and Kimi Kool's BFF, Kali! Your favorite all-Artinian girl goes to the beach... again!!"

"Oh, Kimi Kool! My niece loves those!" Borneo called from the dining room.

"I wish we had those when *I* was a girl, they're just adorable!" Mrs. Hallan exclaimed.

John got up and went upstairs, thinking it was rather strange that Milly was not downstairs already, because whenever Borneo was over she typically clung to him like a big sheet of plastic wrap. Something must be up with her. John first attempted to open her door, but when that turned out to be locked, he knocked.

"Milly, come downstairs for dinner," he said.

"No!"

"Mom demands it."

"Go away!" and he thought he heard sobs.

"Are you okay?" John asked through the door.

"I said, *go away!!!*"

"Okay," and Milly heard his footsteps fading away outside her door.

"Wait! You're not supposed to leave yet!" she yelled.

"But you told me to go away!"

"No, you're supposed to say 'please, Milly, open the door, tell me what's wrong,' and after I scream at you to leave me alone for another few minutes, I finally let you in and tell you about my problems," she explained.

"Why can't you just tell me what's wrong now?"

"John!" she sounded genuinely flabbergasted, "It's the rule!"

"What rule?"

"The rule for girls. That's what we're supposed to do."

"Milly, I'm not going to stand out here begging you to open the door when you already know you're going to do it," said John flatly.

"Some big brother you are!" Milly screamed through the door and started sobbing again, emotionally hurt.

How much more could she bear?! Her days at school were terrible and after all that she came home to a place where no one cared about her! Face buried in pillow, she felt her heart rend as she relived every torturous moment of this horrible day still as fresh in her mind as newly spilled blood, seeping across her psyche like a debilitating flood that would eventually crush her spirit beneath its colossal weight.

It had gone on the same as any other day until last class, when the entire school had been called down to the assembly hall for a mandatory meeting given by the class president, none other than Dee Allderbay: the most popular girl in school. Strutting around in her pink polo, flipping her long brown hair infused with blonde highlights, Dee was a paradigm for her fellow students.

She addressed the dress code today. "Good morning, everybody!" Dee said into the microphone across a hall of babbling students.

"Yeah, Dee!" came a cry in response to that illustrious statement.

"As you all know, the end of yet another school year is on its way. Despite this excitement, we should not forget what is expected of us as Peamount High students. The coming of warmer weather prompts us to wear clothes that may be inappropriate and disruptive to a productive learning environment, and that is why the school will impose a uniform to be worn by all students starting next week.

The uniform for girls will consist of: tight jeans or denim mini, a fitted Hollister* t-shirt, a padded push-up bra, and ugly shapeless tan boots.

The uniform for boys will consist of: faded torn jeans, retro canvas footwear, a hemp bracelet or necklace, and a Hollister t-shirt.

Polos and henleys are acceptable as well. Sweat clothes may be worn on certain days if they have the school name printed on them in association with a sport.

Hair: for girls, hair must be either straightened or up in a loose bun to the side. For boys, hair must be no shorter than two inches from the scalp. Highlights are encouraged in the hair of both genders.

We at Peamount High want to give the students a chance to take an active role in the administration of the school. Therefore, we are creating a new organization, the Peamount Role-Enforcement Party, to be in charge of upholding the dress code. The Student Council and I will select nine students whom we feel best embody the values of Peamount High to be a part of this great leadership experience (which by the way looks really good to colleges)."

"But just what are these values?" Behind Dee, the white screen came down as the EZ ProjectPoint program loaded.

"We've prepared a slide show to illustrate the fundamental values that shape Peamount High."

Click. A handsome photo of their high school filled the screen. There was one word on the slide: "Pride".

"We take pride in our students, who can be recognized by their unswerving devotion to the highest ideals that shape and guide our society."

Click. The next slide said "Freedom."

"Freedom of expression, freedom to be oneself, in a community that is warm and accepting of others' differences. It is encouraged to be different, as long as it's the 'cool' and 'edgy' kind of different, the one that's really popular right now."

Click.

*Of course they have Hollister!

Normally, Milly would be hanging on to every word from Dee's lips in the hopes that if they ever talked someday, she would be able to bring up something Dee had said. But not at this assembly; there were forces acting on her now that overshadowed even Dee Allderbay by a mile.

Milly couldn't help but to glance over again to her right, for the millionth time. His head moved a fraction and he caught her looking at him – her heart instantly palpitated like a bullet shot inside a hollow steel case! *No! Why did you do that!?* she hissed at herself internally, her cheeks turning beet red. *It's only going to make you more nervous, and you know how* that'll *end!* She inhaled deeply to calm herself down, but her entire body still trembled uncontrollably from the shock of being pierced by *his eyes*. She couldn't help but relive their fathomless gaze over and over....

Click. They were now on "Individuality."

The storm raged away inside her, and even though she had no way of seeing what was above her own head, she had the symptoms – the frantically beating heart, electricity all down her body, romantic visions of his face she could not block out – that always came with the onset of her token.

She could hear curious whispering right behind her. "Are they... *ballroom dancing*?"

Why, Bob? Why her most private thoughts!? Tears of misery formed behind her eyes. She knew her heightened emotion was just making the image clearer.

Any time Milly experienced a strong emotional response, it triggered the appearance of an image above her head of exactly what her mind was visualizing at that moment. It was as if a hole was drilled through her skull and into the contents of her brain, a hole through which those contents were projected naked onto the outside world above her head like a movie. She could only sit still and wait for her inner calamity to subside, at which point the image would fade.

The lights flipped on; the assembly was over. Milly's panic flared up again. *Maybe no one will notice*, she thought desperately, trying frantically to numb herself.

"Dude, look!" came a cry nearby. Her head wheeled around lightning-fast. To her right, a boy was pointing to the air above Milly's head while tugging at his friend Marrik McFost's sleeve.

"What?" asked Marrik in irritation as he tied his sneaker.

Milly grabbed her backpack and rammed past everyone in her row in the opposite direction of Marrik McFost's seat. With her back to him, she wouldn't have to see him see the image of himself accidentally glancing at Milly replayed over and over. She only heard Marrik's confused voice behind her saying, "what the fuck?"

Milly held her tears in for the rest of the hour, but as soon as she stepped through her door, it was time to be emotional! *Why do I have to have the worst token in the whole world?* she bemoaned. *I'd take anything – anything! – instead.*

It just wasn't fair! How many times could a girl stand to embarrass herself in front of the boy she secretly desperately liked? She would look into his eyes when he passed her by in the halls and swear she felt a connection – did he feel it too? The longing to know tormented her! Forget it, she told herself. Like there's any chance after today. And even before today, was there any chance? Ever? How could he ever like her when she wasn't like all the pretty, popular girls? When she didn't flirt and wasn't special? Maybe, maybe somehow if she could just get him to notice her.... Ha! Like that would ever happen. Her mother wouldn't even let her wear makeup! She didn't need it, her mother said, because she was already naturally pretty. Yeah right!! That was such a lie! She wasn't pretty; she looked thirteen and her mother knew it! It was sooo unfair to Milly. Didn't her mother know how hard it was for her? Couldn't she empathize? And yet she wouldn't even let her get highlights – she "didn't want Milly to ruin her hair". Well, that was totally unfair, Milly wasn't a baby anymore, she could make her own decisions! But her parents didn't trust her with anything! They didn't even trust her to stay out late! Who her age had a curfew nowadays? No one! But if she came home even five minutes after eleven they'd yell at her as if she had just – just – committed murder or something!! Like it was unforgivable! They were so unreasonable! They didn't even understand the implications of their dictatorial rule: every party she went to she'd have to leave by ten thirty! That's when people started arriving! She'd look like an idiot for leaving so early – what was she supposed to do, not go at all?! Then she'd be missing out on all the fun! Oh wait – she already was!! Thanks to her parents, she was missing out on everything! There were so many vital experiences Milly hadn't gone through yet that everyone else her age had. Like her First Kiss, or the Big Party, or her Clichéd Shocking Transformation. And if she didn't make out with anyone by the start of junior year, she'd never get a boyfriend during high school; and if she never had a boyfriend during

32

high school, she'd never be able to be upset when he broke up with her and bounce back with that unexpected steamy new fling during the summer when she was sixteen; and if she didn't do that, then she'd never have a chance to be so spontaneous again because she'd be past the young-and-innocent age and by seventeen it'd be time to have a Serious Relationship. I mean, she had to keep up! There was a tight schedule to adhere to! These were the stories girls bonded over, the shared experiences that made them friendz for lyfe! How could her parents – how could her mom *– not understand that if she didn't cultivate her emotional depth and gain her sense of self by going through such complicated problems, she'd never have any close friends!? How was she supposed to go through the Standard Set of Teenage Trials and Pangs if her parents were so overprotective? She was tired of being naïve little Milly: compared to everyone else, she was totally inexperienced!!! It wasn't like the moment she was outside their watch she was going to start eating illegally – she wasn't stupid (unlike what her parents thought!). She was totally against all of that stuff, and she knew she wouldn't cave into peer pressure. I mean, she wasn't thirteen anymore – she was fifteen.* Way older. *And what had she done that was so terrible? Nothing! She wasn't pregnant – so why couldn't they just let her go to a party or two? Obviously, she knew that she had to be careful, and that, yes, it was very hard to deal with all the partying, eating, and sex running rampant amongst the peers of her generation like never before in a healthy and mature way, sure – but she could do it! She trusted herself! Why couldn't* they*?!?! Why did they have to* worry? *"Because we're your parents blah blah-blah blah!"* Always *that same excuse! They just didn't understand her – that was it – they had no clue how out of place she felt at school, how no boys ever asked her out, how the most embarrassing things always happened to her, and not to people like Dee Allderbay, or Marrik McFost! Oh, if* only *he would see her like he saw those other girls! Desperate thoughts of what miracles could happen ran through her mind time to time – he secretly loved her and was waiting for the right moment to say it; one day he would feel sorry about the mean, popular girls making fun of her and comfort her, establishing their friendship that would eventually lead to romance; once they were together he would never want to leave her side and would choose her over popularity because it was the right thing to do....Yeah, right;* what wishful thinking! *Milly told herself over and over to kill the fantasy that still lived inside. How could he like someone like her? How could* anyone, *when there were all those other girls with prettier faces, cooler personalities, bigger boobs and nicer bodies? She* hated – <u>abhorred</u> *– whenever her parents told* *her how amazing she was and how all she needed was more self-esteem. Maybe she would have more self-esteem if they hadn't ruined her adolescence!!!*

Milly had finished ranting about how terrible her life was inside of her head, so it was now time for her to break into a fresh bout of sobs and bury her face into her pillow. She did that. Good. In a few minutes, when she would be temporarily out of tears, she would sit up, suddenly feel angry, and fume, in her head again, about how much she hated her parents, how mean and unfair they were, and then finish off with a poignant appeal to how they didn't understand her, how *nobody* understood her, and how she was completely alone – that last thought would tug on a sensitive heartstring and trigger an emotional reaction, and she would have to start sobbing again because of the pain, this time in more desperation. And while she was crying, she would have to remember to think about what strong and powerful emotions she had – this was the tricky part, because it had to be very subtle. She couldn't be *too* aware of how much she relished her suffering, because that would make her happy, and she was not happy, she was very sad.

"Milly!" her mother's muffled call came from downstairs. *What does she want*, Milly thought.

"Come downstairs!"

Oh. Well, she wasn't going to join them for dinner tonight, she was too depressed. They would just have to deal. Yeah, that's right, why don't they try it – see how they *deal* with something.

"MILLY!"

Milly stubbornly did not answer to this raised tone with which her name was being called. In fact, she folded her arms across her chest to be even more stubborn. They could call her a bajillion times, for all she cared, and she still would not go! In fact, they probably would.

...

Why wasn't anyone calling her? Well, fine, that just showed how much they appreciated her! She didn't need them, she didn't need anybody – oh, wait, she was supposed to save that one for when she was running away from home because they wouldn't let her date her new boyfriend. *If she ever had a boyfriend!!!*

Milly broke into sobs again and fell to her bed, hugging her pillow.

34

She stopped sobbing for a moment and listened intently to check if her mother was still calling her. She wasn't.

Huffing, she dismounted her bed and sat down resolutely in front of her computer, staring at the monitor angrily. *I don't need dinner – I'll just go online for the next two hours. Yeah.*

Back downstairs, the chicken was completely gone save for the piece Mrs. Hallan had put aside for her daughter, and they were leisurely wrapping up the evening with some tea.

"Boy, Mrs. Hallan, that chicken sure was delectable," Borneo exclaimed as she came back from the kitchen carrying a tea tray.

"Oh! Why, thank you, Borneo, such a gentleman," she flushed. Borneo smiled bashfully.

"Let's open those tea cookies Borneo brought over," she said, setting down her burden. "John, could you get them, I put them in the pantry."

"Cookies, you say," grumbled Mr. Hallan from his armchair.

"Allow me!" Borneo jumped up.

"Oh, dear, just relax and make yourself at home. So helpful...."

John came back with the box and opened it at the table, revealing its array of powdered lemon tea cookies.

"Would you look at that! Those are Milly's favorites!" Mrs. Hallan exclaimed. Borneo looked pleasantly surprised.

"Where is Milly, by the way," John's father asked. "I haven't seen her once since I got home."

"She's been locked up in her room all day," Mrs. Hallan said with a sigh. "Really upset, she was, she was crying her eyes out."

Mr. Hallan's face hardened in concern.

"Oh don't bother her, she probably just had a bad day at school, you know how she is," Mrs. Hallan reassured.

Borneo looked sympathetic.

"You don't think she's trying to commit suicide, do you?" Mr. Hallan asked.

"Stewart!"

"Well, I don't hear anymore crying," said John.

"John! Honestly, she's your sister!"

"John, go up and check."

"Will do," and John bounded up the stairs again. Mrs. Hallan turned on her husband.

"These ridiculous ideas you have! She's fifteen!"

"Exactly!"

"She's not going to kill herself because some boy wouldn't pay attention to her!"

"Merle, you don't know kids nowadays," Mr. Hallan cautioned.

"She's smarter than that, she knows she's got her whole life ahead of her," his wife yelled in a hiss so that Milly wouldn't happen to overhear.

Borneo looked neutral. No one saw his eye flicker toward the untouched box of cookies in an otherwise stony face.

A minute later, John came thundering back downstairs.

"Well?" his father asked.

"She's not dead."

"Good."

"She's sitting at her computer looking up relationship horoscopes online."

"Did you tell her we have her favorite cookies downstairs?" Mrs. Hallan asked. "Speaking of which, no one's touched them yet. Borneo, help yourself, dear."

"Oh, no, after you, Mrs. Hallan," Borneo politely refused.

"Really, I'm too full. Maybe I'll have one later. Go on!"

Borneo looked politely hesitant. "Well, alright, just for you," he winked, reaching for a lemon tea cookie before the entire response had come out.

"Oho!" said Mrs. Hallan, giggling.

And so it went....

***

The next day, John woke up an hour later than he normally would when he planned to make it to work on time. Throwing on shoes, shirts, socks, pants, not in that order, he ran out of the house as fast as he could.

Something jabbed at his arm out of nowhere. John involuntarily glanced around to see a dirty, unshaven man prostrating a piece of food at him from under his seasonally inappropriate jacket.

"Slagin – " John began.

"Just wait, just look what I got," he attempted to shove the wrapped lump into John's pants pocket. "A nice... fat... quiche. Mmm. Come on, you know you want it."

John knocked him away and determinedly walked on. *Just say no, just say* no... he kept telling himself as he rushed to catch the train.

He was too late. Dammit. Mr. Daltuhn would kill him.

John gasped – a little burst of what might have been hopefulness had been momentarily spawned by that careless thought. John chose to ignore what that meant about how dissatisfied he was with his job. *Okay, it's not what I want to be doing, but what are the chances that if I quit I'd find something better? I'd still probably end up just as miserable. This is the best it's going to get*, he told himself realistically.

"Follow Your Dreams" said random billboards and songs middle school girls listened to. Yes, follow your dreams and then graduate as whatever you can with those ideal dreams still in your head and start living: you're thousands of dollars in debt and stuck at the best job that'll take you. Welcome to reality. Have fun!! It's a hopeless trap – be this or be that or be another thing from this list. I want to be a doctor, one kid says. Congratulations, kid, you're no doubt going to find the cure for Psychosis. Being a doctor is an exciting job – if you enjoy paperwork, stupid clients, incompetent coworkers, and paperwork. Well I'm going to be a lawyer, and I'll end food abuse. Yes, a great job, too, for those who enjoy paperwork, stupid clients, incompetent coworkers, and paperwork.

"Metro's broken, buddy, it'll be down for another hour," the voice from a man next to him cut John out of his thoughts.

Not believing his luck, John heaved a sigh and mumbled, "Better start walking then," checking the time on his antique gold pocket watch. Wait, John didn't have an antique pocket watch, no less one made of solid gold. He shook his head – was this an illusion? – and had to quickly catch the silk top hat falling off. *Oh no*, he groaned.

A deep pink-plum perfectly circular shadow, in whose edge John was standing, emanated from the shop behind him, Gloria's Flowers and Other Such Useless Knickknacks, and a moment later a young girl with an apron over her long white skirt walked out, dreamy eyes in the clouds and wavy hair tied with a fuchsia ribbon that gleamed in the sun.

As she came nearer, John found himself dressed in a jacket lined with silvery silk, his hair combed and waved neatly in place, his stubble gone, and his eyes miraculously a shade of blue that mimicked the sky (which he saw when he looked at his reflection in the clear-as-glass lake to his left). Stars twinkled from a ceiling suddenly black as night.

"Dance with me, John!" cried Bethesda, nearing him.

"I'm not much of a dancer, to be honest," he said, trying to move out of the shadow and finding himself stuck.

"Nonsense!" she laughed, and John found his feet moving most gracefully within the twenty foot radius of lush moonlit garden that encircled Bethesda's body. Everyone else on the streets carefully stood outside the bubble of Bethesda's daydreams lest they be pulled in and find themselves sporting a ball gown or holding a bouquet of red roses – what John was doing now – and watched the scene.

"Are those for me?" Bethesda suddenly noticed the red roses she herself had conjured up for John to present to her, grabbing them from him and tearing the petals off of one.

"He loves me... he loves me not... he loves me...." they disintegrated into sparkles mid fall.

John checked his gold pocket watch again: nine fifteen!

"Bethesda – ! I really – have to get to work – !" but she continued to spin him around, her dirty apron flapping over her long twirling skirt, until she crashed backwards into a pole with a jolt.

"Oh!" Her concentration was briefly broken – or gathered, whichever way you want to look at it – and the daydream evaporated. John ran at least thirty feet in two seconds, relieved to see that he was dressed in normal attire again.

He ran to the next metro station, eager to put lots of distance between his body and Bethesda's. People gave him quizzical looks, I mean, a guy running around the city in a suit, that's pretty weird, malfunctional that kind of behavior is, he must be some kind of freak, not like I, who is normal – but John did not care. Something needed to be done about Bethesda, Mr. Datuhn wouldn't care if a *million* desperate girls with romantic intent aimed at his direction bombarded him with their materialized fantasies. Although talk about living your dreams....

A quiet voice in John's head gave a wry laugh. *Ironic,no? You stand in the street mulling bitterly over the inevitable failure of dreams and the next moment your solid theory is silently disproven as you are faced full-front with the direct manifestation of the complete contradiction to your belief. It's as if your life laughs at you.* John couldn't help but marvel over how blatantly indeed life events had just shattered his ego. He was by no means won over by the side of "dreams"; all that had happened was that two gears had collided in his brain and ground against each other, throwing all his comfortable notions into the air and leaving him unable to pick a side. *Perhaps that's exactly what the moment was for....*

John rushed out of the elevator, across the thirtieth floor, into the deluxe apartment complex in the sky, and up to Mr. Daltuhn's door – which was closed.

Again? It was ten in the morning! Didn't Mr. Daltuhn care that John was an hour late to work? Didn't he want to yell at him, and feel that satisfaction? Well, apparently not. Fuming silently, John turned around and headed straight for the break room, where he plopped into his usual chair.

A magazine from the pile on the table distracted him before he could turn on the T.V. – an issue of *Teengirl*. Wondering who in this building fell within their target audience, John examined its bright orange cover with a neon pink headline that read: "Who Are Your Fav Role Models? Find out on pg. 84!"

He *had* to know! John flipped to this page and read a list of ten female singers and actresses between the ages of fifteen and thirty. The famous actress Zayla Kinner was at number one, and underneath a photo of the brunette beauty was a caption illuminating what a great person she was:

An amazing actress and girlfriend of the way studly Bruce Bonham, Zayla Kinner has also got a great heart. She has donated over a million dollars in charity to various global causes; she is an active environmentalist with her own line of eco-friendly handbags; and she keeps that amazing bod in shape by eating a diet of local-grown organic foods and doing yoga every morning. Zayla is truly the number one role model for a healthy, active, and down-to-earth lifestyle that balances work, life, and love.

Wow, John thought, *I wish I could be like her. She's so successful and pretty. Maybe I could be that successful and pretty if I restricted my diet to yogurt and tofu. Yes, I think that when I do my grocery shopping this weekend, I'll stock up on some of those frozen vegan meals. Hey, maybe I could try one of those new SmartPick dinners I saw on T.V. last night. Yeah, what a great idea!! They* are *a tad expensive, but, you know, so worth it....*

What other goodies were there in this treasure trove of gossip? Other headlines such as

<u>How To Turn A Drab Night Into A Wildin' Fiesta!</u>,

Best Cuddling Tips,

and

Find the Perfect Bikini for <u>Your</u> *Unique* Body (and Score That Hottie at the Pool!)

didn't appeal to him. He put the *Teengirl* magazine down and picked up the one right underneath it. This magazine, called *Cosmetology,* was a bit more adult, as its cover photo of a savvy-looking woman with gold hoop earrings, a fitted button-down shirt, and a foxy expression etched in her arched brows and slight grin denoted. Splattered across the glossy lipstick-red background in bold letters was the headline:

<u>Domenate Your Life: Taking Control of Your Mental, Emotional, and Spiritual Realms (24)</u>

John skimmed the article, pondering its fresh take on male-female relationships. It was very informative when it came to love, but he was still lacking that sense of empowerment and inspiration that gave him the strength to turn his life around, at least until that evening when *Desperate Tokens* came on.

But the only other interesting thing he found was a small piece titled: "Hot Spot: actress Zayla Kinner Dishes Her Favorite <u>Naughty Sex Tricks</u>."

Throwing the magazine back onto the table, John sat down in his usual armchair and turned the T.V. on with the effortless press of a little button on a nifty thing called a remote control. Ah, to be lazy. Wait... he felt something coming to him... no, that would be a stupid name for a company that made reclining armchairs.

He turned to channel fifteen, The News.

"Good morning, welcome to the eleven o'clock coverage of your daily news. Brining you all the latest in what's happening in Vandorn and the rest of Artinia. We're here today with Bobbert Bushnell – ooh, that's me, heh heh – and Tex Masaker. Let's take you to our first story:... our first story:... Tex, I think that's you."

"Oh! Right. Ahem. So there's a new lead on the shootings that happened on Mayfield Street Tuesday afternoon, they rejected the idea that the thirty-eight year old man they found dead by a dumpster killed himself – "

"That's right, it wasn't a suicide. Name was Bay Kent if you missed it. They've questioned his ex-wife, his attorney, and his brother – "

"I personally think each is as likely as the other to have done it," muttered Tex.

"No, Tex, those aren't the suspects," chuckled Bobbert.

"My mistake, Bobbert! I thought you were talking about his ex-wife, his lawyer, and his brother."

"I was.... Anyway, we actually covered that brother of his on the news last year," Bobbert said.

"What a coincidence!"

"Indeed! You recall him?" Bobbert asked.

"Uh, no, I can't say I do."

"Aw, come on: Dante Kent, arrested for attempted rape on a teenage girl. Ring a bell?"

"Um... oh boy..." Tex looked up, his arm on the back of his neck, "I don't know, there are so many... wait, actually... yeah, I do remember him! Aha and now he's on the news again. Boy, talk about your fifteen minutes of fame!"

"You said it," Bobbert chuckled. "Anywho, Kent's financial records were straight. In fact, Kent's ex-wife upheld that he was a terrific ex-husband, never once neglected to pay the hundreds of dollars in child support that went towards her footwear."

"Good man."

"Fingerprints on the gun that killed him did not match the suspects'. A team of highly trained forensic specialists went in early this morning and ran tests using sophisticated chemical thingies, coming up with negative results," said Bobbert.

A pause.

"So in terms of actual suspects...?" Tex turned to Bobbert.

"Well, they didn't find anyone near the scene on Tuesday night, so they just picked a guy. Suspect's name is Jabron Williams. He's six-foot-one, about two hundred pounds, highly dangerous," said Bobbert in tones of seriousness, looking dead straight into the camera. "Anyway, enough of this story, we've got more interesting things to get to, so let's move on. I didn't know Bay Kent – . Our next – "

"Say it, Bobbert!"

"What are you talking about, Tex?"

"You know what I'm talking about! Say it! You know you're dying to."

"No!"

"Say it!"

"Okay, fine: I didn't know Bay Kent, so I don't care. There."

"Goody! In the spirit of a true reporter! Speaking of which, let's head over to Prudmila Sparks, she's out there in the city somewhere with some news story for us. Prudmila?"

"Morning, Tex, morning, Bobbert. I'm standing out here in front of the Vandorn Institute of Art, where hundreds of members belonging to the group AFAC have gathered. They're yelling, they're holding up cardboard signs, they're expressing anger at the authorities – doing everything artists are supposed to."

"Now, AFAC, that stands for 'Artists For A Cause'?" Bobbert asked.

"Actually, it stands for 'Artists For Any Cause. AFAC is an organization comprised of college students from all over the country who devote their lives to fighting for the cause."

"What cause?"

"Well, it depends, really," said Prudmila. "Maybe one of the students could explain," she led the cameraman through the crowd. "Excuse me," she tapped a girl with long straggly black-and-orange hair on the shoulder. "Hi, I'm Prudmila Sparks for Vandorn News, could I get your name?"

"My name is Shanneth Mourber," said the girl.

"Shanneth, what is going on here?"

"Well, it's a big rallying day for the AFAC organization."

"I can see that!" Prudmila exclaimed; behind Shanneth, three girls walked past, each carrying a brightly colored square taped to a wooden stick. One said "Awareness" on it, another said "Liberation" and was covered with stars, and the third said "Love," which was outlined in little hot pink hearts. Their small procession circled the general vicinity, looking very serious as they marched around yelling passionately with the crowd, driven by their determination to spread the message of love and liberation via poster board.

"Thanks to these efforts, have you noticed any significant changes in your environment lately?"

"Definitely, I think our society has become, um, much more aware and accepting."

"Aware and accepting of what?" Prudmila asked.

"Like, of important social justice issues that tie into the principles of freedom and democracy."

"And what does 'freedom' mean to you?"

"Freedom, um, it's doing what you as an individual want, and, um, having the right to be an individual by living in a democratic society that values the individual's personal liberty."

"Uhuh. And what does 'democracy' mean to you?"

"What does democracy mean to me? To me *personally*, I'd say that, like, democracy means having the freedom and power to choose, to have a voice in your government, to live your life as a unique individual."

"Uhuh. And what does 'individual' mean to you?"

"What does – um – to me an individual means, like, just, being who you are, living in a free and democratic society that accepts the diversity of the individual – "

"Okay. How does your organization aim to educate others about these high ideals that shape your community?"

"Well, today we're supporting the Women's Uniqueness World Project, which is a movement whose goal is to create a better social environment for women."

"And how is it looking to do this?"

"Well, we hope that in as little as five years we can ensure an educational course in gender studies as part of the general requirements program for all national colleges."

"Why?"

"Honestly, I really feel this is what both genders need," Shanneth said with vindication.

"And what makes you, one person, feel able to judge what millions of people you do not know need?" Prudmila posed.

"Ah – " there was a pause.

"Never mind. Tell me what sorts of things this course would teach?"

"Well, the Women's Uniqueness World Project has accumulated a lot of valuable statistical data."

"So give me a statistic, any one," Prudmila demanded.

"Um... well, out of a recent study of women who self-reported as feeling abused, seventy-seven percent were listed as 'married', eighteen percent were listed as 'single', and five percent were listed as 'in an open relationship'."

"Huh!" Prudmila's eyes widened. "So, would you say that by publicly displaying this statistic, the organization is sending some sort of message?"

"Um, I think the message here is definitely that women need to be more respected," Shanneth nodded.

"I see. So, does this organization appeal to both sides of the government?"

"Well, to tell the truth, most of us are under the jurisdiction of President Steffen, so it's really towards him that we're gearing our campaign."

"And how receptive has he been to your efforts?"

"Very! He is a great person, so open-minded. He really works with organizations on a personal level."

"Now, your organization is called 'Artists For *Any* Cause'. Could you explain why 'Any'?"

"Well, you see, we're artists, and we're always looking for some cause to support, just so we'll be involved. We really like being in the thick of controversy, it makes us look edgy," Shanneth explained.

"I see. So every time a new cause with the potential to cause political heat wells up in the current – ?"

"That's right, we'll be there."

"Does it matter what cause it is?"

"Um, no, not really. Actually, there is one nuance," Shanneth said in hindsight, "it has to be pretty radical, something that appeals to the younger, hipper generation and shocks the older ones."

"Why to the younger generation? Would you say they are more idealistic? Smarter, perhaps?"

"No, I wouldn't say smarter, I'd say more, um, *enlightened*," Shanneth found the appropriate word.

"How so?"

"Well, I feel the younger generation is more grounded in important ideals such as freedom, and democracy. Students today are willing to fight for them because they've cultivated a deep understanding of them – "

"As you showed us," said Prudmila.

"Aw, why thank you!" Shanneth smiled, flattered, and did a little side-nod with her head.

"So could you give me an example of some other causes your organization fights passionately for?"

"Well, a really big one we threw our support to last month was the campaign to legalize Docpot."

"That's the street term for the beverage Dr. Potter, which is made by the same company that manufactures Crack, Diet Crack, and a whole range of similar beverages, which have all been severely restricted, if not outlawed, by the International Food Laws. The consumption of Dr. Potter, as you know, is limited to one can a week, as with Crack and Diet Crack," Prudmila Sparks spoke into the camera for her viewers at home.

"Yes, we wanted to legalize the unrestricted use of Docpot."

"And how did you approach that campaign?"

"Um, we did lots of things. For one, we gave out little rubber bracelets with 'Legalize' engraved on them."

"And do you think that after you handed out little rubber bracelets to people, society has become more educated about the issues surrounding the legalization movement?" Prudmila asked.

"Definitely. In fact, we're doing the same for the Women's Uniqueness World Project; we've just ordered a shipment for one hundred thousand little rubber bracelets that say 'support WUWP' on them."

"Well, Shanneth, it sounds like you guys are making progressive steps in this campaign. How does your faculty feel about canceling classes for the higher cause?"

"Well, half of the faculty are in AFAC so I would say they feel good about it. The other half, unfortunately, have not canceled classes."

"Ah, so about half of you are skipping class right now. Would you say that an education isn't as important as life experience, then?"

"No no, I think education is *extremely* important, but there are some things that are just more... *real*... and you have to face them. You have to live," Shanneth nodded.

"Mhmm, mhmm," Prudmila nodded. "Partaking in such controversial activities, do you ever feel alienated by society?"

"Well, you know," Shanneth pondered the question while adjusting a couple of safety pins on her shirt, "I feel society is still a callous place for a truly unique spirit to unravel itself in."

"And you'd be referring to yourself here?" Prudmila asked her.

"Oh – no no no, I'm just saying, like, in general."

"Uhuh."

"I do sometimes feel like it's me against the world. But I would never stop just to make society happy. I would rather *die* than be a conformist," Shanneth asserted.

At this point another girl joined them by Shanneth's side.

"Is this one of your friends?" Prudmila gestured to their new companion, who had very curly blonde hair in two braids, square glasses with thick black rims, and a black t-shirt with a faerie on it that was colored in many shades of purple.

"Yes, this is one of my close friends," said Shanneth. "This is my partner, actually," they interlocked fingers.

"Oh! And what is your name?" Prudmila asked the blonde girl.

"Devora McCay," she answered as she caressed Shanneth's palm with her fingertips.

"Devora submitted some of her work to the Women's Art Gallery around the other side," said Shanneth.

"An art gallery! I would love to see that," said Prudmila, and the three women and the camera moved slowly through the throng to a long wall lined with many paintings, sketches, and photographs, all of them filled with deep symbolism representing the mysterious nature of the feminine aspect.

"These works focus on the many definitions of 'woman'. They celebrate female power, highlight our natural beauty, promote healthy expression of sexuality – " Shanneth used hand motions.

They passed by a queue surrounding a painting of a naked woman inside a glass vase.

"... You see, the vase acts as a restraint on her spirit, but with the way it conforms to her body it could also represent her erotic nature, which she is forced to bottle up," a young man explained intelligibly to the small crowd.

They stopped in front of Devora's painting, of a naked faerie sitting on a glowing crescent moon. She had long blue hair swaying in a breeze that could not possibly exist in the vacuum of the cosmos, and she looked down sadly. Glimmering stars surrounded her lonely orb.

"I call this 'Desolate Daemon'" said Devora.

"Very original composition," nodded Prudmila.

"Thank you. This here is a more abstract piece," Devora pointed to a canvas where disconnected female limbs swam in a melon-orange soup. There was a breast joined to a knee and a vagina by the left ear.

"Its title is 'Falling Apart of the Femme'. It took me several months to paint."

"Very rich in symbolism. What inspired this work?" asked Prudmila.

Devora touched Shanneth's arm. "It was when we took our relationship to a higher level that I had an outpouring of creative energy that fueled this piece."

"And what do you call this style?"

"I believe we're in the process of developing the next big creative movement," Devora answered. "We're not sure yet what it will be called. Something-ism."

A tall, green-haired boy trailed by three girls and one other boy passed them just then, waving energetically at the camera and catching Prudmila's attention.

"Excuse me," Prudmila made for him. Seeing her, he stopped, as did his followers. "Excuse me, do you think this rally is a justifiable excuse for everyone here to miss their classes?"

"Aw, it's totally worth it, this is, like, a once in a lifetime opportunity!" said the boy.

"But this happens every week," said Prudmila. "Don't you get bored of doing the same thing?"

"No way, man, every rally is unique," he shook his head.

"You don't feel this causes students to undermine their education?"

"Well, like, most of us aren't even missing class right now. See, Mondays and Wednesdays are when all the graphic design majors have class; Tuesdays and Thursdays are when the art people have class."

"I see. And your name is...?"

"Steven, Steven Arnoff."

"Nice to meet you, Steven Arnoff. And you're not a graphic design major, are you?"

"Nah, I'm a theatre major," he replied as one of the girls ran her hand through his hair, and he began on his way, his casual body language denoting his expectation that the three girls and one boy were going to follow him, which they did.

Prudmila turned back to the camera; behind her, a large group of AFAC members had gathered around Shanneth and Devora and faced the camera.

"Well there you have it," said Prudmila, gesturing to the crowd behind her, which was rather dark as most of them were wearing black. "Here at the Vandorn Institute of Art we are witnessing history as it is being made in our backyard, and it's all thanks to these brave souls who dedicate their lives to fighting for whatever cause is popular at the moment. Though they find themselves alone as they swim upstream, they determinedly plow on without losing sight of their own identities."

"We'll never give in to the majority!" a girl behind Prudmila shouted, displaying nails painted black as she pumped her fist in the air.

"Yeah!!" a dozen students behind her followed suit, also with black nails: they were a statement of how much they hated the conformity bred by popular trends such as pink polos.

"Join us when we come back to see what cause they're fighting for next week. Back to you, Bobbert," Prudmila concluded.

The camera shifted back to a close up of Bobbert and Tex's placid faces.

"What a life! Reminds me of my community college days," Bobbert said with an expression of fond reminiscence.

"You went to community college!" Tex sneered. "You know what that means, right?"

"What?"

"That you're stupid."

"That's not a nice thing to say on air, Tex, thousands of our viewers attend community college every year," Bobbert countered, looking like he was about to throw a chair. "Community college gave me some of the best educational experience of my life."

Tex looked delicately disdainful beneath his wife beater.

"Alright, then, smarty pants, what college did you got to?" Bobbert shot back.

"I didn't go to no college," said Tex. "I took a couple years off after high school and then came to work here."

"How'd you end up on a T.V. News Station?" Bobbert asked.

"I had an uncle who worked here, did something technical. He set me up."

"That was nice of him."

"Yep. He's dead now."

"Oh I'm so sorry to hear that," said Bobbert.

"It's okay; I've still got the job," said Tex.

"Heh. So how's it been working out for you all these years?"

"Oh well, you know, it puts food on the fold-out tray," Tex replied.

"True, true."

"So, uh, we have a few minutes to kill before the first commercial break. What do you wanna talk about?"

"Well... we could take a look at the political situation. Let's start with President Steffen. As Prudmila just mentioned, he's involved in some of the more progressive movements sweeping the nation. I know he recently signed in a bill giving special equality rights to the minorities, homosexuals, and homeless under his jurisdiction – "

"Wait a minute – isn't the entire homosexual population under his jurisdiction?" intervened Tex.

"Probably. Well we wouldn't expect it from Havenford. Keeping his nose out of that, president Havenford is. His half of the country won't mind, though," said Bobbert, then mumbled. "I personally don't."

"The elections are coming up soon; think you'll change sides?" Tex asked.

"I don't see much of a reason to – things seem to be going pretty smoothly," Bobbert said thoughtfully.

"Yeah, it looks likes it's gonna be a pretty uneventful election year. I figure most people will pick the same president," Tex said.

"It's nice though, we've struck a good balance. Both sides are pretty uniform when it comes to the big laws anyway."

"Yeah, wouldn't hear people fighting over the Food Laws," they both chuckled.

"Did you hear about the new project President Steffen is commissioning?" asked Bobbert.

"No. What is it?" asked Tex.

"He wants to repaint his entire half of the Decagon."

"Shoot! Really? That's a lot of paint!"

"Tell me about it – wants to cover the entire white exterior. He's got a big philosophy behind it, too. Wants to show how his half of the government and Havenford's half of the government are different yet fundamentally united," Bobbert explained.

"How's he gonna do that?"

"You know how white light is the un-fragmented whole of seven different colors?"

"Yeah."

"Well, Havenford's half is going to stay white, and Steffen is going to paint his half like a spectrum."

"Gee whiz! That's gonna be one bright building! How do you think Havenford's gonna feel?"

"Does it matter? He doesn't touch that half of the building.... But I bet he'll be pretty pissed. Anyway, Tex, I think we're out of time. Just a quick commercial break, and then we'll be back with your weather report," Bobbert concluded.

John changed the channel; *the news is never any good for catching up on politics*, he thought, submerging into his chair as C-Span came into focus: several hundred old men in black suits slowly filed into a large, spacious room filled from wall to wall with long tables and chairs, preparing to address a very serious topic relevant to the current political situation. The immobile camera from somewhere near the ceiling documented every moment of this procession. It was extremely eventful.

John turned one channel up to C-Span 2. A similar scene: several hundred more old men in black suits sitting at long tables, sifting through papers poking out of manila folders. A debate was in session, and a speaker currently had the floor: "... within the designated districts appointed under the new head of jurisdiction of the southwest region our lawmakers feel that blah blah blah blah blah taxes blah blah...."

John flipped through the channels rapidly until he got to C-Span 14, his favorite C-Span channel. It was sure to have something good, it always did.

"... And that concludes our review of long-standing sex-related laws that are still in effect today but largely unknown by the populace," the man filling the screen said. "Thank you all for tuning in."

John groaned disappointedly.

When Mr. Daltuhn walked into the break room, John had just flipped to C-Span 72, the last C-Span channel.

"...looks *just like violet!* Away with it, I say! There *is* nothing distinct between blue and purple!"

"You're watching today's debate: *Is Indigo Really a Color?*"

"Hallan, I need to speak with you and Borneo," Mr. Daltuhn said.

"About soap operas?" John asked, sitting up hopefully and turning around.

"No. Find him and come to my office," he said and left.

John did as he asked and when he and Borneo walked into his office, Mr. Daltuhn was reclined in his black leather armchair, on the phone, and motioned for the two to enter and sit down in front of his very shiny, polished black desk.

"...No, I can handle a week, max.... Right... exactly... of course not, you bastard!.... 'Bye."

Mr. Daltuhn put his phone down and surveyed them.

"Boys," he began, "Tell me – where are Artinians vacationing these days?"

Borneo and John looked at each other.

"Lainii!" he exclaimed.

John was confused. "That place is a wilderness," he said. "And at least a thousand miles from any continent."

"Exactly. Unlike the well known tourist spots, whose natural beauty has been ruined by the thorough Artinianization those places have experienced due to wave upon wave of tourists, each bringing a flood of successively lower-class people, causing a demand for Artinian shopping centers, this place is fresh, uncorrupted, authentic and pure, barely touched by the soiled hands of civilization. It's fast becoming the hot new escape spot for the wealthy elite. Since Artinia spread democracy to their people five years ago, three semi-exclusive resorts have been built on the virgin isle. And we, boys, will be next. This is where we stake our flag," Mr. Daltuhn said to them, leaning back.

"You want to broadcast NKOZ to Lainii?" John asked.

"Not only that. I want to set up a headquarters there. Not a big one like we have here, something small and more modest. Perhaps five stories. Imagine all the Lainiian-based programming that would become available to us! We could give Borneo his own talk show: Borneo Grimgae in a tropical paradise. Think of the appeal!"

"Mr. Daltuhn, I know you want to expand into new places, but Lainii has an entirely different culture; we could never win them over and undermine their traditional values; the natives would show too much resistance. Or they would just be apathetic, and all our efforts would be wasted," said John.

"That, Hallan, is why you would never succeed as a businessman. You'd be a damn good psychologist or anthropologist – in fact I don't know why you don't get out of here and write a psychology book, or find an overseas government job – but you can never look at anything from a business point of view. *Tourism* – it's not publicized *yet*, but it will be soon! The big wave is rising and we're going to ride it out! See, we're not going there to hook the native population; an undisturbed island is the ideal destination for dissatisfied Artinians, and every year Lainii will become more affordable. We're establishing ourselves among the urban development the influx of tourists will demand, integrating ourselves in Lainiian urban life-to-be by becoming the first big network to make our mark on that fresh soil, like an untouched virgin into which we will plant our seed. It will be a while before we reap the profits, but when we do, oh ho ho! It will all go over the natives' heads, of course, until in a generation when all our mass media and mindless programming will assimilate into the young natives and uproot their traditions and values – but by then I promise you we will no longer be the only network established on that paradise isle."

"Mr. Daltuhn – I don't know if I can help with this knowing that I'm actively destroying an entire culture and replacing it with something fake and mass produced," John said, finding himself fiddling with an uncomfortable sense of guilt.

Mr. Daltuhn looked highly annoyed. "Well, Johnny, can you work with the knowledge that that sad end is inevitable, whether or not we are the ones to initiate it? Other networks are bound to see the opportunity, it's like a neon sign in the sky; if we don't take advantage of it *now*, someone else will. And if *we're* there, at least we can set a good example, give them a hero," he gestured to Borneo, "instead of a food addict. That, Hallan, is the ideal outcome in this case."

John was silent.

Mr. Daltuhn cleared his throat. "So, bottom line, I'm sending the two of you to Lainii for three days," he said.

"You're sending us on vacation?" John asked.

Mr. Daltuhn snorted at this notion, as if it were funny. "Do you really think I would give you two plane tickets at the most expensive time of the year to fly, to Lainii, and stay at the most expensive, all-inclusive resort, *for fun*?"

"I would never assume that, Mr. Daltuhn."

"Well you're damn right not to! You two will be busting your asses down there. Borneo, it's your job to schmooze with the locals. The local tourists, I mean. I'm going to arrange a meeting for you with the Lainiian president – "

"But, sir, I don't think he'd want to be bothered with me," said Borneo, shocked at the prospect of meeting so intimidating a figure.

"Nonsense he'll be delighted."

"What's the Lainiian outlook on Artinians?" John asked.

"The president of the new democratic regime loves Artinia; he practically makes it his mission to import as many Artinian commodities into his country as possible: three modern urban sites are being constructed as we speak, under the supervision of Artinian companies. The malls and banks are already complete, and they are now building several offices, as well as a historic district I believe."

"What do the natives think?" John asked.

"The same, I'm sure; after all, it's a democracy now. You two have nothing to be nervous about! The more confident you are, the better. The Lainiian government thinks all Artinians are confident, charismatic assholes. That's why, Borneo, you'll be doing the smiling, and Hallan will be doing the thinking. Got that, Hallan? Your job is to watch over this one and keep him on task. Same with the camera crew, they tend to get rowdy when they're together, I wouldn't let them loose unsupervised on a tropical island."

Mr. Daltuhn paused. "You leave Friday, six AM sharp."

"As in, two days from now?" asked John, surprised.

"Yes. Now get back to work, both of you!" he yelled.

"Oh, wait wait wait – I have to go home and plan my outfits!" Borneo threw his arms up.

"I'm sending you to a Bobdamn tropical resort and on top of that you have the *gall* – !"

"Mr. Daltuhn, image is *crucial* to the success of this mission! It requires careful planning!"

"Borneo, don't you need help with that?" John asked him pointedly.

"No, why would I need help picking out my clothes?" he looked at John confusedly.

"Alright, Borneo, you can go," said Mr. Daltuhn gruffly. "Hallan – back to work!"

Chapter 04: Just Say No!

"Now, can anyone summarize the Theory of Devolution for me?" the teacher asked her third graders. She called on a little boy in the second row.

"The Theory of Devolution states that as time moves forward, our race continues in a steady decline, degenerating further with each passing generation. Qualities such as survival skills, independent thinking, and originality fade while those of laziness, selfishness, stupidity, and especially self-deception blossom as our race becomes ever more dependent on outside comforts, cheap entertainment, and the instant gratification of every personal desire. Knowledge and wisdom that our ancestors held concerning the living of a decent life, our purpose on this world, and our personal development is continuously being lost and by today has almost wholly disappeared.

In addition, the mark of how far we have degenerated is the oft-heard assertion of the exact opposite of this theory: that our race is more highly evolved than ever and that we are replacing our ancestors' animalistic ways with virtues such as enlightenment, sophistication, mental refinement, humanitarianism, and love. The aforementioned are terms given to what is actually pseudo-intellectualism, trendy new-age beliefs proponed by a cult of followers, a hipster image, and a large amount of complacency, and are all superficial masks currently used to (very effectively) cover our never-more-dominant inner animals."

"Very good, Slater! Class, it looks like our guests are here today, so we're going to stop the lesson and let them take over," the teacher said.

Milly walked nervously into the elementary school classroom in her bright orange *Just Say No!* t-shirt behind her three fellow Peamount students. She let the two tall junior boys and Dee Allderbay, who led the front, obscure her from the class' view. She was the only sophomore. Dee Allderbay hadn't said a word to Milly; in fact, Milly wasn't sure Dee even knew her name.

The four of them had been chosen as this month's model students, and their reward was to teach the kids at the local elementary school about *Just Say No!*, a nationwide program designed to instill into children both knowledge of the dangers of illegal food, and the means to resist it.

"Hi, kids!" Dee began cheerily. "My name is *Dee*, and my classmates and I are here today to teach you about the importance of making good choices! Has anyone heard of *Just Say No!*?"

The third grade class stared back blankly.

"Does anyone know what the Food Laws are?"

"Um, the Food Laws determine what kind of food we can eat and how much of it," the little girl in the pink shirt with a heart on it that Dee called on said uncertainly.

"That's right! In order to be functional members of society, you need to understand the Food Laws well," Dee continued. "The Food Laws were written fifty years ago to solve the worldwide food shortage that came about as a direct result of massive overeating which began with the introduction of sweeteners, fast food, and preservatives into our diets. There is still a food shortage today, which is why food consumption is strictly regulated. Each family is allowed to buy only a certain amount of foodstuffs a week. Today, almost every country in the world follows the Food Laws, with several notable exceptions such as Aruq.

While the Food Laws have saved the world from starvation, unfortunately they've created some big problems. The biggest of these is food abuse. Food is eaten illegally by people who choose to ignore the Food Laws, and it is a very dangerous practice. If you are caught you can go to jail for many years. Also, you can become addicted. Food addiction almost always destroys a life: it ruins one's health, takes over one's time and job, and sabotages one's personal relationships. Thousands of people in Artinia die every year due to health problems or homelessness that happened because they were addicted to food.

Another problem is the black market for illegal food that has developed. Illegal trading, underground restaurants, and laboratories found in basements of street-wise high-school and college-drop-out boys' parents' houses are corrupting businesses and ruining the economy.

The most abused food around the world is chocolate. Chocolate is popular because it makes one feel good, seems to have no bad effects, and lowers inhibitions, making it easier for cowardly people to socialize. People quickly go from eating chocolate once in a while to eating it every day, on the hour. Too much chocolate can make a person dependent on it as a mood-enhancer, so that they are extremely cranky whenever they *don't* have chocolate. This becomes a problem as good chocolate, the tempered kind that melts in your mouth, is hard to find. People spend a lot of money on such chocolate from dealers who up the prices, often receiving, to their anger, chocolate of sub-par quality. Chocolate addicts are recognizable by their excess weight (due both to the excessive amount of chocolate they eat and the sedentary lifestyle they live), their facial acne, their belief that things such as relationships and careers will 'work themselves out', and their frequent use of the word 'chill'. Recently there has been much pressure to make chocolate legal to eat.

The next most frequently abused food is Crack. Unlike chocolate, a very limited amount of Crack and all related items such as Diet Crack, Dr. Potter, Sugar-Free Extra-Sweet Crack, and the like, are allowed, with the limit being one can per week, and only if one is over eighteen years of age. Crack and co. are liquids that frequently come in decorated aluminum cans one has to 'pop'. Crack produces a temporary surge of energy, and becomes extremely addictive when drunk more than once a week. The addiction is very dangerous and is characterized by a thirst for more Crack immediately after one has finished a can, shaking hands when one does not have Crack available, and, eventually, an insensitivity to Crack's high. Crack addicts are easy to recognize by how skinny they are: they consume almost nothing but Crack, which has enough sugar to run on all day.

The last major class of abused food is what we call 'gourmet foods'. Typically they are made of the finest ingredients and sold for exorbitant prices by dealers in the streets. They are 'glamour' foods, abused by rich businessmen who hand them out at exclusive parties as a marker of their wealth. The rarer the ingredients, the richer and more estimable the businessman, and never more so than if the food was imported from overseas. Catching abusers is tricky because they usually appear relatively normal. Gourmet foods include quiche, foi gras, and delicate pastries made with over fifty ingredients.

A *legal* food that's becoming a problem is sugar. It's being abused by teenagers who consume it in small packets of white powder or cubes that can be popped in order to produce a 'sugar high'. Often they do this in small huddles by the school's exterior before class, or sneak sugar cubes to their friends while class is in session as the teacher writes on the board. Also, they have started melting sugar into 'caramel' and lacing it over anything from apple slices to cookies to make them from flavorful."

One little kid raised his hand. Dee called on him.

"My mother buys SmartPick dinners three times a week. Is that illegal?" he asked.

"Research has shown that manufacturing SmartPick does not contribute to the food shortage, so there is no regulation on them," answered Dee.

"Now, eating illegal food, even once in a while, is never okay!" Dee impressed upon the third graders. "People will stop you in the streets and try to sell you chocolate bars or crème-filled donuts; your peers will pressure you into Crack-drinking contests when you hang out together over the weekends; society will make it seem like you need to gain experience with food in order to be educated about true life. All of these reasons are crap. Especially the last one. Whenever someone tries to get you to eat illegal food, all you have to do is *just say no*! We have pamphlets for all of you that explain, over three pages, how to just say 'no'. It's easier than it sounds." Dee made one of the guys hand out the pamphlets to the class.

Another little girl raised her hand with a question.

"Is it true that mostly broad-nosed people abuse food in Artinia?" she asked to the chagrin of her broad-nosed classmates, who turned to stare at her.

Dee looked blank, her mouth open.

"Um – " she was at a loss for words, and the guy who wasn't passing out pamphlets shrugged.

"It's not true, every group of people eats the same amount of illegal food," Milly piped up from the back, catching the ball before it hit the ground. "I mean – no group is more at fault than another. It doesn't matter what kind of nose you and your family have," she quickly fixed her statement.

"That's right, in some countries it still matters what your nose is like, but in Artinia, all noses are equal – innies, broad-noses, curve-noses, flat-noses."

"Yeah, I mean, come on, noses? Are you really going to not hire a guy because you don't like the way his *nose* looks?" one of the junior guys said coolly. "That's like not hiring someone because of what his skin looks like or something," and the kids laughed.

"Thank you, students, for teaching our kids these valuable lessons. Let's give Peamount High a round of applause," said the teacher, and the kids obliged. The bell rang, and Dee and the others moved on to their next class, the fourth graders.

Chapter 05: Lainii

Tired from a late night of watching a riveting debate on C-Span 14 about the proper teaspoon dosage of sugar to be consumed per cup of tea at international dinners, as soon as John, Borneo, and their camera crew boarded the plane for Lainii that Friday morning, John immediately slumped down in the window seat and turned his head away from the throng of giddy people chatting incessantly at six in the morning, and, vaguely watching a gleaming orange slice of sun creep over the horizon, dozed off.

When he woke up, they were flying above a vast city of puffy white clouds, dotted with punctures through which glimmered the blue water far below. The plane was quiet, its interior clean and brightly lit by the rays of sunlight that shone through; off to the side only some moderately audible voices could be heard. Sure enough, it was Borneo, who had long ago gotten out of his seat and was now hanging out in the isle making conversation. The bright blue Lainiian flower-print button-down shirt he wore and the light enveloping his tanned face did something remarkable for his eyes; the crew members he was talking to, at least, seemed very receptive to that.

"Now Nelly, Francine, there's no need to fight over it, I'll take both of your pillows," Borneo was saying to a couple of the flight attendants crowded around him. The two blonde girls, who both appeared to be in their twenties, looked slightly put-out.

"So like I said, I was never much of a surfer, though I've tried it a few times. One time, I tried to take on this huge wave, so big, I got caught in it and almost died – not that I could – but I got pretty banged up – oh, thank you Donna," he turned to a slim brunette who handed him a glass of rum.

"Ah, John, you're up!" Borneo called over to his friend, noticing him stirring groggily in his seat.

"Not entirely," John mumbled in such a way that only he understood what he said.

"Could I get something for my friend over there? Something that'll really give him a punch, tequila maybe," Borneo requested to the girl who had brought him the drink.

"Jodie, you get it for him," Donna said to the redhead next to her while staring and smiling at Borneo, simultaneously pushing Jodie out of the way and moving in slightly to tighten the circle of female workers that enclosed Borneo like a hydrophobic membrane. The result was that before the order was even completely voiced, the poor redhead found herself thrown out of the group, with her coworkers subtly blocking every possible venue of reentry with their bodies.

Throwing a dirty look at Donna, the girl named Jodie turned reluctantly around and remained diligently with her back to their game of eye flirtation to let them know just how pissed she was.

"What would you like?" she asked John, staring at her coral pink nails. John felt slightly sorry for her.

"Could I get some cranberry juice?"

"With..."

"With... uh, ice?"

She looked up. John looked back, struck by how apparent it was that she had had no idea that he was in fact a materialized being.

Satisfied with his juice, and with Borneo now on his third glass of rum and still laughing with Donna, Nelly, and Francine, John leaned back in his seat and took out the magazine he had brought with him. Jodie had sat down in Borneo's empty seat next to him, and out of the corner of his eye John saw her glancing over at him every now and then. Her eyes rested on his shirt for a while, grimacing. But as she kept turning away, and glancing over again, then turning away and glancing back (with increased frequency), she paid more notice not to the shirt but to the lines of the body beneath it, which she did not find repulsive. *Hmm he's not bad*, that kind of body language said aloud. She couldn't have Borneo, but here was another guy whom she hadn't noticed before, and he was all alone; this new development brought with it an element of interest for her. Plus her body was eager to forget its loss and move on, or so her explorative eyes made obvious as the rest of Jodie prepared to dive into this new quest.

She leaned in just a little. "Whatcha reading?"

"*Mortician Monthly.*"

"I – what?" she faltered. Hello, setback!

"It's a magazine I subscribed to back in school."

"Oh, um, what's it about?" Jodie leaned in again, recovering.

"Well, mainly dead people."

"Like dead actors?" she perked up.

"No – well, sometimes – but it's more to do with what happens to the body after a person dies. It's got experiments scientists have done with dead bodies, and weird autopsies, and new discoveries in the field. There are lots of random facts in there, too; like did you know that when you get beheaded, your head remains conscious for about fifteen seconds?"

"Uh... no, I didn't."

"Yeah. Here, let me show you." He flipped to a page near the back and read: "'Legend has it that five hundred years ago when King Chester the Third of Montierra's liberal Congress comprised largely of the wealthy members of the Trenchcoat party cunningly turned his own loyal constituents against him and then gained their support for the execution by beheading of said king, his severed head rolled across the ground, his eyes turned and looked at his body for a few seconds, and then turned back and stopped, although the rest of his face remained perfectly still, despite wild rumors claiming that his ears twitched as well, as if in anger.'"

Jodie looked at John, unable to make up her mind about how to react, but pretty sure that she should be totally repulsed by how weird he was.

"Oh my – um... what's on the next page?" she found a way to change the subject, sort of.

John turned the page, which expanded into a four-part fold-out of a human corpse in the process of being dissected. Jodie caught her breath, ran her pretty pink nails through her hair, and stared at the picture open-mouthed.

"I – I – actually think I have to go... back to the cockpit..."

She got up and left, bypassing Borneo and his entourage; John stared after her. When it became apparent that she wasn't coming back, he turned around and resumed reading his magazine.

Soon, Borneo, exhausted from laughter, plopped down next to him and leaned back, his face smiling toward the ceiling and his eyes closed.

"I think I'll take a nap," he said contentedly.

"Where are your cohorts?"

"Oh, the girls had to get back to work."

"Ah well, there'll be others," John said.

"What are you talking about? Donna and Nelly both gave me their numbers. They're staying in Lainii for a couple of days before flying off."

"So there's a chance yet."

"Definitely! They're great, both of them.... Hey, which one did you think was cuter?" Borneo suddenly turned and faced John, poised to hear his opinion.

"Nelly."

"Nelly? I thought Donna..." Borneo reflected, turning away from John and furrowing his eyebrows in confusion.

"Donna had a kind of malicious look to her," said John.

Borneo snapped up and gave him a look. "I'm only talking physically here! Personality you've got to take separately," he asserted. "And don't give me that look. I *do* care about personality, and I think it's just as important as physical appearance!"

"Okay."

"I'm serious! But you can't say that looks aren't important to you," Borneo argued.

"I'm not. I don't distinguish between looks and personality when I meet a girl – they're the same to me."

"How can they be the same?" Borneo laughed.

John thought about it. "It's like they work together to make something complete," he said.

"I don't get it."

"I'm saying, you can't really know someone if you separate them into looks and personality."

"Is this one of your psychological things?" Borneo asked skeptically.

"No – I mean, maybe – it's more a worldview thing, I guess," John said. He didn't think about the method with which girls ought to be perceived, he simply perceived them. Like Jodie – the coral color she must have chosen for her nails on some earlier date, the way she'd maneuvered her small, sharp body, the way her dull brown eyes had twitched when she found something disgusting.

"Oh please, John," Borneo took a sip of rum. "That's bullshit."

"If you say so," John picked up his magazine again as silence fell between them.

"*Mortician Monthly?*" Borneo queried, leaning over John's shoulder to see the cover.

"I don't get it, why would you want to read something so depressing when we're going to paradise?" Borneo asked him. "You said you hated the monotony in the office, and now you've been given the perfect chance to break it. How can you be so... depressed? Do you know how many beautiful women there are in Lainii?"

"Well it sounds like a great place for you: beautiful, dumb women everywhere."

"Not for me, for *you!*" Borneo prodded John for emphasis.

"I don't plan on starting a relationship with someone I'll never see again after three days," said John.

"Pf! Where does a relationship come into this? Just have fun with them, John!"

"Ah... I see; you want to team up so that we can switch after we finish with the first one," it dawned on John.

"Oh no, you'll be playing it solo. I'm keeping my hands to myself," said Borneo.

It was John's turn to recoil. "What?! Since when?"

For a few seconds Borneo didn't answer, just looked downward serenely, as if contemplating his words.

"I've been doing a lot of thinking lately," he started, "and I realized – I'm done playing the game. I've been doing it for fifteen years and after all that, it's brought me nothing."

"Borneo, you're twenty-three."

"Yeah, and you know what?"

"What?" John asked.

"*I've never been in love!*" he gushed.

"So? Neither have I."

"John, I want something real! Not just some temporary fling like I have every week. I want something meaningful, something based on more than looks. I want to find the one. And you know what else? I have a feeling – nothing more, just a slight feeling – that I'll find her here. In Lainii."

And with that, Borneo leaned back and stared past John out the window at the sunlit clouds they flew by, smiling.

"It was great meeting you," Borneo said to Donna as they disembarked to step onto Lainiian soil for the first time.

"You too," she said coyly. "Call me!"

"I will."

"*You better*," steel glinted in her eyes. They stepped down and headed over to the inside of the airport, John eager to leave her behind.

"Shouldn't you not be thinking about random girls if you're out for the one?" John asked.

"How do you know she's just a random girl?" Borneo countered. John said nothing. He imagined Borneo marrying a sweet girl like Donna. She would probably tell him every day that even though she could be a bitch sometimes, she was really a sweetheart deep down, and knew that she deserved to have a man who would treat her like a princess. She would probably say this when they were arguing about who would do the dishes. And of course since she was a woman and needed to have her freedom, Borneo would smile and nod his head compliantly like a good husband, and go start on the plates, while Donna sat on the couch watching reruns of *Artinia's Next Great Icon* and eating chips. And they would be so in love....

Outside the entrance into the airport they spotted a short, round man in a green suit, accompanied by a thin, slightly taller man who wore a shirt similar to Borneo's and had a stringed wooden instrument slung across his back. The stout one waved to them as they approached.

"Borneo Grimgae! Am I right?" he boomed at them. "The name's Jerry Rombro," he stuck a swollen hand out and firmly shook Borneo's, then John's, hand, "president of the Moonflower Resort, finest in all of Lainii. I've come out here today to personally escort you fellows to your room. And this is Jonki Guida, our guide for the afternoon," he said, gesturing to his companion. The thin man gave a little smile but said nothing.

They and their camera crew piled into a white van that stood waiting for them with chauffer in place, the camera crew taking the back two rows, Mr. Rombro the front passenger seat, and Jonki, Borneo, and John filling the second row.

"To your left you see lavish Lainiian ree-sort and hotels," Jonki explained in accented Artinian as they drove, describing the scene they passed by. Borneo and John looked left. Behind the stretch of palm trees and vines tops of sprawling complexes of white buildings and coral colored roofs burgeoned through, mazes of staircases climbing the walls and zigzagging through aesthetic archways that branched off to white paved pathways.

"That's gorgeous architecture," Borneo exclaimed, enthralled.

Lainii really is *rich*, John thought, looking at the glamorous beachfront resorts stretching toward positive and negative infinity along the coast. He lost himself in imagining a tempting life scenario of watching the sunrise from his own private beach every morning under the shade of a fruited tree....

A fidgeting movement from Mr. Rombro jerked John out of his daydream and his head spun mechanically. He caught a glance of the view out the right-hand window; shocked, unable to comprehend what he was seeing, John stared open mouthed: where he expected to see a mirror image of the glamour on his left he instead saw scattered shanties no bigger than two port-a-potties stuck together, lining the road like a colony of dice that had landed miraculously on their edges. *Are these ancient ruins?* he thought. The construction of them was terrible, some slapped together in ways even the most creative modern artist wouldn't conceive. And the planks of wood with cloths thrown over them made to look suspiciously like entrances...? John saw three small children playing outside one such shanty, and further along he caught sight of a woman, strongly resembling Jonki and their chauffer in appearance, exiting one of the ruins to hang up what looked like wet clothes on a clothesline. And then it hit John....

"Excuse me, but are these – ?" he poked Jonki, who was still busy blabbering about the resorts to Borneo and the others. Jonki stopped and turned to face John.

"Are these... are those structures... do people live in there?" he asked the tour guide in shock. Jonki's face froze in puzzlement for a moment as he looked to where John was pointing.

"No – no – over heer hotel – " he grabbed John's chin, attempting to direct his face away back to the left-hand side. John resisted firmly and pushed the little man's hand away with difficulty.

"Borneo, look at it! Those are people's houses!"

"Whoa, really? Hey, did you know they actually have bars inside the pools at the Moonflower?"

"Excuse me, Jonki – Mr. Guida – but is that how all the natives on the island live?"

But Jonki Guida was adamant. "You look wrong way – look wrong way – hotel left –" he kept repeating.

"Excuse, Mr. Hallan, everything alright?" Jerry Rombro cut in, turning around from the front and pretending to just notice the commotion.

"Actually, no, I was expecting a more extensive tour of Lainii," John tried hard to sound even. "I get the impression there's so much of it we're speeding by."

Rombro glanced casually out of his right-hand window. "Ah, you want to see more of the local culture?"

"Yes," said John.

"I'm sorry, Mr. Guida is hired exclusively for the Moonflower; he's not qualified to provide information in that arena."

"But he's one of – !"

"The Moonflower offers many excursions around the island if you want to get the true taste of Lainii. You can tour the local villages, the jungle, anything you like. In fact there's a good one leaving tomorrow morning. All free of charge for you, of course," Mr. Rombro told him.

"Aw, dude, no way, we're hitting up the beach tomorrow," Borneo gave John a wink that clearly alluded to their conversation on the plane.

After that, the conversation died down and the company drove along in uneventful silence until out from the thick dark green canopy emerged an enormous white marble building with gilded front doors thrown wide open to the marble-floored lobby. Everything glistened under the sun shining through the ninety-foot-high glass ceiling above, including the water in the artificial river cut through the floor running the length of the lobby and out back between two white columns into resort property, where they caught glimpses of pools, lurid flowers resembling miniature sunsets, and many hectic workers in clean white uniforms, all of whom looked similar to Jonki Guida and their driver as they zipped up and down the trails and staircases carrying stacks of fluffy white towels.

"I suggest you boys go get something to eat before the good stuff's gone; Jonki and Dariku will bring your bags upstairs," said Mr. Rombro, watching Borneo's stupefied face complacently. He steered them to the main dining hall.

"This place is wild, man. And we're gonna be wild with it," Borneo threw his arm around John enthusiastically.

John tried to survey the buffet, but there were so many disproportionately fat people blocking his view that he couldn't make out any of the food.

"Looks like all of Artinia came out here," he muttered under his breath.

"I read in the brochure that the ocean here is the bluest and cleanest in the entire world," Borneo exclaimed as they waited in line behind an obese man.

"You read something?" John asked.

"Well not like an article, I just saw the picture and there was a little caption underneath. But imagine – we get to see the best waters our lifetime has to offer, a sight that doesn't exist anywhere else."

"That does sound pretty exotic," John admitted. "Maybe you're – "

"Oh, you know what? I'm gonna go check out what's at that buffet over there," Borneo suddenly motioned to the opposite side of the hall, where two busty looking young ladies happened to be standing. John sighed.

Finally it was his turn. The aroma of sizzling meats and caramelized veggies made his mouth water for some of the exotic fare. He looked down the buffet, wondering what he should sample first: there were hot dogs, burgers, fried chicken, two bins of mashed potatoes, mac and cheese, and coleslaw. It all looked delicious.

He found Borneo again the end of the buffet; he was examining a plate.

"This is bizarre!" he exclaimed. "I've never seen anything like it!"

"Borneo, it's a burger with a toothpick through it minus the top bun."

"Geez, who would've thought..." Borneo said in amazement.

"You can get some regular ones back there," said John, pointing to the other end of the buffet.

"John! We're here to take risks, branch out! *I'm* gonna step out of my comfort zone," he said, and reached for a Lainiian meat patty.

After lunch they headed up to their suite, where John immediately flopped onto his bed to sleep like a puppy through the humid afternoon. Borneo, meanwhile, couldn't contain his excitement. He gingerly entered his own private bedroom and was immediately filled with the sense of being inside a magic box. He ran his fingers over the softly coral puckered wall, savoring the texture, then went back to the main room to their balcony overlooking the ocean.

The breeze swept refreshingly through his hair. *It's so blue, so perfectly blue that it looks like those people are swimming in the sky*, he thought as he leaned against the gilded railing. A forest of palm trees below became sparse and gave way to soft white sands which melted into the ever-changing sea foam at the shore and stretched into the azure waters that became fathoms deep before they disintegrated again into lightness at the horizon.

Of all the places he had traveled to in his brief career, Borneo had never been to one as enigmatically fateful as this. It was as if something were waiting here for him. He could almost hear it whispered on the waves crashing lightly ashore, but the meaning was just beyond his reach....

He went back inside to use the bathroom, entering a space the size of their break room complete with a Jacuzzi, white marble floors, two separate shower stalls, dimmed lighting, violet and coral candles lining said Jacuzzi, and little potpourri satchels tired with red velvet and placed in strategic nooks all around the enclosure.

By a flickering crimson tea light on a ceramic platter, Borneo noticed a rolled up piece of parchment tied with more red velvet. *A secret message?* he unfurled it and read by votive-light: a gala, tonight, at the Moonflower.

"Come on, up you get! We're not going to waste this day lying around!" Borneo said, dragging John off the bed by his feet.

"But I want to sleep," mumbled John.

"We've got business to attend to," said Borneo seriously. "There's gonna be a party here tonight in my honor."

"That's not what 'cordially invited' means, Borneo," said John, taking the paper from his hands and reading it.

"Still. It's our job to go around and promote it."

"Where does it say that?"

"It's obviously what Rombro wants us to do," Borneo rolled his eyes. "Besides, how is it gonna look if we show up to the party and don't know anyone there? I'm supposed to be Borneo Grimgae, the guy everyone recognizes! We need to get out there and spread the word! And where better to start than at the beach?" he winked.

"At the pool," said John.

"No way – all the hotties are gonna be at the beach. The pool is where the old people hang out," said Borneo rationally.

"We can't promote the party to old people?"

"Do you want to?" Borneo countered.

"I don't care," said John.

As they stepped out of the palm tree grove onto pure beach, John realized Borneo was right about one thing – no matter how far down he looked, all John saw were bright towels occupied by bikini-clad females in the nineteen to twenty-seven age group.

Borneo gave him a smirk. "I'm telling you, we're going to meet so many interesting girls here," he said as they searched for a good spot. They settled and took off their shirts. Five seconds later, they saw three girls approaching, talking and laughing as they walked barefoot. They weren't walking specifically to the guys, but the closer they got, the more the girls wordlessly acknowledged the guys, and vice versa. They all secretly knew that their meeting was inevitable.

"Hey there," Borneo called out to them as they passed right by them, determinedly avoiding their eyes.

"Oh, hi!" one of them turned and said in surprise.

"Who might you ladies be?" Borneo asked with a wide smile. They giggled.

"I'm Jennie," said the one who had spoken, who had hair that was long in the back but short with choppy layers in the front, and blonde highlights.

"I'm Kyla," said the one with long hair in the back but short with choppy layers in the front, and blonde highlights.

"And I'm Tess," said the last one, who had short black hair in a choppy fun sexy cut.

"Nice! You girls here on vacation?" Borneo asked them.

"Yeah, for a week. We just came here yesterday," said Tess.

"Awesome! Like it so far?"

"Are you kidding? I am, like, in *love* with this place!" exclaimed Kyla.

"Yeah, it's so beautiful! I wish I could live here," sighed Jennie.

"I know, I love the beach," said Borneo.

"Me too!" Tess beamed. "I'd love to live in this resort."

"No way! So would I!" Borneo exclaimed, and they smiled at each other over their shared sentiment. "I'm Borneo, by the way. And this is my friend, John," Borneo introduced them, pointing to John, who was lying on his towel with his sunglasses on reading *Mortician Monthly* again. John pulled his glasses down and surveyed the girls over them.

"Hey," he said.

"Hey," all three replied weakly.

"Wait, are you Borneo Grimgae?" asked Kyla, looking back up.

"Yep."

"No way!" went Jennie and Tess.

"Way," he winked.

"Oh my Bob, *no one* from school is gonna believe that we met Borneo Grimgae," said Kyla.

"Where do you guys go to school?" asked Borneo.

"University of Southern Vermerilla," said Jennie.

"Awesome! What are you studying?"

"I'm majoring in psychology," said Tess.

"I'm majoring in journalism," said Kyla.

"Nice!"

"I'm majoring in journalism," said Jennie.

"Nice!"

"Actually, a bunch of our girlfriends and us started a club 'cause they're all majoring in journalism, too, so it's a lot of fun. Like last month we interviewed this guy on campus. He's a theatre major, but he also plays guitar. His name is Jake Crash, and he's coming out with his first solo album. It's called 'My Journey'. Have you heard of him?" Jennie asked.

"No, I haven't," said Borneo.

"Oh, well he's really local and underground. But he has lots of fans all over the country. Actually, we got to listen to a demo, it was really cool. His lyrics are so deep, like, spiritual, yet really down-to-earth at the same time."

"Nice. I like that kind of stuff," Borneo said.

"Yeah, me too," said Jennie in a cool voice.

"So what about you, Ms. Psychology?" Borneo continued, turning to Tess. "After you graduate, are you going to go work as a middle school counselor?" he cocked his head.

"No, I'd rather start my own practice in downtown San Diablos after I finish grad school," Tess said.

"Whoa, you guys are in grad school?" Borneo asked.

"Oh no, we just finished our freshman year in undergrad!" exclaimed Jennie, and her friends giggled.

Borneo turned to Kyla and Jennie. "What about you two? Are you gonna end up teaching a high school journalism class fifteen years from now?"

"Oh no, that's not what I want," Kyla shook her head. "I really wanna write for a fashion magazine, like *Belle*, and then hopefully after, like, five years of experience start my own magazine!"

"Five years? Are you crazy!? Do it for a year if you want, but start your own right away! You gotta take risks if you wanna get somewhere!" exclaimed Borneo.

Kyla looked up at him with poignant eyes. "Are you sure? People say it's really hard to start out on your own with minimal experience."

"Don't listen to them," he consoled her, "you're young, you're fresh, and you've got tons of potential. They'll love a spunky girl like you!"

"I'm still trying to find my own voice. I don't want to sound like just anybody. I'm afraid my writing isn't innovative enough to make it in journalism," Kyla voiced her self-doubt.

"Don't be afraid to say what's really on your mind," Borneo advised.

"I'm not! Ask them, I always speak my mind," she said emphatically, pointing to Tess and Jennie.

Tess and Jennie nodded. "Kyla always sticks up for what she believes in," said one.

"Yeah, like, last year, this asshole guy started talking about how gays shouldn't be allowed to get married," said the other, "and one of our really good friends is gay, and he was, like, really upset by it –"

"He almost started crying!"

" – so Kyla went up to him and started yelling at him about how ignorant he is, and how he only accepts people who agree with his views. It was so good, that guy just stood there with his mouth open for like an hour afterwards!"

"That's 'cause he knows I'm right! *Grr*! People like that make me so mad!" Kyla exclaimed angrily. "Jerk." And they all laughed.

"That's awesome," said Borneo, recovering from a bout of laughter. "You should totally write about that. It would be unique. You seem really passionate about it, too."

"You really think?" Kyla asked, smiling.

"Definitely! Anyway, what about you?" Borneo turned to Jennie.

"I want to move to Vandorn someday and write for a newspaper there," Jennie said.

"Like the *Vandorn Times*?" Borneo asked.

"That's, like, my dream! But I know it'll never happen," she hung her head.

"Oh, come on!" said Borneo, cocking his head and giving her a "you gotta believe!" face.

"No, I know there must be a million other people out there who want the same exact thing," she said.

"Yeah, but you're special," Borneo winked.

"Awww, thank you! You're such a sweetie, I love you!" she hugged her new best friend.

"Think you could give me some good publicity when you're writing for the Vandorn Times?" Borneo asked her.

"Yeah right, like you even need it!" she smiled.

"Hey, you never know. Speaking of which, did you girls hear about the party here tonight?"

"Yes! We're *so* excited!" said Jennie.

"I better see you ladies there tonight," he said.

"Definitely!"

"Like we'd miss it!"

"My room has a really nice Jacuzzi. Maybe if the party gets boring, we – "

Borneo suddenly glanced to his right – and beheld a vision so spectacular that it blasted his senses numb with dynamite. It was as if he could suddenly see ultraviolet light, which in its brilliance whisked all the other colors away into monotony:

From the shoreline fifteen feet away emerged a young female who looked as if she had been made by the sea itself. Tall, lithe, graceful as the waves that played around her feet, she had a mane of deep caramel-colored hair that cascaded down her back in waves like a thick, shining waterfall billowing behind her as she walked against the breeze, every movement of her golden body filled with the vigor of her youth. Her figure was exquisite, every bone hinting at rhythmic motion beneath its smooth exterior, her legs wondrous, her hips perfectly formed and enticing, her breasts like warm sacs of beach-sand cocooned in velvet. She looked back at Borneo evenly through large eyes the exact blue-green crystalline color of the waters, which glowed like opals in her golden face.

Over the red bikini that rounded off her thighs and loosely cupped her breasts a lei of passionately pink Lainiian flowers encircled her shoulders and slim waist, adorning it like a banner. She calmly headed toward Borneo, who felt darts of rapture shooting through his heart.

As she passed, "Hi," she spoke. She had the smoothest, most seductive voice imaginable, like molten caramel drizzled over a plate of gleaming fruit.

And then she walked right by. Borneo stared after her, his mouth hanging open; he had completely forgotten about Judy, Kristen, and Sam. They had already left somewhere, though neither Borneo nor John had noticed.

Borneo sat down on his towel and stared off into the ocean. John put down his magazine.

"What's wrong?"

"Did you see her?" was all Borneo asked.

"Who, the lifeguard who just passed?"

"Yes."

"What about her?"

"She was perfect. She was like a drop of sun that had melted and fallen into the form of a woman's body."

"Well did you say anything to her?" John asked.

"No, I – she said 'hi' – but I – I – couldn't think."

"*You* clammed up around a girl?"

"And now I've lost her. I've never met anyone like her and now she's gone... forever...."

"Um... you haven't met her. And she's not gone. I see her standing by the shack. Go over there and talk to her," said John.

"But what if she has a boyfriend – or thinks I'm just some dumb Artinian."

"You're Borneo Grimgae. You can get any girl you want, remember?"

"True." Borneo got up. "Come with me, for moral support," he said to John. Together they made their way to the small wooden shack.

She looked radiant, glowing like a golden island tiki statue. Her long, luscious tresses swaying like ribbons in the breeze, she took a gauzy pink shawl and swung it around – it billowed out like a cape in the wind – and tied it around her hips.

"Look at her, John. I'm going to love her forever, her and only her; we're kindred spirits."

She moved toward a rack of surf boards stuck into the sand and surveyed its offerings, deciding which to choose. Probably sensing that someone was staring at her, she glanced over at them and saw Borneo doing just that. She smiled at him.

"Did you see that?!" Borneo shook John excitedly.

"Yes, good! Now go and say something to her," John pried him off.

But out of nowhere a giant shadow loomed from behind the surfboard rack, a shadow belonging to a huge, young Lainiian man well over six feet tall, with tan skin and straight black hair that hung down his exceptionally thick neck bulging with muscles that John didn't even know existed. This boy-man walked with a proud, straight back, his immense shoulders relaxed and pulled behind his face, which thrust itself forward with its straight nose and pronounced jaw line.

"Who – ?"

"That's Tori Malone, the biggest and strongest guy in all of Lainii," said Kyla, appearing by their side out of nowhere.

"How do you know?" John asked.

Kyla giggled. "I met him in person. He's got a nasty reputation for beating up any guy that gets in the way of what he wants. He's also the champion surfer for six years in a row."

"Six! Why is it always *six*!?" John asked.

"Oh – never mind, it's actually five – sorry."

They watched as Tori Malone came up to Borneo's fantasy girl and placed his big palm possessively on her sunlit shoulder. Borneo's heart sank.

Tori Malone stretched his massive arms up to reach for the highest surfboard, taking it down and sticking it like a trophy into the sand next to the beautiful girl, beaming a manly smile that demanded her adoration, but the girl's face became angry and she pushed Tori Malone away, yelling something at him that John and Borneo couldn't hear. She crossed her arms and approached the board rack with firm steps. Tori Malone chased after her; he appeared to be saying something apologetic, his arms splayed out. But the girl made an affronted face and walked away from him, taking her own surfboard from the middle rack and turning around to the ocean. Tori scowled, staring after her a moment, and then turned around and headed in the opposite direction.

"She doesn't seem to like him much," said John. "But I'd stay away; I wouldn't want to see what that guy would do if he saw you approach her."

"He's not that big," said Borneo, waving his hand carelessly.

Tori Malone's bicep was the thickness of Borneo's lower back.

"Well then, now's your chance," said John, figuring to step back and let be what must be.

"No – I can't," Borneo said, backing away. "Besides... she's gone," he said as he watched her catch a wave and ride it as if she were part of the ocean itself, moving with its powerful and steady grace.

"Come on, let's go back the hotel room," said John after a moment of silence. "We still have that party."

"Yeah..." said Borneo.

He and John turned around and headed back to their room as the sun began to sink behind them, readying themselves for one crazy night....

***

Next thing he knew, John was lying fully clothed on his bed, opening his eyes to a lone ray of light creeping through a crack. He tried to sit up and survey his surroundings – his head felt extremely heavy – but a cloudiness he couldn't shake off weighed his body down. The sound of water running was coming from somewhere.

What happened? he asked himself. *What did I do?*

As his vision came into focus, he saw Borneo bent over the sink, a bottle of pills for the Common Distraction open beside him. Borneo picked up the bottle, threw a dozen white tablets into his palm, put a glass under the running water and –

"Borneo, stop!"

In a flash, John rushed to his side, grabbed his arm, and knocked the pills out of his palm, sending them tumbling down the sink in a cascade of soft planks.

"What are you doing popping five doses like that?! You know you only take two of them once a day for Distraction!" John yelled.

But Borneo's face was a mess; his eyes sad and desperate, his lip quivering, his cheeks flushed.

"I – I can't focus, can't get her out of my mind – I need to see her again, John!"

"Who?"

"The girl from the beach. No matter what I do, she won't leave my mind for even a second. It's driving me insane!!"

"It's been an hour since you've met her."

"Has it?" Borneo cocked his head perplexedly. "I've completely lost track of time – I don't even know what day it is," he stared past John as he spoke to him.

"It's still Friday. We were at the beach, remember? Then we came back here, and I took a nap for twenty minutes."

"Yeah, yeah… where do you think she is right now?" Borneo asked.

"Probably still at the beach on lifeguard duty," said John.

"Let's go!" Borneo jumped up. John quickly racked his mind for a diversion.

"She's probably leaving soon," he said hurriedly. "Besides, she'll be at the party. You'd do better to get ready for that instead."

"You're right. I just need to be myself," Borneo said.

"There you go!"

"And if she's the one, she'll like me for who I am."

"Exactly," John was pleased with his confidence.

"You're totally on, buddy," Borneo clapped John on the shoulder. "Man, I feel so much better. It's like I've found myself again. I'm gonna go pick out what to wear, and I suggest *you* do the same," he pointed a finger at John.

"I'm good to go," said John, checking over his attire.

"Alright, then. Do you think I should go with the red polo that makes me stand out like a young superhero, or the white polo for that crisp, clean, secret-agent look?"

"I'd say the white polo because the white is more visible in the dark, and you definitely want to draw her to you."

"Right you are!"

"Everyone's already here!" John hissed at Borneo when they arrived on the scene two hours later.

Borneo wasn't listening. "She must be somewhere here…" he craned his neck as far as he could.

The party was spectacular. Exotic foods were piled on long tables stretching across the back by the live band, which was in full swing playing an upbeat trumpet tune. Over by a giant bonfire on the beach, John made out a hefty pig roasting on a spit, eyes, guts, and all still intact; the faint smell of burning hair wafted to them on the light breeze. Long leis of Lainiian flowers were strewn between tall flaming torches that burned so brightly they made the sky look like a fathomless ocean of ink.

"I've looked everywhere," said Borneo dejectedly, sitting down next to John at the bar an hour later. Every now and then he lifted his head in hope, as if jolted by a spark of electricity. And then, inevitably, he would let it drop back down, for alas, it had not been her.

He would *never* see her again at this rate, except at the beach tomorrow.

Sighing, Borneo got off of his stool and prepared to turn in for the night, thinking he may as well go back up to his room and fall asleep so that the depression wouldn't eat away at him. He made one final stop by the punch bowl, his hand beaten to the ladle by another, smaller one. Borneo looked up and beheld his dream girl.

She looked more radiant than she had that afternoon. He basked in the aura of her mystery as the moonlight shone on her skin and the firelight danced in her eyes. Particles of a faint fragrance, a blend of pure ocean water, flowers, and stars, tumbled gently from those silky strands that cascaded over her bare shoulders and drifted over to him, beckoning softly.

He looked into her orb-like eyes. "Hi. I remember you from the beach today," he said to her in low tones.

"I remember you, too," came her soft reply. That voice, it drove his body crazy with sultry warmth.

For a minute they stood there looking at each other, smiling shyly.

"Do you... like this party?" he asked her, unable to think of anything else to say.

"I like it now, Borneo."

His heart jolted. "You know my name?"

"Yes," she said with a soft laugh. Borneo's heart zoomed like a cannon let off in his chest.

A slow song had began, the night's last. Its dreamy melody drifted across the dance floor, where the atmosphere became hushed as couples everywhere nestled into each other and the lights were dimmed, so that only the torches remained.

His eyes ran over her splendid figure, wrapped in a shiny dress of red satin that smoldered in the firelight, accelerating the bloodflow to his genitals. He longed to hold her, wrap her up in his arms where they would be forever happy.

Wordlessly, magically, their hands met and their fingers locked gently into each other. Then they slowly slipped apart as she placed her delicate hands onto his shoulders and moved into his space. One of his hands rested firmly against her side, while the other one he

81

placed gently at the bottom of her back where her dress began and continued downward; underneath, her muscles tautened. Lightly, that hand inched across and settled onto her hip, which perfect form he felt beneath the red satin.

His other hand left her side and began to explore. He held her close, gently stroking the smooth skin of her back beneath his bare fingertips.

"What's your name?" he asked her softly. He longed to know it, to say it, to feel its unearthly form on his lips. It must be something evocative of her divine essence, like Lehaila, or Doville.

"Gertrude," she whispered into his ear, her upper lip softly brushing his lobe.

He pulled her tighter. *Gertrude*, his heart moaned.

His lips found hers and they pressed together for a golden moment; he tasted their sweet suppleness in a spasm of ecstasy.

They said no more to each other, only held each other in their arms for those few precious minutes when they could escape into their starlit world of two.

The song ended. They opened their eyes and looked at each other; he was wandering through the long shadows the firelight cast over her face, navigating its crevices and tripping into the shimmering pools of her orbs.

"I – I have to tell you – " he began. But she put a slender finger to his lips.

"I have to go," she said.

"But – when can I see you again?"

"Tomorrow. I promise. Come to the beach."

"Don't go," Borneo whined.

"I must."

And with that she turned around and walked away toward the rumbling dark sea, leaving him standing there alone, a lonely wolf cub left to howl at the moon.

Chapter 06: Love

When John awoke the next morning, Borneo was not in his room. But he didn't worry – he knew Borneo must have gone off to spend every waking moment with his one true love. Realizing he would have most – if not all – of the day to himself, John decided to take advantage of the free tours and, after a sumptuous breakfast in which his taste buds were bombarded with the vivid flavor-sensation of curiously hued rice flakes in a thin opaque-white sauce, he signed up for the Lainiian Wilderness Adventure.

"Welcome aboard the Lainii Express my name is Jack I'll be your tour guide today," said the man in the flower patterned shirt standing by the driver's seat listlessly.

"So... you're here to see the wild, authentic Lainii?" he asked the five people on the bus. The elderly couple in the middle was asleep; the small child was sitting in the lap of its mother, who was reading a magazine and not paying attention to what Jack was saying.

John nodded in accord with Jack's statement.

"Alright then!" the voice sounded bright and cheery, but the eyes could not have been more dead. "Prepare yourselves for an adventure through the heart of the Lainiian jungle!"

"Can we stop and go outside to explore and take pictures?" John asked.

"Sorry that's not allowed resort policy. Anddd... off we go!"

John leaned back in his seat and stared out the window as the bus pulled away, watching the Lainiian jungle pass him by without so much as a wooden shanty to break his monotonous view....

***

In a hidden cove, soft cerulean waves crashed onto the untouched morning sand, imparting their beauty in a majestic rhythm of swells and withdrawals. The pure air was fragrant with fresh smells of ripening fruit and a cool ocean breeze not yet warmed by the newly risen sun. Two sunlit figures ran along its shore, laughing joyously as the ripples of water played at their bare feet.

"That was amazing!" one exclaimed.

"You weren't so bad yourself," smiled the other, whose long golden hair whipped behind her as it lashed through the air.

"I was nothing compared to you," said Borneo, smiling at his companion. She blushed.

"Oh, come on now. I do this sort of thing every day. But for a city boy, you mastered those waves!"

Panting in their quiet natural surroundings, they hoisted their surfboards along and laid them to rest against the first palm tree sticking out of the sands.

"Gertrude," Borneo began, "I'm having the most incredible time with you. I've never met anyone like you!"

"Oh, Borneo – you're so sweet!" she flashed him a shy smile as she caught his eye, red hinting her golden cheeks.

"No, really," Borneo turned towards her, "You're the most interesting woman I've ever come across."

"But there are a million women in Vandorn!" she said.

"Not like you," he looked into her eyes.

Caught off guard by the intensity of his stare, her footing faltered and she lost balance. Borneo caught her lightly, holding her by the arms. As she stabilized, his hands slipped off lightly, down towards her hands; his fingers gently held hers, like a loose web, sparks flying between the fibers.

"Borneo, I – " Gertrude began in a small voice. Borneo leaned in, and she looked quickly up at him; there was an imploring, almost helpless look in the clear aquamarine orbs of that exquisite face, a look that made Borneo's heart melt as he beheld it. She tried to continue what she was saying, but her mouth couldn't form the words. Borneo leaned in closer, pulling Gertrude towards him so that the warmth of his body radiated onto her smooth, golden skin....

Crash!

They quickly dropped hands and looked over – their surfboards had toppled down over one another into the sand. They both ran over to pick them up. The moment had evaporated like delicate mist out of a crystal vial.

"You wanna go get some breakfast?" Borneo muttered as he hoisted his board back up against the palm, making sure it was secure.

"Sure," she mumbled.

Borneo bent down and picked up his t-shirt, brushing off the warm sand that had blown over it to put it on over his bare, salt-water-washed chest, catching a glimpse of Gertrude out of the corner of his eye, just visible behind the palm where she was slipping on a sheer summer dress the exact deep, plum pink shade of a Lainiian rose. Involuntarily, her head flicked around and she briefly almost caught his eye as the airy fabric slid down her hips. His heart hammered. A momentary surge; a quick flash of lightning; an exchange of deepest understanding piercing dart-like into the depths of their souls. It was no more than a split second. Was it his imagination? His rapidly beating heart told him it was not. But now the moment was gone....

They walked side by side in innocent, shy silence, her baby pink flip-flop-clad feet following his rhythm.

They headed over to the breakfast bar and sat down at a cozy table that overlooked the perfect blue ocean and scattered puffs of clouds. As they shared a tall stack of pancakes with maple syrup and two glasses of fresh-squeezed orange juice, their conversation turned back to surfing.

"So how long have you been surfing for?" Borneo asked her, cocking his head.

"Well," said Gertrude, "my dad taught me when I was a little girl. It was a clear September morning," she smiled, a look of nostalgia softening those vivacious eyes. Borneo leaned in, listening keenly.

"The sun had just come up over the ocean's horizon – like that time when you and I were out there, this morning," she chuckled.

"Go on." He cared about every word.

"We went out into the water... he sat me down on my first surfboard. Then he told me to get up. Then I got up. He said, "Atta girl!".... I thought I was going to fall into the water!" she laughed. "And then he let me go. And then... a wave came. He yelled, 'you can do it, Gertrude!'. And... and... I was soaring...."

Her voice trailed off as she gazed into the sweet empty space of memories. But something was different in them, her eyes. A light was flickering out, like a star succumbing to morning.

"Gertrude, are you alright?" Borneo peered at her slightly downward-tilted face. How he longed to save the light that sputtered in those sadly beautiful orbs. She was spinning out of control, yet he could do nothing to help her....

"I – I need to be alone... for a little...." She got up from the table without meeting Borneo's eyes and left the breakfast bar, her magenta sundress whipping after her like a flurry of Lainiian rose petals.

"Gertrude! Wait! Where are you going!?" Borneo shouted.

But Gertrude did not answer. Instead, she ran away, ran to where her heart carried her.

Borneo understood. Her spirit was wild. It needed to be given free reign to run the lengths of the earth, to sprint to the moon and fly to the stars. A rare one, he had found; a woman as untamable and unpredictable as a mare in heat. *She's guided by the pull of her emotions*, he thought to himself, sighing. *I could never control her.*

***

The midafternoon sun streamed through the windows of the bus as they continued to roll along. John glanced at Jack every so often because his eyes appeared to close occasionally. He was probably overreacting, though; his four comrades showed no sign of fret. The elderly couple had out a camera and was preoccupied with taking a decent photo of themselves against a speeding Lainiian background.

"No, Harry, get my good side!" the better half of the pair croaked in a voice infused with decades of cigarette smoke.

"Which side is that, dear?" the man asked politely.

The younger lady had pulled out her cell phone.

"Mama, I'm bored," whined her child.

"Honey, just enjoy the tour," she said emptily as she pushed buttons, smiling a smile that John was sure had no connection with the sound of her offspring's voice. "I'm doing this for you, remember?"

"But there's nothing to do!" it cried.

"Here, look at pictures," she handed it an old issue of *Cosmetology*.

John had not said a single word in the past four hours; his throat felt unusually dry.

Four people looked back at him at the sound of his throat clearing, their expressions betraying that they'd had no idea he'd been there.

"Wha – who needed a bathroom?" Jack snapped awake, asking groggily.

John jumped on the chance. "I do."

"Alright, gang, we're gonna make a quick detour. I gotta use the john, too," Jack announced.

Ten minutes later they stopped by a dirt path that led deep into the jungle.

"Harry, what's going on!" the elderly woman demanded as they followed Jack. John came up last, behind the mother and her child.

"Well, this is more exciting than sitting on a bus with no air conditioning for four hours!" the woman remarked as she plowed through the bushes.

"Yeah," said John.

"You from Artinia, too?" she asked.

"Yep."

"Where from?"

"Vandorn."

"Oh, cool. My ex-husband lives there."

"Oh... does he like it?"

"I guess. He does management for some company or something, I never knew..." she trailed off rather carelessly. "What do you do there?"

"I work for NKOZ."

"*No way!*" she turned around, her mouth open.

"Way."

"Oh my Bob, so are you, like, on T.V.?"

"No. I work with Borneo Grimgae. Do you know of him?"

"Isn't he like the hero or something? Young boy?"

"Yeah. He's here with me now, but he's back at the resort doing some... promotional events."

"Like what?" she seemed interested.

"Um, establishing ties with the Lainiian natives."

"Nice," she nodded.

Their half-dozen-large party emerged from the green onto a small, white beach, untamed except for a medium-sized shanty comprised of several "rooms".

John emerged quickly from the bathroom, walking away from the rest to skim the edge of the shoreline while he had the chance.

The woman was sitting cross-legged in the sand, still reading her phone, while her child played happily by the gentle waves that washed in.

"Honey, be careful!" she shouted to it, looking up.

"Who knew you got service in Lainii," she said with a smile as John passed by.

"I didn't," he threw out his arms, glancing at the phone she'd just lay beside her in the sand.

"I'm Carol, by the way."

"I'm John."

"Nice to meet you, John," she said, shaking his hand as he sat down beside her. They remained silent for a while, staring out at the water.

"I hope we stay here a while, my son is at least having fun," she said.

John glanced back at the shack; Jack seemed to be taking his time.

"Must be a nice break from working in a big T.V. network for you, huh?" she asked, turning to him and smiling, her sunglasses pushing strands of her somewhat chemically damaged hair out of her face. Her shoulders, adorned only with the straps of her black tank top, were covered with freckles and sunspots, the result of years of similar beach visits.

"It is," John nodded.

"I just had to get away from everything, after the divorce, you know?"

"Uhuh," said John. "So, what do you do?"

"I work in sales. Also a full-time mommy for Vincent over there. Oh, and I'm trying to start my own line of handbags, but I haven't got a business bone in my body so I don't know how that's gonna work out," she laughed.

John nodded. They sat in silence, staring out at the sea, breathing in rhythm with the waves. John sensed how her whole body rose and fell with the movement; its battered being, now past the days of its prime and aging, could for a few moments release its sadness and tension and open itself to the natural world, letting its forces flow in like an elixir that made every time-earned sunspot and age line okay to exist with a love she did not know. There was an inexpressible clash, between the lifetime she'd built up, full of prejudgments and coarse daydreams embedded into her through the routine existence she'd fallen into once the halcyon college days had thrown her body out into the harsh world of adult life but left her mind with the fragments of dreams and her heart with disconnected strings of longings, creating an unsurpassable disconnect that robbed her dry to be easily dipped lower and lower into dispirited contentedness with daily cheap thrills, and how those years of low living bore no weight here. At least, this was what John thought about. He wondered if this perception was real for Carol, too. She was watching the unending, unerring majesty of the waves' rhythm seemingly entranced.

Carol's phone beeped. A cackling laugh burst out of her mouth as she read the message. "Oh my Bob, that's so funny...."

"So are you in Lainii for long?" she asked John after she texted a reply.

"Just until tomorrow."

"Where are you staying?"

"At the Moonflower."

"Oh, really! Us, too!" she smiled brightly, adjusting her sarong over her bare legs as the breeze swept it up. "What floor?"

"Third."

"We're up on the fourth floor. Room four-thirteen. That was actually the date of my wedding." She laughed loudly. "Hence I don't like to spend much time in it," she laughed again. "I haven't had a chance to explore the night life yet, what with – " she cocked her head toward Vincent. "But I'm thinking to head down for the show tonight after I put him to bed. Get around, maybe meet some people."

"It's nice to just walk around," said John. "And it's lit at night."

"Sounds romantic. You taking the lady around?" she gave him a sly look.

"Uh... thinking about it."

"Very cool!" she nodded, smiling.

They stared at the sea again. A minute later Carol packed up her phone and her Vincent, waved 'bye to John, and returned to stand by the bus. John could no longer rely on not being forgotten by Jack and left behind, as only one fifth of their group was now missing and four out of five really ain't a bad return...so he, too, made his way back.

Harry and his wife were holding up the tour as the wife set Jack to take the perfect photo of the two of them.

"No, don't push the button until I tell you!" she croaked. "Harry! Get over here! Hold me, Harry! If you could for Bob's sake make me feel like a woman for once in my life!"

"Incompetent idiots!" she muttered at the top of her voice, snatching the camera from Jack when they finished.

"Honey, that's the flash, you need to press the off button if you don't want to waste all the battery," Harry nudged.

"Well whose fault is that if you didn't bring an extra pair!?" she yelled.

They clambered back onto the bus and resumed their journey, watching the scenery rush by as they rolled ever closer to the heart of the wilderness....

***

The fiery sun was just beginning to set over the exotic little island known as Lainii: the blood red orb emanated its last rays over the velvety earth, casting long, plum shadows over paradise nooks; large night-blooming flowers began to unfold amongst their leaves and release the intoxicating perfumes lying dormant in their spires; tall, cool grasses stood in waiting to be laid upon by secret lovers meeting each other under cover of the mischievous night; billions of tiny grains of sand synchronously relinquished hold of the heat they'd held captive, as if exhaling one last deep breath before closing their eyes in submission to a tempting slumber.

Still, he pressed on. He had to find her.

Worry not, said a voice in his head. *Your heart will guide you.* Undaunted, Borneo continued with renewed spirit, feeling himself get closer with each step.

As it turned out, it actually wasn't that hard to find because it was the same place where they had been surfing that morning.

There she sat on the sand, alone, watching the waves approach her dainty feet, yet never touch them....

How beautiful she looked, the last glimmers of sunlight bouncing off the dark gold strands formed into a long, loose plait that hung down her back, tied with a ribbon of silk azure. How amazingly the turquoise tank dress she wore, with matching necklace, radiated against the orange-red hues of the setting sun.

He approached.

"I knew I would find you here," came his voice in deep, sultry tones from behind. She did not turn around, but remained staring at the sea, hypnotized.

"Ger-gertrude? It's me. Borneo.... I'm here."

Still, she refused.

"Look, Gertrude, I get it. You're an enigma – you're like a labyrinth I'll never be able to find my way through! I know I'll never understand your true depths, but I just want you to know, that I – I – I'm falling in love with you."

Gertrude turned around to face him at these words, and Borneo saw that her eyes were sparkling with tears. Oh! How Borneo's heart contracted in pain to see such delicate beauty suffer! He yearned with all his being to hold her, to take her in his arms and kiss away her pain.

"Gertrude, don't cry," he whispered softly, trying to be strong and mask his own pain as he in one fluid motion pulled her to him so that they held each other in a warm embrace, their knees buried in the sand.

They kissed, kissing into each other, searching for each others' souls in an endless quest.

Gertrude's hands, they were exploring, feeling every inch of Borneo that stood before her, against her. She searched inside his innermost depths, caressing his hair, running her fingers through it in deep ecstasy; her hands moved down, grazing his neck, grasping his shoulders, over his chest, his ribs, down his abdomen....

She found his soul.

They were one now; in a sudden surge of heat, Borneo felt it with all his heart, this incredible connection that he had never felt before. He knew her, saw into her, and she knew him. She was it – she was the one for him, and in that long moment of purest bliss, he knew. Knew that he would love her forever, knew that she felt just the same, knew that his search was over and he could die happy, having experienced the joy of loving another's heart....

"... Oh, Borneo, take me away from this place," said Gertrude to him, her head resting upon his shoulder as they sat side by side in the sand watching the stars peek out.

"But don't you like it here? This is paradise!" he exclaimed.

"I do like it here, but I feel so... chained! I want to see the world!" exclaimed Gertrude, eyes glassy with wonder as they gazed upon the cerulean sky. "I know that probably doesn't make any sense," she said sheepishly.

"No, I understand completely," said Borneo, caressing her shoulder to show her he, in fact, did. The sounds of bugs chirping and buzzing danced about them in the quiet evening air. Suddenly, Borneo was struck with a brilliant idea.

"Come back to Artinia with me! I could show you Vandorn, it's the biggest city in the world!"

"Oh, Borneo, that would be so exciting!" exclaimed Gertrude, turning to him and clapping her hands together. "But I couldn't..." she turned back away.

"Why not?"

Gertrude said nothing.

"Is it Tori?" Borneo guessed. Gertrude nodded.

"I'm afraid to leave him," she said in a small voice. "What if... he doesn't let me go?"

"I'll protect you," Borneo whispered, and she snuggled closer to him, her face nuzzling his collarbone. He could feel her worry.

"But Tori offers me a good, safe life here. He'll make a fine husband. Why should I not want to marry him?" Gertrude told herself aloud, but Borneo only heard the pained denial. He pulled her toward him, looking deep into her eyes.

"Because he doesn't understand you like I do," he said. "Say you'll come with me," he whispered, touching her face with his fingertips.

"I'll come with you," whispered Gertrude, breathless.

"I leave tomorrow at sunset. In less than a day we'll be on our way."

They both knew that they must part ways for now; for Gertrude had to pack. It was almost too unbearable for Borneo to be apart from his one true love. He consoled himself by thinking only of her and the precious moments they'd shared that day as he walked placidly along the beach, his pants rolled up casually, his hair whipped by the breeze, and a gentle smile on his face as it looked out to the boundless sea. He stumbled upon something lying in the sand.

"John?" Borneo asked, looking down. John lifted up his new sunglasses and looked at Borneo, squinting from the glare of the very last rays of the sun that melted over the waters.

"What are you doing lying there in the sand?"

"I was taking a nap. We got back about an hour ago and you weren't in the room so I figured I'd go looking for you, and then I couldn't find you so I just sat down and ended up dozing off. Must've been worn out from the day's adventures. What've you been up to?" John asked his friend.

"I spent all day with Gertrude. She's amazing, John. The more time I spend with her, the more I know that she's really the one."

Then he gulped. "John, I've gotta tell you something. I'm bringing Gertrude back to Artinia with me," he said.

"Um, that was sudden."

"She's packing her bags right now. I was just on my way to meet her," Borneo explained. "Want to head over to her place with me?"

John shrugged indifferently and got up.

"So what tour did you go on?" Borneo asked him.

"The Lainiian Wilderness Adventure."

"Sounds intense!"

"It was." John picked up the plastic bag lying beside him. "Check it out," he shoved it toward Borneo.

"Whoa!" Borneo held up a mirror whose back and rim were covered with glued-on seashells.

94

"Authentic Lainiian shells, found nowhere else in the world. Twenty bucks, but I promised Milly I'd get her something. There's a keychain somewhere at the bottom for you, too," said John. Borneo rummaged around. He pulled something out with a disgusted face.

"Oh, that's my empty smoothie cup, forgot to throw that away," said John. Borneo picked up another lump and smelled it.

"Looks like you didn't finish half your burger, either," he said.

"Eh, I wasn't hungry. Should be some fries in there, as well."

Borneo nodded, assuming that he could help himself, because he was starving.

Gertrude lived only five minutes beyond the resort. They approached her tiny house, with only one light on, surrounded by dozens of others just like it to collectively form the little village. Gertrude rushed outside to meet them, running straight into Borneo's arms for a passionate embrace.

"Are you ready?" he asked her gently after they unpeeled.

"Almost. Let me get my last things and then we can go," she said, running back inside. Borneo and John stood alone outside the steps, feeling themselves strange and unwanted visitors. But they soon discovered that they weren't as alone as they thought; two other men, talking in low voices in the Lainiian tongue, emerged from out of the dark-nesting trees and walked towards Gertrude's front door. They stopped talking when they came upon the two Artinians, and stood staring at them.

"Who are you?" the older one asked in thickly accented Artinian.

"I – um –" began Borneo. Just then, Gertrude came out of the house and stopped. Her run changed to a cautious procession down the front steps.

"Papa!" she said in soft tones to the man who had spoken to Borneo and John. "How was your fishing trip?"

"Gertrude, who are these two men?" Gertrude's father asked his daughter.

"Now, papa, don't be mad," she began, placing her hands on his shoulders to soothe him. "This – this is Borneo, he is a friend of mine – "

"A friend?" her father repeated, and the other man by his side, much younger and taller, let out a laugh at these words that echoed through the village. Then the young one said something very quickly in Lainiian, and Gertrude's father went "oh!" and then also laughed.

"Tori tells me this is the famous Artinian who comes here to 'civilize' us," he said in grand tones. Borneo looked from one to the other, confused.

"Pleasure to meet you, sir," he finally said, extending his hand for Gertrude's father to shake. Gertrude's father stood there looking down at Borneo's hand, until Borneo put it away after a nudge from John....

"What is that?" Tori Malone pointed to the bags on the porch steps. They had been so loud that by now people in the surrounding houses had come outside to see what was happening.

Neither Gertrude, nor Borneo, nor John said a word.

"An explanation, please," Gertrude's father demanded, "for why all of your belongings are outside our house!"

"I – " was all Gertrude managed.

Borneo cleared his throat. John backed away a bit.

"Sir," Borneo began, "Gertrude and I were talking and, well," he took a breath, "I would like to take her back to Artinia with me."

Silence fell like a brick. Gertrude's father's rounded on his daughter. "Do you mean to tell me that you plan to fly away from your home with a boy you met two days ago?" he asked her.

"Actually, we met yesterday," interjected Borneo.

"Sir," Borneo jumped in again quickly when they felt a surge of heat radiate from the Lainiian's neck, "this isn't how it seems! Your daughter and I, we love each other!"

Gertrude's father swelled with rage. "You foolish girl! You think you love him!? This isn't *love*, this is something entirely different for which I think you know the word! I thought I taught you better, but you're still a stupid child running after your emotions! You know nothing of love! You could make the biggest mistakes of your life running after your 'love' and then spend the next three decades trying to fix them! This boy will leave you in the city to starve! He'll find another – ten others – whom he 'loves' more than you, and then where will be all your great love!? *Go back inside the house and stay there until I come and speak to you!*" Gertrude's father yelled at her.

"But father – ! This is my dream!" she cried, spilling tears.

Borneo moved to shield her from his hurtful words.

"Gertrude! Don't cry! I know your dreams. He – he doesn't understand you like I do!" he put his arms around her as she buried her face in her hands and quaked.

There was a surge among the rest of the village from all the other fathers of Lainiian daughters, who knew enough Artinian to follow the conversation.

"Dirty Artinian!" one of them uttered, scandalized.

"Ah, wait, this is the one who cannot die!" cried another. The others let out cruel laughs.

"That – that's right!" said Borneo, looking around at them defiantly.

"Let us test if it is true!" Gertrude's father called out to appreciative yells. Then he shouted something in Lainiian.

"Papa, no!" Gertrude gasped at the words, eyes wide between splayed fingers. "Please," she threw her arms around his neck, pleading, "he doesn't understand our customs, he is from a different world!"

"I know the people of his world, Gertrude, and the more of them die, the better!"

John glanced at Borneo. This had to be a joke, right? Before they could resolve that, one of the bigger men grabbed both Borneo and John by the backs of their shirts and threw them onto the ground, where they landed on the dirt in thuds. Borneo was on his stomach, massaging his head, when Tori Malone bent down beside him and flexed his fingers, baring a snarling grin.

"Nooo!!!" Gertrude tore herself away from her father and flung herself across Borneo's chest, a barrier between his body and Tori Malone.

The villagers gasped. *She would die for this arrogant, ignorant stranger?*

Meanwhile, John lay there unprotected.

"Move out of the way, Gertrude!" said Tori Malone roughly.

"*Never!*" she screamed.

He rolled his eyes and picked her up in an easy swoop.

"Get off me!" she screamed, kicking and beating his muscular chest with her fists as he carried her to a spot of grass ten feet away.

Squirming, Gertrude fell out of his arms and landed hard on the floor.

"*Ow!*" she yelled. "You *threw* me!?" she gasped, turning to stare at Tori in shock. *How could he? After all the years he'd known her, all they'd been through, the secrets and special moments they'd shared?* Her beautiful eyes locked onto his cold, callous ones. Fury and disbelief pounded her heart like the waves of a storm a tender shoreline.

"How could you treat me like one of your dead fish? You promised to be my best friend for life!" she choked back tears that shone out of her eyes disbelievingly.

"Wait, what?" said Borneo.

"Gertrude, I – " Tori began like a helpless five-year-old, holding out his arms.

She covered her face with her hands and ran sobbing into her house, hurt, slamming the door behind her.

"Gertrude, wait!!!" Borneo called out, his voice cracking; but no one emerged from the house and a minute later a light came on in an upstairs room, from which the faint sounds of sobbing emanated. Borneo turned to John, mouth open. John was shocked, too. Not because of Gertrude, but because they were going to die. Actually, only *he* was going to die! With a jolt he absorbed this second blow and began to perspire.

"Tori, would you like to test your strength?" asked Gertrude's father.

"Let's let the dog warm them up first," Tori said. "I like to save my strength for real men."

John and Borneo saw a shadowed figure emerge from one of the buildings, holding something large and furry by a thick collar that snarled loudly. Gertrude's father yelled a word in Lainiian and the man let the beast go. John and Borneo scrambled up as fast as they could.

"Get out of here!" Gertrude's father yelled at them as they bolted.

They ran to the forest, plunging into the thick blindly, dodging tree trunks and jumping over roots they didn't know where there by instinct as the vicious beast chased them.

"Do you think we lost it?" John panted a minute later, glancing back, only dimly feeling the humiliation of Gertrude's entire village laughing uproariously at their pathetic getaway.

A growl and a bark from right next to them shocked them.

"Ahh!" Borneo screamed. "John, do something!!"

"I don't know!" John called back, sensing the dog right behind them. "Quick, up this tree!" he yelled as they passed one with wide, low branches sprawling out. Borneo jumped up the lowest one instantly, grabbing at everything wooden.

John turned, his back pressed flat against the trunk as the dog's angry eyes aimed at his face. He reached into his bag and pulled out the half of a burger, waving it before the hungry animal. It caught its attention. John threw it far to his right and the dog ran off after it with a whimper.

"Borneo, jump down! Now's our chance!" yelled John. Borneo obliged and they ran, John throwing his whole bag behind him as a precaution. They ran until they were sure they had lost the dog, not slowing until they reached the trail that took them back onto resort grounds. As Borneo's fear faded, glum overcame him and he hung his head.

They stopped outside the west side of the front lobby, by a path that led to the theater. Music could be heard filtering toward the rim of the main building; there must've been a show going on inside. A sudden uproar of laughs confirmed this.

"Do you think I should visit her tomorrow?" Borneo asked.

"NO."

"But how can I speak of love, then? I need to prove myself to her."

"Let's recuperate and check out the entertainment first," said John, attempting to distract his heartbroken friend.

They walked through the archway and saw that the entire place was packed with vacationers in halter-top or button-down shirts seated around candlelit tables watching a troupe of resort staff performing some comedic skit onstage. John and Borneo took one of the last empty tables in a far corner. Neither of them really watched the show.

Borneo sighed. "I'll never get over her."

"Sure you will," John replied bracingly. "Just... give it time."

"Borneo!!" came a sudden cry from their far right. Both guys glanced up and saw the three girls they'd met at the beach yesterday, smiling and waving frantically at – Borneo. As soon as Borneo acknowledged them they got up and walked over.

"Hey!!" exclaimed Jennie, sitting down next to Borneo while Kyla took the seat on his other side; Tess reluctantly took a seat between Jennie and John.

"Aww, Borneo, why do you look so sad?" asked Kyla. Borneo shrugged.

"Let me make you feel better," she cooed, and turned around in her chair to give him a neck rub. Borneo barely flinched.

"You'll just make him tenser. A foot massage will relax you more," said Jennie from the other side, and proceeded to tenderly pick up Borneo's feet, place them in her lap, and remove his sandals to rub his toes.

"I know palmistry!" exclaimed Tess with extreme excitement; she reached over John and Kyla and grabbed Borneo's right hand. "I wonder how long your life line is! I bet it circles all the way around your hand!"

As the three girls played with Borneo like he was a limp rag doll, and as Borneo responded just like a limp rag doll would, John watched the candle in the glass votive on their table, its flame dancing barely above the pool of melted wax. Borneo's voice cut across John's foggy thoughts and snapped him back into reality:

"Hey, John, we're gonna go over to the heated pool. Wanna come? Kyla says she can make anything she touches glow in the dark." There was an eruption of giggles behind Borneo. Unbeknownst to John, they had all stood up from the table while he'd spaced out.

"No thanks. I'm gonna go up to our room."

"Aww, alright. We'll miss you!" said Borneo; no one else commented.

They parted ways, John walking to the main lobby, where a few stray souls sat in lamp-lit armchairs drinking and talking in low voices. He went back to their room and onto the balcony, where he breathed in the cool air and listened to the sound of the ocean below, savoring how the world slowed down here, where silence was the norm and tranquility the preferred state.

There's no need for the constant rush to catch a train to keep on rushing, he thought. In his usual life he so rarely felt the kind of rightness he felt a grain of here.

He looked at the sea of stars he never saw in the city glimmering far above him, infinitely far away, leading to worlds unknown and unimagined.... He could only wonder what else was out there.... How diminished his life seemed amid this vastness he perceived a corner of. And yet, his one small life was mostly filler! How much time he wasted doing not what he wanted! thought someone inside of him who woke up and looked around wide-eyed every now and then before he went back to sleep.

What he needed was a sense of urgency to douse him like cold water so that when he returned to Artinia Monday morning he would not fall back into listlessness and forget this moment. What he needed was to remember this sense of peace he felt here as a goal for his routine life.

He opened *Mortician Monthly* to his saved page and, by the lamplight, read:

Creative Fiction

By S. "Nightwhisper" Mourber

Undead Love, Part 2

Blood dripped from the walls. Echoes cried through the night. Whispering. Screaming. Silence.

With padded feet he doth enteréd, smiling through the night a sick smile of deathly decay. He opened the door. His long, black nails gently scratched the rough surface. His golden eye peered in. A sliver of light. The hum of a song. Gentle.

She gasped.

"I came here to say goodbye, Cayenne. I am leaving," spoke the creature deeply.

"Show your true form!" Cayenne commanded.

The terrifying beast metamorphoséd. There stood a being of beauty in his place, glowing pale like the moon.

"I cannot stay," said the lovely being to Cayenne in her mystical voice, throwing back long hair that was silky like a silk dress. Almond-shaped eyes so deep so dark. Mysterious they shone.

"Oh, Genyuah! We cannot part!" cried she the innocent one.

Daggers in her heart.

Stone met her warm beating breast, so cold it made cessation to the flow of her blood. Eyes so lovely they cried silver rain of agony. Cayenne's tears fell onto Genyuah's neck.

"If I stay, they will kill me," spoke Genyuah. A look overtook Cayenne, one that Genyuah, for all her powers as a Mindreader, could not figure out. Cayenne had always been too much of a mystery, even for her skills.

"But they cannot kill you because... you are already dead."

Thunder. Lightning. Silence. The blood fell from the walls. A drop landed on Genyuah's shoulder. She licked it off, savoring the taste.

"I did not want to tell you because I was afraid you would leave me. But now it is the only thing that can save our love!" cried Cayenne.

In a flash she was gone. Into the night. It absorbed her like a fallen soul weighed down by the pain in her heart. Her heart was stopped! And she had not known! Betrayal!!!

Cayenne had been the only one to break down her defenses. In the three and a half millennia Genyuah existed only Cayenne had reached so deeply with her peering green eyes full of innocence and touched so deep inside her. No one else could! Genyuah had searched the underworld for someone to understand her and found no one. Emptiness. How dark it was inside her heart, and only Cayenne had lit it with her tiny spark. Taming her wild spirit. The subtleties that lay between them –

Genyuah screamed into the night, her wings carrying her through the storm. Whirlwinds. Tornadoes. Rain lashed at them, hurting their tender surface. The only part of her that wasn't hard stone.

She couldn't bear. The pain. Any. Longer. How long could she escape the emptiness of the Darkland?

Halt. A sudden stop. Frantic eyes searched the stormy night. At last she found it: a rusty dagger. Joy.

It would bring her joy....

She must know. If she...? Not worth. For much else.

Her mind was clarity. She dove down with the intense rush of night air through her wings and through the pores of her skin. Claws grasped the dagger that blazed with intention. Then raised herself higher. Higher than every tower. Higher than every ghost of a bird that flew in the Darkland. It would bring her joy....

The dagger pulsated inside her clenched fist. It spoke a bare whisper that she could almost not hear.

I wish... too...

... to reach so deeply inside...

... and have my place of repose...

... inside...

... your...

... heart.

Genyuah plunged the dagger into her chest and fell from the sky. At last... it would bring her joy....

Rain dripped on her forehead. She pulled out the dagger. Black-red blood dripped from the hole in her chest, glutinous substance that would replenish itself faster than she could breathe. It had failed. Dooméd, she was! Still alive!

A soft chuckle from the night.

"Ah, Genyuah... poor Genyuah..." more chuckle. From out of the void stepped Donnio. Her nemesis.

"So you've finally learned. Poor being. Destined to roam this wretched hole for eternity. Unless... you can't roam."

"And who would stop me?"

"I would. I would take away your freedom. I would rip your wings off from your very back, leaving your skin to curl and shrivel. I would enslave your body in a cell and watch you hover between death and... other death. I would highly enjoy it."

"I would like to see you try, you pathetic excuse for a daemon. You know you're no match for me."

"Ah, yes... the all-powerful Genyuah. Master Mindreader of the Third Degree. Metamorphosid extraordinaire, able to change shape with half an Intention. Skilled Nightbender and Swordweilder. It seems there is no limit to your power. But I know your weakness, and I know how you will fall," said Donnio.

No... he couldn't possibly.... Genyuah recalled, for she knew what he spoke of. Two millennia ago, when she was still a young novice training in the skills of Mindreading and Metamorphosing, she had discovered her greatest weakness. Her chief limitation. It could not possibly – "

With a crash and a bang, the hotel room door burst open and Borneo and Kyla toppled out of it, making out furiously. John glanced up, beholding this sight. The groping duo haphazardly found its way into Borneo's bedroom, crashing into a lamp and the T.V. stand along the way, but eventually making it inside.

The door slammed shut.

Calamitous sounds rent from inside and the bedroom door burst open again a few minutes later. Borneo and Kyla rolled across the floor, wrapped like a burrito, their lips pressed together so hard they disappeared from their faces as they moved their cavorting slowly but surely to the lavish bathroom.

John remained on the balcony for a long while mulling over everything and nothing. Finally sleep claimed him and he went back inside, his silence disrupted only by the occasional sound of unbridled passion.

***

The next morning, Borneo had his meeting with the president of Lainii. He wore his best polo and ate a sumptuous breakfast.

"...I just love how she gets me, you know? It's what I've been looking for my whole life. John, these eggs are amazing, you gotta try some."

"No thanks," said John.

"Aw... alright, well, I'm off," he said, clearing his plate and skipping lightly from the table.

This time it was Borneo who fell asleep as soon as they boarded the plane; his head rolled to the side, wearing a contented grin. John, on the other hand, could not sleep.

"Borneo, you know what I wasn't here, for the first time in a long time?" John asked his groggy friend.

"Hm?"

"Bored."

"How is Vandorn, the biggest city in the world, not exciting enough for you?" Borneo asked.

"It's not my kind of excitement," said John.

"Try going out," Borneo brushed him off with a yawn.

"No. I need a change, Borneo. I need to do something that makes my life worthwhile."

"That's easy!" Borneo chuckled.

"Oh yeah?" asked John.

"Yeah. Just fall in love," he shrugged, and then dozed off to sleep.

Chapter 07: The Great Wheel

Bob is ununderstandable. One cannot know Bob. Bob is not a *thing*, a *shape*, or even an *idea*. That is because Bob has no borders; He has no spaces, no form, and no definition.

Bob cannot be grasped as a whole; He has no surfaces or protrusions to grasp onto.

Bob has no duality. He has no rival or opponent, for nothing is separate from Him.

Bob is beyond Space and Time. There is no more of Bob in the entire universe than there is in a grain of sand. There is no more of Bob in a century than in a second.

Bob is both beginning and end, both nothing and everything. Bob is zero and Bob is infinity. Are not both endless?

Yet for all that can be said about Bob, it cannot be said what He *is*. One may hear His voice, know of His quality, but it is impossible to see Bob Himself.

For He is Essence – that which can be given no explanation; that whose origin cannot be traced; that which is everpresent and indestructible.

One's true self is one's essence. Therefore one *is* essence. One is a part of Bob. One's outer shell – the appearances, strengths, weaknessness, one defines oneself by – are not of one's essence.

There is a something that decides everything, the factor that tips the scales. But this something is *nothing*. This is the force of Bob. This force is a mystery. Bob is Mystery itself.

Bob is direction. We who have no direction must therefore seek Bob. He is the something always left to be found, around the bend, beyond the horizon, hanging over our heads where we cannot quite reach.

Bob must be sought, but He is that which cannot be found. Therefore eternal longing is of Bob.

***

Long ago, Bob created the universe, including our world. He created all from the mountains to the atoms to feelings to realms of thought and possibility.

He has a tool with which he maintains the universe: the Great Wheel. It stands vertically, balancing on its edge as it spins, always falling but never fallen.

Everything in the universe has its counterpart place in the Great Wheel. There is no war, no galaxy, no amoeba, no thought, nothing that falls outside the Great Wheel.

It is "rhyme and reason"; and as it spins inexorably, every piece takes its turn in its needed moment. This is the harmony of the Great Wheel.

Thus the universe is locked in a neverending dynamic dance like the glittering of the stars to keep in step with the Great Wheel's turn. The universe *must* reflect the Great Wheel, for if it did not, the universe would have no sense. And it must, for Bob *is* Sense.

The seedling of every manifestation springs from the Mind of Bob and stands before the Great Wheel, which it must spin to find its place. All things must fulfill their purpose in order to keep the Great Wheel turning. When the purpose is served, its form disappears and the seedling rejoins Bob.

The essence of we mortals are such seedlings, and we, too, are here with a purpose, unique to each of us. Only by fulfilling it will we return to Bob. But we are anomalies, for we are out of touch with the rhythm of the Great Wheel, blocked by fleeting desires that pull us in a hundred directions every moment and create our seeming senselessness. If we sense beyond them we will perceive the harmony that pervades through all and will know how to step in accordance with the Great Wheel.

Although one can understand the Great Wheel, one cannot understand that which stands *behind* it. This is Bob. Bob is *why*. But *why* cannot ever be given a name; one can only know that *why* exists.

***

Bob has agents who assist Him: the Lauki. They are His messengers and servants.

Opposing the Lauki are the Shugina, agents of Pat. Pat is the force that draws one away from Bob. Pat denies Bob. But it is futile, for Pat is also of Bob, and by law must one day return to Him. Therefore in life there are always two directions: towards Bob, or away from Bob.

Pat was once an agent of Bob, but he turned against Him. The moment this happened, an enormous explosion took place, and Pat's great body cleaved off, releasing volatile material into the universe. Three consequences ensued:

1. The creation of Polarity. Towards or away, light or dark, yes or no, attract or repel. We are bound by Polarity, but it is not the ultimate truth. Pat does not want us to realize the illusion, for as long as we are swayed by Polarity, he exists. And Pat's very aim is to exist, to be separate from Bob.

2. The material that flew off left Pat with a tiny, weak body. Ever since, he has sought to regain all of the lost material to rebuild himself.

3. Bob's pressing universal need became the safe disposal of that turbulent material that flew off at great speed, threatening to wreak havoc on everything in its path if left uncontrolled. He did not see fit to return it to Pat, and instead decided to send it to

the far corners of the universe, to several distant planets settled in the remote fringes, which He thought would make good waste disposals. One of these planets was ours. This volatile material is released little by little through each mortal in the form of a token. It is by the Great Tension of Bob that the material is kept in restraint and not released all at once. Thus it is the mortals' duty to act as valves for this material and lessen the Great Tension.

Before the Great Divide, mortals did not have a token and were born into this world in a natural and empty state. But now, every mortal on our planet possesses a token. A token is a "something" that defies natural law, the mortal's personal anomaly. It may take on any form, except for immortality, for there is only a finite amount of this material.

Before a mortal of this planet manifests in the universe, he must stand before the Great Wheel; as it spins, one's token is chosen and one falls into place in the Plan. At the moment of birth, a Lauk is sent down to implant the token into the center of the mortal's being. There it will stay for the duration of its life, giving the material a home. During one's lifetime, one must burn through this material, transforming it into action. When one has transformed all of it, one becomes free from one's token. One becomes a natural mortal, undistorted and unburdened.

A token is both a gift and a curse. It is a gift because it is one's unbroken thread to traverse the world of confusion to come to Bob and alignment with Purpose.

But it is a curse for two reasons. First, one may become a slave to one's token and let it control one's life. Second, a token inherently causes a mortal to perceive a skewed version of reality. We live in two universes: our feet are in the universe as it is, but our minds are trapped in a parallel universe of our own creation, a parody of the real universe. Each individual lives in his own universe and rarely do two universes coincide. The source of this is one's token, that special anomaly which distorts. Only by conquering one's token may one see the true reality. The token is like a veil that colors one's world subjective. Mortals were once aware of the distortion in their perceptions. But now they believe that what they see *is* the truth. In fact, no two mortals ever experience reality in the same way.

If one has not conquered one's token by the time of death, one remains bound to his token and sinks to the Lair of Pat. Pat reabsorbs the token and regains a portion of his body, and the mortal, still attached, remains bound to Pat, longing to return to his source, which longing is mirrored by Bob's.

Pat grows stronger every time he regains a piece of his body. Therefore, he seeks to divert the mortals from their purpose to advance his own: to become separate from Bob and turn the universe on its head.

In the beginning, mortals were aware of their purpose, but over time Pat's influence overtook the planet and mortals forgot the true reason for their anomalous state. They perverted it into the belief that their tokens existed because they were "inherently special." Interestingly enough, each mortal did not think that all mortals were special but that *he alone* was special and important. Each mortal began to see himself as the main character in his world. This belief has become so deeply held, it is the greatest obstacle to conquering one's token, and the greatest weakness that causes one to succumb so easily to the influences of Pat.

Bob seeks to help the mortals return to Him, so he sends the Lauki to assist them. But, likewise, Pat sends the Shugina to prompt mortals to indulge their weaknesses and to cease being inspired by their token. For the duration of one's life, there is an ongoing battle between the Lauki and the Shugina. Every action that occurs is a war of these two opposing forces that must reach settlement. Even the most complex of our mortal entanglements can be boiled down to the pull of opposites. What is it that tips the scale one way and not the other? That, no mortal will dare answer....

Despite Bob's help, the mortals are weak in their resistance to Pat, and the more follow him, the stronger his presence. If his presence dominates, the world will have to be annihilated, for the mortals no longer serve the purpose of Bob.

In its final days, the world will turn on its head. Everything not normal will become the norm; lies will act as truth; freedom will be slavery. Thereby can one know when time is running out.

Chapter 08: The Token Law

Milly and her best friend, Tai, crept quietly down the Hallans' stairs, their fuzzy slippers muffling any sound as they tread carefully toward to the kitchen.

"What do you want for breakfast?" Milly looked down at her friend from the counter top she was kneeling on in her princess jammies.

"Pancakes!" Tai licked her lips.

"My mom needs the rest of this week's eggs... sorry," said Milly apologetically.

"Man, I should've slept over tonight!" Tai hissed. "Then tomorrow we could've had whatever we wanted. Do you have *anything* left?"

"We've got ice cream!" Milly exclaimed excitedly as she jumped down from the counter and opened the freezer.

Still in their pajamas, the two girls carried their huge concoctions of vanilla sundaes draped in chocolate fudge and caramel sauce (which the Hallans had plenty of left over) over to the living room where they sat them gently onto the coffee table, then plopped themselves onto the couch.

"Now this is what I call breakfast," said Milly.

"Anything good on?" asked Tai. Milly turned to the T.V. Directory channel to see the listings, which rolled along the bottom half of the screen as an infomercial for something indispensable to the home gym played on the top half.

"Just cartoons," groaned Milly, resisting the sudden impulse to turn to that channel because she'd feel stupid if Tai knew that she still watched old children's cartoons.

"*Seven Stranger Danger* reruns from last season are on," exclaimed Tai with a degree of interest. "Did you watch last season?"

"No..." Milly answered.

Tai clicked her tongue. "Oh my Bob. It was *so* good."

Milly and Tai's attention was easily distracted by the commercial that came on in place of the stale infomercial, advertising the upcoming season of one of the most popular shows on television.

"Be sure to tune in to the new season of *Artinian Artist* this July! With your favorite host, Johnny Dale!"

Johnny Dale appeared on screen, smiling genially and waving while holding a microphone in his other hand, loose strands of his wavy dirty-blond hair almost brushing the tops of his chiseled cheeks.

"Oh my Bob!!! I'm so excited for *Artinian Artist!*" Tai exclaimed, jumping out of her seat.

"Me too!" screamed Milly.

"We should see it live this season!" Tai exclaimed.

"My parents would never let. Those tickets are so expensive," Milly groaned.

"Tell them you'll pay for half of it," said Tai.

"How? I don't have a job."

"The *Teengirl Magazine* website has tons of ideas for summer jobs," said Tai. They put away their now empty bowls and rushed upstairs to Milly's computer.

Twenty minutes later...

"Thx...ur...pics...r...cute...2...;)" Tai typed.

"Do you know him?" Milly asked over Tai's shoulder about the boy onto whose page Tai was leaving this comment.

"Yeah! We talk online all the time," said Tai, clicking the 'send' button. "I kind of like him," she divulged.

"I didn't know you were meeting guys," said Milly naively.

"Oh, yeah! We're going to video chat tonight."

"Wait... so you've never actually met in person?... Then how can you like him?" Milly asked, mildly confused.

"What does *that* matter?" Tai turned sharply to Milly. "It's not one of those superficial physical relationships. I don't need to meet him to know that we have a connection! We click. We agree on so many things."

"Oh.... Do you, uh, think he likes you, too?" Milly asked, trying to smooth things over.

"Yeah," Tai smiled reluctantly, as if shy to admit that someone might like her. "I can just hear it in the way he says stuff, you know?"

"But... you can't hear him...."

"Well, I can *imagine* what it sounds like," she explained.

"But then... aren't your conversations only a product of your imagination?" Milly posed with trepidation.

"What are you saying?" asked Tai, her manner that of a lioness waiting for her unassuming prey to step naively into her den.

"That, well, doesn't that make your whole relationship not... real? I just don't think you can have a meaningful relationship online. You don't see the person, you don't hear him; you imagine the whole conversation based on words you see on your screen! You're basically talking to yourself. Any emotion you feel is not based on a physical interaction between two people but on your own belief in an illusion, and is thus also illusory in nature. How can you really know the person if your whole relationship is in your head and your emotional attachment is not to him but to a mental representation you created of him that doesn't even exist?" Milly asked.

"Oh my Bob, I *hate* when people say that! Do you know how many people meet each other online? Are you saying that millions of people have 'fake' relationships?"

Milly didn't answer.

"Bob, Milly, you're so judgmental!" exclaimed Tai.

"I didn't mean – !" Milly started. "So... how do you know he likes you?" she picked up from there instead.

"It's the little things, you know? An ellipsis here... an exclamation mark there. And sometimes he ends his more *grin* *suggestive* remarks with a winking smiley face. And he's been doing that more and more lately!" Tai smiled. "You should make an account on YourSpot.com. Everyone at school has one!"

"I can't. My parents are afraid old men will stalk me," said Milly miserably.

"That sucks," said Tai.

"My parents are the lamest!" Milly whined. In the meanwhile Tai went back to her own YourSpot page. Suddenly she jumped up and shouted.

"Oh my Bob! Dee Allderbay and I are friends on YourSpot! I sent her a friend request four times and she finally accepted!"

They clicked on Dee Allderbay's YourSpot page; Milly's monitor turned a blinding shade of pink. Tai scrolled down to Dee's photos and clicked on an album titled "Party It Uppp!"

"Ooh! This is from that huge party at Spencer Blake's house last Friday. I heard all about it," Tai informed her slightly less in-the-loop friend.

Click. Dee, Delilah, and three other popular, tanned girls, all with straight hair and highlights, one-armed hugged each other in a row while designer pieces of cloth hung off their bodies and cans of cheap beer stayed in their hands.

"Is that Melissa Ethers on the right? Next to Samantha Johnson?" Milly asked.

"No, that's Delilah Summers, Dee's BFF. Melissa is second from left. And... that's not Samantha Johnson," said Tai, leaning in to get a closer look at the photo. "That's Brittany Jansen... Samantha Johnson isn't even in this photo."

"Yeah she is, she's all the way on the left," said Milly.

"No, that's Julie Stevenson," corrected Tai.

"Are you sure?" Milly studied the details... diamond stud on the *left* side of the nose, not the *right*....

"Wait, we're *both* wrong! That's Morgan Mason!" she exclaimed.

Click. Dee Allderbay, three of her girlfriends, and four guys in polos and sideways-worn baseball caps, nonchalantly holding their beers, were gathered around a long table set up with red plastic cups in some kind of triangular pattern at both ends; some were looking at the camera, and others carelessly not. It was an ideal random candid party photo.

"They're playing Beer Sling!" Tai commented.

"What's Beer Sling?" Milly asked curiously.

"You don't know what *Beer Sling* is?" said Tai, cringing her face and raising her eyebrows, before turning back around to the monitor and shaking her head one or two times, not more.

Click. Dee taking a masterful shot at Beer Sling and firing the tiny ball into a far cup with her sling shot.

Click. Milly and Tai clicked through seventy more photos until they got to one that made Milly's body lurch in upheaval: Dee Allderbay kissed Marrik McFost lightly on the cheek as Marrik looked at the camera with a sultry non-smile and steady eyes. Milly's heart pounded furiously inside her chest as she stared at that perfectly sculpted face, feeling, behind the towering brick wall inside her that kept her standing wistfully outside the elusive garden in which the popular kids played, the smidge of a deep-resting instinct – animal jealousy, a creature in the innermost pit of her gut growling as Milly's eyes clamped onto Dee Allderbay's hand, which thoughtlessly rested on that broad, dependable shoulder, the other hanging loosely at the end of the slim arm thrown behind her, holding a beer.

Milly lunged over Tai and clicked, before her emotions could get the best of her.

It had been the last photo. They moved on to her next album, entitled, "Waking Upp Bitchessss!"

Click: Dee lying in bed after waking up, holding a beer. Click: Dee brushing her teeth, holding a beer. Click: Dee and her mom in their kitchen, arms around each other, a can of beer in Dee's.

"Hey, I have a new message!" Tai cried.

Hey All, Born here,

Lainii was amazing, It was so fascinating to learn about a new culture. Was it a challenge? Well, you know, I'm immortal, and Lainiians traditionally believe that that is not possible. But in spite of our differences, I've made many great friends I'll treasure for the rest of my life. Hear me talk all about it this Thursday on Vandorn News! As always, I look forward to your emails, so keep 'em comin'!

Hugs, BG

"You're friends with Borneo on YourSpot?" Milly asked Tai, astounded. Tai proudly clicked on Borneo's page to show her that she could view his profile.

In number of friends, Borneo ranked fourth on YourSpot.com, with one million and nine – oh! – one million and ten.

Milly sank glumly onto her bed, resigning herself to a life of friendlessness, because, thanks once again to her stupid parents, she would never have the opportunity to spend three hours a day looking through photos on YourSpot.com!

***

"This is excellent," said Mr. Daltuhn, leaning back in his chair complacently when John brought him his mail the following day. "The network's never been better and with Thursday, we'll be golden," he threw his head out the window and smiled at a giant billboard showcasing Borneo modeling a new line of designer tuxedos, which had appeared sometime during Borneo and John's absence.

"Don't you change that channel!" John's mother called from the kitchen that Thursday night as she finished putting dinner into the over so that she could watch, too. John threw the remote onto the other side of the couch and leaned back. Just then, the house phone rang and John picked it up.

"Hey, Hec. I'm about to watch the news," John replied.

"Borneo's interview? I'm watching that, too. Did you see that debate on C-Span 72 on the length of teaspoon handles? That was sick! I'm personally a proponent of the long-handled spoons, otherwise they get too hot when you're stirring your tea."

"When was this?" John asked.

"Uh... Saturday night," said his friend Hec on the other line.

"Oh, I was in Lainii on Saturday," answered John.

"You were *where*!?"

"Lainii."

John used the interruption of a Kimi Kool commercial to fix himself a drink in the kitchen:

As an upbeat pop tune played, one Milly would probably have recognized, animated Kimi Kool walked forward in front of a bright blue sky. She smiled with unmitigated joy as her long yellow hair swayed about her in one piece.

"Summer's in the *air!*" Kimi Kool exclaimed brightly, winking a crystal blue eye that was the same color as the flower on her pink bikini top.

"It's my favorite time of the year!" she laughed in a way that enjoined her audience to laugh along.

An enormous white house came into view, its front double doors flanked by two adults and four small children of varying sizes. Kimi Kool stood facing it with her back to the audience, her long hair covering her body so that it was visible only from the miniskirt down.

117

"Guess what, everyone!" Kimi Kool yelled excitedly. "School is over for the summer!! Hooray!" she flung her arms up in joy.

Her family joined in with her.

"Congratulations, Kimi!" beamed Mrs. Kimi Kool (sold separately).

All six personages were clearly very excited that Kimi Kool had finally come home from wherever she had been, for the unintelligible jumble of sounds they expressed denoted happiness, alertness, and loving care. After a few moments the first distinguishable sentence was uttered.

"We have a surprise for you!" said the handsome man holding Mrs. Kimi Kool's arm.

Spotlight on a hot pink convertible. Kimi Kool shrieked with delight.

"Thanks, mom and stepdad!"

All beamed.

Kimi Kool found herself standing behind her new car without having walked there. The camera admired Kimi Kool's new car from every angle. Top view. Profile view. Three-quarters view left. Five-eighths view right. Then it showed it zooming away without the assistance of a driver.

"Whee!" Kimi Kool exclaimed once her car had magically appeared by her side again. She jumped in and cruised out into the bright world. As the wind swept back her hair and the road wound on, she turned to face her audience.

"Now I have the freedom to go *wherever* I want, *whenever* I want!" she announced, slamming on the gas.

She drove to Hollister.

She walked back out of the store, laughing, five large shopping bags in tow; she threw them into the backseat and continued to drive on. There was a conspicuous lack of important background scenery, such as roads, in these frames. Suddenly, she pulled up to where three of her best friends happened to be standing.

"Neat car!" exclaimed Shelley.

"Hop in!" said Kimi friendlily.

"We can finally do summer the right way!" said Lacy.

"Let's go to the pool, girls!" exclaimed B.J.

"Okay!!" went the other three happily.

The pink convertible drove into the sunshine, four heads of yellow hair blowing in the wind.

The music ended. While an announcer spoke, the screen showed the actual Kimi Kool doll, all twelve glorious inches of molded plastic she was, wearing its Summer Fun Outfit of pink bikini top and denim miniskirt.

"... Summer Fun Kimi Kool! Every girl's gotta have one! Kimi Kool Summer Fun Car sold separately...."

"We should go down to the bar and get a beer later," said Hec.

"How about tomorrow?" John answered, sitting back down. "Oh! It's coming on! I've got to go," and he hung up.

"Scoot over, John," fussed his mother. "Stewart! Hurry up!" she called. John's father came thumping into the living room.

"I'm missing my evening smoke for this?" he growled.

"You can smoke your cigar some other time," said his wife, slapping him gently on the knee as he sat down next to her.

"Where's Milly?" Mr. Hallan asked.

"In her room. I don't think she'd be too interested in – " John started.

"Quiet, it's starting!" his father barked.

Right off the bat they knew something was off: there was no background music. The Hallans threw each other looks of concern.

"We're here to bring you a special report," said the news anchor, looking as if he'd spent a year without sunshine. *Borneo couldn't be that big*, John thought.

"At eleven AM Vandorn time, the Decagon received an anonymous memo warning of a bombing downtown at three PM today."

Mrs. Hallan gasped automatically.

"No bombs were found on the scene, the block between the junctions of Mallow and Eight Street and Mallow and Seventh – "

"John! That's only a few blocks from where you work!" Mrs. Hallan exclaimed, looking wide-eyed with shock at him.

"No, it's really not that near at all," John promptly launched into an unconcerned-sounding reaction. "And especially when you think about how many buildings there are insulating us, if a bomb went off there we'd barely feel the impact so it's actually quite far away," but

John only set off a stream of visions of domino-effect collapses in her mind.

" – and will remain blocked off as investigations continue into the night. However, since the prospect of any real danger seems dim, authorities have assured that the area will be cleared for tomorrow's morning commute."

"See?" John pointed to the television.

"Maybe you should stay home tomorrow," his mother said worriedly.

"Mom, I'm not in school," he said.

"But this is a bomb threat! You don't know what might – anything could happen!"

"I told you, even if a bomb did go off, the shock would barely reach NKOZ," John soothed. "I mean – that's not what I meant to say – " he fumbled at the growl from his father. "They wouldn't clear the area if it wasn't safe, right?"

"You're getting yourself worked up over nothing, Merle," John's father cut in. "It was probably just a bunch of stupid teenagers who'd eaten too much chocolate."

" – Rumors have already connected the memo to the well-known international terrorist group LASS. Meanwhile at the Decagon, Presidents Havenford and Steffen have turned to Colonel Kevin Rutt to lead the safety response, which may mean an increase in security measures – "

"Trust them to use anything as an excuse to monitor our lives," Mr. Hallan grumbled darkly.

As the news report went on to repeat what little information they had about the bomb threat in as many sentences as possible, they retreated to the kitchen, where Mrs. Hallan was soon rapidly discussing the news with a girlfriend over the phone.

"Milly, did you watch the news?" Mr. Hallan asked his daughter, who was setting glasses onto the table.

"No, dad, fifteen-year-old girls don't watch the news!"

"Yeah, they hear about important things like bomb threats from their friends at school the next day," John informed.

"There was a bomb threat? Where?" exclaimed Milly, looking around.

"I thought you weren't speaking to me because I didn't bring you a souvenir," said John.

"Mooom! Was there a bomb threat?"

"Yes! Near John's job!" cut in Mrs. Hallan quickly, holding the phone down on her shoulder before picking it right back up and continuing in serious tones.

"Not that near," corrected John.

"And no, I don't care about a stupid souvenir, I'm mad that you forgot about me!" said Milly.

"I bought you a souvenir! I already told you what happened," said John.

"Yeah, right, I'm supposed to believe that," huffed Milly.

"But it's true!"

"Please, John, exciting stuff like that doesn't happen to you!"

***

As he'd predicted, John's quest for his morning coffee was significantly impaired. He walked out of Schmidtstein's quickly and, for the first time, took a shortcut through a narrow street he had always avoided to make it work on time.

John already felt the adrenaline flowing out of the cracks in his freshly broken routine. He could do this every day. He smiled. Then he knocked into something hard.

"Hey! Watch where you goin',' man!" shouted whoever John had just walked into. His and John's eyes met.

"Well well well," said who turned out to be a large-nosed youth with black hair tied away from his face by a red bandana. "You ain't too bright, is you?" he smirked at John, whom he seemed to recognize.

Before John had time to respond there was a gun pressed to his forehead.

"Do you know me? Because I really don't think I know you!" John exclaimed, quite alarmed.

"Damn innies all look the same; that same smug expression like you's better than us. I'd know yo' face from a mile away!" he spat.

"Why you yellin' all over the place?!" came a new voice, both angry and hushed, and much deeper than the boy's. It belonged to one of two lumbering figures that stepped out of the shadows at the alley's other end. Both were large-nosed and wore red bandanas on their heads like the boy. Together their shoulders equaled one of their bodies in length.

"Look what I found me, Akshansh! It's one of them cops who thinks we done the bomb threat!" the youth hissed.

"Wait, what? They didn't say anything about searching citizens on the news," said John.

"Right, like they gonna tell you that. They keep that shit undercover, let you 'good innies' go free and catch the 'bad guys' and 'street thugs'," said Akshansh.

"But I'm not a cop!" said John.

"He *lyin'*!" snarled the youth.

"Shut it, Devesh!" snapped Akshansh. And then he froze. He waited for something, looking up and down the dim alley with suspicious eyes as every other muscle stood unflinching as if he had been sculpted of copper.

John also listened intently. He thought he heard the softest of rustles, so quiet as if to snuff itself out. Akshansh's forehead creased. And then –

Out jumped a man quick as a flash of lightening, landing behind the giant thug, pressing a short blade to his thick neck, and holding his arms behind him in an unbreakable bind before anyone reacted. The assailant was a flat-nosed stranger who, though only about Devesh's size, was more toned than he, leaner and quite agile.

"Toki!!" bellowed Akshansh, and before he could conceal his surprise behind a mask of anger, six more flat-nosed assailants materialized from the shadows. All of them had green handkerchiefs tied around their left biceps. The one they called Toki stood silently behind the giant, smiling a thin, sinister smile.

"Let him go!" bellowed Akshansh, drawing his gun.

"I think not," Toki scoffed lightly. "But I sense by your fear that you'd be willing to bargain. How about I take this one – " Toki pressed the blade harder against the large-nosed man's neck, " – and we won't turn you in to the cops, who have quite a reward for your head as it stands."

Akshansh swiftly moved to hold the gun up to Toki's forehead. "How's this for a bargain: you don't kill him, I don't kill you."

"I tried to negotiate," said Toki, then slit his captive's throat. He fell to the ground, dead, and in a split second Akshansh put two fingers into his mouth and whistled; instantantly five more broad-nosed men came running down the alley.

Looking alarmed, Toki and his men bolted out of sight, followed by the broad-nosed crew, who left their dead on the street to rot.

John stood in the now deserted alleyway, paralyzed, just him, the dead body, and the dead body's gun. After a moment's hesitation, John picked up the gun and pocketed it carefully.

He came to and ran as fast out of the alleyway as he could, stepping back into the street's broad daylight to merge with the clueless crowd he could sink into like a warm, safe bath, dissociating himself from the scene he'd just witnessed.

It was a new day, walking through the city with a gun. He had always prided himself on not carrying one, as so many people at odds to protect themselves did. But it was high time to drop those ideals, he reasoned sternly. At least he wouldn't have to waste the fifty dollars to buy one and use that money for metro fare instead.

When had he shifted imperceptibly to only caring about metro fare and how to plan his clothes for the weather? *Five years ago I ached to travel the world, now I pray on bended knee to leave the office half an hour early on Fridays and thank Bob when it happens....*

"...Never thought something so exciting would happen in our lifetime!" exclaimed an unfamiliar voice as John walked into the break room, still shaken, where Mr. Daltuhn, Luke, Nelson, and three strange men stood.

"Darek, you bastard! You don't call your country almost getting bombed exciting!" Mr. Daltuhn laughed.

"Please, Daltuhn, you don't really believe that?"

"'Course I do! Always known damn broads have got it out for us."

"Any idiot can tell the whole thing was a hoax," said the man called Darek.

"Are you calling me an idiot? You're fired!"

They all laughed.

Just then Borneo burst in through the break room, almost knocking coffee out of John's hands.

"Can you believe this!" he yelled in astonishment. "They didn't show my interview!"

"Borneo, there was a bomb threat yesterday," said John behind him. Borneo spun around to see who'd dared counter him. It turned out everyone was staring at him.

"I know and it's terrible... but couldn't they have shown it afterwards?"

"I daresay they spent the rest of the time discussing LASS," said a man of fine bone structure with glasses, raising his coffee away from Borneo's swinging arms.

"What's LASS?" asked Borneo carelessly.

Everyone's jaws dropped.

"Daltuhn, you better not let the world know how sheltered your boy is!" chuckled one of the other men.

"LASS is short for the Levitation/Aviation Secret Society," said the bespectacled man mildly, turning to Borneo. "They're an international organization formed exclusively by men whose tokens pertain to the power of flight."

"So?" demanded Borneo.

"They're only the most well-known terrorist organization in the world!" exclaimed Darek.

"Yeah, and they've kind of got a thing against Artinia, as in, they want our guts," said the third man.

"It's 'cause like half of them are in Aruq," said Darek.

"Damn bastards got noses so big they can smell our food from the other side of the world," growled Mr. Daltuhn.

"Mr. Daltuhn, what are we going to do?" he looked at his boss with great concern.

"Nothing?" Mr. Daltuhn turned back around as he made to walk out of the break room with the three men.

"But this was my biggest interview yet! Can't you just talk – !"

"Boy, let me tell you something. In this business you have to know when to push someone and when to leave them be. And I suggest *you* try that right now!"

"Unbelievable!" Borneo threw his arms up when they were gone. "All this bomb threat business is going to make me old news!"

He slumped down into a chair and pulled out his laptop.

"*Not even three hundred emails?!*" he cursed in anger several minutes later.

"John, did you hear me, I didn't even get three hundred emails today!" Borneo called out to him.

"Oh no," said John, turning a magazine's page.

"John," Borneo said, "what if this is the end?"

"The end of what?"

"Of my career."

"Well, you'll have a long time to rebuild it."

Borneo did not find this joke funny. "I'm serious! What am I doing wrong?" the question tormented him.

"Nothing! People are a little preoccupied right now! Just give it a few weeks and everything will be back to normal," said John.

"A few *weeks*?" Borneo yelped like this was forever.

By lunchtime an agglomeration of hungry people had amassed in the break room to heat up their condensed soups and *SmartPicks*, crowding around the television as they waited.

"...This just in: in response to yesterday's bomb threat, the government has passed a security measure requiring all Artinian citizens to register their tokens," the anchor reported.

John choked on his coffee.

"The measure, called the Token Law, will go into effect by Friday, September first, when all registration papers will be due."

"*What!?*" was the reaction in the break room.

"The information will be kept on record at government offices and may be used to monitor suspicious activity, but will not infringe on privacy. How are the people responding? Let's go to Anita Slater."

"Hi, Rick, I'm here with Ethel Marburg, a resident of Vandorn for over fifty years," said Anita Slater, gesturing to an elderly lady with bright red lipstick and several shopping bags.

"Ethel, how do you feel about the bomb threat?" Anita asked. Ethel grabbed the microphone from her and put it to her shriveled lips.

"My grandson – *my grandson* – he works downtown, and I am very worried about him. He is twenty-six years old – "

"How do you think the government should respond? Do you think this is something that can be ignored, or should we respond forcefully?"

Ethel caught her breath, paused, and said, "I think the government should respond forcefully!"

"There you have it. Back to you."

"This goes against everything in our Constitution!" someone in the break room cried.

"*Registering* your token!? Is there no sanctity left in the world?" another exclaimed passionately.

"We can thank those Bobdamn liberals!" a man beat his fist on the counter.

The entire floor was a-buzz over the news. John marched past people arguing between cubicles, but Mr. Daltuhn's office door burst open violently before he could knock. A scared looking woman looked imploringly at him as he hastily escorted her out.

"But will I get sued if I – ?"

"I don't know! I don't care! I don't give a damn if you write a fake token and I don't give a damn about your real one! Just don't bring a lawsuit onto my head!!" he yelled. "Move along, Hallan, I just got a call about Nelson having an anxiety attack! Religious nut...!"

"I can't imagine how it is for him. Telling another person his token is like showing them his genitals," said John, following Mr. Daltuhn's rapid steps.

"I don't care what psychic scarring this causes him, if he doesn't fill out the damn registration I can't have him here!"

"Really?"

"Yes, really. Why, what's the matter?" Mr. Daltuhn turned around.

"Well, I have some news for you, then," said John.

"Better be good news," Mr. Daltuhn growled. John's lack of response conveyed that it was not.

"Quickly, Hallan," Mr. Daltuhn said.

John looked around; he didn't want anyone listening. He opened their office door to give them some privacy.

Both men dropped their jaws at the sight that met their eyes: as the wind bounced the blinds and ruffled papers on the desks, Borneo stood at the open window, his head, shoulders, and half his torso leaning out of it as his hands clenched the sill.

"Borneo!!" John shouted.

"What in the name of every Bobdamned thing under the sun do you think you're doing, idiot boy?!" Mr. Daltuhn yelled. Borneo turned sharply around so that he stood facing them, looking manic.

"I can't take it anymore!" Borneo shouted. "No one gets it! No one understands how hard it is! No one gives a *damn* about what *I* have to go through!" he exploded.

"What?" John cocked his head.

"You heard what I said! Now get away from me, all of you! Get away before I jump!"

The two other people in the room backed up several feet.

"Enough of your stupid antics, boy! Get away from that window and get back to work!" yelled Mr. Daltuhn with a distinguishable note of panic.

"If you *cared* maybe you'd know that I *hate* this job! I've had enough!" Borneo yelled, his back making one plane with the open window. He turned around, leaned out, and yelled, "I CAN'T TAKE IT ANYMORE!"

Down in the streets, people heard the yell from high above; they looked up, gasping in horror at the sight of one third of a man leaning out the window.

"I CAN'T TAKE ANYMORE OF THIS LIFE!!!" came down another strangled cry. He was leaning so far out he looked like a see-saw about to tip the other way.

Borneo's head tipped down and his eyes landed on the sidewalk directly below, thirty stories of empty, dizzying space away....

Both John and Mr. Daltuhn saw his hand slip off the ledge and his body begin to slacken. His head collided with the windowsill in a nasty crunch as he slipped to the floor and retched before fainting.

Chapter 09: Freedomism

BORNEO GRIMGAE: ATTEMPTED SUICIDE

Artinia's immortal herowas seen leaning out of a thirtieth story window in NKOZ headquarters in downtown Vandorn screaming '*I сдп'т тдкэ дпумфяэ фг тнix̌ liгэ!* by no less than two dozen civilians around four thirty yesterday afternoon.

Has he ruined his relationship with his fans? Borneo is an icon for many and a role model for children across the nation (continued on page 3)
....

COUNTRY RESPONDS TO TOKEN LAW, pg. 2

John put the newspaper back and proceeded forward in line, sighing as he wondered what Mr. Daltuhn would do about this mess they were in. He had already smacked Borneo across the head with a copy of that same newspaper Friday morning before retreating into his office for the rest of the day. The continual babble over the phone they had heard behind his wall was the only sign that he himself was not replicating Borneo's attempt.

Mr. and Mrs. Hallan had reasoned that Saturday morning would be a good time to do this week's grocery shopping as the store was likely to be empty early on; unfortunately, so had everybody else. John, with whom the senior Hallans were testing their theory, had been standing in line for half an hour already, and looking ahead, he judged he had about that much more to wait. The available reading material he might use to pass the time was such that he would rather wait quietly. Indeed, standing in line at the grocery store, John never did more than glance over the magazine covers preceding the checkout. Some were pretty amusing; one seemed to discover shocking new revelations about sex every month. Didn't John want to be touched in seven secret spots six months ago already? Oh, no, this was different – this was the five naughty things he wished a woman would do to him in bed.

The lady behind him picked up a copy of the very magazine he'd just been laughing internally at and flipped open to the middle,

129

reading peacefully while her young daughter sat in the cart quietly with her headphones on.

As the line moved, another magazine caught John's eye. <u>The Storm Inside: The Inner Workings of Borneo Grimgae</u>, said the latest issue of *The Current*.

John picked it up and opened to the article:

> We thought he was happy. We thought he was okay.
>
> We were wrong.
>
> *Borneo Grimgae tried to kill himself*. Okay. You made it past the first stage, and you've accepted it. Now comes the tricky part — why? Why would someone so happy suddenly want to end his life? The puzzle is intricate. The clues are few. And you yourself are burning to understand how they fit together. That's why we've asked world renowned psychologists to help us analyze what's really going on inside Borneo's mind.
>
> 'Borneo's character is extremely complex,' says Dr. Jeremy Finkelstein. 'Between the two layers of personality, inner and outer, is what we in the psychological community call the Equilibrating Maintenance System (EMS). The EMS works like a filter, deciding what gets pushed to the surface and what gets buried underneath. The EMS-based personality is the hallmark of modern man, a tool that many now consider healthy for social manipulation and play, and its development is actively encouraged in young children by modern educators.
>
> In a healthy person, the EMS finds a balance between the good parts and the bad parts. However, because he is always in the spotlight, Borneo feels compelled to be only 'good'; his EMS is overworked as a result and may even be broken beyond repair.'
>
> But according to Dr. Imji Fuka, that's just the tip of the iceberg! 'Borneo is a unique case; much of him is hidden in shadow. The reason for this is that while most people live for themselves, Borneo lives for others. He sacrifices himself for society's good because he has the rare capacity to represent our ideals. But he has become a role model at the expense of his own spiritual and emotional needs, a heroic – yet tragic – feat. Most people would've collapsed from this kind of strain within a week; Borneo held on for over a *year*! His devotion to his fans has made him oblivious to his

own suffering, which, to any keen observer, has been obvious for months.'

Look for Dr. Fuka's highly anticipated upcoming book: <u>The Brilliant You: the Underlying Structure of YOUR Personality</u>.

John burst out laughing. Throwing the magazine into his cart, he moved further toward the check-out.

***

"So an immortal boy with feelings and thoughts of suicide! Describe that for me!"

"Sometimes even *I* want to laugh at the irony of it, Jackie! I know it's illogical, but the cold hard truth is that depression doesn't care whether or not you're immortal. I guess I never really thought it would happen to me. I was going along fine, bottling it all up, and then – bam! – it hit me."

"Well let's talk about it," Jackie leaned in, her face becoming concerned. "What's going on inside of you?"

"I'm alone. I'm confused. You see, no one really understands me. And I ask myself, *is it worth it to go on?*"

"And obviously you've found that the answer is no, it's not worth it?"

"Look at it this way: if I feel no connection to anyone in the world, what's the point of living, right?"

"Mhmm, mhmm," Jackie nodded. "Can't anyone help you?"

Borneo shook his head. "No. I just... I'm too far gone, honestly," he chuckled.

"So when did you first consider suicide as an option?"

Borneo looked up, trying to recall. "Um... probably about a week ago," he nodded.

"So you want to kill yourself, but the fact is, *you can't die!* What do you *do* with that?"

"You've got me!" Borneo threw his arms up.

"That must make it even more unbearable that *normal* suicide!"

"Tell me about it," Borneo smiled weakly, rolling his eyes in shared understanding with Jackie.

"I have to say, this situation is *fascinating*! Can we just talk about the philosophical implications for a moment?"

Borneo straightened up. "It's like I'm constantly dying, but I can never die. Yet if I no longer feel anything inside, isn't that already a form of death? So I'm dead – but I can't be. I'm dead, but I'm living forever. What is the difference, then, between death and immortality? Aren't we all eternally dead? Aren't we all immortals?"

Jackie was silent for a moment as she let his profound statements sink in.

"Can you describe the exact moment when you realized you wanted to commit suicide?"

Borneo looked thoughtful.

"I was standing by the window, having a moment of despair.... And then I realized: nobody loves me. It was a moment of clarity in the midst of confusion, like the eye of a hurricane – "

"Ooh!"

"Suddenly I knew what I had to do, what was the *only* thing to do. But then..."

"But then...?"

"I realized – I *couldn't!* And *then*...."

"Yes? And then?"

"I broke."

Silence.

Jackie turned to the camera, looking serious and somber.

"We'll be back after these commercial messages."

"... Do you have body fat? Then you're unattractive!..."

***

Borneo's depression had the entire country gripped by Monday. The only person who seemed unperturbed by his plight was Mr. Daltuhn. Indeed, he reveled in the extra media attention slathering

Borneo from this slightly different angle. People from other floors came up to congratulate him and marvel at such a lucky turn of events, whereupon Mr. Daltuhn would act pleasantly surprised himself at how things just seemed to work out so uncannily.

Borneo came in that morning a mess; his hair was unwashed and his face was unshaven; he sat in a corner of the office and spoke to no one.

Completely ignoring the three dozen bouquets piled high on his desk, he opened his laptop and started typing astonishingly quickly while music of a depressing nature issued from his speakers.

John walked over and stood behind him, watching:

> Welcome to DeadDiary.com! Create your basic account for FREE!
>
> Username: Total_Eclipse
>
> Interests: Total Eclipses, Fate, Lust, Love, Poetry, the Dark Side of Humanity |

"Yes John? I'm in the middle of writing?" Borneo said.

"What are you writing about?"

"It's personal."

"Personal enough to publish online?"

"It's only available to people on my Friends list," said Borneo.

"Borneo, that's forty-three people," said John, looking over Borneo's shoulder.

"And?"

"Nothing. That's just pretty impressive for an account that's been open for five minutes."

"Yeah, well, these are rather personal thoughts, so I had to choose my confidants selectively," said Borneo. But a few minutes later his face was buried in his hands and his state-of-the-art laptop was quivering in his lap.

"Borneo, you're not really depressed," said John from his seat.

"Yes I am!" Borneo looked up, affronted. "You have no idea what it's like! All you know is your happy little world!"

"Okay."

"Just leave me alone, John!" Borneo demanded.

"Okay."

"Don't say another word to me!"

John said nothing, but got back to work. There were several minutes of complete silence.

"And stop trying to help me!"

John made no response.

"That's it! There's only one way out and it's through this window!" Borneo announced dramatically, carefully closing his laptop. He walked up to the window and threw it open. A forceful wind blew past Borneo and through John's hair, making him look up: Borneo was standing on the ledge.

"Wait!" John shouted. "I – I know you're in a lot of pain, Borneo, I know how hard it is for you!"

"Oh yeah?" he turned his head and looked at John, his feet squarely on the ledge, poised to take a thirty-story dive. "Five minutes ago you didn't believe me when I said I was depressed! I thought you were my friend, but even *you* don't understand."

"I – I *do*. You're lost, you want someone to save you but the irony is that no one can because no one realizes you're trapped inside *yourself*. See, I get it," John consoled.

"That's not it at *all!*" Borneo crossed his arms.

"Yeah it is," John said dubiously. "It's more complicated than it seems on the surface. There are parts to you that are buried deeper than the ocean floor. Right?"

"You oversimplify it!!" Borneo burst out insanely.

"But I understand you!" said John.

Borneo leapt down from the ledge and grabbed his bag. "All you understand is how to make me hate myself more! *Have a nice life!*" he said with as much emotion as he could muster, and before John could stop him, he opened the door and walked out, slamming it behind him.

"...*Wait! I meant, I* don't *understand you!!*" he heard John cry through the wood a moment later.

But it was too late.

He tightened the hood of his black hoodie as he leaned against the grimy window, letting his face fade into oblivion on the other side of the impenetrable wall between himself and the world.... He turned on his mePod. It was a happy tune. He changed it.... People approached him in his seat, saying words, making smiles. How good they were at pretending.

I wish I could just be one of the many, he thought to himself as he got off and went nowhere in particular, passing by blissfully naïve faces. Twenty feet behind him where he could not see, a teenage boy, also listening to a mePod, incidentally to the same song Borneo had been enjoying, had the exact same thought as he threw his bangs over his eyes.

Somehow Borneo ended up at the mall. The colors and patterns swam by him in a dreary blur – and then something caught his eye: the clothing store *Abyss*. Its entrance was framed with daggers and inside it looked dark.

"...and then my mother was all, 'why can't you just be normal?' And I was all, 'what is normal? Working at Hollister?'"

"Good retort."

"Can I help you?" the one who'd been retelling the story, a tall, lanky youth in a black zip-up hoodie and tight black jeans asked Borneo as he entered.

"No," said Borneo curtly.

"I know that look on your face. It's the look of torment," said the customer with whom the lanky employee had been talking, a pudgy youth in a black t-shirt and several piercings through his ears.

Borneo shrugged. "I doubt you'd understand," he said as he picked up a t-shirt with a photo of the rock band Dystressed on it.

"Try me," said the pudgy grade-school youth.

"I've never been more lost in my life, and sometimes I feel the only way to end it all is, well, to end it all," said Borneo.

"I know what you mean, I've ceased to feel the pang of my own desperation," the pudgy one related. "If I feel nothing, what's the point of being alive?"

"Well, see, I *can't* die; I'm immortal," said Borneo.

"That's pretty twisted in an ironic, poetic way," the youth said, mildly impressed.

"Oh yeah? Try yearning for nothing more than to be a part of the world, and yet relishing your private status as outsider," said the lanky employee. "That's where I am. In this trap I created for myself."

"That's nothing," said a new voice, belonging to the boy who'd been walking some distance behind Borneo, who had just stepped into *Abyss* to overhear their conversation. "At least *you* don't fall asleep to the sound of your parents lashing out nastiness about who's fault it is that you turned out such a freak," he said. "I wrote about it in my DeadDiary last night, but when I reread the entry this morning I had no idea what I was talking about."

"It must've been genius," said the pudgy one.

"Wait, *you're* XxDeath_ChildxX?" asked the employee.

"Yeah."

"Do you really have a mermaid named Esmeralda living inside your mind?" he asked as he and the pudgy customer crowded around him, blocking Borneo out.

"*Yes.*"

***

"Good morning, Borneo," said Mr. Daltuhn the next day.

"Bless you, my child," Borneo nodded, going gracefully on his way.

Borneo walked placidly into their office an hour late to find John, Luke, and Nelson standing around. He walked over and hugged John like family. When he finally let go, John took a few steps back, bewildered, and sat down in his chair. Borneo sat on top of his desk.

Mr. Daltuhn came in after him. "Borneo, what is the meaning of this!" he demanded angrily. "We do not come to work an hour late, sit on desks, and keep the facial hair of a hobo!"

But Borneo laughed softly, as if in pity. "Mr. Daltuhn, Mr. Daltuhn," he shook his head. "I forgive you for yelling. I know you are ignorant of the Way. Most people are."

"What in the name of Bob are you talking about?"

"I had a revelation yesterday that saved me from the neverending spiral I was in," he said.

"What kind of revelation?" asked John.

"*Freedom*," said Borneo grandly, throwing his arms out.

"Absolute freedom," he said after a few moments passed in which no one responded to his previous statement. "Social conventions inhibit our spirits. I take my example from nature. Look at a bird, John – it's free to fly, no one is stopping it from being a bird. But look at us – we must be like this, dress like such, do so-and-so. It's wrong. I say we do whatever we want. Without limits or bounds," Borneo paused, leaving room for someone to clap.

"But, Borneo, society wouldn't be able to function if everyone acted on each of his or her random whims," said John.

"Who said we need society? Society is the ultimate evil. I'm going to assemble an association of individuals to get rid of it once and for all!" Borneo exclaimed.

"...A society against society?"

"Precisely."

"Borneo, drop the act. You got your popularity back!" John was getting frustrated.

The words pierced him. "This isn't about popularity! I've been through a lot in the past five days, John. They've changed me! And if you don't believe me I'm never going to be able to help you."

"What – "

"See, most people make it more complicated than it is. Take it in its simplest form: freedom. Doing what you want, whatever the consequences," Borneo explained. "Most people think they want a family and house and a job – "

"You don't seem to," John cut in.

"Well, my wants are more cosmic in nature now." he explained.

A few hours later, Nancy-Beth poked her head into the room. "Sir!" she said. "Sir, the concierge says there are five people trying to get up to the thirtieth floor. What should we do?"

"Are they bringing more bouquets?" Mr. Daltuhn asked.

"No, it looks like – several college students and one middle-aged man," said Nancy-Beth.

"Oh! That's for me!" Borneo exclaimed, jumping off the desk. "Let them up, Nancy-Beth, it's fine."

"What is this?" Mr. Daltuhn demanded.

"I told them we're meeting here, you don't mind, do you? Thanks!"

A minute later, a small troupe paraded across the floor, gathering odd looks from the bedesked employees; some of the band looked highly intimidated, others – a college student and the middle-aged man – stared around impressively.

"In here, guys!" Borneo pointed to the break room, dragging John along with him. They piled into the small space, making it feel rather cramped, all of them wearing red pins that said S.A.S on them.

"So, thanks for coming to our first official meeting, it's great to finally meet everyone. Shall we go around and introduce ourselves?"

The middle-aged man, who had a large pot belly, went first. "Hi, everyone, I'm Stanley – you know what? Why don't we sit on the floor, we'll be cozier that way," he interrupted himself. Everyone sat on the floor.

"So – ah – I've been a resident of Vadorn for over forty years, love the city – *love* the city – but can't stand the people!" he finished with a chuckle, mopping off some perspiration on his head. All the college students and Borneo chuckled along.

"Heyy, I'm Matt," said the next guy, making a sideways peace sign with his fingers. "Um, I'm in college, getting my degree in political science....Got a lot of big plans for the world," he nodded.

"What in the name of Pat is this!" Mr. Daltuhn barked at them, storming in.

"Oh, Mr. Daltuhn, this is the first meeting of the Society Against Society!" said Borneo brightly.

"The society against – *what*?"

"Society! A project of mine, don't worry about it. John here is a founding member."

John shrugged evasively.

"Everyone, this is my boss... but not for long!" he laughed, and so did they. "Mr. Daltuhn, would you like to join us?"

"No, I would not!" Mr. Daltuhn turned red and walked away.

Borneo sighed. "Alright, let's move on to the agenda."

"We definitely need to recruit," said Jan as she passed around herbal teas to the circle.

"Born here's got some cred, he'll pull in more people," said Matt.

Borneo nodded. "I'm gonna send out a message on YourSpot this evening. We might get *a lot* of people; where should we hold our next meeting?"

"Ooh!" said Jan. "There's this adorable chai shoppe by the meditation center I go to – "

"Are you talking about Mystikals?" Stanley cut in.

"Yeah!"

"I *love* that place. You know – I think I've seen you around! Do you go on Saturdays?"

"John! Are you taking notes on our first meeting?" Borneo suddenly asked.

"Borneo – I have to get back to work," said John.

"Come on, John, what's more important? Fighting for freedom, or work?" asked Jan.

"Yeah!" said a second girl. "Freedom! Freedom!" she started chanting and they all joined in.

"Freedom! Freedom!"

"'Bye," he walked out.

"Guys, numbers aren't that important," Borneo continued. "We need to take *action*."

"You mean leading by example?" asked Stanley.

"Exactly. I mean, we're all here because we don't follow society, right?"

"Personally, *I'm* fed up with being what society expects me to be," said Jan. "I hate it. There are so many standards and rules. Nobody can just be themselves."

"Yeah."

"Uhuh!"

"Society's lame."

"I think college has really opened my mind, though," Jan continued, and the other two girls nodded along to that statement while Matt said, "definitely".

"College is, like, the only place where I can escape it. When I go home, though, my parents – *ugh*! We're *so* different. I just wish I could find someone who's more like me," said Jan.

"Do you mean as in marriage?" Stanley inquired.

"Well, I don't believe we necessarily have to be *married*," said Jan. "Just as long as it's the right person."

"Yeah!" the girls agreed.

"Finding your soulmate's important," Matt nodded.

"*Really?*" went the second girl in surprise.

"Yo, guys care about finding the one just as much as girls do," said Matt.

Stanley gave a little chuckle. "Matt, I feel it's because modern society doesn't acknowledge men's more feminine selves," he said. "I personally am a very sensitive person who finds release through creative pursuits such as poetry."

"Do you share your poems with your wife?" the second girl asked him.

"Oh, I never married. To me marriage is another artificial contruct society tries to force on us, and I don't believe in forcing people into something they don't believe in."

Everyone nodded.

"You know, it struck me that once we eliminate society, millions of souls will be liberated," said Jan.

"Oh yeah, there'll be a huge release of energy on the planet," Borneo confirmed.

Two of Borneo's coworkers walked into the break room just then.

"...Reports aren't coming in until next week, Sanchez has us running around like dogs."

"Tell him not to be so concerned with it when the season is so high. Do you have that Faulker report I asked you about?"

"Yeah, I put it on your desk...."

They glanced momentarily down at the crowd on the floor and then left with their refilled coffee cups.

"It's part of our natural evolution toward higher being," Jan continued, "when we automatically come closer to Bob."

"Bob's the only one I'll listen to. Like, when people try to tell me to do something... they're so wrong," said Matt, shaking his head, while everyone laughed.

"Trust me, when you've been in the city as long as I have," said Stanley, still chuckling, "you just want people to stay the Pat away from you!" he chuckled again, holding up his arm to demonstrate how he kept his distance. "I mean, I'm friendly and open, but some people... are just assholes," he shook his head. "Can't stand 'em."

The others nodded slowly, staring at him for a long moment.

"Oh! Look at the time! It's already three," said Borneo, checking his watch and jumping up.

"Oh shoot! I have a class," said Jan, standing up in a hurry. The sudden realization of the hour was causing a commotion.

"Me too," said the second girl, shaking hands goodbye with Matt.

"Yeah, and I have to get home – and – " came from Stanley.

"Great meeting, everyone! Same time next week at Mystikals?" said Borneo as they departed.

"Yeah! See you!"

"Bye!"

***

Borneo hadn't written in his DeadDiary for three days. Things finally seemed to be getting back to normal.

"You could check your spirituality forum, maybe someone argued your point," John suggested to him that Friday as they sat in the break room, talking about how they'd had nothing to do all day.

"Oh yeah, later," said Borneo. "Can I tell you about this one girl I found, on the twelfth floor? Her name is Jill and she is *hot!*"

"Why don't you invite her to the bar with us today?" asked John.

"Ooh, good idea. Who else is coming?"

"Just Hec I think."

The weather outside was gorgeous and they had nothing to do but joke around with the delightful prospect of going to the bar in a few hours' short time.

"Want me to ask Jill if she can bring a cute friend?" Borneo winked.

"I don't care," said John.

"Come on, John, we need to get you – !"

"*WHAT IN PAT'S MIND IS WRONG WITH YOU!*" Mr. Daltuhn stormed in, angrier than either of them had ever seen him. "You had an interview on the news yesterday! Where were you!?"

"It wasn't my time," Borneo shrugged. "Look, Mr. Daltuhn, we might not have the same philosophy – "

"I don't care about your Bobdamn philosophy! I want you to drop this idiocy once and for all and go back to normal! Or go back to being depressed, that was working fine, too!"

"Mr. Daltuhn, I can't change my *soul*."

Mr. Daltuhn's face turned such a livid shade of red it looked like all of his small arteries had exploded beneath his skin. "Soul!? How can you have a soul, Bobdammit?! You're an ignorant, selfish, attention-seeking kid whose only redeeming quality is being popular!"

Borneo's face dropped.

"And I've had enough of your games! You're becoming more trouble than you're worth, and if you don't drop these antics right now, then you're – you're fired!"

Even though everyone got told once a week that they were fired (for prophylactic), it was nothing as hearing him say it to Borneo. Borneo himself could only sit and stare, dumbfounded, his ego shattered in pieces around him on the floor. He got up and left the break room hurriedly.

John followed him.

Borneo had stopped at his desk, his hands on it, his face panting.

"Listen, John, the real reason I didn't do that interview isn't because it wasn't the right time, it's because I just don't know if I can take all this extra publicity I'm going to receive when my system goes public," he was shaking.

"Borneo, you thrive on publicity."

"I *already* feel overwhelmed by responsibility, and when my new book comes out – ? My depression from five days ago still comes back to me and I think it might be better just to end it all – "

John rammed opened his drawer and thrust the gun he'd picked up days ago into Borneo's hands.

"Go ahead. Do it. Shoot yourself."

Borneo's jaw dropped. He stared from John to the gun in his hands, all trace of insanity and despair suddenly wiped from his face.

A few hours later a soft knock sounded on their office door and a girl walked in, smiling.

"Heyy!" said Jill. "Oh my Bob, what are you doing!" she exclaimed when she saw Borneo and Luke sitting on the ledge of the open window, each with a leg dangling out to the air, as they cracked jokes.

"Just hangin' out," said Borneo. Then he burst out laughing when he realized what he'd said.

"Aren't you scared?" she asked.

"Why should I be," Borneo shrugged with bravado.

"Well, *duh*, I was talking to Luke," Jill smiled.

"Actually, yeah, I am kind of scared," said Luke, looking down, and he got off the window and went back to his desk next to John.

"Come here, babe, I'll show you something cool," Borneo nodded and stood up on the ledge.

"Borneo, maybe you shouldn't," said Jill, approaching.

"Yeah, you've been doing that a little too often lately," said John.

"Don't worry, I'm – oh Bob!" Borneo gasped, slipping. Jill screamed. Borneo grinned, righting.

"You – !" Jill lunged at him, fists out in fury.

"Come on, give it your best," Borneo grinned down at her. His back was to the open air. He let go of the walls with both hands, then caught himself quickly as Jill screamed. Then he let go again. But endorphins must have dulled his reflexes, because this time he fell out of sight.

***

At the morgue, John waited silently in the lobby while Borneo's body was transported for its autopsy. He'd been silent since his arrival, numb to the reality of what had happened. Several of the morticians joined him now. John noticed that they were all quite young, in their twenties and thirties. And the one sitting next to him, who had sleek dark hair and looked like the youngest of them all, had pulled out a copy of *Mortician Monthly* and was now reading with interest.

"Is that the new issue?" John asked him. The dark-haired mortician looked up, a bit surprised to hear John's voice.

"Yeah, just came out this week. You read *Mortician Monthly*?"

"Yeah."

"I've never met anyone outside our circle who reads it," he said, amused.

"My old college roommate was studying to be a mortician and he got me into it," John explained. "Do you all read it?"

The blonde girl sitting with her back to them turned around and smiled.

"You're not a mortician if you don't read that," she said.

"This issue isn't as good as last month's, but there's some decent stuff," said the young guy.

"Last month's issue was what got me though Lainii," said John.

"When you two..." he trailed off as John nodded.

"I can't believe Borneo Grimgae's *dead*," he said after a pause. "Were you his close friend?"

"Yeah, we worked together; that's how I met him."

"When you say you worked together, do you mean you both worked for NKOZ, or like *together*?" he asked.

"We sat right next to each other," said John. The morticians' interest suddenly spiked.

"What do you do at NKOZ?" the girl asked interestedly.

"I guess you could say I'm assistant to our boss... though I haven't been doing much assisting with anything as of late," he reflected. "It's all been Borneo. To be honest, I have no idea what we're going to do without him now...."

Their mouths were open and they looked at each other, then back at John.

"How old are you?" the girl stared at John as if seeing him in a whole new light.

"Twenty-four," said John.

"He's even younger than we are," the girl to her coworker in astonishment. "*And* he was Borneo Grimgae's best friend."

"Really, it's not as impressive as it sounds," John tried to explain. "I didn't do anything important – "

"They should be bringing him up shortly," they were interrupted by a third mortician, a tall, muscular broad-nosed man with dark, closely shaved hair and an intimidating face that nonetheless betrayed a soft interior to his person.

"Edgar, Cassie, you can take him down in five minutes; Morina and I are still setting up," he said and then left.

John went downstairs ahead of Edgar and Cassie, who went to put on their masks and gloves. As he rounded the corner in the long hallway leading to the operating room, he involuntarily walked in on the other two morticians, having a moment in a secluded corner; they stood in a close embrace, the broad-nosed man John had just seen running his hands through the woman's long, dark hair that waved over her shoulders.

"I will love you forever, Morina, you are my sunshine," he said in low tones.

"Oh, Ankur, that was so beautiful; your words are like poetry... like song... like... *like music to my ears*!" she cried.

"That is so sweet, my love, just like you," he said.

"Oh, Ankur!" she swooned.

"I would die for you, Morina."

"Ankur, no! You're not supposed to say that line yet! Don't you know you only say that later on when we find ourselves in grave danger? But now, it is so unnecessary."

She took his hands off her shoulders and they walked together into the room.

"So he survived all of that stuff by sheer luck!?" Cassie exclaimed as she sterilized equipment.

John walked in and joined them to stand over the dead, sheathed body of their beloved late hero.

"What was his token, then? If he wasn't immortal, what was his gift?"

They removed the white sheet, looked down, and their eyes popped. One of the women giggled, while the other gave a whimper of regret. And then they knew.

Chapter 10: Death

Borneo's actual death shocked the country even more than his attempted one. Forums burst with discussions of the cosmic implications of an immortal's death. The only person who seemed totally unfazed was Bethesda, whom John caught prancing dreamily in the streets in a flowy skirt in her habitual bubble of delusions as he and his family journeyed across the city to the biggest Hall of Bob, where the funeral services were held.

Half the Vandorn populace had turned up for the biggest social event of the year: Borneo's family, friends, and thirty of his closest reporters and their camera crews were there to mourn his passing. John spotted Mr. Daltuhn near the front, keeping a queue of reporters at bay with deterrent glances.

The minister stepped onto the podium and the crowd quieted. Silence now filled the high-ceilinged room that echoed their breaths.

He began:

"What can we do, knowing that one day we will die? With the knowledge that all of our pursuits and desires will in the end amount to nothing, that even the progeny we leave behind will one day wither, how are we supposed to live? Where do we find value, if everything with a beginning comes to an end? And we must admit that everything in life has a beginning. We probably all ponder such questions in moments like these," he paused, looking around the Hall. "But I do not have the answers; I have only the questions."

"This is not the first time it has been asked, nor will it be the last; after all, people forget the sobering truths that hit them once the impact fades and their minds return to wondering what messages those two or three special people they have strings tied to sent them.

No, perhaps I am wrong. Perhaps you are *not* thinking about anything else because you are currently in such shock that temporarily nothing else can occupy your mind. Perhaps you are even feeling somewhat righteous because not only can you think of nothing else, but the things you thought before your reality received this blow now seem pointless and insignificant, and somewhere underneath your skin you are embarrassed that you even bothered yourself with such trifles, which any soberminded human being realizes are not worth a speck of care when we are faced with real and inevitable death.

Against our better judgment, we believed that immortality was possible, and now reality has hit us with our own naïveté. But I do not think there is anything strange in our believing the impossible. No, I say the strangeness lies in our own hypocrisy: the underlying secret belief in our *own* immortality each one of us harbors. Do not we feel total disconnect with our impending death as we argue, struggle, complain, waste time, seethe in negative thoughts and emotions every moment of the precious unknown time given to us? Do we not act as if we have a permanent tomorrow to fix our problems in? We do, until the moment when death stands at our side and reminds us of its silent suddenness. Then how quickly we remember that we are alive! And when we see our lives from death's impartial perspective, how clearly for a brief flicker do we see the *worthlessness* of all we do! But the next moment we push that down and divert the discomfort into emotion-ridden thoughts such as 'oh I am so sad he died!' which eventually progress to intellectual debates about life after death and other questions we think are 'deep.' You know you are avoiding the true issue, which is the worthlessness of all you do. Why do we so fear facing the unpleasant truth when all we risk losing to it are our illusions? Only by facing the reality may you strike upon the chance to change it. Otherwise you will go on carried with the wind and the tide from one random phase and place to the next, until your own 'tragic' death befalls you. And yet, why is death a tragedy? To me it is not the death that impends we should grieve, but the life we waste.

Who knows when they will die? Not I, for certain. We might laugh at all the people who plan for their future. The clever economist sits at his desk planning for his retirement, and his children approach his lone chair and beg him to play with them; but he ignores them; he doesn't have time for their childish games when he needs to preoccupy himself with the future; and anyway they are ignorant of reality; he tells himself he is planning for their sake; but if he is honest with himself (and we all know how often that is the case), he will find that the *real* reason he does not play with them is that his body does not wish to get up from its comfortable seat and make the effort to run around with his children. And – horror of horrors! – his neighbor would see him looking like a fool. The man must pay for his life with his effort, but he is broke. Tomorrow, this same man dies. His children will grow up without the happy memory of playing with their father one spring day, and where their hearts could have been filled with a moment of joy to anchor them throughout the hardships in their years to come, they will remain a little bit emptier. I do not preach for you to 'live for the moment' – it is in our nature to worry about the future. But a good future is achieved through a good present, not through a neglect of the present.

Returning to the original question, I do not know any more than you what we can do to give our lives meaning and make ourselves permanent – immortal. Perhaps there is nothing we can do. But then why do we not simply throw it away? Why is it our instinct to care what becomes of us? Must there not be some reason we are alive, even if it is for a brief flicker of time?

After you die, what will come of that emotion you felt yesterday? What will remain of all your hobbies, your strong and correct opinions, the trifles that made up your entire world? They will evaporate into thin air. Was it worth it to argue with that person, and feel your hungry monster satisfied when you crushed his ego beneath your own while pretending outwardly that you were 'righteous', suppressing the smile that yearned to creep over your face? Hate me not, for I speak of what is inside you; and if you feel hate than it is hate only towards yourself. But would your – our – time not be better spent on creating happiness rather than the drama that feeds our egos? Creating a warm atmosphere for all to live as they truly are without hiding themselves? Being generous rather than stingy when the food we don't share gets excreted by tomorrow but the bond we form from sharing it lasts a lifetime? Would that not be the something more permanent we are seeking? True, it would fade with us – but as I have said, I do not know what to do to make ourselves permanent. I know only how to make our temporary time worthwhile. Time worthwhile is spent not fighting with oneself, but living in accord with the principles that already exist in one. Perhaps all we are here to do is to leave this planet peacefully, and teach others how to do the same so that they may enjoy life and not dread death. After all, the beautiful flower fades, but was its presence not worthwhile? I do not know, my friends. I can only ask."

All in the Hall nodded in solemnity. One by one everyone got up, forming a long line that slowly advanced to the casket for one last look. John felt a tap on his shoulder and turned around to see Mr. Daltuhn, jerking his head to the side. John abandoned his spot and followed him outside the room into the hallway. They stopped in a corner.

"Hallan, there was something you wanted to tell me earlier, regarding the Token Law?" said Mr. Daltuhn. John looked around the Hall; this seemed an inappropriate time.

"I don't have all day, I have a lunch date at two," his boss said impatiently.

"You know how you said Nelson can't work for us if he doesn't fill out his token forms?" John began.

"Yes."

"I can't fill them out, either."

"Why not," Mr. Daltuhn demanded.

"Because I don't know what my token is."

Absurdity made a canvas of Mr. Daltuhn's face. "That's impossible! *Everyone* knows what their token is!" he exclaimed with a burst of laughter, not believing him.

"I don't."

"No, there must be some mistake," Mr. Daltuhn shook his head as if John was just not getting all the facts. "You're twenty-four! How can you *not know*?"

"Borneo didn't know his for a long time," John pointed out.

"Maybe you're the immortal one," Mr. Daltuhn grinned.

"It's okay I don't want to find out," John replied quickly.

"I've never heard of such a thing! Haven't you ever wondered!?" he looked at John queerly.

"Never," said John tonelessly.

"Well I don't know why it's taking such a long time to reveal itself to you. I had mine since I was two! Pretty obvious once I walked through the wall into my parents' room that night. Heh," he laughed, reminiscing, "*that* killed it. Could've had a little sister.... Oh well."

There was a pause as John waited.

"I guess I'll write 'unknown', then," he said when Mr. Daltuhn gave no response. "What's the worst that could happen?"

"Are you out of your mind!?" Mr. Daltuhn yelped. "Have you any idea how suspicious that will look? And especially now with all this bomb threat and LASS bullshit – "

"Oh, they've already forgotten!"

"If they see someone with an 'unknown' token they'll investigate at once! That's as rare as being immortal!"

"Fine, I'll make one up," said John.

"Are you kidding!? You think they'd issue the Token Law without being able to detect fruad? They'll find out if you lie! They have – machines!"

John raised his eyebrows.

"Look, I'll deal with it. Just keep it a secret. The only other people who know are my family," said John.

"I'm not crazy enough to go telling people. First, they'll think *I'm* crazy. But secondly, they'll – they'll take you away to some freak lab and run tests on you, and I don't want to lose you. You're a good asset."

John's eyes widened; he was touched. Mr. Daltuhn had never before acknowledged his appreciation for him.

"But if you don't find it, I might have to," he warned. "So get on it."

"Get on what?" John was confused.

"Finding your token!"

"But that's impossible!" John laughed. "You don't *find* it!"

"Well you had better be the first," said Mr. Daltuhn.

"This is as plausible as you telling Luke to have those reports done by yesterday," John remarked. "You should've just told Nelson to do it, he was sitting right there and not doing anything."

"Luke was pissing me off," Mr. Daltuhn grumbled as they walked back.

After the services, John and his family went out to lunch at one of Mrs. Hallan's favorite restaurants, since they were "already dressed up and might as well make use of the occasion."

"That's my girl. So practical," Mr. Hallan said, rubbing her arm affectionately.

"John, hurry up! We're crossing!" she called, still blushing and smiling.

John was admiring the Hall's architecture. It was an old stone building, one of the oldest in Vandorn, and atop the roof stood an iron Cross of Bob, the ancient, sacred symbol of their religion whose origins dated back millennia, represented from then to this day on Halls of Bob all over the world. The Great Wheel, standing vertically, was crossed by the horizontally laying Wheel of Consequence; where they met in the middle was said to be the seat of Bob:

It represented perfect balance, the state of delicate harmony that pervaded the universe. On either side of both ends of the Great wheel was a Lauk, guarding it in holy service of Bob. In the same way a Shugin held the Wheel of Consequence, serving the work of Pat and his purpose.

That was the original design. But perhaps the sculptors of early times thought that that would be much too painstaking to reproduce on all of the sacred Halls of Bob popping up across the world like mushrooms, so they simplified the symbol to what it was to this current day:

Chapter 11: The Search Party

Once, a wealthy noble family hosted a big party, to which they invited everyone in the village: all of their relatives, all of their friends, religious men, political men, businessmen, and even ordinary men off the streets were called to attend. It was an event of the most joyous celebration, and one that would not soon be forgotten by the villagers!

Since every adult was attending the party, no one was left to watch the children, and they had to bring them along. The host family thus singled out a large room in the far recesses of their house for the children to play in. They filled its every corner with amusements – games, snacks, toys, books, colored pencils, grotesque amusements, and play-dough: in short, everything a child could want – so that even the thought of leaving the room would not enter their heads while the adults took the night off from their daily responsibilities to relax, sing songs, trade anecdotes, and tell inappropriate jokes.

When the guests arrived, they dropped their children off at that room and then left to join the party. The children kept each other company, distracted by the toys. But late into the night, some of them had gotten bored with the trinkets and were curious about the noises of laughter and singing they heard from far away. They left the room and wandered through the house's dark corridors until they at last stumbled upon the party. It was going on in many rooms at once and the children waded confusedly through them, unnoticed by the adults. The sights filled them with wonder: here, a group of men playing music on strange instruments, there, sparkling bottles filled with liquids of azure blues, forest greens, and deep ambers, and everywhere lights that swathed the walls in dim gold. Then in one room the children saw something most strange: an old man sitting in a corner on the floor. Unlike the other adults, who drank from only one cup at a time, this man had three cups around him, each filled with a different liquid. Fascinated, the children approached this oddity.

A boy pointed to the cup containing red liquid, and, thinking it was blood, asked what it was.

"That is my wine," said the old man.

A girl pointed to the second cup, containing yellow liquid, and, thinking it was pee, inquired as to what that was.

"That is my tea," said the old man.

Another boy pointed to the third cup, containing clear liquid, and, thinking it was poison, asked the old man what was in there.

"That is my water," said the old man.

Of course, any sensible adult would have known at once what was inside each of those cups. But the children were disappointed to find out that the contents of this old man's perplexing cups were so ordinary, for they expected strange contents for a correspondingly strange man.

Then one of the boys pointed to a dark and heavy-looking closed container with a spout on one end that sat between the old man and his many cups.

"What about that?" he asked the old man curiously.

The old man's eyes came alight. "Ahh! This is a very special object!" he said. The children begged the old man to tell them the secret of this seemingly ordinary teapot.

"Alright, alright," he said at last. "Come close to me."

The children gathered around the old man, and he whispered to them: "If you promise to be good, I will show you some real magic."

The children promised, staring up at the man with wide and attentive eyes. The old man picked up the metal teapot and asked, "Do you know what is inside here?"

The children shook their heads in unison.

"Inside here is anything I want. This teapot is a magic teapot! It gives me whatever I desire. Watch," and he proceeded to demonstrate its rare power by taking his now empty tea cup and tipping the pot's spout over it; it instantly yielded more of the yellow liquid that had filled the cup before.

"You see? I wanted more tea, and it gave me more tea."

The children were astonished.

"Can you make it pour out candy?" asked a little girl excitedly. The old man shook his head, "No."

"Why not?" she was disappointed.

"Because I do not want candy. I want tea, and since my teapot gives me what I want, it will give me tea. If you had your own magic teapot, it would give you whatever you wanted it to give you," he said.

The children sat quietly around the old man, watching him drink from his cups calmly. After a while, the third cup, the cup filled with water, became empty.

"Make your magic teapot pour out water," said one little boy.

"I cannot do that. This object looks like a teapot, so I only want it to pour out tea. Otherwise I couldn't call it a teapot. If a teapot poured out water, it would confuse everyone, and we wouldn't be able to give it a name. And an object without a name has no place in our world.... But this is a very good teapot, come to that, so I want it to pour out very good tea." He refilled his tea cup with tea from the pot and let the children try it; they all agreed that it was indeed very good tea.

But one pessimistic little boy said, "I think you're lying. Your teapot isn't magic; it's just an ordinary teapot!"

The old man was affronted. "Not magic!?" he cried. "Of course it is magic! It does exactly as I wish! Your brothers and sisters, parents, and schoolteachers almost *never* do as you wish. Where else have you seen such magic as this, which has granted me my desires without fail?" he argued.

"Can we see what's inside your magic teapot?" asked one girl.

"No, if you look inside a magic teapot you will see nothing; it is too dark."

"How much tea is in your magic teapot?" asked another boy.

"*How much* does not matter. What matters is where it comes from," replied the old man.

"Where does it come from?" the boy asked.

"It seems to come out of nowhere," said the old man, looking inside the dark teapot. "My teapot makes something out of nothing, and *that* is *true* magic!"

But the pessimistic boy remained unconvinced; he said to the old man, "My mother has a teapot just like that. What makes yours so special?"

"What makes my teapot so special is that it is made with a secret ingredient, the stuff of magic; your mother's is not."

"And what is magic made of?" the boy asked curiously.

The old man said, "To show you I would have to take apart my teapot, and I will not do this. For you see, once you take a magic object apart, you cannot put it back together again. The magic is lost forever."

Disappointed by this news, the children hung their heads.

"But if you bring me another magic object, a *real* one, I will take it apart and show you what true magic is made of," the old man said.

"There are other magic teapots?" a girl asked.

"Oh yes! There is a special land, far, far away, just filled with magic teapots. There are enough for each of you to have ten magic teapots plus ten magic teapots to give ten of your friends! And not just magic teapots: magic cups, magic spoons, magic dresses! Magic anything you want!"

The children all looked at each other in astonishment.

"I got my magic teapot from that land. But only those who really want to go there can find it. If you only *think* you want to find the land of magic teapots, you'll never find it. Before you want it, you have to want to want it."

"Did you want to find the land of magic?" asked a boy.

"Of course, otherwise I could never have found it. But it took me very long, and I got lost many times. It is such a secret place, I almost missed it. You never know when or where you will find it, because it always moves around. It is like the wind: here out of nowhere one moment, a doorway leading to riches unimaginable, and gone the next, leaving the world barren.

Sometimes, a little magic teapot or magic rock or magic flower or even an entire magic building escapes from that land and comes into our world, but it hides away. We have to look for the pieces of magic here, and they will tell us how to get to the land they came from. But beware! Many objects pretend to be magic, but they're only lying and trying to trick you. Don't listen to what they say! Only listen to *real* magic objects."

"How can we tell real magic objects from fake ones?" asked a boy with grave concern.

"Oh, it's easy. You'll know real magic when you find it. What's tricky is telling the difference between *thinking* something is magic and *knowing* something is magic; a lot of the time what seems like magic is just a good trick.

It will be a very long time before you stumble upon true magic, but you must always keep looking. There is only a very small chance that you will ever find it, but if you give up then there is *no* chance. I will give you one clue, and you can remember it for the rest of your lives: if you find true magic, then you will *already* know what magic is made of."

With that, the old man finished his story. The children were convinced that they had seen true magic as they never had before and couldn't contain their wonderment. They ran off to tell their parents and friends about the mystical old man who had a magic teapot that gave him anything he wanted, and that he had obtained it from this mysterious place which had now become the destination of their lifelong travels.

Of course, the parents didn't believe them, but several of the other kids in the children's room did. Together, those children banded as one and set out to find the land of magic teapots, or at least a relic from that land that might've chanced to escape and take refuge in a remote corner of their world. It was difficult because the man hadn't described at all how to tell a magic object apart from an ordinary one; so they didn't know what they were looking for. Nor did the man tell them where or how to search; so they looked everywhere and in every way.

Meanwhile, the other kids stayed in the room and played video games.

They searched the house high and low, in every doorway, every nook, even in the darkest of places, which, though frightening to explore, were the best hiding spots. Everything they met was potentially magic, for it *might* be hiding magic inside it – one could never know until one searched. They could almost see the magic behind every corner. And when they didn't find it there, they looked farther, seeing it out of sight. There were many times when the children wanted to quit, but they remembered what the old man had said about looking for a long time.

Alas, their search ended unsuccessfully that night, but by its end, this small group of children had searched the house so thoroughly that they had come to know it better than its owners did.

After the party, many of those children either forgot about the search party or got tired of it and went back to playing games. But a few could not forget the old man's story, so deeply did it settle inside their hearts and minds. They constantly imagined the magic land, and the more they dreamed about it, the more they yearned to find and see it for themselves. This shared ambition bound these few children together and they became devoted to that one aim; they set out to search the world for the land of magic teapots, starting with their own town. When they found no magic there, they went away in hopes of finding it somewhere else. If they didn't find magic in a place, they left and continued onward, toward the horizon. They went from town to town, repeating this cycle many times – but no matter where they went, they never stumbled upon what they so ardently sought.

As they got older, they kept their mission a secret from others, for most adults scorned at the notion of a magic land. "Live in reality!" they exclaimed, shaking their heads at these insane individuals who spent their lives throwing their efforts into a void. But the search party went on its way.

They stuck together in spite of obstacles, meeting many tricky objects who claimed to be magic, just like the old man said they would. Some of these objects were so convincing that they captured one or even some of the search party. But someone would always be just clever or intuitive enough to see through the ruse, and he or she would save the fellows. But occasionally, a falsely magical object so tempted one that it pulled him along with it far enough away from the group that he left it forever; it was a sad day when the band lost one of its own, for it was almost impossible to find the search party again once one parted: it always moved. However, there were many individuals they met who had also heard of the old man's story and were on the same quest. The search party learned to recognize one of its own, outward strangers but inward kin, who then joined them and made the party stronger. They visited every village, absorbed every culture. They came to know the places they visited better than their inhabitants, for rarely did the villagers seek for anything in their own homes. They learned many things and accumulated vast worldly knowledge. People were in awe of all they knew. But the search party did not care for what they knew; they cared for what they did not know. They continued to seek in spite of the hopelessness of ever finding what they sought. And after many years, they had not found even a magic pebble.

Never did they meet another who had been to their destination, and after many, many years, still the only person they knew of who had been to the magic land had been the old man from their youth.

As for that old man, he waited with his magic teapot, which continued to unfailingly supply him with the tea he so desired, until one of the little boys or girls who'd grown up and gone off to search for magic would finally return and say that he or she had at last found where the true magic lay.

Chapter 12: Actors, Ultd.

A heaviness had fallen over the floor, as stagnant as the humid summer air.

"Is there any point in coming?" Luke asked as he walked into the break room, where John was reading *Mortician Monthly*.

"He's going to fire us any day, it's not like there's anything to do," he grabbed his third Diet Crack out of the fridge. "That is, if we ever see him again."

The last any of them had seen of Mr. Daltuhn had been at the funeral, over a week ago. He stayed locked up in his office all day, brooding, John guessed, over the collapse of his entire empire.

Life on the thirtieth floor continued as usual, albeit with a subdued air. As for John, Luke, and Nelson, there wasn't much for them to do. John himself had been alternating between reading and watching T.V. all week.

"...We will return to *A Modern History of Terrorism* after these messages," said the T.V., turned to C-Span 14, as it ended the clip of people running chaotically around outside to the sound of bombs going off.

"...In the meantime, help fight against terrorism. Buy our patented

bumper sticker. For the low, low price of $19.99 you can support your country!"

"Hallan, come to my office," came Mr. Daltuhn's voice. John spun around and gazed upon the ethereal apparition that was his boss. Mr. Daltuhn had the closest to puppy-dog eyes John had ever seen on him. What this meant was the absence of anger from his face. So in essence he looked normal.

"I fear this is it for us," he began when they were inside. "Without Borneo we'll be forgotten in a year or bought out by some bigger network."

Pity welled up in John's chest toward him, but a little thorn in his mind restrained it, saying, *wait*....

"Mr. Daltuhn... I can't help but feel we should mourn Borneo before we mourn our financial losses," he voiced.

"We mourned him last Sunday," Mr. Daltuhn replied.

"People die all the time," he said to the look John was now giving him. "Trust me, when you get to be my age.... One death is one death, but the blow to our company affects thousands."

John had to admit that Mr. Daltuhn made an undeniable point.

"Now, I'm going to need your help in getting us out of this slump," he turned businesslike. "First thing's first: we need to create a scholarship in Borneo's honor."

"The Borneo Grimgae Memorial Scholarship for Young Heroes," said John.

"Good. We'll pick a kid once a year, say he embodies the values Borneo stood for, and give him a thousand bucks. I like it."

"We can announce it through his YourSpot page. The whole country will know by tomorrow."

"Good, good. I don't know what YourSpot is but good," Mr. Daltuhn approved. "Now, to find the network another face. There must be someone else as appealing out there. Think, what small-town firemen with hearts of gold can we exploit?"

"Mr. Daltuhn, maybe another hero isn't what's best," said John. "We're moving on. We need to get someone from a different angle, break away from the past."

"Well what other angle is there?"

"Talent! It's all the rage. Take musicians for example. Hardly anyone gets recognized for accomplishments in sports or art these days; the easiest way to become popular is by writing music."

Mr. Daltuhn was intrigued.

"In a year we'll be done publicly mourning Borneo, and we can safely have a brand new star without looking like assholes who just sought to replace the old guy," explained John.

"A year!?" Mr. Daltuhn yelped.

"Well we can't bring him in tomorrow."

"Why not? People have memories like goldfish."

But John shook his head. "It's too unnatural. It'll be blatantly obvious that the whole thing is a money-driven ploy and people will be repulsed by that. But if we make a smooth transition from one to the other, people will think it happened on its own. And even though they'll still know underneath that it's all fake and money-driven, the fact that it seemed like a natural process won't generate a strong enough shock to keep them from being swept up by the thrills. Time hides intentions," said John.

"Then how do we install a replacement without looking like we're replacing Borneo?"

"How about a songwriting competition in Borneo's honor," John suggested. "The one who writes the best song in his remembrance will win! The song will be a hit, and while we're looking like good people for honoring Borneo, the artist's name will become known. People will think that he's genuine and does it for the love of the music and his late hero. They'll be inclined to like him. And in a few short months when we've filled our quota of 'remembrance', he can easily stand on his own as the next big thing due to the good standing he's already built up!"

"People will think *they* made it happen! It's brilliant, Hallan!" exclaimed Mr. Daltuhn. "We'll need to work out the practical details, hire songwriters, a record company – the Actors, Ultd. Agency has just branched into the music industry – but first we need to find our man. Or woman. Hallan, after you look up Actors, Ultd., I want you to make a list of every struggling musician in Vandorn between the ages of sixteen and twenty-five. I realize this is a long job so I'm giving you until tomorrow. Now get to it!"

***

By the following Monday, the notice calling for the "finest musicians of our day" had been sent out – and oh how the public had responded.

"I'm relying on you, Hallan!" Mr. Daltuhn told John before they began the first round of interviews. "I need you to look through these losers like they were made of glass! Got it?"

"Yes, sir."

Mr. Daltuhn walked down to the lobby where dozens of hopefuls were waiting. The crowd was comprised mostly of young men in their twenties, sporting graphic t-shirts and shaggy hair, and many with guitars.

"You lot all look similar. What are you into, rock?" he asked, greeting them.

"Nah, man, I follow my own beat," ten of them said in unison.

"Well, I'm Edmund Daltuhn, and it's me you'll be talking to today. So, shall we get started? First up we have 'Blayke Griffin'. Is there a *Blayke Griffin*' here?" he asked, reading off a sheet of paper.

Two of the musicians stood up at the same time, glancing at each other with mild surprise.

"That's Blayke spelled 'B-l-a-y-k-e', so whichever of you takes the alternate spelling, you're up first," Mr. Daltuhn said.

Both guys made a simultaneous movement forward.

"Oh, uh, we both spell our names alternatively," said one of the Blayke Griffins to Mr. Daltuhn.

"I see.... It says here that this Blayke Griffin dropped out of high school to pursue his dreams of becoming a rock star," Mr. Daltuhn read further.

"Yeah, man."

"Right here, yo."

Mr. Daltuhn was getting aggravated. Next time he would send John to deal with these hoodlums!

"This Blayke Griffin is eighteen years old!"

"Oh, that's you, man," said one to the other, taking a step back.

"Follow me, son," Mr. Daltuhn led Blayke Griffin away.

***

Interview number 3:

D: "So why do you want to be a musician?"

3: "You know, man, I just wanna make it big. It's my dream. I got nothing else, and all my life I been a failure. My mom's always nagging me, 'Get a job, Jimmy! Stop wasting your time on these silly dreams! There's a real world out there!' But she just doesn't understand; nine-to-five, holed up in some cubicle doing meaningless shit – that's just not me. I can't explain it, I'm just – I'm *different*."

Interview number 12:

12: "Music is my *life*. There's some *amazing* stuff out right now that not that many people know about because it doesn't conform to the media's standards, and that's what I'm really into. You know, man, the underground stuff. Not all that pop crap, *derisive snort*."

D: "So if you became a big hit and your producers tried to commercialize your style, you wouldn't alter yourself to satisfy the tastes of a bigger crowd?"

12: "Oh, no way. I mean, I'm all about synthesis and collaboration, but I gotta do me."

Interview number 27:

D: "How serious are you about making music your career?"

27: "Like I said, music is my one true passion. I can't say my parents are happy about it, they want me to get a job and settle down. They just don't like the instability, but that's really what living is all about. *Chuckle* the number of times I've heard, 'why can't you just be like everyone else?' is ridiculous *head shake*."

D: "So it's not just about fame for you?"

27: "No way!... It's about girls."

D: "Mhmm. What do think makes you truly memorable?"

27: "You know, I've never really considered that, but I don't think it's a problem 'cause trust me, I'm like no one you've met before."

***

And they were back to square one.

"Wasted efforts!" he yelled at John.

John said nothing. It had been unpleasant to burst Mr. Daltuhn's bubble, but he wasn't about to plunge them into a worthless pursuit.

"Maybe we're wasting our time seeking a replacement when we should be looking at programming instead," said John.

"Absolutely not," his boss rejected the idea adamantly.

"Fine then, let me do it," John said impatiently.

"*You?*" Mr. Daltuhn's head fell forward and he roared with laughter. "Oh, you've lifted my spirits. You're the *last* person I'd pick for any work related to the public! Well, no, I'd pick you before Nelson, but you're close to last. Hallan, you're many things, but charismatic and appealing isn't one of them."

"That's two things."

"See?"

There was a knock on the door.

"Come in!" Mr. Daltuhn called.

A girl John didn't know walked into the office, carrying a cup of tea on a platter. She set it down on Mr. Daltuhn's desk and kissed him on the cheek.

"Thanks, sweetie," said Mr. Daltuhn as she walked out, nodding at John in greeting.

"New secretary?" John asked when she was gone.

"My daughter. She just graduated. Gave her a job, called it 'research'," Mr. Daltuhn explained.

"Oh," said John. "So... are we done?"

"Yeah. Now get out!"

***

The teacher was paying the students no attention from where he sat at his desk reading a newspaper, glasses up. Today was devoted to module 11.4, and tomorrow they would advance to module 11.5.

Even though computer science was Milly's least favorite class, she managed to crunch through the day's assignment in five minutes.

She sat in her seat, fanning herself as little beads of sweat formed on her forehead. They still had half an hour. In the row in front of her four guys had congregated around one computer and were being unabashedly loud.

166

"Dude, this class is so pointless," said one of them, leaning forward to better see the screen they were looking at, his Hollister t-shirt stretched across his back.

"I know, this is such a fucking waste of my time," said another one so loudly he practically yelled, tendrils of his messy blonde hair poking out from beneath his sideways cap.

"Eric, take your hat off!" yelled Mr. Badgely, distracted by the volume of Eric's voice.

"No."

"What do you mean 'no'? You – you better, or I'm going to send you to the office!"

"'Kay."

"Alright. That was my last warning!" said Mr.Badgely.

"Dude, *what* are you doing! There's one right there," yelled Eric to the guy sitting in front of the screen, playing a game that revolved around shooting kittens.

"Yo, stop messing me up!" he said, concentrating on the game and throwing his shaggy hair out of his eyes.

"Get it, Justin!"

A little cartoon calico ran across the screen. Justin fired by pressing the enter key, thereby causing a cartoon grenade to be thrown at it. The kitten exploded with a digital "mreeooow!!"

"Hahahahahahaa!!!!" The four guys laughed, staring at the monitor.

"That was sick, dude."

"Yeah, do it again."

Amy turned around, "You guys are *so* immature," she said, rolling her eyes in annoyance. Then she turned back around to Brenda.

"Anyway, I'm, like, *so* excited for the sixth book to come out! I *know* that Caroline and Hilton are gonna hook up."

"Yeah!! They make, like, the cutest couple *everr*!" said Brenda.

"Ohmybob, I heard the one after this is gonna be *the last Chitchat Chick* novel!" Amy exclaimed.

"Are you serious?? But Melania, Rei, and Haydn are still in their love triangle!..."

Milly hated computer science, and the heat of the day was not improving her mood. Her body couldn't take it anymore; the consequences she faced paled in comparison to this torture!

Glancing around to make sure no one was paying attention, she quickly took off her long-sleeved henley and stuffed it into her backpack. Instant relief flooded her body. But – Milly glanced down nervously – all she had on underneath was a plain yellow tank top of no brand name! Her mom had gotten it at the department store. She'd bought her one in every color; she said color looked good on Milly's pallid complexion.

She glanced around again nervously to ascertain that still no one was watching her.

Milly simply didn't have enough Hollister shirts to wear one every day! She had three, which she rotated as craftily as she could. But half the time she needed them they were in the wash! It was lucky for her that henleys were allowed, or she'd have been kicked out by now for sure, because her mom point blank refused to get her any more clothes from Hollister. "Is this supposed to be a public school or what?" she had complained when Milly brought home a notice from school for refusal to follow uniform regulations after wearing a plain blue t-shirt. That episode had sufficiently terrified Milly: she was paranoid of slipping in her education! After all, she had to go to college and graduate school and land a job making millions of dollars, and what college would take a delinquent who was kicked out of high school!? From that day forward, Milly put all her brainpower into being more careful. Week after week she'd been dodging the unyielding glare of the P.R.E.P. by her artful tactics, which had to compensate for her lack of Hollister shirts. She had been able to get away with not wearing them all the time by walking around in her jacket and saying she was cold, or taking full advantage of the sweatshirts and henleys allowed to be worn on occasion. She had become so skilled at it that she could go three straight days wearing a different colored henley as long as she wore a Hollister shirt on the fourth. That got them off her back. Occasionally she would wear her best Hollister t-shirt on Monday, wear a sweatshirt Tuesday, and wear henleys the rest of the week. At that point, she had roused the Peamount Role-Enforcement Party to their feet and they hounded her, ready to pounce at any moment. But they pulled back from the ledge when she showed up in Hollister t-shirts two days straight the next week, wore a henley the next, and, as a reinforcement and "false-alarm" signal, wore her other Hollister t-shirt the fourth day like a good girl. Then they smiled at her and left her alone.

But she was walking a very thin ledge! And *now*, with the unbearable heat, her wardrobe options had been virtually halved!

Today was the first day that she was blatantly breaking the dress code. The only thing that saved her was the approaching end of the school year, a time during which, she hoped, the institution might be too lazy to care. Milly had learned this year to abandon all hope of people acting "out of the kindness of their hearts." Her peers had taught her. The greatest danger she faced right now was her enemies becoming bored.

Amy Bagshow, she knew, was a member of the P.R.E.P. And in sixth period computer science she was the leader, for she had the privilege of being friends with the circle that was friends with the circle that was friends with Dee Allderbay. It was she whom Milly was worried about. Milly tried to remain invisible in her seat as if there was nothing conspicuous about her, resisting the temptation to glance at Amy and her friend Brenda with all her might though in her nervousness she itched to see if they were looking at her.

"Justin, is that all you do all day?" came Amy's voice.

"No, he jerks off, too," said Eric, making Amy laugh.

"Shut up, dude!" said Justin as he pressed another key.

"Aww, Justin, is it 'cause you're not getting any," said Amy.

"Ooooh," went the guys, as Brenda and a couple other girls giggled.

"Downtown hookers don't get much in the eyes to a ho like you, Amy," retorted Justin.

The girls' mouths dropped.

"Oh my Bob!"

"You are *so* disrespectful to women!"

"*Apologize*, Justin!"

"Whatever," Amy said coolly, tossing back her blonde hair, "I don't want fake, insincere apologies from a jerk like him."

"You're so strong, Amy!" went Stacy and Kaylie in awe, causing Amy to smile modestly.

Brenda moved in to sit on the lap of her boyfriend, Carter, one of the four boys and in a blue Hollister tee that stretched over his pecs tighter than his girlfriend's t-shirt hugged *her* body; she ran her fingers through his shaggy brown hair.

"Sweetie, you need a haircut," she said. "I'm gonna take you to my hairdresser this weekend, 'kay?"

"Sure," muttered Carter.

"Dude! Are you gonna let your woman control you like that?" shouted Eric.

Carter blushed. Brenda's mouth dropped open.

"I'm not controlling him!" she said shrilly.

"Yeah right," said Eric; Justin and the other guy, named Brett, kept their faces straight to not so much as flinch at Brenda and Eric, staying purposely on the screen.

"Dude. Dude! Right there," Brett muttered, and Justin fired.

"Carter, can you please tell him that I don't control you?" Brenda demanded.

"Brenda doesn't control me, Eric," said Carter.

"Carter!" Brenda cried.

"What?" said Carter, shocked.

"That's not how you're supposed to do it!"

"Well, then what am I supposed to say?"

Brenda just looked at him in shock for a prolonged period of time, the way a female lead character would look at her jerk boyfriend in a teen drama the moment when she realized the *truth*, with the camera straight on her face and that hot new raunchy offbeat guy having just made his debut in the last scene. "You just don't *get* it," she half-whispered disbelievingly.

And then she turned away.

Carter turned to his friends with an expression of utmost confusion, but they were all staring determinedly at the monitor.

"Whatever, Carter," Amy stepped in. "Obviously you don't really care if you didn't even get mad at your friends for insulting Brenda."

"I care! I *am* mad. Yo, Eric, don't say that shit," he said.

Amy rolled her eyes. "Oh please, that was *so* fake! If you really cared, you would've said something like 'don't you *dare* talk about my girlfriend that way, you asshole! You're a douchebag who's just jealous of what he doesn't have! Brenda's the sweetest girl in the world!'"

Brenda gasped, "Just like the way Nick got *sooo* pissed off at Logan when he made fun of Tabitha on *Seven Stranger Danger*. He is *so* sweet!" she exclaimed wistfully.

"Oh my Bob he's like the best boyfriend ever," said Amy.

They sat there discussing last week's episode of *Seven Stranger Danger* for a while, allowing the boys ample time to play their computer game.

"...Yeah, I found the *hottest* photo of him! It's on my phone, I have to show you," Brenda giggled. "Carter, can you get my bag from across the room?" she asked.

"I'm kind of busy," Carter brushed her aside as he aimed at a tabby. Brenda huffed.

"Fine. *I'll* go get my bag," (what a ridiculous notion) she said, getting up and walking to her seat. But she didn't return; instead, she plopped herself down in the chair and faced away from them all, especially Carter.

"Carter, why are you being such a bad boyfriend?" Amy asked.

"How am I being a bad boyfriend!" he exclaimed half an octave higher-pitched.

"Um, you just made Brenda cry."

How Carter wished Amy would go away; Amy was extremely annoying, along with all of Brenda's other friends. Bob, he hated girlfriends' friends. Next time he was going to find a loner chick who *had* no friends. But then she'd always want to be around him, and he would see her everywhere he went. *Dammit!* Was there no escape!?

"Can you please go talk to her. I'm asking nicely," said Amy, crossing her arms.

Carter half-sighed half-growled and reluctantly got up. The other three guys exchanged glances.

"Hey sweetie, what's wrong?" Carter asked gently, putting his arm around Brenda.

"I don't want to talk to you right now," said Brenda to the wall.

Carter resigned himself to a long conversation....

"...I don't care more about my friends than about you!" the guys heard Carter exclaim a minute later.

"Oh my Bob, can you just go away!?"

"Whatever," said Carter, and he got up and left.

Amy, Kaylie, and Stacy quickly left the boys to congregate around Brenda, where the four of them started talking rapidly in very low voices about some mysterious topic.

Milly began to get nervous; she no longer had a row of boys to shield her and only an isle of empty space separated her from Amy and her posse. Her cheap tank top as bright as the sun was just a glance away, and to make matters worse, Amy was facing her.

A sudden outburst of giggles made Milly glance over before she could stop herself; she caught the girls in the process of turning away from something right across Amy to look at four other, separate things. Brenda examined her nails, Stacy looked at the wall, Kaylie looked at the floor, and Amy looked at some other people.

Milly went back to doodling on her math homework, blushing slightly. Meanwhile, the girls kept up an intensive stream of whispers, periodically glancing around at random things – the wall, the teacher, Milly, the door, Milly, the ceiling.

Don't pay attention. It's probably all in your head, she told herself.

Before she knew it, a large shadow loomed over her.

"Hey, Milly!" Amy said brightly.

"Hello," she replied, looking up at the four girls crowded around her. Stacy and Brenda sat on the table with their backs to the boys in the row in front, thus placing themselves right near them without making it seem like that was their intention.

"Whatcha doin'?"

"Doodling," said Kaylie from over Amy's shoulder.

"Milly, I wanted to know something," Amy said. The others put their hands to their mouths in shock as if they couldn't believe she was actually doing whatever it was she was about to do, going softly, *"Oh my Bob!"*

"Um... what?"

"Did you get your shirt at Hollister?"

"Um, I don't think so," said Milly in a small voice.

"Yeah, that's what I thought. But you know it's supposed to be from Hollister, right?" said Amy.

Milly looked from girl to girl.

"Well, Hollister shirts are really expensive. I don't have enough money to wear one every day."

"That's no excuse!" Stacy chimed in. "Hollister always has sales going on. You could totally get some cute shirts for cheap. I got this one for twenty-five bucks," she said, pointing to her plain purple tee with "HCO" written in the corner.

"Are you girls talking about clothes again?" Brett turned around from the computer to face Amy and the girls.

"So what if we are?" demanded Stacy, making a cute little face at him.

"That's all you girls ever talk about," he rolled his eyes.

"You're so judgmental, Brett!" went Amy. "I swear, guys are such assholes – right Milly?"

All eyes on the latter.

"Um... I don't know... I don't really know every guy so I can't judge...."

"Thanks, Milly," Brett grinned at her. "She's the only cool one out of all you girls," he said to Amy and the others. "You're cool, right Milly?"

"Uh... sure," Milly shrugged, looking quickly between Brett and Amy, very uncomfortable in the crossfire. She glanced at Mr. Badgely, who wasn't paying them attention. A desperate wish that he would suddenly turn around and demand that she move to a seat on the other side of the room raced across her mind. Of course it didn't happen.

"Aww, you made her blush," Amy cooed, smiling widely with an accompaniment of the iciest eyes.

"I'm not blushing!" said Milly, blushing harder.

"Yeah you really are," nodded Stacy.

"It's probably because he smiled at her," said Kaylie.

The three other guys had turned around to face their conversation now.

"Oh, look, they're done their stupid game," said Brenda (*oh thank Bob, relief, change of topic*, thought Milly's heart), glancing at Carter, folding her arms, and then looking away. Carter got up out of his seat and went around the row, coming up behind Brenda and putting his arms around her to show he cared. Amy clapped her hands.

"Yay! Carter finally decided to be a good boyfriend!" she said, while Stacy and Kaylie giggled along.

"Carter, man, you're whipped," said Eric.

"Shut up, dude," Carter mumbled, turning as red as Milly. "You're just bitter 'cause no one will put out for you."

"I'm *bitter*?" Eric exclaimed, laughing. "That's a low blow, dude."

"Like the kind you're not getting."

"Alright – " Eric stood up as Amy's eyes darted hungrily between them.

"Guys, why are you fighting 'cause of some dumb bitch?" asked Brett. "Don't you see what's going on here? She's just doing it for kicks."

Eric and Carter both backed down.

"Sorry, man," said Carter, blushing again.

"It's cool," said Eric. And before the girls knew it all the boys had turned back to the computer.

"Thanks for sticking up for me, Brenda," said Amy, who was tearful.

"Amy! I – !" Brenda began apologetically.

"No! I don't want to hear it! I'm tired of your excuses! You *never* stick up for me!"

"That's not true!" Brenda cried.

"Yes it is! All you care about is Carter!"

"No!"

Carter turned around and raised his eyebrows.

"I mean – I care about both of you the same!" Brenda cried in anguish.

Amy's face contorted in fury. "*You care more about your boyfriend of three months than your best friend of five years!?*" she screamed. "Thanks, that's what I get for always being there for you!"

Brenda looked like she was about to cry; she turned to Carter and the rest of the boys, but they were employing this ingenious strategy of being both part yet not part of the conversation.

"Amy, I think Brenda was about to stick up for you, but she didn't have enough time before you started – "

"Before I started *what*?" Amy rounded on Milly now.

"Before you, um, told her that she didn't stick up for you."

"Stop defending her, Milly, it's not like you stuck up for me, either."

"Yeah, Milly, how can you bring up Brenda not sticking up for Amy when you didn't even stick up for her?" Carter came to Brenda's defense.

"Well I'm not her – !"

"What? Friend?" Amy leered. "I see how it is. I was *going* to be nice and not report you for breaking the dress code, but since we're not *friends*...."

Terror flooded Milly; it must have shown above her head in an imagined scene of herself being scolded in the principal's office while wearing that yellow tank top. All eight of them laughed at the unfolding movie.

"Oh my Bob, I'm just *kidding*, Milly! I'm not really going to report you!" Amy said as her scowl switched to a smile like a streetlamp while Milly turned deep, deep red.

"She was *so* scared!" said Brenda to Amy about Milly, who was sitting right there.

"Aww, I'm sorry, sweetie," Amy now put her arm around Milly. "It's okay if you don't like Hollister, it's good that you have your own style," she nodded. The girls giggled.

"I'm serious, why are you guys laughing?" said Amy.

"Just stop, Amy," said Justin, shaking his head.

"What!? I'm being nice!"

The bell rang at last, freeing Milly from her bondage. She had learned a new lesson today, about helping people. But they had gotten right to her self-esteem. And it – it was low.

***

"Think, people, *think*! We need something new, something fresh!" Mr. Daltuhn paced back and forth in their office.

"I've got it!" came an exclamation. It was Luke. Luke was offering an idea, perhaps for the first time ever.

"What if we make movies? Or, like, hire a team to make them and say they're 'our' movies? We can have a story about... penguins! Chocolate-loving penguins. Only, let's make them surf! Oh! And let's make it like a hip reality T.V. show type thing, where the penguins speak in dialogue that sounds like people from *Seven Stranger Danger*! And the entire soundtrack will be indie songs!"

Silence and blank stares.

"...That's the fucking most retarded idea I've ever heard! Who in this whole Bobdamn universe would spew out such inane fecal waste from their mind?! You're fired!" Mr. Daltuhn shouted over the table. Luke sat back down, dejected.

"Hallan!" Mr. Daltuhn barked, "may I ask why you're reading *Teengirl* magazine?"

"I finished *Cosmetology*."

Mr. Daltuhn grabbed the magazine out of John's hands.

"No work to do?" he leaned his face into his.

"Well, yes," he admitted.

"Never fear," said Mr. Daltuhn, and he went and got the usual: a large cabinet of files. "And while you're at it, you can fill in for Nancy-Beth, she's out for the day," he set him up at the secretary's desk in front of his office.

"No interruptions! I'm in the middle of a meeting!"

Who could he have a meeting with now, John wondered.

John heard two male voices coming from the other side of the door, but he could not make out a word they said. After twenty minutes of lonesomeness he looked up at the sight of Mr. Daltuhn's daughter, whom he hadn't seen since she'd walked in on their meeting almost a week ago, walking with Luke.

"Bet you miss school. Wild parties and all," Luke grinned.

"Not really, I didn't go to that many parties," she said. Luke's grin faltered.

"I miss seeing my friends every day. And I miss being a student. Quote unquote real life isn't like college at all."

"Yeah, I feel ya," Luke nodded

"Do you really?" the girl cocked her head.

"I mean – it was a figure of speech – "

"I know, it's just that people say that but don't really mean it."

"So what did you study?" Luke changed tactic.

"Oh, a whole bunch of things. It took me a really long time to decide what I wanted to do. I actually still don't know, to be honest."

"Uhuh," Luke nodded, his feet imperceptibly shuffling toward the door to their office.

"It's like, instead of starting out lost and gaining direction, I started out pretty sure, but the closer I got to graduation the more it all fell apart until I was more lost than I was as a freshman! My parents were *horrified*, and then one day when I visited home I was sitting on my bed and I had this *huge* epiphany – "

"No way!" Luke's eyes widened, and he walked in the office and closed the door.

The girl stopped there for a minute and stood before the silent wood. She turned around and met John's eyes watching her from the secretary's desk. She walked over.

"Hi," she said, stopping in front of the desk. "Is my father in there?" she pointed to the door behind him.

"Yes, but he's in a meeting."

"Oh. I never introduced myself earlier. I'm Erica," she said.

"I'm John," said John, shaking her hand.

"Do you want some help? I have nothing to do," Erica said, looking down at the files spread over the desk as John sorted through them.

"Sure."

Erica grabbed a chair and sat down, taking a stack for herself.

"This is pretty monotonous," she said after a few minutes.

"Yes it is."

"Is this what you do every day?"

"Pretty much," John felt himself start to blush a few seconds later. "This isn't what I want to be doing with my life," he informed.

"What do you want to – ?"

Mr. Daltuhn's office door suddenly opened.

"...And he said the people will feel *guilty* about it!" Mr. Daltuhn boomed with laughter, holding his door open.

"Oh, that's rich," said an unfamiliar male voice with an attractive tone.

"*There* he is!" Mr. Daltuhn smiled, looking down at John. From behind him a man John had never seen walked out. John was struck by a whiff of dark electricity about his person. He wasn't hugely built, but tall and slender in the statuesque rather than scrawny way, his build accentuated by the perfectly tailored suit he wore with a gold wristwatch just poking out from his left cuff. A neat mop of rich black hair with a healthy shine framed his swarthy, handsome face, whose pointed features radiated a subtle cunning. He could not have been older than his mid thirties said the youthful vitality emanating from his being.

"I was just telling Sajan about our efforts to find the network a new face," Mr. Daltuhn explained. "We tried musicians first – a bust," he shook his head. The stranger named Sajan chuckled, surveying John and Erica with his dark eyes.

"And this is my daughter, Erica, who just graduated from Vandorn University," Mr. Daltuhn said.

"Did you leave behind a legacy for your father to be proud of?" Sajan winked at her.

"Well, I wrote for the newspaper," Erica shrugged.

"Ah, so you fulfilled your quota of involvement," Sajan nodded approvingly.

A young lady purposefully approached their group in quick, high-heeled steps, stopping abruptly upon seeing Mr. Daltuhn in conversation and waiting patiently, files over her pencil skirt.

"Ah, Sandra," Mr. Daltuhn turned to her.

"Here are the reports, sir," she handed them to him and stood next to the stranger, waiting for Mr. Daltuhn's reaction. Mr. Daltuhn groaned at the overwork. Sajan Walker looked over his shoulder and let out a low whistle.

"Trying to kill your boss, there?" he grinned at the girl. She looked up and met his eyes.

"Well it's not *my* fault," she smiled back nervously.

"Sandra, this is Sajan Walker," Mr. Daltuhn introduced them quickly, "he was just stopping in to chat."

"Oh my Bob, *the* Sajan Walker?" Sandra put a hand to her mouth.

"Oh, Bob, I hate when this happens," Sajan Walker lowered his head modestly.

"I didn't recognize you from your article photo!" Sandra said to him.

Sajan laughed. "Yes, they captured my good side."

"Oh, please," she rolled her eyes and smiled.

"Sandra, was it?" he looked at her, his eyes penetrating hers. "Well now that you know what *I* really look like, I'll have to remember *you*. That way when we have one of those fateful chance encounters in the streets, we won't just pass each other by after a fleeting look of vague recognition, but will stop and perhaps say 'hello'."

"Oh – you wouldn't remember me," Sandra blushed. "You're – "

"What?" he said, the corners of his mouth raising. "Too 'famous' to associate with normal people?" he teased. "Nonsense," he tapped her arm.

"No!" she laughed, deep fuchsia creeping over her face. "That's not what I meant! It's – *me*. I'm just not that memorable."

"Oh, that's baloney. You're Sandra, with brown hair and hazel eyes and a trendy pencil skirt and you work on the thirtieth floor at NKOZ. That's not too much to commit to memory."

She adjusted her hair.

"Well, I really must get going," Sajan said. "I've got some packing to do before my flight to Bouclé," he turned to Mr. Daltuhn and gave him a firm handshake.

"You're leaving *again*?" Mr. Daltuhn exclaimed.

"It's a chore, but it's what you do for the job," he sighed.

"You're telling me," said Mr. Daltuhn darkly. "That reminds me of a story I have to tell you, but not now, you have to run."

"How about over dinner next week? My treat."

"I won't say no!"

"Excellent. I'll see you then. Good day to you all," he bid the rest.

"Nice meeting you," Sandra flashed a smile, but no glances were sent her way before Sajan took his leave down the hall, a straight-backed magic stick followed by everyone's eyes.

The rest of them headed to the break room for lunch.

"Oh my Bob!" Sandra immediately dashed to her friend. "Kathleen, you'll *never* believe who was just here!"

"Who?"

"*Sajan Walker!*"

"*What?*" said Tom, the tall man with a strong jaw who had been talking to Kathleen. "The man I aspire to be was here on this floor and I didn't know about it?"

"Did you talk to him!?" asked Kathleen.

"Yes! He looks even better in person than in the article! I didn't think it was possible."

"Article?" John mumbled, overhearing.

"Must be the one in last month's *The Current* where they voted Sajan Walker Vandorn's Number One Bachelor," Erica said.

"Ah, I wouldn't be up on the latest gossip in that arena," said John.

"Me either, really."

"So, who exactly is he to merit an article?" asked John.

"He's the owner of Kimi Kool, the creative force behind the commercials, miniskirts and all," said Erica.

"And he has to be one of the finest specimens of man on the planet," said Kathleen as she and Sandra approached the two of them to heat up their SmartPick lunches in the microwave. "With his manor, his philanthropy, his innate charm...."

"And he seems surprisingly genuine. He said he liked real, down-to-earth women who don't overvalue fame and superficiality," said Sandra.

"It must be so hard for him to find a normal girl, can you imagine how many crazy women go after him?" asked Kathleen, and they both burst out with insane laughter.

"I know it seems cliché, but when I read his interview, I could really see myself falling for that kind of man," Sandra remarked.

"Oh, he's *definitely* a model for my ideal mate," Kathleen nodded. "I mean, he doesn't have to be a *millionaire*, but, you know, he has to be able to support a family... and an allotment for nice shoes doesn't hurt."

"Financial stability, completing higher education, and he has to be decent looking," Sandra rattled off. "And I'm sorry, but I could never marry someone who supported Havenford... *or* owned a gun. Those are just two 'no-no's for me."

"Until you start settling," cut in Erica.

Their heads spun onto her.

"I could never settle!" Sandra looked scandalized.

"Not now you can't, but when you're forty and all your friends are married and have families and you're alone, it won't look like such a bad idea."

"No," Kathleen shook her head vehemently.

"Yes," nodded Erica. "The fire that fuels your idealistic dreams dies with age and you'll start rationalizing why settling is the way to go. New beliefs just as strong will replace old ones without your notice. Or, you'll just lie to yourself that you didn't settle, that you do love the person, that they are what you wanted, and that you didn't give up on your dreams."

The women stared at Erica in shock.

"Happens every day."

Chapter 13: Priceless Tokens

The best day of the year was here: Friday June eighth – the last day of public school; a day where nothing was accomplished in classrooms, where order broke down into careless chaos because in a few short hours it would not matter. Mismatched outfits that needed only a pair of sunglasses to look like they belonged at the beach colored the hallways unsystematically. But Milly was stuck in computer science working on her last assignment.

"All done? You're a good worker, Milly, I hope to see you in my level two class next year," Mr. Badgely smiled at her from behind his computer. She grinned awkwardly back.

Amy Bagshow gave a soft snort and rolled her eyes from her desk as Milly walked by her in her new sea green Hollister t-shirt. Milly suddenly became aware of how oily her hair felt. *It must look so bad.* Then she remembered that Marrik must've noticed it, too, when she passed by him on her way to class that morning.... The way his t-shirt had moved so naturally with him as he'd walked ever closer... his hair falling in front of his face and the way he'd carried on conversation with his friend but had looked at *her*....

She allowed herself to fall into this pleasant reverie as dim conversation barely reached her ears from the people next to her, a group of average kids in Hollister t-shirts and jeans, sitting around talking excitedly about their weekend plans.

"You should go, Erin, it'll be awesome," said a guy named Sam sitting casually in his chair.

"Who's coming?" asked Erin D.

"*Everybody* – Sarah, Sarah, Stacy, Jessica, Stacy, Ryan, Andrew, Morgan, Alex, Alex, Alex, Alex, Andrew, Michael, Andrew, Michael, Alex, Michael, Jennifer, Jenny, Jen B, Morgan, Jen C, Jen G, and Jennie."

"What about Alex?"

"He's out of town."

A commotion then happened as Dee Allderbay walked into their classroom like a flurry of leaves. She seemed not to care about looking good since it was the end of the school year and there were more important things to think about, and was thus dressed casually.

"Oh my Bob, Dee, your pants are so cute!" exclaimed Amy from across the room.

"Thanks!" said Dee, twisting around to better show off her bright yellow sweatpants, which had the word "GREEN" written on the butt in blue letters.

"Mr. Badgely, I need to use one of your computers," she said.

"Go right ahead, Dee!"

"Oh my Bob! Dee! Did you see what happened on *Seven Stranger Danger* last night?" Amy called out for the whole class to hear.

"Obviously I did, or we wouldn't have talked about it this morning," said Dee.

"I know, but wasn't it *shocking*!?"

Erin D. rolled her eyes and turned to face her friend, Erin B.

"I can't *stand* her. She thinks she's like, the shit or something just 'cause Dee talks to her. Dee doesn't even *like* her, she told me herself," said Erin D.

"Who even cares about popularity anymore? It's not like we're in middle school," agreed Erin B., and the three of them erupted over their shared wisdom acquired with age.

"Are there *any* not shitty computers in this room?" came Dee's angry voice as she walked past their row.

"You can use mine, I'm not using it," Sam stood up quickly from his seat, then went to stand beside Erin B. and Erin D. Dee sat down in his seat.

Milly couldn't stop being aware of the fact that she was sitting next to Dee Allderbay, sitting there awkwardly doing nothing. *What* Dee must think of her!

"*Bobdammit!*" Dee yelled. "Mr. Badgely, my computer froze!"

"Here, I can fix it," Sam walked over. "This computer and I are practically one," he cracked a grin.

"Whatever," Dee said, holding up her manicured hands and stepping back. Sam worked away on the computer while Dee sat on a chair in the corner texting continually.

"I fixed it, Dee," he said after ten minutes. "Dee, I – Dee?"

Dee looked up from her phone. "What? Oh, thanks babe."

"So, did you hear what Casey Matthews did to Sean in the bathroom the other day?" Erin B. asked her friends, half-glancing at Dee expectantly; Dee typed away without paying them mind.

"What?" leaned in Erin D. excitedly.

"Even worse than what she did to Marrik McFost second quarter."

Milly's heart jumped out of her chest.

"Ew. Who would even wanna *touch* that dirty whore," Dee Allderbay scoffed without looking away from her screen.

"I know, right," said Erin B, laughing along. "It's like she tries to be as dirty as she – "

Dee Allderbay saved her work and got up.

"Dee, are you coming with us to get ice cream after school?" Amy asked Dee as she was leaving.

"Um, call me," said Dee as she walked out the door.

What *had Casey done to Marrik in the bathroom??* Milly fell into preoccupation once the ripples had smoothed over the troubled pool of their classroom. *Could it be something dirty? No, Marrik wasn't like that.*

Somewhere, deep inside her heart, Milly knew that Marrik McFost wasn't the boy she thought he was, that she had conjured his image up for herself in her own mind; and yet every time she passed him she couldn't help but feel *something*, a feeling she just couldn't ignore.

When Milly came home that afternoon, finally done with her sophomore year of high school (the worst year of her life!!!), she ran upstairs to her room and brought a magazine back down, opening it before her family to show them what she had been talking about. Looking over her shoulder, John saw that the magazine contained dozens of pictures of flesh-colored sticks posing at odd angles to show off clothes.

"There they are, that's them," said Milly, pointing to a small square of a page that showcased an array of brightly colored sweatpants that all had the word "GREEN" written on the butt in contrasting shades. "Those are the ones I need to buy before I go off to camp. Tai and Gretchen and I decided that we'd each wear a different colored pair. Mine are going to be purple."

"I notice there aren't any green-colored ones," said John.

"*Duh,*" said Milly. "The company is called 'Go GREEN'. You can't have GREEN pants that are green, that wouldn't make any sense!"

"Um."

"They're awfully expensive," said Mrs. Hallan.

"But *everyone* has them! It's the most popular thing right now!"

"To 'Go GREEN' without going green?" John intervened.

"Mom, don't listen to him, John doesn't know what he's talking about," said Milly.

"Yep," said John, stepping away. "A sure sign that the world has gone insane: the name of a color written in a different color onto pants of yet a third color."

As the rest of his family went to the mall to get the pants, John headed along familiar streets toward a familiar destination: Mabel's House of Hunger, the former-restaurant-turned-bar that had refused to change its name. The new owners had decided to keep it as a joke, and as a means of luring unsuspecting customers through their doors – people would mistakenly assume that they were going to a restaurant and instead walk into a bar. They would become confused and might even panic for a moment, always to the amusement of the bartenders standing behind the long, usually filled counters. One could almost hear the expectations shattering as the innocent civilian lost his footing, his mental world harshly disrupted as something had blatantly not gone according to plan; their faces would say, "*what the fuck!?*" and their eyes would be wide. One could always recognize a first timer. Then someone would have to patiently explain this most comical situation to the poor customer, who would be forced to bear the genial laughter and pityingly smiling faces of dozens of strangers as he stood rooted to the spot in what was perhaps the most shocking moment of his week. Some people laughed along awkwardly and then felt like they needed a drink to assuage this craziness – lucky they were at a bar!; some called the owners and customers weirdos to cover up their embarrassment and left, hating the place for daring to make them look like a fool when didn't their lives evidently prove the exact opposite (who had just closed that deal worth a million dollars today, thank you very much?)?; and some left because they had brought their children to a friendly family diner (or so they thought!).

It had happened to John, too, the first time he went in there. But they were more surprised than he, at his reaction that is. He'd walked in, looked around, clearly cognized that his surroundings were not what he'd expected them to be (as denoted by the widening of his eyes and raising of his brows), and sat quietly down at the bar. The bartender, who'd never seen John before and had noticed the characteristic pause in movements that came with unfamiliarity with Mabel's House of Hunger, recoiled: this stranger seemed totally unaffected. "Can I have a beer?" he'd asked, simple as that. And the bartender had handed him a beer, staring at him in perplexity. Maybe someone had forewarned him, yes, that was probably it. But, as they started talking ("This isn't much of a restaurant, is it?" he took a sip), it became evident that no one had tipped the stranger off, that the guy hadn't had a clue, and that, when asked if it hadn't come as a shock to him, just shrugged.

Events like that only happened now for the occasional tourist. A year had passed since the genius inception of this local hang-out spot that offered somewhere to go after ten PM, and this little jewel of upside-downity had become a source of peculiar comfort for its regulars, the epicenter of a certain subset of Vandorn society.

By the time John walked in it was already pitch dark outside, crowded inside. He slid into a barely open space at the counter.

"Took you forever," said Edgar. He already had a glass of beer in front of him, as did Cassie, sitting on his left and still in her work clothes.

"I walked," John explained.

"Hey, John," said Cassie, smiling at him. "Ugh, I can barely squeeze myself into this mob," she uncomfortably squirmed in her chair, ponytail of blonde hair flying about her face. Edgar took his palm and smoothed back his dark hair, then propped his chin on his hand, his straight nose almost touching his chilly glass. His eyes glanced at the brunette who'd just squeezed through on John's other side.

"Hey, John, mind if we, uh, switch seats?" he asked would-be-casually. John, who'd been waiting for his beer, jerked around with a "hm?"

"I would, but I don't think I can get out of here," he said, indicating the wall of babbling bodies closing him in. "Why?"

Edgar's lips tightened a moment, but that was the only change to his face. "It's just a bit cramped on this side, but it's cool."

A soft little sigh (he didn't know how he heard it through the surrounding din) to his right made John glance over; he beheld a tidal wave of rich brown hair shining in the lamplight. Then he beheld the girl it belonged to, dark eye makeup and cherry red lips and all. She was remarkably thin, except for her chest, and wore gold bangles on her wrists.

"Are you alright?" John asked, noticing how her shimmering eyelids were half-closed and her long crimson-tipped fingers were hanging about loosely, as if she were helpless.

"Oh!" said her eyes as she glanced up in surprise at this caring stranger.

"Yes, yes," she said.

"Thank you for asking," she said half a minute later.

"No problem," said John, turning around again.

"What's your name?" she asked him.

"John. What's yours?"

"Danielle."

Danielle's round of shots came through with the bartender. She took hers and downed it, then smacked her lips. John watched her.

"Want one? I'm buying," she told him.

"Uh, no thanks, I'm not big on those."

Pause.

Time to exit John's head and enter Danielle's:

I need someone to save me; I've been so alone; some days I can't even bear to look at myself. The problems of my day are temporarily absolved by my shower but as I step out they all come flooding back into my wretched body as I stand alone in my room, where my now ex-boyfriend slept last week; I'm so drained, I can't think, I can't eat, I can't even take my laundry out of the dryer! I've been self-abusive. I have no energy for life so I lie in bed, crying.... My black satin slip is dirty so I put on my red one. It shimmers in the feeble light of my room, cascading over my freshly shaved legs. I wish someone would tell me I'm beautiful....

"But I'll buy you one," said John.

"Aw, really? That's sweet of you! I'd never ask normally," said Danielle.

"You didn't ask. I offered."

"I know, it's just that I feel bad when someone buys me a drink. It's like, I'm single, yes, but I'm an adult and I can take of myself, you know?"

"Yeah," said John.

"I guess people just seem to think I'm vulnerable," she shrugged, glancing downward.

"I didn't think you were vulnerable," said John. "You're wearing gold jewelry and nice clothes, and you said you were single so obviously you're not relying on someone else to pay for all that."

"Oh," she laughed like a songbird, "don't be deceived, these are all cheap. The only one worth something is this one," she pointed to a gold bracelet that looked unique among the rest. "My ex gave it to me. I know it's silly that I still wear it, but..." she trailed off, looking downward again.

"It's not silly. It's a nice bracelet. If I were in your place I'd still wear it, too. Plus it matches with your earrings and your shirt," John remarked.

"Well, *he* thinks it's silly. He thinks people shouldn't wear things their exes gave them. He called me the other day," she sighed. "My friend thinks it's a sign that he wants me back," she chuckled nervously, endearing John yet also showcasing her inner torment through her eyes with the half-glance she gave him.

John shook his head. "No, it seems like he just wants to prick you. Trust me, if a guy wants you back, he'll either tell you or avoid you at all costs," he explained.

"Yeah, I really have to move on. I know," said Danielle. "It's just hard...."

John nodded.

"I need a genuinely good man. It seems like men just use me for my body," she said in a slightly sad tone. "I need to find someone who won't take advantage of me."

"That sounds like a good plan," John agreed.

Danielle gave a sardonic laugh; the notes were like dilapidated chimes yearning for a gentle hand to set them right again.

"Please, John..." she said, shaking her head as she laughed casually and sent tendrils of her shiny hair lightly brushing his forearm, "they don't exist.... Where am I ever going to find a good guy?" and then she looked up at him, imploringly, her eyes saying what her words did not; the dim lamplight gently reflected within their dark, liquid depths.

"Beats me," said John. "Yeah, you're right. They really don't exist." And he laughed, too, realizing it.

The bartender came by again.

"Can I get another one of whatever she had?" asked John, pointing to the empty shot glass sitting in front of Danielle.

"Coming right up," said the bartender.

"There you go," said John to Danielle, smiling. "Hope you enjoy!"

"Hey John, Morina and Ankur got us a table, let's go," said Edgar, tapping him on the shoulder.

"I've gotta go, my friends are over there," said John to Danielle, who hadn't touched her drink. "You're welcome to join us if you want to."

"I'm alright, I think I'll hang out here," said Danielle with a smile. Her eyes rested on a centimeter past John's head; a young guy with curly blonde hair and broad shoulders had taken Edgar's seat just a moment before.

"Alright. Well, see you later then," said John, and off he went to join his friends.

***

Mrs. Hallan hummed as she made breakfast, Mr. Hallan silently read the newspaper at the table, and Milly made a list of everything she would need to bring to Camp Putentach with her, which was easier than actually going around and gathering those things. John took a seat next to his father when he came downstairs the next morning and opened the Boble with his morning coffee.

"Son, why do you keep reading the Boble? It's all I've seen your nose buried in these past few weeks," said Mr. Hallan.

"I'm looking for something," said John, preoccupied.

"What?" asked his dad.

"Something that can help me...." The truth was, if there was one source able to get to the truth about his token, it would be the Boble, John thought, the only canonical text on the matter.

The phone ringing broke the silence. Mrs. Hallan picked it up.

"Hello?"

"Merle! Oh my Bob – Merle! – have you heard!? Turn on the news!"

"What is it Jackie?" Mrs. Hallan said severely, making Mr. Hallan and John glance up.

"There's been a terrorist attack on Vandorn! LASS tried to blow up the Tower of Onyx!"

Mrs. Hallan turned on the T.V. The four of their eyes met a scene of people on the streets screaming and crying and pointing upward.

"...Three members of the International Terrorist Organization known as LASS attacked the Tower of Onyx in downtown Vandorn less than one hour ago," Anita Slater was saying. "The effects are frightening, debris everywhere. There is mass confusion on the streets...."

They now showed the seventy-story Tower of Onyx, the city's largest financial center, stretching like a black thorn into the blue sky. Small fires were burning out of three spots along the building's body, filling the air with charcoal shaded smoke.

"Each member strapped bombs to his chest and flew into the tower at full speed, and was killed upon impact. The collisions created large dents and broke several windows. Of the victims, five are dead and twenty-seven injured. Two died from the direct impact of the breaking glass. Two more died from the ensuing flames. One experienced a heart attack earlier that morning in an unrelated incident...."

"Oh, thank Bob it was a Saturday," said Mrs. Hallan with a hand to her mouth as they watched the three-hundred-foot high cloud of smoke rising onscreen.

"Milly, where are you going?" Mr. Hallan asked sharply. Milly turned around like a burglar caught in the midst of robbery, hand on the stair railing.

"Are you going on your computer?"

"I just wanted to see – "

"Have you no respect!?" their father boomed. "This is no time to gossip about boys! You are going to sit down with your family!"

" – I wanted to see the *news!*"

"You'll have a month to talk to your friends about the news!"

"Stewart, about sending her to camp," Mrs. Hallan objected, glancing at her husband.

"*What?*" Milly exclaimed.

"It might be too dangerous, Milly," said her mother.

"But mom!" Milly cried, taken aback, "that's not fair – !"

"I don't want to hear it," she closed her eyes, deaf to the sputters of adolescent dismay.

"Nobody's parents are going to stop them! You guys are so overprotective! You-you already paid for it – !"

"Your safety is more important to us than money," said Mr. Hallan.

"It's not like they're going to attack Camp Putentach! Won't I be safer in the middle of nowhere than in the city that just got attacked?"

She leaned back, expecting her parents to turn to each other and think over this solid argument which, to her, was totally irrefutable whichever way one looked at it.

"John, grab her arms; I've got the legs," Mr. Hallan said.

John stood up. Milly ran back to the table, taking her seat again bitterly.

"You can bet security will be tight as my belt now," Mr. Hallan said darkly, looking between John and his wife.

"*This burger wrapper looks mighty suspicious... it could be linked to the terrorists' plot,*" John muttered under his breath.

"John! How can you say such things!" his mother gasped.

"I was kidding! No one but an Artinian would have any connection to a burger...."

In spite of the attacks, the commute on Monday morning was crowded as ever. John pushed and shoved to make his way through, already late from getting caught up in Congress' emergency meeting on C-Span that morning:

"'An assembly has been called to discuss a plan of action in response to Saturday's attacks. Congressman Stanford has the floor.'

'Thank you, Congressman Anglebee. I am inexpressibly upset by these events. I believe we must do all we can to rectify the damage inflicted on our country.'

'Thank you, Congressman, for that input,' said Anglebee.

'I'd like to address the issue of national safety!'

'Yes, Congressman Thurnum?' Anglebee said.

'General, how do we know that the threat is only external? What if these terrorists had inside help?'

Murmurs of speculative assent.

'Now wait just a minute,' a voice called out. 'Before you tap our phones – '

'Tap your phones? Ha! For the past fifteen years!'

'We cannot interfere with the rights granted to us by our Constitution!'

Murmurs of speculative assent.

'I don't know why you're being paranoid, Congressman Chambers, no one is going to take away our rights. I for one would gladly submit myself to a harmless inspection for my countrymen's safety. It is like the Token Law – '

'Which is a gross violation of privacy – !'

'Congressman Chambers, let me pose a hypothetical scenario,' Thurnum shouted over Chambers' shout. 'Would you not feel safer if an inspection assured you that your children's teachers are not terrorists, pedophiles, or criminals?'

'What pedophiles and criminals – ?'

'Are you saying that pedophiles and criminals are not a problem in our society?'

'This is completely irrelevant to – !'

'Bring in the statistics!'

'Order, order in the meetinghouse!' Congressman Anglebee, the General, banged his mallet. 'Congressman Thurnum, pedophiles did not bomb the Tower of Onyx, but if pedophilia is a topic of interest for you, you may enter it into the suggestion box for future discussion.'

The camera caught a shot of an elaborately carved wooden box in the corner of the room.

'General, there's no telling how far these measures will go! First the Token Law, then the threat of search, then losing the privacy of our very homes! People on the streets are worried,' said Congressman Chambers.

'Worried about another attack!' cried Congressman Jobe.

'Look,' a third intervened. 'We are not talking about the distant future – we are talking about what to do *now*. The presidents need an answer and they can't move without our plans.'

'Then why don't we let *them* come up with it?'

'Quit your whining, lazy buffoon! Because it's our duty!'

'Congressman Hudgebub – ' the General began with a sigh.

'*I'm* a lazy buffoon – !?'

'Perhaps,' said a new voice, 'the answer is to *unite* our country politically for a time.'

Silence fell upon those words. Congressman Alaleem went on.

'We are one people socially and economically, but we maintain a great divide. Could it not be that this barrier is the source of our problems?'

'What are you saying?' Congressman Thurnum asked, eyeing Congressman Alaleem suspiciously.

'I am saying that it might be better to have one president temporarily lead the country instead of two. One strong leader to unify us on all fronts against the great danger we face.'

There was a pause of silence.

'Are you insane!?' shouted Congressman Dale. 'This is undermining the most basic premise of our Constitution!'

'I agree!' cut in Congressman Foreman.

'We've been fine for over three hundred years!'

'We can't force half the country to be run by a man they didn't vote for!'

'Alaleem's idea is a bunch of hooey!' cried Congressman Hudgebub, the oldest and veiniest of the Congressmen.

'Congressman Hudgebub, that language is not appropriate for congressional meetings!' said Anglebee.

'Hooey!' Hudgebub repeated, brandishing his walking stick at Anglebee.

Anglebee banged his mallet.

'Enough! I say we take a vote. The question is: should we offer Congressman Aalaleem's proposal to the presidents or not?'"

The vote was taken. In the meanwhile, John got dressed, checked his email, and made his lunch. Just as he finished his sandwich, clear voices issued from the T.V. set again.

"'The votes have been tallied,'" said Congressman Anglebee. "Those in favor of informing the presidents, thirty-three percent. Those against, sixty-seven percent.'

'Majority rules!' someone way in the back shouted.

'You know what, that's a pretty big percentage. I say we inform the presidents anyway and let them decide,'" declared Anglebee. He banged his mallet.

"...And here I thought what a nice twelve-year-old boy, until he winked at me and told me to 'stay sexy'," said Erica that morning after John had run in hurriedly.

"Maybe it was the clothes you were wearing," said John, bustling with coffee.

"I wasn't wearing anything – !"

"Well there you go."

"I meant nothing like *that*."

"Alright, everyone, into the meeting room!" Mr. Daltuhn commanded, walking past swiftly. They, Nelson, and Luke made their way over and sat around the table, isolated from the rest of the floor behind windows of glass.

Mr. Daltuhn looked most stressed. Not only were ratings plummeting as shows like *Artinia's Next Great Icon* took a backseat to the news for once, but they were still no closer to salvaging the network. He cleared his throat:

"This past month, after looking through the research you've come up with, the data you've presented to me, and analyzing the trends moving this industry, I've decided that we are going to expand in an entirely new direction – "

John cut in. "I know, I know – we have to innovate, we have to focus on the modern, technology-oriented mindset of today's youth and move forward with a more fast-paced, tech-savvy, reinvented image. We need to make new versions, instate sleeker designs, embrace modern trends, pretend to really like multi-ethnicity, start reality T.V. shows showing how random common people go shopping at Floor-Mart, connect with the public, depict free-spirited artsy chicks who are into women's health magazines and environmentalism and sit around eating yogurt and doing yoga, use savvy language, and embody the changing values of our forward-moving society."

"Boy, stop being an idiot and sputtering nonsense from that insipid peephole you call a mouth!" Mr. Daltuhn replied angrily. "We need to go into the *past*! We're going to totally go against every modern trend and put back on the air all the old values we haven't seen on T.V. in fifteen years. You know what I mean; we're going to get rid of computer animation, we're going to have a moral at the end of every episode, and by Bob we're going to show normal, functional families with two happily married parents and their biological children! Vintage is in, people!" he finished.

Mr. Daltuhn was clearly going insane. John hoped that after a little while he would forget about what he said at that meeting, and indeed he brought it up no further. Yet John couldn't help but feel that the idea still clung to him, like a thin mist around his aura.

As there was nothing for him to do, John took the day to go to the library and do some research of his own. He had exhausted his Boble for tidbits on tokens, but when discouragement had plagued him, he remembered that his was not the only version! Since the dawn of its conception, the Boble had been translated, retranslated, edited for removals and additions, and even reunited with lost whole sections of itself that had been miraculously discovered centuries later! John need not despair – there were hundreds of variations of the Word of Bob!

The library was practically devoid of people other than some schoolchildren on the first floor. John had no idea where amid its seven levels it might hide books on tokens.

"Try self-help," the concierge told him. "Top floor."

John climbed the round, spiraling staircase in the middle of the building up to its end, stepping out onto a stretch of burgundy carpet with a sign stationed at the front:

Autobiography, Biography, Journals >>

<< Religion, Self-Help, Restrooms

John turned left and walked slowly among the quiet isles, the carpet muffling his footsteps, the afternoon sun streaming in through the windows casting long shadows over the white walls of the high-ceilinged room, making the quiet of the vacant space quite eerie, and the sense of being alone there quite strange. It seemed few people or librarians ventured here; the shelves and armchairs looked long unused. A lone ray of light illuminated a layer of dust settling over a jumbled stack of Bobles on a shelf by the corner window.

John picked one up and sat down in this solitary nook. He flipped the book over and then opened it; it was an edition from almost a century ago, the stiffness and cracks in the corners of its black leather binding testifying to its age. There he stayed as the passage of time was wiped gently away. After a while the Boble found itself on the table before him and *Mortician Monthly* found itself open on his lap.

Suddenly something made him look up. There was another person at the end of the isle. It was Erica. She looked at John with an expression of surprise that mirrored his.

"I didn't realize there was someone else here," her voice carried as she walked toward him.

"Neither did I," said John. "So this is where you go during the day?" he asked.

"Usually," she said.

"To the seventh floor?" John looked around, wondering what kind of company research prompted the use of the material stored here.

"Most of the time I'm down on the third floor, but I come up here sometimes. It's peaceful," she looked up at the high ceiling.

"Are you doing research, too?" she asked.

"Uh, of a kind," he said. She looked down at the glossy pages open on his lap, one of which had an advertisement for premium coffins.

"It's just a magazine I read," John mumbled.

"About dead people?"

"Yes."

"Cool."

He stared at her.

"So, uh, what kind of research are you doing?" she asked.

"Oh, it's not for the network, this is something personal," John said.

"Ah, I see," she said.

There was a moment's pause.

"On tokens," said John.

"Having some trouble?" Erica asked.

"You could say that."

"Oh, do go on," she sat down on the arm of his armchair, intrigued. John regretted having said anything now.

"It's a little strange," he tried to mumble it aside.

"Tell me," she insisted.

John paused. "You really want to know?"

She nodded.

"I don't know what my token is," he said.

Erica didn't react. She didn't even blink at this news.

"That's unusual," she said.

"Yes," he muttered darkly. "But more importantly, I need something to write on those papers. That's why I came here and read this," he nodded to the Boble. "I thought maybe it would have some helpful hints on finding it."

"But a token isn't something you *find*," said Erica.

"I know! But what else is there to do?"

"Maybe your token is already there, but it's so slight and subtle you just never noticed it before," she suggested. "It's completely possible!" Erica said to the doubtful expression he now gave her. "It happens to people with mental tokens all the time."

"But I'm *twenty-four*. At this rate it's more likely I just don't have one," said John.

"Oh please, stop pitying yourself," Erica snorted, cutting across their sacredly quiet surroundings and getting off the armrest. "Have you looked at the self-help section? There's tons of stuff written on tokens," she walked over to the other end of the floor.

"No, that's a section I try to avoid," said John, getting up and following her.

"Try this," she said, handing John a copy of *Become a Better Token-Bearer*. Its cover displayed a photo of a smiling man who inspired people with his white teeth and strong jaw. Here was clearly a better token-bearer. John flipped through it, but it seemed to have nothing of use to him.

"Well then this won't help either," said Erica, putting back a copy of *What It's Like to Break Mirrors With My Eyes*.

"There are almost as many self-help books on tokens as there are on relationships," John remarked, stalking through the volumes of token-related concerns.

"Ooh!" Erica pulled down a thick volume titled *Priceless Tokens*. "It's a collection of the weirdest tokens ever recorded!" she said with hungry interest, flipping it open. "'...*A man who could make his physical appearance change before other people's eyes by the words he spoke. Anyone who came into contact with him saw him truly as he was only the first time. After that, he would start speaking to them, and his words were so fluid and persuasive that they had a magical quality about them, which literally changed his physical appearance in his beholders' eyes.*'" Erica went on, "'*He had three beautiful wives, and he never stopped talking. He spent his life in constant speech lest the spell wear off and someone see through the curtain that shrouded him.*'"

"Sounds like he burned through that one," said John.

"I don't think so. I think it burned through him," Erica replied.

"What do you mean?"

"I mean, if he'd really owned it he would've been able to resist the urge to talk, and reveal himself at will. This way, he was its slave. It must have been lonely for him; no one knew who he really was...."

Erica flipped onward.

"Here's a strange one with the power of flight. It says this woman could fly, but only if the sky was cloudy, the temperature exactly seventy-three degrees, the large moon half full, and never after she had eaten meat less than three days ago."

"That's not so extraordinary, aside from the weird conditions," said John.

"Well, that's not all: while she could only fly under specific conditions, when they were met she flew higher than anybody should be capable of. On several occasions she flew higher than airplanes, and seemed impervious to the cold and lack of air."

"How did she discover that exact combination?" asked John in wonderment. "It's like a combination to a lock."

"Chance?" Erica shrugged. "I don't know. Listen to this one," she continued onto the next page. "'*This woman had the incredible gift of being able to embed a thread of her own sinew under the epidermis of any person she chose, binding the person to her against his or her will. After that moment the victim could never be truly free from her unless she herself broke off the connection. She divorced five times and died immensely rich."*

"I'm glad she's dead," John muttered.

"Ooh, this is my favorite!" said Erica. "This man could absorb the token of anyone in his vicinity! Whatever it was, while they were near him he took on their ability as his own, like a token chameleon."

"Then what was *his* token?" John asked.

"That was it," said Erica, blinking up at him, unsure of what he meant.

"Yeah, but *what* was it? That sinew lady – her token stood on its own. But he needs other people to define his. By itself, his token is essentially nothing, yet it changes things," he couldn't wrap his head around it.

"That's the beauty of it," Erica smiled.

John flipped over to the next page.

"I like this one," he said. "This man could cancel out anyone's token. No matter what it was, their ability disappeared whenever they got near him; they became essentially normal people."

"Heh. This guy had the ability to turn into a tree," said Erica, flipping ahead. "One spring day he walked up to a willow and suddenly there was another tree just like it where he had been standing."

"And?" asked John.

"That's – that's it. Apparently it only worked one way."

"How do they know he didn't decide it was easier being a willow tree than a human?" asked John.

"That's a good point. I guess we'll never know," Erica shrugged. "Ooh! Check this out! *'There still lives today a man with the remarkable ability to enter any world that has universally been acknowledged as existing, but which no one can reach. Well he can. He has been to many such mysterious places, as for example the Land of Missing Socks and Hair Scrunchies; the Holy Origin of Social Norms; the Final Distant Resting Place of Our Sewage, Excretory Waste, and Other Things We Throw Away Without Thought For Where They End Up; and the All-Mystical Ever-Unreachable Reality*

200

Containing the Peaceful Existence of Things We Told Our Spouses, Parents, and Teachers. In the future, he says, he plans to visit the Sacred Land of Your Paycheck, the Collective Home of All the Brilliant Ideas, the Rainbow, and Mirror World (the world existing on the other side of the mirror that you'd enter if you could go through the mirror, like he can). This man's name has been kept confidential for his safety from the thousands of jealous people who have read his online memoirs (which he writes from a different location every time) and who want to kill him. He has stated, in a private interview with the author of this book, that his one regret is that he must visit all of these fascinating places alone.'"

"That's amazing!" said John in awe. "Way more amazing than this next guy who grew money from his limbs. This guy couldn't even pay that guy to take him to these places; just goes to show that money can't get you everything."

They flipped the page over and burst out laughing. There it showed a middle-aged man with dollar bills growing off his arms instead of hair. Next to him stood a beautiful young woman clutching his arms and looking simply ecstatic.

He finally began to live a peaceful, happy life, the caption said, when he became old currency, worth absolutely nothing.

Chapter 14: Wheel!... of!... Consequence!!!

As one knows, there are two directions: towards Bob, or away from Bob. Although lore tells of the path toward Bob as the Uphill Path and the path away from Bob, toward Pat, as the Downhill Path, that is not the case.

The true paths are known as the Invisible Path and the All-Encompassing Path. The Invisible Path is the way to Bob, and is like a staircase that hangs in midair with no bridge between it and the ground. It is unseen to the mortal eye, and to jump on it requires a parting with the world, the ground.

The All-Encompassing Path marks the way to Pat, and it is everything else. From the mortals living as criminals to the virtuous who mark their daily progress along the Uphill Way, patting themselves on the back for choosing "right" among their fixed notions, all are slowly making their way downhill. The All-Encompassing Path steeps slowly downward to the very bottom, where Pat resides in his Lair. It takes a long time to reach its end, and one can almost always turn around. If a mortal goes the other way on the All-Encompassing Path, he or she may reach its edge, where the slope is flat, and become free from its downhill pull. Only when one is free from the pull may he or she strike upon the chance to jump onto the Invisible Path that hangs overhead.

But if one travels too far along the Way toward Pat, the slope becomes too steep, and one starts falling. This is the Point of No Return.

Just as Bob maintains the Universe with the Great Wheel, so does Pat, too, have an instrument with which he exercises control: the Wheel of Consequence. It rests flat on its side, immovable and unchanging. Behind the Wheel of Consequence resides Pat on his throne, keeping souls away from Bob in his quest to become greater than Him. But it is futile; Pat will never be greater than Bob.

No mortal is free from the Wheel of Consequence. Just as Bob sends down a Lauk to implant the token at one's birth, so does Pat send a Shugin carrying a line with a hook on the end. It embeds this hook into the mortal; the other end of the line is attached to the Wheel of Consequence. From then on the mortal is bound to the Wheel until death.

As the mortal goes through life, with every step he takes his string winds around the Wheel. If he wanders with no internal compass, aimlessly, his string intertwines with the spokes to form a tangled web which he must painstakingly undo, knot by knot, working through every wind and crisscross. But if a mortal lives with purpose, if his mind, his heart, and his actions have come into alignment with the Great Wheel, his string remains untwisted for all his days.

Not a single moment is missed. One who believes he can "forget about it" is only fooling himself. Everything is counted. There is not a moment that does not matter, and not a moment that matters more. Just as the Great Wheel is the map of the universe, so is the string's path on the Wheel of Consequence a map of one's life.

Sooner or later, everyone frees his ties from the Wheel of Consequence and becomes free to reunite with Bob. Even Pat himself must one day rejoin Bob. From his Lair one can only go up, and therein is even the Lair of Pat itself Bobly.

Chapter 15: Ideals

After just one week, virtually all shock caused by the June ninth attacks had dissipated and the country had returned to relative normalcy; oh don't worry – plenty of photos that would later find their way into the backs of high school yearbooks in memoriam of the event had been taken. But Time, like always, had dulled the shock. People returned to caring about getting the best deals on summer bathing suits for their children; to machinating a week off from work to take the family to their cabin; to fretting over the uselessness of rusty garden supplies.

Kids and teenagers, who'd been smart, had stopped caring about the attacks *way* before the adult population; they had the sense to ignore these trifles and get back to their own lives: Robbie flipped all the swings on the playground over the bar! Aww, they're not showing new episodes of my favorite cartoon today! When my parents go to sleep, we're gonna sneak downstairs and watch the sex channel!

But these were child's play – teenagers laughed at such silly endeavors, fondly recalling their own childhood caprices from way back two or three years ago. Enough laughing – serious issues needed attending. *How* am I going to make him like me when he's dating another girl (I'll never get over him!)? If I'm not – gasp! – valedictorian – gasp! – next year – sharp inhale! – my life – hyperventilate! – will be – hey, sweet car, must be the new model. How am I gonna hide my grades from my parents? I dunno, but here, have a chocolate bar, it'll make you feel gooood.

And if they were going off to college in the fall, they were facing issues of *real* importance that younger kids didn't understand:

I just don't see us staying together, we need to explore our own lives. But you'll always be in my heart. 'Bye now.

...Now that I'm done with high school... life... has no meaning. It's empty. *I'm* empty. Where do I go from here? I need to find my calling... something I can put my soul into.... I need to start a band. I'm gonna write about the deeper truths in life, stuff I've come to learn... the first song will be called "How That Bitch Broke My Heart."

Which were almost as serious as the issues facing college graduates who now stood on the threshold of the adult world:

...Now that I'm out of college... I wanna take a year off to do something meaningful with my life before I sink into the quagmire of mediocrity forever.... Maybe I'll record a solo album.... I'm gonna write about all the things I've learned these past four years... the first song is gonna be called "Women Have No Soul."

And the rest had spent more than a week watching the same stale news retold in different exciting words to cover up the fact that no new substance had made it in since day one. Hearing two anchormen discuss the issue for twenty minutes without saying anything had become routine, an expected monotony that had blended into the gray-toned mosaic backdrop of Artinian life like a piece of worn glass.

"...Should be a fun treat for everyone, the third annual Vandorn Elementary School Sing-a-Long, you can catch that tonight at seven. Now onto more news, there was quite a stir in the Decagon this weekend, did you hear, Candace?" John heard at breakfast Monday morning.

"Oh I heard, Paul. My husband watches C-Span."

"For those of you who missed it – or who perhaps don't watch C-Span in the middle of the day – "

"In other words not dorks like my husband, but normal people – love you, honey!" she blew a kiss.

" – President Havenford announced his support for Pro-Choice, the movement that formed several days ago in response to Congressman Alaleem's proposal and which supports keeping the two president system. The presidents are currently debating Alaleem's proposal on the Round-the-Clock Presidential Debates airing on C-Span 3," Paul said. "So what do you think about having one president, Candace?" he asked, turning to her.

"Um – you know, Paul – I think one president is, a, um, interesting idea, I don't know if anything will come of it. I think that along with the attacks it's certainly given the country a shake!" she chuckled.

"Oh yes! More on that to come, but right now let's take a short break for these commercial messages."

A Kimi Kool Artinia Free commercial came on. Kimi Kool stood on a rock, wearing a t-shirt in the design of the Artinian flag paired with low-rise jeans, her hair blowing back in the wind and her face looking boldly out toward the horizon.

"I'm proud of my country," said a voice-over in Kimi Kool's voice as Kimi Kool continued to stare onward.

"*Artinia.*" A patriotic orchestral piece started to play.

"The land where I can be free!" Zoom in on Kimi Kool's impassioned face as a gust of wind swept back her hair at one-hundred-and-eighty degrees, breaking it up into strands that miraculously bypassed her eyes.

"*...Collectible* Kimi Kool Artinia Free doll, limited time offer! *Support your country!...*"

Milly bounded down the stairs, through the kitchen, and past John, throwing the last of her luggage into the pile by the door. Luckily for her, their parents had calmed down with the rest of the country and deemed it okay for her to spend the month at Camp Putentach, where she would be secluded from civilization by a mantle of quietly rustling trees, sleeping in a stout log cabin with a dozen other adolescent girls. And across the lake where the geese swam would sit the boys' camp, which they would spy on through binoculars during free hours, giggling excitedly when they caught the boys doing the exact same. Except Milly would refuse to partake out of terror that one of the boys would recognize her as the creepy stalker who'd spied on him and call her out in front of everyone at the first dance, just like that one summer it happened.

As soon as they reached the camp, Milly ran out of the car and up the familiar road to find her new bunk, one for the older girls; these were strategically placed around the canteen containing Camp Putentach's tampon vending machine. Last year Milly hadn't had her period yet (a fact she'd had to reveal to her bunkmates when one of them asked to borrow a pad, which she had assumed Milly was stocked on since she never went to the vending machine to get any. The girl promised not to tell anyone that Milly didn't have her period yet – after all, she was fourteen! And she kept her promise – but, in a bizarre coincidence, she'd seen this one unpopular girl no one liked eavesdropping on that very conversation where Milly had revealed her shameful secret – Milly hadn't seen this sneaky girl because, as her bunkmate reminded her, her back had been to the window, and she must have ran and told all the other girls. That was how Milly's entire bunk found out.

But no one made fun of her. Everyone blooms in their own time, they'd consoled, adjusting their bra straps.

"Really, it's such a hassle, I hate dealing with it every month," said Natasha.

"You're so lucky you don't have it yet, Milly. I wish I didn't have it," said Dana.

"Me too. I get the worst cramps," complained Tish. "And sometimes I get cramps *afterwards*."

"Oh my Bob, same!" exclaimed Patricia, eyes widening behind her glasses.

"Do you guys ever get nauseous, too?" asked Sherrie.

"*Yes!*" said Natasha and Tish at once.

"We need to exercise," Natasha said sagely. "We should make a running schedule, when girls live together their menstrual cycles synchronize!").

But this summer was different. This summer she was a woman.

"Milly!" came an exclamation as Tai ran into the cabin followed by a group of girls, several of whom Milly did not know. "You should've been here yesterday, Pam took us on a trust walk!" she said.

"What's that?" Milly asked.

"It's when we're blindfolded and hold hands as Pam leads us around camp until we stop at a clearing by the lake and sit under the stars having deep meaningful conversations until three in the morning."

"I missed that!?" She had missed the crucial First Bonding Experience! Now she'd be an outsider, listening to inside jokes that she wasn't a part of and feeling awkward because she didn't know what they were laughing about!

"At least you're here for Girly Night," said Gretchen, panting. "Sorry I'm all sweaty, Milly, we're just getting back from soccer," she said as she gave Milly a hug.

Milly was relieved; her least favorite part of summer camp was the team sports they were forced to play.

"I'm leaving Meredith in charge tonight," called out a girl who looked older than the rest, placing her shoulder on an athletic blonde girl panting heavier than the rest.

"You must be Milly, I'm Pam, your counselor," she shook Milly's hand. "Oh shoot! I'm out of tampons! Sam, will you go down to the cantina and grab me one?" Pam asked, turning around to a spunky looking girl with black hair whom Milly also didn't know.

"Sure!" Sam said brightly, putting on patterned orange flip flops and heading out the door.

"*Don't forget the mayo!*" Pam said exaggeratedly, and Sam burst out laughing.

"Uh... mayo...?" no one had ever informed Milly about this part of tampon usage.

"It's just a joke from yesterday, don't worry about it," said Pam dismissively.

Milly looked around the bunk; all of the other girls had been with them the previous summer.

"Natasha's not in our bunk?" Milly asked.

"No, she's in another bunk with Tish. They made friends with the 'popular' crowd," Tai said with some spite.

"Good," Milly said; she didn't like Natasha.

When Sam returned they changed into their bathing suits and walked down to the pool together.

It was there that Milly got her first glimpse of Natasha; she had really hit a growth spurt, both vertically and horizontally. She and several other girls were reclining in lounge chairs in untied bikini tops, working on their tans, lording over the rest with their mature, shielded stares.

"Milly, you gonna jump?" Tai called out to her from the water. Milly glanced back at Natasha; Tish was applying tanning oil to her back; they did not use lotion.

"I'm gonna work on my tan," Milly shouted back.

"But you're wearing a one-piece!"

"Look at how pale my legs are!"

Trying to be as inconspicuous as she could, she spread her towel out on a nearby chair and lay down. She had never "tanned" before; within ten minutes she was so hot, so bored, it was more than she could stand! But she kept at it. She supposed one got used to the suffering. Natasha's crew appeared fine with it; they were enjoying pleasant conversation while lying on their backs.

"...I got *so* trashed on those, I had like seven. I almost threw up all over my red halter dress."

"Oh my Bob that dress is so hot. Where did you get it?"

"Lacy's."

"I *love* Lacy's."

"Oh my Bob. Me too."

The pain in Milly's poor little heart that pined for such bonding experiences was almost too apparent *See how normal girls her age were supposed to act? Why couldn't she be that way? She wasn't mature enough – she needed to be more mature.*

"...But be careful the first time. It took us a couple of tries before he could get it in."

Milly gasped to herself; *how could they say such things out loud!? After all, having, you know, it, was the most private and personal thing there could be. At least, that's what Milly always thought.* Milly sighed. *Maybe this is just how you were supposed to act when you were grown up. She didn't agree with it, but everyone seemed to become this way when they got older! Was this the true way to be? Did they have it right? Should she* not *disagree?*

Wait a minute – her own family wasn't like that, and neither were her best friends... but how prominent were they within society? Not very. It seemed people who held the same values Milly did never rose high in society. That was one thing Milly couldn't understand, no matter how she twisted her mind around it: why was society led by those people who gave their values up, and not by those who kept them? All those deeply-held ideals that she instinctively felt resided in everyone, like a common thread connecting each and every person from inside. She had seen time and time again how people forsook what they knew was right in order to "win". And what was worse, then they denied what they'd done, and pretended like they had never believed the things they believed before so that they could continue without shame to act in the way, not according to their values, to make social life easiest. Then they convinced themselves that the role they came to play was really who they were, *and that all the things they said, did, and wanted before had disappeared into oblivion... But* Milly *was convinced that nothing was ever forgotten, nor that it disappeared, that everything counted, and that who they truly were remained buried deep inside them, denied and suffocating slowly, and that from the time they transitioned into adulthood, one's whole life was spent wearing a mask and playing an act, nothing but lying to him or herself about who he or she was in every respect, burying his or her true self deep underneath so many layers until it was unearthed one fine day by that unexpected comment that struck right at the core and pulled it all back out again in a mess of confusion and pain. She believed that no matter how much time had passed, people still believed all the things they knew as children, despite all they said and did in the "real world" as adults. Yet no matter how well one lied, one could not change the truth!*

But those that lied best became the leaders, the right, the influential, the ones sided with. Why was it this way? Why did this class of people, like Natasha and Dee Allderbay and the P.R.E.P, and not people like her, lord over the world? Make the rules? Determine "truth" and standards for the rest of the society?

Milly closed her diary as she finished pouring out all the thoughts that had been swirling around in her head ever since they were at the pool.

"You actually brought your diary with you?" Gretchen asked her.

"You know Milly, she's always writing in it," said Tai, who was on her own bed right next to Milly's.

Milly got out of bed to change into her pajamas.

"Are you seriously taking your diary into the bathroom with you!?" came Gretchen's incredulous voice as she watched Milly walk over.

Milly turned around. "Yes".

"Oh my Bob, you don't trust us that much? We're your best friends!"

"It's not that I don't trust you," Milly asserted. It was just that she didn't trust them.

Meredith, Sam, and Dana returned from the canteen with bagfuls of popcorn for their bunk. Pam had already gone out for the night.

"Okay, what are we watching?" asked Sam, setting the popcorn on the floor around the T.V.

"*Cliquey Chicks!* It has Julian Wiles," said several girls at once.

"But Adam Beaumont is in *The Diary*," asserted others.

"Let's take a vote!" Meredith stepped in over the shrieking that had erupted. "Who wants *Cliquey Chicks*, raise your hands....Who wants *The Diary*, raise your hands." She looked around. "That's seven, who didn't vote?"

"I actually wanted to watch something else," Milly said.

"Well, we're deciding between those two," said Meredith.

An awkward silence followed.

Two hours later, all the popcorn was gone and *Cliquey Chicks* had come to an end; the credits were rolling but the girls didn't turn off the T.V. because they were laughing too hard.

"Okay, guys, I think we should have a pillow fight now," said Meredith, checking her watch. All eight girls instantly started having lots of free-spirited fun. In just one night they were brought so much closer together, Milly could practically feel the bonds of everlasting kinship forming between their skins. It was as if she had gotten not seven new friends, but seven *sisters*.

They sat clumped around the floor in a lopsided circle, wonderfully exhausted.

"Hey, guys?" Milly asked, breathing heavily, pillow in her arms.

"Yeah?" responded a couple of her sisters.

"What's the deal with the mayo thing?"

"What?" several of them looked confused.

"Some sort of inside joke?" Milly said.

"Ooh, it's just something from yesterday, don't worry about it," said Tai.

"But what *was* it?" Milly wanted to know.

"Ugh – Milly, no one feels like explaining."

"You know, I'm kind of glad Natasha's not in our bunk anymore," said Sherrie. "She was kind of mean."

"Yeah, especially to you, Milly," said Gretchen. "I don't know why you never stood up to her."

"I guess I just didn't think of her as being mean to me," Milly offered up this lame excuse to keep from admitting that she was scared of sticking up to Natasha.

"Bull," said Gretchen at once.

"No it's not!" Milly protested.

"Seriously, Gretch, you were the one complaining that Milly doesn't trust anyone and now look at you," said Tai.

"Yeah!" said Milly. "I heard Natasha talking at the pool about having sex."

Patricia's mouth dropped. "She's our age! I didn't even have my first *kiss* until last year."

"Me either!" said Sam.

"What about you, Milly?"

All eyes on Milly.

"Um... I haven't had one yet."

"Well... that's okay," said Sam.

"Yeah, we can fix that at the dance this Friday," said Dana excitedly.

"No!" exclaimed Milly, scandalized.

"Why not? There are tons of cute guys!"

"I don't care," said Milly. *How could she care about boys, or rather, any other boy, when she cared for one already? That would be like cheating, and true love didn't allow for such impulses....*

"You'll have as good a camp story as the kind they write about in young adult novels!" said Dana.

"I don't understand how you can kiss someone who's not your boyfriend," said Milly.

"Come on, Milly, people at school hook up all the time," said Gretchen. "I'll probably end up doing it at some point."

Milly couldn't believe what she was hearing from her friend. "Well I won't," she said resolutely.

"You can't be that in control over it. Sometimes these things just happen," said Meredith.

"Yeah, like when you're really horny right before you get your period!" Dana exclaimed, generating a shockwave of reactions with the word "horny".

"Oh my Bob, I *never* know when I'm going to get it!" whined Patricia. "I'm *so* irregular."

"Same!" Milly burst in.

"Mine lasts for a *week, every month*," Sherrie whined.

"That sucks! Mine only lasts three days," Sam said.

"You're *so* lucky!"

"Oh no," Meredith suddenly remembered. "I forgot to bring tampons with me."

"It's okay, I brought a ton," said Gretchen. "I have enough for, like, all of us."

"Are they regular or slim? I can only use slim," said Meredith.

"Duh, regular is for after you start having sex!" said Dana.

"And pads are for before you start making out with guys!" Gretchen laughed.

"Hey! I'm scared to use tampons," Milly said defensively.

"It's no big deal. You don't even feel it after a minute," said Gretchen. "Tell me when you get your period, I'll explain how to use it."

"It's okay, I'm fine with using pads," Milly said.

"No, you need to learn how to use a tampon," Gretchen asserted.

"Okay, so we've talked about our experiences with boys, we've talked about our periods – what else do we need to cover before the night is up?" Meredith said.

"How about our hopes and dreams?" Milly suggested.

"We covered that last night," said Meredith, shoving the idea aside.

"Oh, I know! Let's go outside in the middle of the night!" exclaimed Sam.

They opened the door and quietly snuck out of their bunk. It was that quietest time of night when the world slowed to stillness, only the chirping of crickets or the creak of a plank breaking the sacred silence around them. In these private hours Milly felt like she was walking along the underbelly of the world. She breathed in the rarefied air and felt the porch's warm wood beneath her bare feet. Through its touch her skin absorbed the subtle complexity of a million different flavors, as if in the planks was preserved the essence of every moment that had passed through them. Her soles drank in every story at once without words or forms.

This is amazing, Milly thought to herself, looking up to a breathtaking sight of millions of stars locked in a dynamic dance.

The camp around them slept as the eight girls huddled around their porch in perfect comfort, talking in low whispers about deep things, dreams and ideals, as the night often makes one do.

There was a flurry of giggles, then, "What about you, Milly? What's your ideal romantic scenario?"

"I don't wanna say, it's too embarrassing," Milly whined.

"We're not gonna make fun of you! Come on, you never tell us anything!"

"Well," Milly felt herself blush, "I guess it would just be me and him, sitting quietly together somewhere," she blushed more.

"Where?" one girl whispered.

"I dunno... like, a lake or something... somewhere peaceful and, you know, secluded. And... well *I'd* have been sitting there alone, and then he would know that I was there and find me." Only Milly's whisper pierced the silence. "And... we'd know that we lo-like each other without words, and we'd just sit there, holding hands, and, like, being one I guess you could say," she crunched through it, undiluted shame burning inside her like acid; how stupid she was for harboring such an unrealistic ideal. When she thought it in her head, it seemed – it felt – perfect, but now as she said it out loud she could hear how inane it sounded to the world.

"And he'd lean over and, um... kiss me, gently... and, um... that's pretty much it." Milly blushed so hard her face hurt. She burned. "It's never going to happen, though," she chuckled to relieve some nervousness.

"Yeah, it's too unrealistic," Gretchen agreed.

Wait, what? What did she mean, it's "too unrealistic"? *Milly* was allowed to say it was never going to happen, because then she could be pleasantly disproven; but *Gretchen* wasn't! For, deep down, Milly still believed in this ideal vision! She didn't want reality to take off the rosy sunglasses that shaded her eyes from the world! No! She didn't know what she was talking about! It *could* happen! He *did* love her behind it all!

Milly could not fall asleep, so she stole back outside after everyone had gone to bed. There she sat on porch, crying, gears colliding inside her.

How could it never happen!? True love was supposed to be perfect! And anything less wasn't true love! There wasn't supposed to be the mess of reality debasing what was pure – hook ups, caring about looks, treating sex like it was the equivalent of going shopping. And yet all around her – that was what happened. Even Gretchen was descending the staircase of standards, giving up and falling into the sea.... Milly could not express how much it saddened her to watch everyone eventually give in. Would she herself eventually follow suit? Would she be the last one still clinging to ideals that seemed more like fantasy with each passing day?

Maybe others simply realized something she did not, some undeniable fact of reality she was naïve to. Perhaps she just hadn't matured yet, and perhaps as she did, she would understand why others behaved the way they did.... But who was she kidding – she didn't really believe that! She believed that what others did felt wrong! There had to be someone, somewhere, who agreed with her, and that someone was the one she loved, her other half....In reality, Marrik was probably like the rest. She didn't know if he hooked up with random girls, maybe they were just rumors... oh come on, that sounded laughable even to her. She'd just have to come to terms with the fact that, in all probability, he did hook up with random girls and he wasn't as pure as she hoped. But she was being so judgmental! He was still pure on the inside. He was different from everyone, he was special. The way his head tilted downward instead of upward... he was looking within himself. Oh, would they ever be together? She fantasized about the day it would happen, as she felt sure it must....

Milly wiped the tears off her face, spent, and crawled back into her bed, falling asleep much quicker than she thought her tormented state could allow.

Chapter 16: So You Want to Be Yourself...

Interview No. 1:

Q: So why do you want the job?

A: I'm a committed and dedicated worker. Once I set my mind to something, there's nothing that can stop me. But at the same time I'm open to change.

Interview No. 2

Q: Why should we hire you?

A: Well, not only am I passionate, but I'm a team player who brings one hundred percent to the table.

Q: But what sets you apart from the rest of the team?

A: I would have to say my dedication *nod*.

Interview No. 3

Q: Do you feel like this is an important career step?

A: Absolutely. I feel that this position will take me a long way on my path.

Q: What would you say is your worst quality?

A: Hm... probably caring a little *too* much about my job!

***

"None of them," John said, slapping the papers onto his desk.

"I didn't think so," sighed Mr. Daltuhn, yearning to stretch out of his confining suit. It was the suit he wore on interview days.

"I'm sick and tired of these damn phonies! If I hear one more word about 'dedication' I'm going to – !" someone knocked on the door.

"There's the last guy, John, open the door for him."

John opened the door. A scraggly, thin man with matted hair, a worn t-shirt, and dirty jeans walked in. At Mr. Daltuhn's motion he sat down in the chair opposite.

"So you're here about the janitorial position?"

The man nodded. "I need money for Crack and rent. Mostly for Crack."

Pause. "You're hired."

"Cool."

Finished the day's assignment, John went into the break room and turned on the T.V. to watch the presidential debates.

"...Delectable potatoes, really," Havenford was saying to Steffen as the two of them sat at a dining table.

"Thanks, Antonio made them for me. He's *amazing*."

"Hmph.... Dj'you see the article on 'flying brain monkeys'?" Havenford unrolled his newspaper as a servant brought out the soup.

Steffen rolled his eyes. "*Total* hoax."

"Damn teenagers..." grumbled Havenford.

"Anyway, down to business," said Steffen seriously.

"Oh, can't we just enjoy a nice brunch together?" Havenford let out a hushed exclamation.

"But – *Mark*, we have to discuss – " Steffen motioned to the camera " – we're on the air!"

"Alright, alright," Havenford put down his newspaper and took off his glasses. "Let's go over the points again...."

John sighed and turned the T.V. off.

"No C-Span 3 today!?" came Erica's mock surprise.

John turned around.

"They just keep going around in circles with Havenford trying to convince Steffen to abandon Alaleem's idea and Steffen being indecisive."

"Why doesn't Steffen just agree? It's not like he wants a one president system," Erica said.

"Well, there's a lot of pressure on him with Pro-Life," said John.

"Who?" asked Erica.

"The countermovement to the countermovement. They formed a day after Pro-Choice, but they didn't get popular until AFAC picked them this past weekend."

"So they *want* one president?"

"Yep. And they want it to be Alaleem. There's supposed to be a huge televised rally later today, I can't wait."

"...Weren't you going to spend your free time looking for your token?" Erica asked.

"I looked under the table, behind the chair, – "

"Maybe you should try the television," she muttered.

"Yeah, I was going to try there today."

She gave him a look.

"Yo, why aren't we watching the news," Luke broke the fresh silence as he walked into the break room wearing a round Pro-Life pin that gleamed on his chest. Jake Crash's "Save Her", the summer's number one hit, blasted from his mePod.

He turned the T.V. back on. A clip of a Pro-Choice rally was playing.

"That's the deluded majority for you," Luke sneered at it, running a hand through his tousled his hair that looked like it had been kissed by the sun while he'd been playing beach volleyball that weekend. "Half those people won't even talk to you if you're not innie. Do we want a country run by people like that?"

"How would they be running the country if they're keeping the status quo?" asked John.

"Duh, John. If Pro-Choice wins, Havenford silently rises to power as Steffen's constituents become the silent voice."

"You realize Pro-Life winning might put *Havenford* in more power if *he* gets elected as sole president," John noted.

"No way," Luke shook his head knowledgeably. "Steffen or Alaleem. Havenford doesn't stand a chance in a national election. Ninety-five percent of his Cabinet is male innies above age fifty," he informed.

"Did you look up that statistic before you left for work?" asked Erica from behind her magazine.

"For your information I looked it up five minutes ago on my phone, which gets internet," he waved his mePhone in front of her face.

The news now switched to Prudmila Sparks standing in amidst an immense crowd gathered under the hot sun.

"I'm at the site of the Pro-Life protest, host to more than five thousand people and some of the most intense rallying this city has ever seen!" she said through the commotion. Next to her stood a young supporter. He was a college boy who looked like he'd been windswept with fervor for the cause with those sunglasses over his hair that he hadn't had time to take care of because he'd had to be at the rally early this morning, and clearly such important issues came before one's appearance, so he'd just thrown on his Pro-Life t-shirt that was tight enough to subtly accentuate his pecs, shoulders, and especially his biceps, like a Hollister t-shirt, but slightly looser than a Hollister t-shirt since he didn't care about looking good or getting girls in light of the bigger cause he had to fight for, which was what truly mattered. She turned to him.

"Why do you think the majority of Pro-Life supporters fall in the eighteen-to-thirty age group, whereas most Pro-Choice supporters come from the thirty-five-to-sixty range?"

"I believe that the younger generation is better able to accept new ideas," he nodded. "One president might be a radical notion, but everyone here believes it can work if we all put in the effort. And as you can see by our being here, *we're* ready to make that effort."

"Hold on, let's analyze that statement," Prudmila backed up, and everything around her froze. All shouting and screaming of the rally stopped and stood still as she alone and the college student blinked in front of the camera. Prudmila spoke clearly into the silence:

"How does your being here show us, the world, that you are willing to put in the effort? How do you draw that connection? You are here today for the fun part of the process, but that doesn't mean that you will be around next year for the difficult work," said Prudmila in the moment where she stopped Life to clear up a critical matter before it went any further. She tipped the microphone toward the college student.

"This isn't just *fun*, this is *work*!" he said, flustered. "We are taking this one step at a time, and the first step is to spread awareness!"

Life started again. The noise resumed.

"Free hot dogs!" yelled someone in the back over a queue of supporters waiting in line.

"Back to you, Bobbert."

"Thanks, Prudmila. We now go to our guest, Mr. Sajan Walker, president of Kimi Kool and this year's number one bachelor," said Bobbert. In the seat next to him, Sajan grinned sheepishly.

"Sajan, what are your thoughts on the situation?"

"I fully support Pro-Life and Congressman Alaleem," said Sajan. "I know Congressman Alaleem on a personal level and I'm confident that he would make a fine leader."

Erica looked at the screen suspiciously.

"Did they not get his good side?" asked John, noticing her grimace.

"I just have a bad feeling about him."

"Your dad seems to disagree. They hang out all the time now."

"I know," said Erica darkly. "I think he's dangerous."

"How could he be dangerous?" John almost laughed.

"Come on, John, think: what do all men with a lot of time and a lot of money do?"

"Mast – "

"Right! They *dabble in the occult!*"

"That's actually not what I was going to say."

"John, that's what men with a lot of time and *no* money do," she sighed.

"So, what, you think he's in some secret society that controls the world behind the scenes?" he asked.

"I don't know, but I want to go to the library and do some digging."

"...Why don't you just look online?"

"That's what made me suspicious in the first place! I couldn't find anything personal on him. No sordid love affairs, no family history, not even a DeadDiary."

"Maybe his DeadDiary is friends only."

"John – he doesn't even have a blog."

John's mouth dropped.

"You're right, he's a freak. If you need an excuse to look at more of his photos we can go to the library tomorrow and look him up."

"Please, he's not my type," she said loftily.

"The charming, handsome type?"

"The insincere, manipulative type."

"Dude! No way!" Luke's yell again interrupted them. "*Havenford was just found dead!*"

"*What*??" they both rushed over to Luke as he used his mePhone's touchscreen to pull up the article.

"But we just saw him eating brunch!" exclaimed John.

"Does it say how? Was he murdered?" asked Erica.

"I don't know, I only know what the article tells me!" Luke said irritably.

Everybody on the floor crowded around Luke and his mePhone, which gave updates every fifteen minutes as they posted more information about Havenford's death, his family, his potential suicide, and his secret history of prescription pill abuse (in that order).

"...I didn't think that stuff could get you addicted," said Erica as they walked out that evening, just having read the most recent exposition of Havenford's dependency on analyzing-stimulants.

"Oh yeah, anals are really potent. They're great for a lazy mind, but make a habit of them and you'll be overanalyzing everything," John was saying. "He probably used them to help him with debates. You know, make better arguments."

"It would explain the filibusters," mused Erica. "Are you headed home?" she asked him before they split off.

"No, I'm going over to Mabel's to meet up with some friends," John motioned behind him.

"Oh, I've never been there before."

"Really? It's my favorite bar.... My only bar.... You should come with us, if you're not busy."

"I'm not busy."

"So that's it, then. It's over for Pro-Choice now that they lost their leading member," said Cassie as John and Erica squeezed onto stools beside their group.

"No, Morina, it *was* the right time!"

"Ankur – nobody confesses their love in the street when there's a *green light!*" Morina looked at him. "It's just common sense!"

"Ay, woman, you don't understand the drama!"

"What drama? All the cars that are gonna run me over?"

"Yeah! It's the *passion!*" said Ankur.

"Oh Ankur," she rolled her eyes in annoyance. Then she pulled him down around the neck and kissed him passionately while he almost fell off his stool.

"...Pro-Choice has officially scored the allegiance of the Recursives, who joined the rally today led by the Head of the Recursive Community, Amil Farr," Bobbert Bushnell was saying on the television that blared above them.

"Whoa! No way!" said Edgar at the T.V.

"*Way,*" nodded Bobbert.

"I don't understand why they need to involve religion in a *political* debate," Morina exclaimed vehemently, turning away from Ankur to stare angrily at the television.

"Baby, it's the Recursive Council's choice, they can do whatever they want," said Ankur.

"But is it fair of them to speak for *every* Recursive?" she turned to Ankur and asked, her voice carrying across the bar. "*I'm* a Recursive, but maybe I support Pro-Life."

"Do you?" asked Cassie, wide-eyed.

"Well, no, but it's still not fair!" said Morina. "They're just creating more conflict. And now they're putting the Chancees into an awkward position."

"Well the whole thing is stupid – their 'great divide'. I mean, if the Recursives are right, the Chancees' whole belief system is false! And vice versa! Yet each believes so wholeheartedly in their own way. Why don't they focus more on reconciling their views?" Cassie asked.

"Philosophers haven't been able to find a way to do it," John shrugged.

"See, neither of them contradict the Boble. They only differ in things beyond its scope, so neither can be proved wrong," Morina explained to her.

"Right, but if they're not taking their claims from the Boble, then how can they justify them as absolute truths?" asked Cassie.

"Oh no, not another debate about religion," said Edgar.

"Yeah, I'm down with Edgar on this one," Ankur agreed. "Let's talk about sports. Or the weather. We can even talk about makeup!"

"Well, I read in *Cosmetology* – " John began.

"No! I want to talk about religion! I haven't had a serious religious debate since college! We are having a religious debate!" demanded Morina. She banged her fist on the counter.

"Aw, Morina, you scared away the people," said Ankur as three guys who'd been sitting near their group suddenly seemed to find it a better idea to sit on the other side of the bar.

"Anyway," Morina continued, "*both* are equally credible from the standpoint of the Boble, but to me personally Recursivism makes more sense. I'm not a Recursive simply because I was *born* into it, I'm a Recursive because I *choose* to be one. I see more *depth* in it."

"Okay, but it still isn't part of the canon," said Cassie.

"Neither is Chanceism – "

"But Chanceism, at least you can look at life and come to that conclusion, that it's all random – like they're basically saying *we don't know*. 'Cause we don't, we don't know how one's token gets chosen – "

"Well, *I* feel like I know," said Morina. "I truly believe that we are meant to have the token we do based on experiences we have had in the past which are beyond our consciousness – "

"But being born over and over? That just doesn't make sense! What scientific proof is there for that conclusion?" Cassie argued.

"To me *randomness* doesn't make any sense. To say that our essences stand before the Great Wheel and spin to a random spot is ridic – *something* has to determine where it lands – !"

"Right, *accident*!"

"But how can something *so important* be determined by something so trivial?"

"That's the great irony of it! The Cosmic Joke!" Cassie's face came alight.

Morina was shaking her head. "No. To me it makes more sense that we go around the Wheel lifetime by lifetime until we complete its full course. It means we overcome everything, and that we are headed towards completion. That gives life *direction*, it gives us *purpose*."

"Who said our lives have to have purpose?" asked Cassie as she took a gulp of her beer.

"I *hope* they do!" said Morina, rather scandalized.

"I could think of a few lives that don't serve much purpose," interjected John. Edgar and Ankur chuckled.

"*Every life has to have a purpose*," said Morina firmly, returning to the conversation.

"What if our purpose is just to die?" shrugged Edgar.

"Well that's gay!" said Morina loudly.

"Is gayness a problem for you?" Edgar asked with a smile.

"Whoa, one controversial topic per discussion, please," said John.

"What about you, John?" Morina turned to him. "What do you think?"

John paused for a moment, reflecting. "Well... I really liked the idea of the Cosmic Joke, and also the idea about completing the Great Wheel full circle... but I don't know how to connect the two of them."

"Boy, that was an exciting answer. You really added a lot to the debate," said Edgar dully.

"I mean, I was born into a Recursive family, but I don't think one is right or wrong, and I'm not saying that just to avoid taking a side!"

"Uhuh."

"That was an interesting debate," said Erica as they walked back home that night.

"I don't get too involved in those," said John, "having learned my lesson too many times about revealing my truest opinions."

"Ah, I see. Well, if you ever want to unload the burden I won't judge," she smiled.

John paused a moment. "I think the whole question is bullshit," he then said flatly, "because no matter what side they're on their theories are just attempts to placate their own uncertainties. When you get down to it, that's what it's really about and in light of that I don't think the truth even matters."

***

"He and Milly have been flirting all week," said Gretchen.

"Have not!" said Milly.

"What about that letter he sent you on Saturday?" asked Dana slyly.

"That was just about a question I had that he didn't get a chance to answer!" Milly defended, blushing.

"He sent you a *letter*?" Sherrie's mouth dropped open.

"Yeah, but she hasn't even replied," Dana rolled her eyes.

"Milly! It's Wednesday!" Patricia exclaimed. "Jeez, the boy was just trying to be nice!"

"What did the letter say? Was it really personal?" asked Tai.

"No!" *How* she wished they'd leave it alone.

"Then why don't you let us read it?"

"Because it's – nevermind!" said Milly angrily, staring at her bowl of noodles.

"*Milly* and *Marvin...*" Dana started singing.

"You should dance with him at this Friday's dance," Sam insisted.

"She already rejected him at the last one," Gretchen answered before Milly could respond.

"He asked you to dance and you said no!?" Sherrie's eyes popped. Milly shrugged aloofly, maintaining her stare at her food.

"But, Milly, it's just a dance," said Patricia.

It most certainly was not *just a dance; more like a betrothal.*

"Besides, you like him!"

Milly's head shot up.

"No I don't!" she tried to sound as genuinely surprised as possible. *Man, I pulled that tone off well*, she reflected to herself.

227

"Not even a little?" coaxed Sam.

"I mean, I like *talking* to him," she said.

"Ooh!" the whole table erupted in giggles.

"Milly! You should ask him to have lunch with you!" Dana said excitedly as Milly found herself surrounded by her entire bunk.

"Lunch, alone, with him? I can't! That's too... personal!"

"You take *everything* too personally!" said Gretchen. "That's your problem! You need to be more casual."

"How?" Milly cocked her head.

"Just joke around with him like do with your guy friends," said Sam.

"Punch him playfully, that's what I do," said Meredith.

"I don't really have any guy friends," said Milly. *She wasn't like Meredith; she could never have a million guy friends.*

"Look, I don't even want to go on a date with him."

"It doesn't have to be a date. It can just be a friend thing," Sam explained.

"Yeah, Milly, you're always complaining that you don't have enough experience. Here's your chance!" said Gretchen. "*We'll* all come home with exciting stories from summer camp and what will you have? Nothing!"

The horror of such a prospect doused Milly like cold water as she realized the implications of Gretchen's words.

She reflected, "Well... a friend thing would be fun... but I don't want *him* to think it's a date!"

"Just act like it's no big deal, like 'whatever'," said Sam.

"Yeah, say 'whatever' a lot," said Gretchen.

"Is that casual?"

"It is. You want to make it seem like you're just one of the guys," Meredith counseled.

"Think insults and injuries are funny and cool," added Dana.

"Don't make a big deal over *anything*. Casually drop other guys' names so that he knows you're *just friends*," said Patricia.

The bombardment of advice was overwhelming. "What if I mess up and act really awkward?"

"You won't," Gretchen said. "You're not trying to impress him; if anything being awkward will help."

"Right..." Milly told herself. She wanted to do this. She really did. And so she resolved to be casual and approach Marvin the next day; after all, she needed to get in a good camp story and fulfill her quota of Teenage Girlhood.

***

Okay. She knew her mission. Her chance was now. Tomorrow before the dance would be a perfect time to have lunch with Marvin. It was all planned out in her mind.

There they were, standing around on the field together, talking. Milly approached.

"Hey, Milly," said Marvin as she boldly stood between him and Emmanuel.

"What's up," she said, baseball cap shielding her face from the sun.

"We were just seeing who's stronger," said Emmanuel, flexing his arms.

"Whoa! Look at those!" Milly exclaimed when Emmanuel showed her his biceps. She wasn't *really* impressed by them, but she thought she should pretend to be and make a big deal of it just for kicks, because it seemed like that's what other people did.

"I'm still stronger than all of you, though," she asserted.

"Milly, can you even bench forty?" Emmanuel asked her.

Milly had no idea what that meant.

"Uh... forty what?"

"Pounds. You know, the bar?" said Emmanuel. Marvin chuckled.

The what??

"Psh! *Yeah.*"

"Uhuh, Milly," Marvin grinned at her.

"Can *you* bench the bar?" she counteracted.

"Milly, I could pick you up with one arm," he stretched out an arm as he made a movement towards her.

229

Milly punched him.

"Ow! What was that for!" he said.

Emmanuel chuckled; Milly laughed along loudly.

"What are you, a wimp?" she asked, laughing still.

"She told you, Marvin," said Emmanuel, giving his friend a look of raised eyebrows that totally bypassed Milly's awareness.

Milly liked this, standing around in the bright sunlight, joking casually. This was nice. I mean, this was really casual.

"So, Milly, you excited for the dance tomorrow night?" Emmanuel asked.

"Whatever," she shrugged.

"Are you, uh, going with anyone?"

"I dunno. It's no big deal."

"Really?" he raised his eyebrows.

"Yeah, I'll go with whoever. I'll go with all of you if you want," she said.

"That's... interesting. Make sure to dress up for five boys, then."

"Psh, I'll probably just show up in this," she said, looking down at the old gym shorts she was currently donning.

"Oh..." he said. "Oh, look they're back. Come on, guys!" he sprinted off to meet the rest of their friends returning from soccer.

Marvin and Milly were slower in leaving.

"What, were you not good enough to make the team?" Milly joked, walking behind him a little.

"No, I don't play soccer," he said.

"Oh, so *that's* your excuse." She punched his arm again. His face flinched in her direction, but he didn't look at her.

Good, that must mean he doesn't think I'm a big deal, thought Milly.

"Hey, wanna have a friend thing tomorrow?" she asked him.

"Um... what's a friend thing?" Marvin asked, turning around.

"Like, you know, lunch."

"Are you asking me out?"

"*No*," she snorted, as if *ew, why would I do that?*

230

"Oh. Well then... no, thanks."

"What? Why not?"

"I don't want to. If you wanna go out with me, though – "

"Oh, I don't do dates. Only casual things," Milly said.

He looked at her queerly. She smiled back at him to show it didn't mean anything to her.

"What are you, five?" he asked her.

"Wh – no..." Milly said.

He shook his head. "Whatever. I'll see you around," and walked off at a quicker pace.

Milly stopped and stood there in her boyish shorts and Meredith's baseball cap staring after Marvin's retreating back, everything crashing around her.

What happened!? Milly didn't understand. She turned on the spot and ran; where she was going she did not know – but she had to get away. She relived their last moments over and over as she fled down forested paths. *What was I thinking!? I made such a fool of myself!*

Milly found herself at the entrance to an old, rather unused cabin on the grounds' edge: the guidance office. She barged into an empty waiting area. No one was there.

He's going to go tell everybody what an idiot I was and everyone will laugh at me behind my back! I was so stupid to listen to my friends! Why am I incapable of being casual!? The sober realizations of what had just happened now crashed over her, moments too late.

She blinked around to dry the fresh tears leaking out of her eyes, her attention caught by an array of brightly colored brochures about self-esteem, pregnancy, or your menstrual cycle. One was titled "So You Want to be Yourself...."

This might be just what I need, a dash of hope ran through her as she picked it up and unfolded its purple pages:

So You Want to Be Yourself
A Guide to Being the Real You

Growing up can be a stressful experience fraught with peer pressure and low self-esteem. This often makes teenagers act in

231

ways they don't want to so they'll be accepted by their peers. But the only *real* solution to adolescence's trials is to *just be yourself!* How does one *"be oneself"*? Here are some useful tips!

- Only buy the Hollister shirts you really like, not the ones everyone else is wearing. Make sure your Hollister shirt enables you to express who you are.

- Don't change the music on your mePod to reflect your friends' taste. When you browse meTunes feel free to explore genres that are less mainstream. In fact, some of your peers might think you're pretty unique!

- And remember, just because everyone picks option A doesn't mean you should feel pressured to follow suit. It's your life, and you have total freedom to choose options B, C, or D.

Sometimes it is best to have a good role model. Here are some examples of kids like you who aren't afraid to be themselves:

- Take Josh: he has a lot of passionate political beliefs, but he's sometimes intimidated to address controversial topics in public. Should he back down? No!

- Look at Ashley: her parents certainly aren't what you'd call "average". Should she be embarrassed by them when they come to pick her up from school? No!

So you see, grasshopper, being yourself is the key to a happy adolescence! Just *be yourself* and others will appreciate you for who you are.

***

Milly threw the pamphlet back and left without a word, back to her cabin where her diary, a much better counselor, was waiting for her in its secret hiding place which is so secret even *I* don't know where it is.

***

"You're not supposed to be here," said Gretchen when Milly sat down at their table for lunch the next afternoon.

"Stop being sarcastic, I know you know," Milly replied moodily.

"Know what?" Gretchen asked, confused.

"That I'm not having lunch with Marvin."

"Did you reject him *again*?"

"No, he didn't want to have lunch with me," said Milly.

Everyone's mouths dropped.

"*What?*"

"Didn't you guys know?" Milly looked around at them.

"No," they all shook their heads.

Milly could've sworn that all morning they were being carefully polite to her to avoid making her feel embarrassed. "Well, just ask the guys, Marvin probably told them everything," she said.

"No, Dominic hasn't said anything to me," said Gretchen.

"Oh. That was nice of him," Milly was a mite perplexed.

"What happened?" asked Tai as everyone leaned in.

"I made a huge fool of myself. I tried to be casual, but it came out completely fake! I couldn't go back to the soccer game and be around him; I went to the guidance office and then back to our cabin and then I went to the lake and cried for like an hour."

"I had no idea you were so crushed! You didn't say anything about it all night!" said Tai.

"What a jerk!" said Meredith angrily.

234

"No, no, it wasn't his fault," Milly assured them. "I mean, he can't help it if he doesn't like me. Besides, he could've been a lot worse about it; I should be grateful that he didn't spread the word and make me look like an idiot publicly," she said, more to herself than to them; and she took great comfort in this realization. "It's not the end of the world if *one person* doesn't like me, right? And I still want to be friends.... I should apologize when I see him tonight for acting so weird," Milly said thoughtfully. "Plus, on the bright side, I overcame a fear. This experience made me stronger, and that's something to take away," she said positively. She already felt better, emboldened with the hard-won self-confidence needed to embrace the bright July sunlight streaming through the dining hall windows, carrying with it the promise of new beginnings.

"No!" Gretchen shouted. "Don't *apologize* to him!" Her scandalized cry brought Milly crashing down from her self-induced high. "Why would you feel grateful to an idiot who rejected an amazing girl like you!?"

"What?" this made no sense.

"I'd be mad," Meredith nodded affirmatively.

"But – " how could she be mad at him for a personal decision? As far as she was concerned, it was her job to accept his answer gracefully – "isn't the important thing that I overcome the self-depreciating attitude I automatically take on in such situations and overstep my ego by not harboring either blame or self-hatred?" Milly questioned.

"I guess," said Gretchen.

"Milly, why don't you think, 'I am really great, and anyone would be crazy to reject me'?" asked Sam.

"... Should I?"

"Yes!" everyone burst out as if it were the most obvious thing.

"So I should demand to know why he rejected me?" Milly asked.

"No!" Gretchen warned. "Under no circumstances should you be the first one to approach! He should come to you."

"Why?"

"Because otherwise he'll know you're not over it."

"But I'm not – "

"If he sees you surrounded by your friends, laughing and having a good time, he'll realize you're confident enough to move on and begin to wonder whether he made a mistake in rejecting you," Tai recited *Fifteen* magazine's love advice column for her.

"So what do I do if he approaches me?"

"Avoid him," said Dana. "It sounds paradoxical, but you have to be aloof. You might even want to ignore him completely."

"So I shouldn't mail him the reply to his letter I wrote?" Milly asked.

"No!" they all shouted, scandalized. Milly recoiled: she'd had the urge to mail it the next morning as a sign of friendship. But if everyone perceived the gesture so weirdly, wouldn't Marvin do the same? Milly didn't know how to think about this. It had seemed like such a good idea in her head, but everyone's negative reactions threw her own judgment into the most extreme of doubt! Judging by their tones, *they* were certain. Whereas she, Milly, was certain of only one thing: that she was not certain of anything.

... And maybe she wasn't even certain of that!

***

Milly was not having fun at the dance. She'd done everything her friends had told her: acted like she was having fun, ignored Marvin, been aloof.

And yet, unless her mind was deceiving her, the strategy was failing completely! Marvin hadn't glanced her way once the entire night: from what she saw, *he* was the one having fun!

That's the last time I'll listen to my friends, Milly thought angrily again as they stood conversing on the fringes of the basketball court/dance floor. *I should have done what I wanted.*

Just as she was about to storm out of the dance, Gretchen came out of nowhere and grabbed Milly's arm.

"Come on! We're going to the lake!" she hissed in Milly's ear.

"But that's off limits after nine!"

"*Camp story*, remember!?"

"Oh yeah!" Milly broke into a run with her. They fled the scene of the dance and bypassed the trail back to camp, taking a less-traveled dirt path on the outskirts of the woods as the pop music faded gently behind them.

"Shh!" they heard a male whisper as they hurtled through the trees into the clearing at last. "Stop giggling, you all!" It was Emmanuel.

"*I* wasn't giggling. Stop, guys, we'll get caught!" said Meredith to her bunkmates.

Everyone went silent.

The boys – their boys – were standing by the dark lake, throwing stones across its ink surface. There was Marvin, taking a turn with a stone of his own. He didn't even glance back at the sound of their footsteps.

Look at how pretty the surroundings are! Milly forced herself to think with wonderment. She skipped excitedly off to the lake's bank to stare into the liquid darkness. It shimmered with little golden lights from the buildings on its distant edges, and rippled gently as Milly's fingertips skimmed its surface.

"Pretty, isn't it?"

"Mhmm," she said before she could stop herself. Marvin had approached her space.

Be aloof! Don't be friendly, she reminded herself sternly as he stood next to her.

"So, only two more days of camp," he said again.

Milly shrugged without looking at him.

"This is probably my last summer here."

"Really? What are you gonna do next – " and then she cut off abruptly. *Darn it!*

"What am I doing next summer? Probably working."

That sucks, thought Milly. But this time she controlled herself and made no outward response.

"I'm gonna miss the people here," said Marvin. Milly half-glanced to her right at him, her heart thumping; she knew where this was going.

"We should stay in touch," Marvin said. "Although maybe you should give me your phone number since you don't do so well with answering letters," he grinned.

Milly was caught; she didn't know how she should respond. So she shrugged again. And then she moved some grass around with her foot while her arms were folded, as if she were really bored and he was no one to her and she didn't care about him or anything he thought.

"So... can I have your number?"

"Why?" she asked in a tone of surprise as if his request was completely out of place because they, like, barely knew each other and why would she give a stranger her number?

"So that we can talk..." he said slowly.

"I probably won't even answer, I'm terrible with phones," Milly waved it away, shaking her head, to explain it away yet make it seem like this was a trifle to her and she had gotten past his rejection – no, like his rejection had never happened – and, to her, they were just two people who had no significant connection whatsoever.

Marvin sighed.

"Alright, Milly, I understand," he said, and turned, and started walking away.

"Are you alright?" Milly asked in pretend surprise, as if she couldn't for the life of her understand what had come over him no matter how deeply she searched within the recesses of her emotions, which knew the truth of the matter. She wanted the outward manifestations to convey as clearly as possible that there was nothing between them, that all their personal and slightly uncomfortable interactions had never really happened and had *definitely* never been seen as anything noteworthy in her mind because they hadn't affected her whatsoever, and she was totally oblivious to everything (even though of course she wasn't *really*; in fact, just the opposite was true). And to top off the performance, she showed concern for this random guy next to her who was suddenly blue for no apparent reason because she didn't want her fellow human beings to be upset, even when they were strangers she didn't have any connection to.

At that question, Marvin snapped right around and faced her.

"I don't get you, Milly!" he said passionately. Milly's careful balancing act swayed on its tightrope from the gusty breeze of his words.

"There's nothing to get!" she righted it, vainly re-crossing her arms.

"So that's all there is to you? A confused little girl who acts like a different person every day?"

She just looked at him, paralyzed.

"Why don't you act as *you* are?" he asked.

"I *do*, around my friends – "

Marvin turned abruptly around and walked away from the spot without another word.

What just happened? Milly asked herself, utterly confused again. She repeated the last tidbit of conversation to herself – and gasped, realizing what her "aloofness" had led her to do. She had an impulse to chase after him and explain, finally be honest – but she found it too hard to act on such an impulse for fear of what might happen. And so she let the impulse die as she remained standing by the lakeshore among the crickets. Now only its aftertaste pulsed through her being, ever dimmer with each passing moment, and ever less able to rise again as defeat swept over her in its place. So she remained there, looking out at the dark water.

***

Milly didn't say much at breakfast. She felt sobered from the events of the week by the quiet Saturday of Camp Putentach. She couldn't get rid of the feeling of defeat, but strangely, she also felt somehow new. The passing storm had left things quiet, letting her breathe and reflect on what was now gone. There was nothing to do but accept it and move forward.

One thing was for sure: she'd had enough with trying to act like this, or trying to act like that – anything but acting like herself!

What's wrong with the way I want to do things? she demanded of herself angrily.

She finished eating and stared around at her friends, still working away on their breakfasts.

I don't have to wait for them; what am I, dependent?

"I'm gonna go pick some wildflowers. I'll see you guys back at the cabin," Milly announced happily, getting up from the table.

"Okay," said Gretchen, chewing her food, looking up at Milly.

Milly put away her tray and skipped outside in the morning sunshine, happily and boldly going on her own way.

Everything was so alive! She smiled at the beauty of life around her.

A group of laughing girls who passed by Milly caught her eye.

Why didn't I invite someone else to come with me? the thought struck Milly as she glanced back at them. *I could've just asked if anyone else wanted to come along instead of going off on my own, yet I didn't even think of it! What's wrong with me!?* it boggled her.

Whoa! said a cautionary voice in her head. *One complex at a time....*

Chapter 17: The Chapter That's Really a Chapter

"Just three minutes! I had to turn off the T.V. for three minutes and miss the not-to-be-missed C-Span moment of the year!" exclaimed John as they strolled down the sunny streets that Friday afternoon, having spent all day cooped up in the library.

"I'm sure it's online," Erica said.

"Hopefully," John sighed. "And if not, it'll at least be in the next issue of *Mortician Monthly*, I can assure you."

"Are you sure you never wanted to be a mortician?" she asked him.

"I'm sure," John said flatly. "I just like the magazine."

They walked freely along. Street performers played mediocre guitar, people bustled past fast in conversation, vendors swatted away flies. It was a beautiful city day.

"I wish Mabel's lived up to its name," said Erica, rubbing her stomach as they passed by the bar.

"There's a restaurant next door, The Restaurant That's Really a Restaurant," said John.

"Is it good?"

"Dunno, never been there. I hear it's upscale."

"We should go."

"Okay."

Before John could react, Erica grabbed his hand and turned them sharply ninety degrees and up the steps toward the restaurant's doors.

"I didn't realize you meant right now," he was mildly taken aback.

The massive windows let the light of sun stream inside and fall over the vines hanging over whitewashed archways and little patio tables at which couples dined and sipped coffee, their feet scuffling over the garden-stone-paved floor. It gave the impression of dining outdoors by a vineyard. Judging by the clientele, it was the vineyard of a private estate, and John quickly reexamined his clothes, which were several notches too casual.

"...If I were him, I'd want to visit other planets. I wonder if he can do that," Erica said once they were seated and had placed their orders.

"Okay, I can understand reaching the Land of Missing Socks – but other planets!? That's just impossible!" John shook his head. "Although that's probably exactly what makes it possible," he added as an afterthought.

"Do you think the person who could absorb others' tokens would have his ability, too?" she voiced the sudden thought.

"Technically he should," said John as he munched on the free bread.

"Too bad they didn't know each other, then the poor guy could've had someone to travel with," said Erica.

They sensed him before they saw him; the pointed cologne was not offensive, but accurate as an arrow.

"Well, look who it is!" said a voice above them. Sajan Walker, dressed in a button-down shirt and a pair of breezy summer slacks, his arm snaked around a beautiful, slim blonde, stood before them. A golden tie adorned his neck, a bold statement that he warped into sophistication with the perfect complement of a few pieces of dark hair falling out of their jaunty part. Diners at neighboring tables stared at him; his assured light smile betrayed his awareness of his own effect.

"Nolene, this is Edmund Daltuhn's daughter, Erica," he said. "And this is John Hal – Hol – er – ?"

"Hallan," said John.

"Right! They both work at NKOZ, interning I think."

"No we're not," said John as Nolene surveyed them haughtily with her ice blue eyes.

"I didn't expect to see you two so far from the office," he said, gracing them with a mischievous grin.

"Oh, we've been at the library since morning, uh, doing some research," said Erica, stealing an uncomfortable glance at John.

"Ah – *morning*. That's what you miss when you're self-employed," sighed Sajan.

"It took someone *how* long to get out of bed today?" Nolene playfully pinched his arm.

"You're lucky you have that structure," Sajan nodded, ignoring the flirtation. "Waking up at noon throws off my whole day."

"How do you bear it," said John.

"Well, it's a give and take. On the other hand you have the freedom over your life, and that's what I like best. It's not the money, it's how the lifestyle suits my personality, I'm one of those self-regulated types," Sajan explained, turning to Nolene for confirmation, which she gave via nod. "Self-employment isn't for everyone, though. I mean, *I'd* never be able to go back to a nine-to-five corporate, but that's just me."

"Do you even remember what that's like?" Nolene asked, a note of admiration rumbling underneath her skeptical words.

Sajan laughed. "Not really. It must've been since I was, what, your age, John" – he looked up, recalling – "no, younger!"

"Well, Sajan, we weren't all blessed with the artistic genius it takes to break out. Whenever I see a Kimi Kool commercial I *marvel* over the creative juices that needed to spill to make such a refined work of art," John looked at Sajan. Erica looked at him.

"Oh, John! Talent is five percent, *maybe*. The rest is direction. You have to know where you're going from an early age, and none of that switching careers business, that'll land you in a rut," Sajan said.

"I always knew I wanted to be a model, ever since I was a little girl," Nolene nodded.

"And Sajan must've always known he wanted to design commercials for seven-year-olds' dolls dressed as prostitutes," said Erica.

Silence.

John and Erica's food appeared in front of them out of thin air.

Nolene looked up and gasped. "Is that Congressman Alaleem?" she pulled on Sajan's arm.

"It is! I have to go say 'hi'! Good seeing you kids!" and he and Nolene hurried off.

"...Congressman? What a pleasant surprise!" they heard in winning tones in the distance.

"Ah, Mr.... Walker?"

"I told you to call me Sajan. What brings you and your lovely wife to this part of town?"

"We have reservations for lunch."

"I told you we should've made reservations, Nolene," came Sajan's lament. "The wait is ridiculous, we've been here for forty minutes."

"Really?" Alaleem gasped.

"Well, we wanted balcony seating. We'll just try back when it's less crowded."

"Oh, Sajan, that's such a shame; you hype this place up so much," said Nolene.

"Well it *is* my favorite," he chuckled.

"Oh – why don't you two join us?" came a forced voice.

"We'd love to, Congressman, but I've dallied enough. I should get back to my office. Next time you're in town, Nolene, I promise. She's never been to Vandorn before."

"Never? Then I insist! Their steak is phenomenal."

"I can't argue with that," Sajan acceded.

"Sajan, take some time out of your busy schedule, enjoy life!"

"Well, alright," came Sajan's chuckle.

"Ah – we would like to add two to our table, please," said Alaleem.

"Certainly," replied a hostess' voice.

She led the quartet around, past John and Erica's table to an upstairs balcony; neither Sajan nor Nolene made eye contact with them to indicate that they had just spoken a minute before.

"Boy, do you see how Mrs. Alaleem is staring down Sajan's date?" asked Erica quietly as they watched the older woman turn her nose up at the full view of Nolene's slinky-backed dress before her.

"I'd like to see how critical she would be if she could dress the same," John replied. "Then she'd call it confidence, throw in something about women's rights, and get her picture plastered on a magazine as a role model for women today."

The conversation carried down quite audibly from the balcony overhead.

"...Honestly, I find it ridiculous that we *don't* already have a one-president system. We're supposed to be the most advanced country in the world, yet we stick to an outmoded structure that keeps alive the prejudice and discrimination we've been working for decades to get rid of. It's never *been* a riper time to change!"

"I couldn't agree more, Sajan. I wish you would take that passion onto the streets."

"You and I both! My cousin is one of the founders of Pro-Life."

"Really?"

"Yes. I was just telling her how much I wish I could partake – unfortunately, expanding the company overseas has had me flying to and fro Bouclé like crazy."

"Congratulations!" exclaimed a surprised Alaleem's voice.

"Oh, thank you. It's the crème atop the torte, really. In the last three months alone I've *tripled* my revenue!"

"What are you going to do with the extra?" Alaleem asked.

"You mean the protion I don't give to Pro-Life? I was thinking of building another house overseas. Nothing too fancy, just a stone number with a wraparound porch in the countryside. Either that or a new car."

"Have you seen next year's models?"

"Last year," Sajan took a bored sip of wine. "Though to be honest, it's been my dream to have a place in the mountains; I'm an outdoorsman."

"Ah! I am as well!"

"Get out! Have I taken you on my yacht before?"

"You have not."

"Congressman, it's a *date*!" they chinked glasses.

The setting sun cast plum shadows over the still houses as they looped slowly around Erica's neighborhood to dispel the weight of dinner in their stomachs, talking about nothing and everything. John felt as peaceful as he had in Lainii so many months ago, watching the cerulean sky deepening above them. Nothing disturbed the summer silence, save for a gazebo full of preteen girls: they were giggling and gossiping loudly, faces lit by the lamplight and breast buds poking through their Hollister t-shirts.

"I dare you to scream 'penis' out loud!" said Maggie as John and Erica walked by.

"Okay!" said Ally. "PENIS!!!!!!!!!" she screamed at the top of her voice.

"Heeheeheeheehee!" chorused a quartet of girls.

"You know what would be even funnier? If you screamed 'vagina'!" said Joy.

"Watch this: PENIS AND VAGINA!!!!!!!!!!!!!"

They rolled around on the floor of the gazebo, laughing their heads off. A cell phone rang, playing "Pick dat Shit Up (Off da Flo')" by Hoodlumz. Ally picked up her cell.

"Hey, wazzup?... nuthin much... chillin at the gazebo. You gonna come?... Yeah, you *better* bring your sexy ass here!... Alright, 'bye, lol."

"That was Roger," she said.

"Ooooh!"

"Oh my *Bob*, Casey, you're so immature," Ally rolled her eyes. "Have you even kissed a boy?"

"*No*, Casey doesn't get any!" said Maggie, crossing her legs the other way because her g-string was bothering her....

"...By now you would've seen millions, and if you looked out at the ocean it was like a sea of stars over an enormous field of rolling black waves," said John.

"I've never seen more than two stars at once," said Erica.

"That's what was *really* great about Lainii. Not the fancy resort with its bars in the pool, that stuff was boring. At least for me."

"It would be for me, too," she said. "I'd much rather know what it's like to live out of one of those shanties than in a lavish resort where everything is handed to you and it's boring. It's strange," she turned contemplative, "that working constantly for the most mundane things is what fills life with richness, probably that same richness people seek by buying mansions."

"It's still the same want... people just look for it in the wrong place and don't know it," said John.

"But if you even just think about it, owning a mansion is an enormous burden after you get past the bragging rights. All the practical things to take care of, and inevitably realizing that most of it is a waste of space. Poverty is the true freedom. But we're taught to want mansions."

"I don't want a mansion.... But I wouldn't want to live in a hut either," said John, and Erica laughed.

"Where would you want to live, then?"

"To be honest, it doesn't matter to me. I could live in a mansion or a hut or an apartment or anything in between but I think life would basically remain the same," he answered. "That's kind of how I feel about everything. Like, there's nothing I *really* want. And then I don't know where to go."

"Ah, I have the opposite problem. I want everything... but the end result is the same," said Erica.

"So you don't know what you want?" John asked, then paused, and smirked. "Not surprising," he muttered.

She hit him lightly. "Of course I know what I want," she said.

"What do you want?" he asked.

"I just... *want.*"

John walked through his front door in buoyant spirits, humming to himself, just in time to coincidentally match pitch with the Kimi Kool commercial playing on T.V:

Kimi Kool sashayed her hips across the screen against a background of neat city streets lined with quaint boutiques and chic cafes. There was not a speck of litter on the ground. None of the dozens of boring, expressionless inhabitants milling about were as uninhibited as she, who alone could dance in the streets to the music that enlivened their world with complete disregard for social norms. Everyone else was too constrained by society.

Kimi Kool's frayed-denim-mini came dangerously close to exposing her butt as she moved about freespiritedly. But she had black leggings underneath. They were a perfect match to her tight black tank top that had the word "REBEL" printed across the front in rhinestones, and the rings of black eyeliner that rimmed her big blue eyes. She winked one at the camera.

"Nothing can stop me from expressing who I am!" Kimi Kool declared as she walked along the street, ogled for her bold statement by the less important and more conventional cartoon dolls in plain t-shirts and khakis. She spun around in the middle of the street with her arms out, while a woman standing nearby covered her child's eyes.

"...*New* Kimi Kool Social Rebel doll!" the voice-over exclaimed as the commercial showed how to dip real-life Kimi Kool's hair into cold water to produce neon pink streaks in it.

"You're back already?" John asked Milly as the regular program resumed.

"Shh!" she hissed from the couch, where she sat watching a nervous hopeful auditioning before the judges on *Artinian Artist*.

"*...Babydoll, you sound just like last season's winner.*"

"*So I'm in?*"

"*You're in!*"

"Where are mom and dad?" he asked.

"I dunno," said Milly flatly. "Why are you in such a good mood?"

"I just had a good day," he shrugged as he passed her going upstairs. He went to his room and flopped onto his bed, his peace too soon disrupted by a sudden argument that erupted down the hall.

"*You just spent a month with your friends and you want to have a sleepover!?*" Mr. Hallan was yelling.

"*Dad – !*"

"All she does is watch T.V. and go on the computer, Merle!" Mr. Hallan yelled to his wife.

"That's not true!" Milly yelled back, crying.

There was the slam of a door.

MilE45: hey, i can't sleep over tonight :(

CutieBabe33: aww

MilE45: my parents are sOoOoOo unfair!!

CutieBabe33: yeah

CutieBabe33: hey wanna make a yourspot account for u??

MilE45: yeah! i don't care what my parents say, i'm not a baby anymore!

CutieBabe33: what r u gonna use 4 ur account name?

MilE45: ...Milly

CutieBabe33: no thats boring!

CutieBabe33: do something fun, like millyroxursox

MilE45: eww...that's stupid

CutieBabe33: how about Milé

CutieBabe33: it sounds sophisticated

MilE45: but that's not my name

CutieBabe33: ugh wtvr do what u want

MilE45: but

MilE45: i mean do other people just use their names?

CutieBabe33: barely

CutieBabe33: but its ur page

 MilE45: check it out: yourspot.com/mile45

MilE45: i decided to just use my sn

CutieBabe33: y did you put up a photo of a flower as ur default pic?

MilE45: it's pretty!

CutieBabe33: ur soo weird

MilE45: i don't have any good photos of me!

CutieBabe33: here:photobox.com/taidie4567/photo473

MilE45: ew! i look sooo ugly

CutieBabe33: photobox.com/taidie4567/photo474

MilE45: ugh are you kidding?

CutieBabe33: omb!

CutieBabe33: photobox.com/taidie4567/photo512

MilE45: ew that's the one where i'm making that weird kissy face

CutieBabe33: omb you look so good there put it up!

MilE45: i hate it

CutieBabe33: i can fix it

Tai opened her photo editing software and clicked on the "Beer Can" button, an option that allowed one to add a can of cheap beer to any photo. She dragged the little icon to Milly's lips, saved it, and resent the photo to Milly.

Name: MilE45

Age: 16

About: Hi! I'm Milly and I'm a 16-year-old student at Peamount High in Vandorn. I'm going to be a junior this year and I'm really excited! I have an older brother named John (he's sooo annoying! You know how older brothers are :P). My favorite food is apples. I'd like to be a writer or illustrator when I finish school, but if that doesn't work I'll just bum around and do nothing (like my brother). Just kidding! I won't really do that. And just kidding about my brother, too – he's got a job and everything. Well, not everything, he still lives at home. Anyway, I really like writing, playing with animals, collecting seashells, and baking/eating muffins. I do not like sports or computer class. I guess that's pretty ironic because I'm on a computer right now, but oh well :P. That's about it, I guess. Also, I really miss Camp Putentach!

MilE45: look i already have a friend!

CutieBabe33: everyones friends with the creator

MilE45: oh

CutieBabe33: i wrote on ur wall

CutieBabe33: write back on mine!

MilE45: kkk!

***

John and Erica burst through the doors of the thirtieth floor, laughing, John with a cup of coffee in one hand. Luke, Nelson, and Mr. Daltuhn stared at them as they walked into the meeting room, and they immediately quenched their laughter as they took seats around the table. John caught Mr. Daltuhn's eye and quickly looked in the opposite direction.

"Hallan!" John's eyes snapped back onto him, alertly. "I want you out of here at the end of this meeting! No dawdling around. You hear me?"

"Yes, sir," John nodded.

"Ooh, is he fired?" asked Luke.

It was Wednesday – two days until token registration was due. Having accosted John with a demand to know that he'd found his token, and finding out that the answer was 'no', Mr. Daltuhn took matters into his own hands and forced John to make a trip John had known deep down was coming: to the Token Directory.

The Token Directory was the Artinian headquarters for research on tokens. Artinia was among the only countries in the world to house such a building, as it had been considered for millennia all across the globe a sacrilegious thing to tamper with tokens, a topic so sacred it must be left untouched. Thus Artinia had become the first country to move past that belief. But a horde of other countries was currently following in Artinia's foorsteps by building Token Directories of their own.

It sat in the heart of the city, a boulder sinking into the concrete. John wove through a jungle of tall, gray-tinted buildings threaded with narrow alleys to reach it. Innermost Vandorn seemed to implode on itself.

He headed through the revolving front doors. The lobby resembled a museum, with dark gray, glittering, polished stone floors and a large front desk area of the same that curved around a third of the wall. John approached this desk. If not for Mr. Daltuhn's name he would not be allowed inside.

"...Oh, here's your pen back," he heard a voice say while he waited for the receptionist to confirm his identity. Three men had just stepped out of the elevator across the lobby, two of whom wore suits and the other who was in a gray coverall uniform with a military badge pinned to it. It was he who had spoken.

"Thanks! Thought I lost it," one of the other men reached for the pen. "What the – "

His hand grasped thin air. The military man let out a cackle, the image of the pen still in his hand.

"Bobdamn you, I hate when you do that!" yelled the man in the suit as the three of them walked out the door.

A minute later, the two suited men returned without the third, who was seemingly a visitor to the building.

"Bob, I hate when he comes over here," muttered the one still missing his pen.

"Must get lonely on Shun," said the other.

"Yeah, that's not a day job I'd wanna have...."

With a wristband, John was authorized to proceed. The silence was not peaceful, but unsettling. John looked around and picked up the *Official Guide to Tokens* issued by the Token Directory. He flipped to the section titled "General Categories of Tokens," and read:

All tokens can be classified into one of several categories: Physical Tokens, Emotional Tokens, Mental Tokens, and Abstract Tokens.

Physical Tokens are the most commonly occurring kind, and are a bodily anomaly or an ability rooted in the physical world. They are visible to the naked eye, and can be readily accessed and controlled by the possessor. There come in the widest variety, ranging from extra limbs to x-ray vision, to flight or the ability to set up a force field around oneself, to channeling a force of nature. The possessors of such tokens often find them useful, and they are always applied to the altering of the physical reality. They have a large range of power, with some being innocuous and relatively ineffectual, and others being destructive, especially if uncontrolled. As of last year, eighty-three percent of the total world population possessed a Physical Token.

Emotional Tokens are much rarer than Physical Tokens and, unlike Physical Tokens, can only be triggered by a strong emotional response. Therefore they are not described as a physical anomaly, because when latent they are nonexistent, even though they can have a physical manifestation. Emotional Tokens may also work by invisibly altering the emotional states of others, and therefore generally have a more strongly psychological effect on either their possessors, people around their possessors, or both. They are more difficult to control but usually more powerful than Physical Tokens. An estimated five percent of the world has this type. The most common manifestations are to force others to empathize with one's own feeling, to force others to profess feelings, or to display one's feelings in some unique way.

Mental Tokens are, unlike Physical and Emotional Tokens, completely invisible to the outside world, existing only in their possessors' minds. They are therefore the most difficult to assess, and are usually determined by the seeming lack of token in one. They manifest as a mental ability not inherent to the average human mind, as for example the ability to run three distinct streams of thought at once. Some Mental Tokens can be easily identified with outside help, such as the ability to probe others' thoughts, recall others' memories, and communicate telepathically. Other Mental Tokens are very difficult to notice, as they are subtle differences in perception and the possessor may not even realize they possess an abnormality of thought. In such cases, usually the Token is discovered by actively comparing differences in thought processes among people to find the anomaly. Roughly twelve percent of the world's population possesses a Mental Token.

Abstract Tokens, or Weightless Tokens, are those classified as not being a *thing*, or having an essence that can be pinpointed. They are the rarest and most poorly understood type, and any Token unable to fit into one of the above categories is labeled Abstract. Examples of this type include: the ability to mimic Tokens, the ability to nullify Tokens, and the ability to give one's Token away. As is evident, such Tokens cannot be given a shape or form of their own, but rely entirely on external circumstances. It is estimated that less than point one percent of people possess such a token....

John walked out of the Token Directory into the late afternoon sunlight, dejected and tired. There stood Erica, waiting for him outside the building. One look at his face told her everything.

"It's alright," John shrugged, smiling, as she patted his arm sympathetically.

Suddenly he felt the burden removed from his shoulders and the oppressiveness of downtown Vandorn evaporated like a wisp.

Outside in the warm air, he could smell the waters of the harbor on the other side of the building. He knew the way the murky waters lapped up against the sloping slate walls of the industrial park, opening to the blue-green waters of the bay and out toward the chilly ocean. Far out in the bay lay Shun Island, housing the old military detention center. Many fantastical things were rumored to reside there, from secret experiments to unreported torture to housing of futuristic weapons and portals into other lands. It was there that the military man John had seen hours before worked.

"I thought they closed it down," said Erica when she and John stood facing it by the dock, watching the water. The island was beyond their sight.

"There are rumors that it's still open and the government is running all sorts of experiments on it with top criminals they've captured," said John.

Erica looked at him rather skeptically. "Wouldn't people *know*? I mean, airplanes fly over it," she said.

"Why would they keep it off-limits, then? The whole thing is blocked."

"How do you know?"

"In high school we'd try to canoe there. Some kids made it all the way there and said they came up to nothing more than a fifty-foot-high solid wall of concrete. And they couldn't blow it up, or fly over it, or anything. It was well protected."

"Did you ever try to go there?" Erica asked.

"Once."

"What happened?"

"My mom woke up in the middle of the night, sensing I was gone. I didn't think it worked while she was asleep; unfortunately, it's *extra* sensitive when she's asleep," sighed John. "The police found me a couple blocks from my house."

Thus the island sat tantalizingly out of reach, a real-life unsolved mystery in their mundane world that still held John's curiosity.

"I've never met someone who works on Shun Island before. I thought they'd be more... clandestine. This guy just seemed like an ordinary Joe, a bit of a bum even," said John.

"The ability to make mirages *is* pretty rare," said Erica.

"Yeah, good thing, too," said John under his breath.

"Who knows, maybe this whole world is that guy's mirage, and he keeps it up so we don't all go insane," said Erica, a slow grin creeping over her face.

"Well, if that's the case, I'm not complaining," he glanced at her. Erica's grin turned into a quick smile, and they turned around and started walking back, hand in hand, headed toward the sunset.

Chapter 18: The Cult of the Greater

Long ago, when the world was new and the first mortal civilization at its peak, there was only the Great Wheel, presided over by Bob. Bob ruled the mortals from His realm, assisted by His Immortal Agents, who dwelt in His realm with Him. Of these Immortal Agents was one whom Bob held closest to His Eternal Heart: Pat. While the other Agents roamed the Realm in bliss, Pat would often peer into the world below and observe the mortals, watching them with an inquisitive and curious spirit. Much of what he saw perplexed him, but nothing more so than their suffering. So he said to Bob:

"I have often observed the mortals from afar, and they seem to always be 'suffering'. I do not understand it, for I have never suffered before."

Bob replied: "That is because there is no suffering in My Realm."

Pat said: "I pity them; I can see that this 'suffering' is what keeps them from bliss. The other life forms on their planet do not suffer; why must they?"

Bob saw that this question caused Pat much concern, for he was the most sympathetic of the Immortal Agents, and so He explained to Pat: "Despair not, for their fate is not hopeless. There is a Law I have given them which functions in their world: the Law of Bob. By following this Law during their lives, they may reach our Realm and obtain bliss," said Bob.

"What is the Law of Bob?" asked Pat.

"The Law of Bob is to follow one's conscience; not 'conscience' as their society defines it, but what they know in their hearts to be the right course of action apart from outer circumstance. For the mortals such conscience is the supreme undeniable truth. Only one who brings it to the surface in spite of the surrounding what they call 'reality' will reach Me and be freed from his suffering. But if a mortal fails his conscience, betrays it in action, or buries it inside himself to claim another as truth – woe unto him and his life! For he is doomed to bask in the mire of suffering for all eternity and never to reach

Me!" spoke Bob. "All mortals innately know the Law of Bob. It is knowing this Law but being unable to follow it, or to ignore it, which breeds their suffering."

Bob spoke further: "I will send you to their world as a mortal so that you may live as they do and understand their suffering. And to prove that the mortals may reach Me I will give you a task: in their world there is a mountain called the Mountain of Mysteries, jutting out into the sky above the flat plains on which they live. You must climb this mountain, and at its summit you will again meet Me, and I will take you back home to our Realm. Therefore you will know that it is possible."

Pat accepted Bob's task. He separated from Him and came down to the world of the mortals.

The mortal life is difficult from the outset, thought Pat as he bore his first taste of suffering the first night, feeling cold, hunger, and fear. He found shelter with a hospitable family who fed and clothed him for no reward. A strange feeling welled within Pat, and he came to realize that such relations were what made mortal suffering bearable.

From this family, who allowed Pat to stay with them, Pat learned of the need to find work in order to obtain the money he would need to live independently in their world. He set out to the nearby city the next morning and soon found such work.

Though food and shelter had alleviated his pain, the work he did to keep it at bay brought suffering just the same. He looked around at the natural world, struck by its beauty, and wished nothing more than to spend his days wandering it. But he could not, for his work constrained him to spend his days working to advance another mortal's aims instead of his own, and by the time he came home at night he had energy for little more than sleep.

For a long time Pat kept up this lifestyle until he acquired enough wealth to detach from his host family. *At last I am independent,* he thought with relief.

But soon enough he encountered other forms of suffering: not all mortals were as kind as his host family, and most were not above trickery or deceit when their own interests were at stake. Though often friendly, they forgot that for the pursuit of their personal desires. These relations repeatedly caused Pat humiliation, dejection, and anger, for they were so unlike what he had known in the Realm of Bob. *The mortals say, 'it is a cold world,'* he thought, *yet it seems not to be the world which is cold, but they.*

After a while Pat learned to maneuver through these obstacles and became accustomed to self-reliance, and went along more or less normally until he chanced to meet a certain female. Their relations were different from all his others, and a stronger, more vibrant force than any Pat had known drew them together. She was the one mortal whom Pat felt had his best interests in her heart, and he had hers in his own, for he always thought of her. The fulfillment of this relationship obliterated all suffering, and Pat felt he had found the key to a happy mortal life. *What more could I want?* he wondered as his heart bounded with joy. But fate separated the two of them, and though Pat did not want it to end, he could not hold on. Alone, Pat experienced the most intense suffering he had ever known. He began to think of many things that had never bothered him before; his inevitable death, his nothingness, the complexity of mortal affairs and many questions besides tormented him. He became consumed by worry and anxious mental states. This constant suffering could see no end; but day by day, Pat began to slowly even out.

At last at the end of two years, Pat understood a great deal about mortal suffering. His experiences had made him sober-minded, and he stopped minding the suffering of everyday life; he came to regard it a healthy way of life, one that strengthened the mortals. He assimilated into their society fully, captured by the allure of temporary delights, busying himself with women, with gambling, with wine, with schemes to make more money and with talk amongst the intellectual circles of the day. He had forgotten the reason he was there in the first place. But after a while he grew tired of the routine; the women were all bland, the intellectual talks came to nothing. *Is this all there is to life, to live, die, and be gone?* he wondered. He felt it could not be so, but he did not know what else there was. He began to remove himself, frequenting the taverns no more and ignoring the calls of his friends. Then one day, gazing into the distance, he caught a glimpse of a tall mountaintop, the Mountain of Mysteries. A clarity such as he had never known in his mortal life overwhelmed him! He remembered the task which Bob had given him, and for the first time since he'd separated from Bob, Pat felt renewed.

Yet he had done nothing for Bob's task thus far, and did not know how to climb the Mountain of Mysteries. Pat said to a mortal with whom he had good relations, "Look over there, at that mountaintop in the distance. I need to climb it and I seek the best means."

The mortal looked at Pat as if he were mad: "No one can climb the Mountain of Mysteries! It's impossible!"

"But I have been assured that it *is* possible," said Pat.

"And let *me* assure you that every mortal who has tried it has died!" said his friend.

These statements disconcerted Pat greatly, for they opposed everything Bob had told him.

But because of their good relations, the mortal told Pat that he would need a carriage, a horse, a guide along the beginning of the trail, and many smaller provisions and tools from food to a tent to a lamp and much else besides – none of which Pat had. And so Pat set to work on obtaining all he needed. He cut out everything else in his life and lived exclusively for this aim.

Apart from the melee now, Pat began to observe the world as he never had before. He realized that he had known it but superficially. Most of all, he was curious to see the Law of Bob at work.

But the more he looked for it... the less of it he saw. Instead he saw the opposite; at every turn the mortals committed atrocities against each other, and even worse, against themselves. One pushed down another, and the other allowed himself to be pushed down, going on pretending like it didn't matter, pretending he didn't care; but no amount of pretending touched the defeat that settled inside.

Every mortal he encountered, Pat felt this defeat through the look on his face, the regrets that permeated him from within. Whether they lamented their lives or ignored their feelings to show the world a pleasant face, everyone suffered the same, and this, for Pat, was the most painful suffering of all.

Why? he asked himself desperately. *Why are the mortals like this?* He got ever closer to the mortals' inner world in trying to answer this burning question, and the day he finally learned to see through their eyes, he struck upon a horrible reality: no mortal was the same on the inside as he was on the outside. No matter who, beneath the surface there always lay a secret self buried deep inside and hidden from the world. In there were the mortal's most treasured beliefs and yearnings, rejected by the outside and trampled over in favor of a society-approved demeanor. But they never truly disappeared, and all the days a mortal denied them, he lived his life as an act. The days turned into months, the months turned into years, and the years turned into a lifetime spent living not as one wanted.

No one is free to follow the Law of Bob in such conditions! They are urged to imprison the one thing that can save them from their cage of appearances, their "self" of standards, opinions, and actions they do not truly agree with. But how can the world exist this way when there is the Law of Bob?

Outward life showed no signs of the underlying calamity, and the mortals ridiculed Pat's crazy claims. But Pat could not reconcile their assertions with what he felt in his heart.

Then one day he struck upon the unspoken structure that ruled the mortals' society, making its standards and writing its unwritten laws: the Cult of the Greater. It seeped through every walk of life, cropped up in every society, and pulled in one direction: away from Bob. It was the force that urged mortals to push themselves down in favor of what the Cult deemed acceptable. Those who adhered most to the Cult of the Greater and ignored the Law of Bob were rewarded with earthly positions of power and influence, while those who attempted to follow the Law of Bob were devoured alive.

No mortal was free from the Cult's sway. The majority were followers, running after those ahead, who gained their own followers and then thought themselves leaders. Sadder still were the mortals who resisted the pull who one by one eventually gave in. But saddest of all were those who sat closest to the Cult's heart, who had gained dominion over the material world, but who had buried their true selves deepest.

Never had such a great clashing taken place within Pat, between what was and what he felt should be. This caused him the greatest suffering he had ever known, until he felt he could endure the pain of empathy no more.

Day by day he began to despise the rule of the Cult and everything that drove a mortal deeper into its well. His pity turned to hatred. His heart grew numb, enveloped by callousness it until he scorned the world that had once filled him with wonder.

One way or another, Pat finally acquired all he needed to trek the Mountain of Mysteries. The time had come for him to leave the mortal world forever, and after a long and arduous struggle, he finally reached the top. There at the peak stood Bob, waiting for him.

"The time has come for you to rejoin Me," Bob said.

But Pat did not move.

"You said the Law of Bob was the Law of this world, but I have seen nothing of it! The world is cold to Your Law; instead of listening to their conscience, mortals bury it; and those who try to follow it are devoured alive, while those who betray it get rewarded with the world's riches! And do You know why? Because the world is ruled by the Cult of the Greater, the force that pulls one away from You!" he burst out.

"I never said it would be easy," said Bob.

"But it is *hopeless*! In the process of life everyone abandons his heart! They give up the part of themselves worth keeping alive for acceptance by a world which doesn't care for them, for dreams that are not their own, for a life they did not ever want, and for satisfaction of a hunger that can never be satisfied! They become slaves! Slaves to jobs, slaves to money, slaves to people and slaves to custom! And when they cannot stand to feel the incongruence between their inner and outer lives, there is a myriad of beautiful escapes to keep the defeat inside at bay that lives inside them because that one part still feels the truth of their situation: that they have given in! To feel this is unendurable!" cried Pat.

"Let go of your hate, Pat; it has consumed you. Let it go and you will know a higher truth of the world," said Bob.

Pat laughed. "There *is* no higher truth of the world than its materialism. The truth is that the 'truth' we seek is only an illusion to divert ourselves from the harshness before our eyes! There is no Law of Bob: there is only the world as you see it and you either face it or not!"

"Your heart is hardened to blindness. Open it to Love and take My hand. It is your next step, for you have completed your mortal destiny and have place here no more," spoke Bob, extending His hand to Pat.

Pat stood an inch away from Bob. But his heart was covered with enamel so thick even the Love of Bob could not pierce through to its tender depths. He looked over the mountain back down at the world, shook his head, and turned around.

Pat walked down the mountain, back to the ground, lower and lower into the mortals' realm until he reached the lowest point. Nothing touched him, no feeling, no empathy, no pangs of connection. He who had once been so full of sympathy felt none of it anymore. Pat denied Bob and everything He spoke, and there he sat forevermore, at the center of the Cult of the Greater, pulling all down towards his realm.

enlightenment magazine

inside this month's issue

5 things enlightened people do

wear eco-friendly clothing
pretend to know how the latest technology works
balance mind, body, and spirit
eat vegan
blog

top 10 religions *you* should know about

elections: your all-access guide to who you should like and who you should dislike

related: Arnold Carrs Band plays at Alaleem's Rally, photos pg. 24

love news: the committed long-term relationship

why it's better than marriage
who's doing it (everyone!)

doc-pot: may have surprising medicinal benefits

plus

this month's poll: is Artinia helping Aruq?

vote and maybe win a FREE enlightenment magazine tote bag! Made with 33.4% recycled fibers.

coffee with Dan Brownn

soy, no whip, please!

Do you remember what your mother read while she spent day after day humming away in the kitchen, apron around her waist and a spoon absentmindedly stirring a big pot of dinner in one hand? The twentieth 'work' of yesterday's best-loved romance novelists, women as equally bored and desperate for adventure. They told the tale of a ruggedly handsome, two-dimensional man who just happened to be single, a poor, melancholy heroine who was unbelievably beautiful, and the thin plot that wove them together for all eternity – or at least until you finished the book. But no matter – you got the same satisfaction by picking up the next one. And the next. And the next. Get my drift? Those books were smut. With today's rapid intellectualization, readers requires more than cheap thrills to satisfy their cerebral cravings. Thus I offer you my curious August selection of Thought-Provoking Books sure to keep a happy mind with plenty to chew over:

1. *Travels Through the Lonely Desert*: the spiritual journey of a middle-aged man who's lost everything and escapes to a lifetime of wandering through the Avada Desert. There he meets his soulmate, the retired pilot Devon Chasewelder, who seeks solace and a place for quiet contemplation. Through their newly formed deep friendship, both discover parts inside of themselves they never knew existed. An enticing read that will make you question the conventions of love.

2. *The Unlocked Cage:* set in modern-day Aruq, a young woman's journey of self-discovery and her fight for her own freedom in the midst of a repressive regime. Unimpeded by her restrictive society, Abanna's spirit proves stronger than the boundaries that long to contain it as she boldly defies tradition with her involvement in an activist youth group. She refuses her arranged marriage; she experiences her first feelings of love with a young rebel relentless in the pursuit of his dreams; she discovers herself and her true calling in life; she has fun wearing makeup. A riveting and intellectual read that will open your mind. *Great for making yourself seem culture-savvy!*

3. *Vampire Love Story*: Malora and Stefano are meant to be. They have loved each other since their first bite. But their love isn't superficial like everyone else's – it goes deeper than their bones. It goes to their very blood.... Their passion is so strong that they are a threat to the cosmic balance. Will the world be torn apart by their refusal to part – or by the pain of their parting?

score the summer's *hottest* eco-friendly gear!

T-shirts that say "peace" and "recycle", <u>metal water bottles</u>, and coffee mugs with witty quotes on them!!!

Also on page 8, quirky magnets, too many planners to choose from, handmade bookmarks, and the finest selection of imported herbal teas!

self improvement

You meditate upon waking, you eat only organic foods, and you make a point of it to read at least one book a month – give yourself a pat on the back. But do you now find yourself wondering what else you can do to appear better than everyone around you? The answer is to learn a new language! One of the most important skills to have today is to know multiple languages. It makes you look sophisticated, it impresses your neighbors (especially if they are monolingual), and it lets you become buddy-buddy with your hip foreign coworkers.

The best way to pick which language you are going to learn is to look at which foreign languages are most popular in your setting –

"Hallan! Put that damn magazine down!" Mr. Daltuhn yelled as he rushed through the break room past John. John laid the glossy new magazine back on the table.

"Hurry! We can't be late!" barked his boss.

Today was a very important day indeed. The project that had had them running around like Crack addicts for the past week was finally coming to fruition. John grabbed his coffee and rushed after Mr. Daltuhn, who was already standing in the elevator, pushing the number 6 button. John just made it inside as the doors closed.

Mr. Daltuhn turned to him. "Well, it's done," he sighed, changing his tone. "I sent in your paperwork with everyone else's. Are you sure it's safe?"

"I put it down as the ability to automatically perceive situations as mathematical formulas," John recounted for the third time.

"They'll wonder why you're not working for the Air and Space Directory with all those other mental token brainiacs!" said Mr. Daltuhn.

"I'll tell them my love for the television industry drove me to use my talents for NKOZ."

"What if they want to use you for military planning?"

"I'll just make things up! I only said I *perceive* things as mathematical equations; I never said they were correct! For all they know I could be crazy. Besides, there are tons of other people with that token," John assured.

"Well, nothing we can do now. At least that burden is off our shoulders. Well, maybe not yours, but at least mine," Mr. Daltuhn said, comforted. Then he shook his head.

"I still don't understand how you can be so passive about it. If *I* didn't know what my token was I'd go crazy!"

"It doesn't bother me at all," John said flatly, looking at the elevator wall.

"That's because you don't care! You're a good guy, Hallan, but you don't wanna make a name for yourself. You're too scared of putting your foot in the mire, so you keep yourself conventional."

"Hm. So what about the election coming up? Who's got your vote?"

"Not that dirty broad-nosed son of a – "

The elevator doors opened.

"Sajan appeared at a Pro-Life rally yesterday, it was in this morning's paper," said John, who'd opened the newspaper at breakfast to a massive Pro-Life article headed by a half-page photo of Sajan Walker in a crowd of people donning a Pro-Life t-shirt, sign in hand.

"Idiot," muttered Mr. Daltuhn.

John had only been to the sixth floor once; he almost never went down to the filming studios. A short walk took them to studio 6B, where Erica, Luke, Nelson, the camera crew, the hired actors, and the caterers were already waiting.

John's phone rang just then. "Just a sec," he told Mr. Daltuhn as he hung back in the hallway.

"Dude!" it was Hec. "Are you psyched or what!? Election's in less than a month! I can't believe Steffen's refused to take sole presidency."

"Why? It's unprecedented and most of his constituents are against it. He'd lose their votes if he didn't assure them he was keeping the two-president system."

"I know, but there's been so much pressure on him from Pro-Life, and he and Alaleem are in close circles."

"Yeah, but Pro-Life's not *that* big," said John.

"I dunno, man, they're all I see on T.V.," said Hec.

"They're just getting all the attention to make it *seem* like they're a big deal. In reality most people haven't changed sides. If there was more time they could sway enough people to the one-president system, but by the end of the month? No way."

"Well, word is if Alaleem *does* get elected he'll turn Steffen to a unipresidential system anyway," said Hec.

"Yeah, he probably would. Listen, Hec, I gotta go, we're filming today – "

"Alright. Hey, you guys wanna meet up at Mabel's with me and Rachel after work?"

"Sure. See you later."

John dashed into the studio where he saw – to his surprise – his straight back clad in a crisp plum button-down, his dark hair shining under the bright lights, Sajan Walker, making hand motions as he brought his artistic vision to life.

"Pretend to be laughing casually. Like the camera just caught you in mid-laughter," he ordered an actor. "Widen your eyes in surprise, you're portraying someone who's real and down-to-earth... hands in your pockets!... Can we get in more of the scruffy jaw line?... I think we'll take five," Sajan clapped his hands. The actor walked off, immediately extracting his mePhone from his pocket.

Sajan sat wearily in the director's chair, where he was approached by an attractive blonde actress. After a minute she burst out laughing, smiling and patting him on the arm. Luke stood against the wall ten feet away, struggling to appear aloof but shooting glances at them every few seconds. On the opposite end stood Erica, looking bored. She caught John's eye and promptly made a beeline for him.

"Hi," she smiled, approaching.

"Hey," he couldn't help but smile in return, only the part of his peripheral vision keeping tabs on Mr. Daltuhn not focused on her; the man in question paced back and forth by the set, talking loudly on his phone:

"Can't, Sal, I've got the whole team in here....You know I'm a pro at keeping it under wraps! I'm like a shark. Swim under the surface and them bam! I jump out and bite ya!"

"Alright, places everyone!" Sajan commanded.

"Alright, everybody, take two of PermaLock New Double-Seal Freezer Bags!" Mr. Daltuhn yelled, standing next to the Director's chair, putting his cell phone away. The owner of the PermaLock Plastic Bags company, a rather fat middle aged man with a lot of stubble, sat off to the side looking lazily between Sajan and Mr. Daltuhn, taking no visible part in the production.

Mr. Daltuhn had agreed to help film a commercial for PermaLock's newest product, Double-Seal Freezer Bags, effectively sending the thirtieth floor into chaos as it mobilized for this undertaking. He happened to mention the project to Sajan over lunch one day:

"...I'm in meetings with the artists all week to tweak our newest concept design. Thank Bob for weekend yacht getaways, right?" Sajan had chuckled.

"Of course," replied Mr. Daltuhn. "My life is stressful, too."

"Oh?"

"Yes, big project coming up, it's taking up all my time," Mr. Daltuhn had drawled. "I'm helping Arnold Shaffer with his new commercial. He's the president of PermaLock, if you didn't know."

"Oh, Arnie! We used to work together, you know, back when I was starting out. It's been ages since I've seen him – I never did buy him that drink I promised."

Pause.

"Oh, then would you like to come to the filming?"

"Well I don't want to intrude – "

"I under – "

"But I'd love to!"

"Ah – it's no trouble at all."

"We'll go out for drinks afterward, my treat."

"Excellent! I love drinks!" said Mr. Daltuhn.

"So are you still working on the concept?" Sajan asked.

"No, we've got that pretty much figured out."

"Let me guess – Arnie wanted a dichromatic color scheme?"

"Yes, actually – "

Sajan threw back his head and burst out laughing.

"Oh, he hasn't changed a bit. The man's ideas could use some revamping. Did you know that his sales have gone down by twenty percent in the past three years?"

"What? No I didn't know that," snapped Mr. Daltuhn.

"*I* personally think it's his slack advertising... but what do I know."

"Well, maybe you could give him some pointers," Mr. Daltuhn said nonchalantly.

Sajan sighed. "I don't know, Arnie never listened to me. *I* wanted the Kimi Kool cartoon, *he* wanted claymation."

"Please!"

"Alright, I'll do what I can. But only because you're my friend."

"Oh, thank you, Sajan! You're a savior! Drinks will be on me."

"Fair enough."

"Did you want to say 'roll'?" Sajan now turned to Mr. Daltuhn and asked.

"I – yes."

"Alright, go ahead."

"Roll!" Mr. Daltuhn barked.

The cameras pointed to the right side of the set, a kitchen in various tones of beige, where the blonde Sajan had been talking with earlier, an Artinian woman with no distinguishing features, stood holding a generic brand of plastic bag filled with marinated vegetables. Two small children, also blonde, ran to her, who made to open the bag and promptly spilled everything on the counter. All three assumed disheartened expressions.

"Cut! Excellent."

As the thirtieth floor staff stood off to the side watching amusedly, the crew rearranged lighting and cameras onto the left side of the set, a bright purple kitchen with shiny, grass green appliances, very clean, modern and cheery. A flat-nosed lady in her mid-thirties, her black hair arranged in a modern ponytail with some straightened strands falling out of it, stood behind it, holding a PermaLock Plastic Freezer Bag filled also with marinated vegetables.

"Aaannd – " said Mr. Daltuhn.

"Mitsu, a little to the left! *Perfect*, that made all the difference!" Sajan directed. "And action!"

Two small children, a boy and a girl who also appeared to be flat-nosed, ran up to the lady, who let the bag carelessly sway in one hand as she bent down to ruffle their hair. Up and down it bounced, never opening. The lady finally brought the bag around and opened it for the children, who were very happy to see that they were having marinated vegetables for dinner. Then on cue, a tall, handsome man walked onto the set holding a generic brand plastic bag filled with spaghetti. He accidentally spilled it as he made to hug his wife, who gave him an exasperated yet loving look while he shrugged in an "oops" manner. Then she handed him a PermaLock Plastic Freezer Bag and looked at the camera, shaking her head. (Most of) this family got it right by using PermaLock.

"Cut! Good show, everyone! Let's break for lunch!"

John and Erica joined the slow-moving queue at the buffet, glimpsing Sajan and the two actresses who'd played the mothers chatting by the bar while Luke hovered around them like a satellite.

"...Texting, video messaging, YourSpot. I can't even keep up anymore!" Sajan was shaking his head.

"I *know*, it's *ridiculous*! My ten-year-old nephew just got a mePhone for his birthday!"

"I don't even know the difference between a mePod and a mePhone! Don't they do the same thing?"

The actresses laughed.

"It's amazing what technology can do now, but do I really *need* to change my phone every three months?" Sajan posed.

"Right, right," they agreed.

"Call me old school, but I'll always love sitting down around a television more than watching a show on my laptop. It just has more of a feel of 'family' to it. Even if I'm alone."

"Aww!"

"I guess it's this stupid sense of nostalgia I carry around," he laughed to himself and shrugged.

"It's not stupid!" exclaimed the blonde. "Besides, I bet that nostalgic T.V. is a flat screen as long as your body," she said mischievously.

"You know me too well," he winked at her.

"I need to get my boyfriend to start his own business, maybe then he'll make enough to buy *us* one," Mitsu complained.

"Honestly, the importance our society places on money – it's overrated," Sajan shook his head. "I know it's the oldest cliché in the book, but has it ever brought real, lasting love?"

"Sajan! Enough sentiments!" came the bark of Arnie Shaffer as he and Mr. Daltuhn approached Sajan and the actresses. "I'm here to talk business!"

"Ladies, excuse me," Sajan said politely, then turned to face Arnie with a genial smile.

"I hear you've had a sales boost!" boomed Armie.

"You've had a sales boost?" Mr. Daltuhn said promptly.

"Summertime, girls need more dolls I suppose," Sajan shrugged, taking a sip of his drink.

"I'm thinking an investment – "

"No can do, Arnie, it's all gone."

"All of it!?"

"Spent," Sajan nodded.

"On what!? What could you possibly need, a fourth house?" Arnie laughed.

"Only for the purpose of providing more jobs for the unemployed," countered Sajan.

"A philanthropist *and* a Pro-Life supporter?" Mitsu smiled admiringly.

John could practically see Luke's Pro-Life pin double in luminosity.

"Ah, yes, I forgot you're involved with that," Arnie wrinkled his nose.

"*I* think it's brave," defended the blonde, looking angrily at Arnie's squat form. "Sajan was even at the rally this Saturday!"

"I thought you said you flew out to Bouclé Friday night! How did you make it back in time?" exclaimed Mitsu.

"I took my private jet, of course," Sajan said matter-of-factly. The actresses' mouths dropped.

"I'm joking! I don't – " he sputtered " – have a private jet!" as if the notion were absurd unless he were some rich elitist fancying himself above common folk. Their circle erupted with laughter.

"John, get me another, would you, same kthanx," Sajan broke from the merriment, holding his glass out to John as John made to get another sandwich.

"I got it!" Luke pushed Erica out of the way as he ran forward.

"You're the man, Luke! *This* is why I gave him a ride today."

"Sajan, how do you do it all?" asked Mitsu in awe.

"Sacrifice," Sajan nodded. "Like, you know, that sleep thing," he waved his arms, and they laughed.

"Poor baby, you need a break," cooed the blonde.

"Oh there'll be plenty of time for that later, right boys?" he winked at Mr. Daltuhn and Arnie.

"Right! It's been too long since we've shared a happy hour," said Arnie. "And you still haven't taken me around in that sweet little car of yours."

"It's *sick*," accredited Luke.

"What!? Then you're riding with me when we leave!" Sajan declared.

"Shotgun!" called Arnie.

"Ladies, I'm sure you'll be very comfortable in the back," he said as the actresses turned to each other in giggling glee.

"Mr. Daltuhn, can I get a ride with you?" Luke muttered off to the side.

***

"...I pre-removed the naked ones, so don't get your hopes up."

"But why," said Erica disappointedly.

"Because I'm trying to disperse the embarrassment evenly: today is awkward early puberty, thus at a later date you will see naked baby photos," said John.

"Alright," she accepted as they walked into Mabel's after work that evening, Erica disappearing into the bathroom while John sat down by Hec.

"Wipe that smirk off," said Hec, who was already sitting at the counter with a beer. But John hardly cared; he felt as happy as their bar's calm, comfortable interior looked. The sun shining in from behind him sent its horizontally slanted rays streaming through the window and falling around his head to illuminate the counter his hands rested upon.

"Just wait," said Hec darkly, "soon you'll come back to reality and it'll be, 'John, I thought we agreed that you would cut down to one cup of coffee per day!'; 'John, why do you like going to the bar so much?'; 'John, I wish you would look at me like you did when you first liked me'."

John laughed. "Where's Rachel?" he asked.

"She didn't come."

"Why not?"

"Uh... we're on a break."

"What!? You were together this morning!"

Hec sighed. "We got into a huge fight after you and I got off the phone, and we decided it would be better if we didn't see each other for a while."

"Sorry, Hec," John sympathized.

"I mean, it's not really out of the blue, stuff's been building up. She expects me to be perfect all the time! I forget to put my plate away once and she starts yelling for an hour! I'm human! I don't have every token, you know? And then she starts on how I don't have enough ambition – ! I don't think she even loves me for who I am. It's like she wants me to be this suave intellectual who reads classical literature when he's taking a break from discovering the cure for distraction! I'm sorry, but that's not me! Is it so wrong to want to be loved for who you are!?" Hec ranted fervently.

"*I* don't think so," said John.

"But I don't even know who I *am* because we're always doing what *she* wants to do! I just can't handle this right now, I'm already stressed out from work. I need some time to get my head together and just do the things I want to do," said Hec.

"Well, that could be good," said John.

"I mean, I miss her like crazy, but I'm going to use this time to reclaim myself. And if I'm my own person it'll be better for the both of us in the long run."

"Definitely," said John.

But despite these assurances Hec's head hit the countertop piteously. John turned on the news.

"...Billionaire heiress Lillian Holt, daughter of Theodore and Caralee Holt of the Holt restaurant chain, a good girl and celibacy poster-child, has recently taken a bad turn! The nineteen-year-old was caught driving home drunk from a party in Cherry Lane last night. When approached by the police, she resisted questioning and behaved 'belligerently'. Now to our update on the presidential debates...."

"I saw enough of that face today for a lifetime," said Erica, rejoining them and looking up at where Sajan Walker was being interviewed.

"...Sajan, as a leading player in the Pro-Life/Pro-Choice battle, do you see this movement catalyzing any big changes in our society?"

"Absolutely, Paul. Social stress has a way of bringing dormant issues to the surface and that's what we're seeing now."

"Do you think this is what's behind the mysterious crosses found spray painted on the sides of buildings this past week?" asked Paul. "For those unaware, the symbol, two perpendicular bars crossed on the upper half of the vertical one, is suspected to bear religious significance and looks like this:

"Sajan, what do you say to Recursives of Artinia leader Amil Farr's comment: 'It is a message of discord used to terrify the public: the Wheel of Consequence sits higher on the Great Wheel, disrupting the balance, while the Lauki and Shugina have been removed.'? Do you think this symbol is a big enough threat to merit the use of the biggest police task force we've seen in decades?"

Sajan looked thoughtful before replying, "Honestly, I think the biggest threat is the illusions we still keep around after millennia, despite the incredible sciencfic advances our society has made."

"Illusions? Such as what?"

"Why, the biggest one – religion. The notions of 'Bob' and 'Pat' having influence over our world – even that they exist! And the Wheel of Consequence? A clever trap to control our every move."

Shocked reactions erupted from many bargoers watching the program. "Pretentious prick!" John heard among the mass of cries. The tempest of angry remarks drowned out the remainder of the program until it ended and gave way to a Kimi Kool Social Rebel doll commercial.

***

Mr. Daltuhn stormed into their office and slapped a pile of papers onto John's desk. He was still in his week-long anger rampage.

"What's this?"

"Up-to-the-day sales analyses of Kimi Kool for the past three months. Sajan Walker's sales are through the roof!" In his other hand he held a rolled up newspaper folded to the story: "Sajan Walker: Enemy of Bob?"

"I don't understand!" Mr. Daltuhn burst out. "The whole country hates him yet his sales are skyrocketing! I want to know how he's doing it!"

"How is that going to help us?" asked John as he examined Kimi Kool sales and saw a sharp, swift increase starting from the middle of the summer.

"Once we figure out his secret, we can apply it."

"You know what's weird?" asked Erica as she looked over John's shoulder,

"His sales have gone up most in the central region, where they've traditionally been the lowest."

"I didn't think Kimi Kool's style catered to the more rural market audience out there," said John. "For years they've preferred the older Sadie dolls; less hip, but more skin coverage. I guess moral resistance is breaking down everywhere."

"Maybe Sadie sales might give us a tip," said Erica.

"They pale in comparison to Kimi Kool's, I can tell you that much. The birth of Kimi Kool was the death of Sadie. In fact, I heard rumors that it was going out of business. Is it?" asked John as Erica visited the Sadie Dolls website.

"No, but it *is* under new management: 'Sajan Walker became the new owner of Sadie Dolls at the end of June'!" she exclaimed.

"See, guys? He's just a great businessman," said Luke. "He might have a couple missteps with the media but it doesn't mean he can't do business."

But if John was certain of one thing, it was that Sajan had no such missteps. Sajan was not accidental – he was calculated, and John was sure that everything he'd done had been exactly what he'd intended.

"Look!" Erica gasped. She had pulled up an article titled: "The Burning of Kimi Kool":

> Hundreds of protesters across the nation's interior have demonstratively burned Kimi Kool dolls in response to company owner Sajan Walker's recent incendiary religious comments. Resentment of Walker has been growing since his public support of Congressman Alaleem and the Pro-Life movement.
>
> 'I bought ten Kimi Kool dolls in June, clothed them like decent girls, and put them on posts!' said Jim Keane of Bratcha County. 'We are sending this man a message that we will not let him corrupt our morals.'
>
> 'I'd prefer my daughters playing with the old Sadie dolls,' Lauren Burne echoed the sentiments of many 'sensible' consumers, who have since switched to the old doll 'until Kimi Kool gets her priorities straight'.

For a tiny moment John glimpsed straight through the cracks so exactly that he understood every detail of Sajan's plan.

"Mr. Daltuhn, I know what we have to do!" he yelled, in the throes of epiphany. "We've been going about it all wrong!"

"What are you talking about!"

"*Hate!* Sajan's been using people's hate to tap into the other half of his available reserves! And we, too, can capitalize off of people's need to dump their negativity onto an object!"

"How do we do that?"

"*By hiring Lillian Holt!*"

"She's despicable! It would ruin the network's image!"

But John shook his head. "It doesn't *matter* if she's loved or hated! Attention is all the same! In an instant the coin can flip! Don't you see, Mr. Daltuhn, attraction and repulsion are but opposite sides of the same monetary coin," John finished sagely.

Mr. Daltuhn smacked him across the head with the newspaper. And then he hugged him. "You're brilliant, Hallan!" he cried. "Call everyone into the meeting room, we've got a new show!"

Chapter 20: Magic Artinia

"Are you going to post those pictures on YourSpot?" Milly asked during lunch.

"YourSpot?" Gretchen turned around. "No one uses YourSpot anymore."

"Yeah, I deleted mine ages ago," said Jean.

"Me too," said Emma.

"But – I just got mine. Tai, you just helped me make it! You still have yours, right?" Milly was extremely confused.

"Yeah, but I'm gonna delete it soon. It's just annoying."

"Dee Allderbay deleted hers," nodded Emma.

"Besides, everyone uses faceplace now," said Gretchen.

"What is faceplace?" asked Milly.

"It's a social networking site."

"Like YourSpot?"

"*Noooo*," went Milly's friends in unison, shaking their heads.

"It's *so* much cooler," said Gretchen. "Not that many people know about it yet."

"Maybe I should make a faceplace page," Milly wondered aloud.

"Milly, don't be a copycat. If you like YourSpot, keep using it," said Gretchen.

"But what's the point if I don't have anyone to talk to on there?" she said.

But Gretchen shook her head at Tai, who understood what she meant and rolled her eyes.

"First day of junior year?" John asked her that evening as they sat around in the living room.

"Yeah, and I can already tell it's gonna be the worst year of my life," Milly said gloomily, staring at the television.

"...Season five of *Artinian Artist* continues tomorrow, with your new host, Mostafim Abdul Raja!" the commercial showed the new host with his spiked hair and button-down shirt, holding a microphone and making an exclamatory face which involved an open mouth and a look of shock. Then a smile.

"Whatever happened to Johnny Dale?" asked Milly.

"Oh, they replaced him a long time ago," said John.

"Why?"

"Just trying to get their ratings up," he shrugged.

"...Welcome back, if you're just tuning in, this is one of the most exciting installments of The News you're ever going to see! President Steffen has just been pronounced dead of unknown causes and Army General Kevin Rutt has temporarily assumed the Presidency for both Havenford's and Steffen's chairs."

"*What?*" exclaimed John, jumping up.

"...Elections have been postponed due to the country's instability and President Rutt has put the Token Directory under government operation, authorizing monitoring for any suspicious activity...."

John stared at the screen disbelievingly.

"...This move grants the government unprecedented power in matters pertaining to tokens. Many are calling it the grossest violation of privacy of the century, but Rutt maintains that safety come first in this dangerous time when the country is in chaos and LASS is an imminent threat."

"In other news, Lillian Holt has made a comeback with her new hit show, *The Life of Lil*. The reality show's pilot, which followed Lillian from her exit from rehab to her re-immersion into ordinary life, premiered yesterday night on NKOZ to astronomical ratings! Tune in next week when Lillian takes Vandorn nightlife by storm for her twentieth birthday."

Inside John went cold. Just when he thought his problems had been solved, he found himself in more danger than ever....

***

280

In light of their show's success, Mr. Daltuhn held a party that Saturday night on two floors of the Regale Suites Hotel downtown, the most posh hotel in the city.

John arrived at Mr. Daltuhn's doorstep that night to see a limousine parked outside the spacious driveway, its driver leaning against it smoking a cigarette.

"The limo is here," he said as he walked through a conservatively furnished sitting room of middle-aged men in dark suits wearing overbearing cologne and smoking cigars: the network executives.

"Alright, gents, looks like we're going to have to call it game!" Mr. Daltuhn shouted to a general groan.

One by one they got up and stretched, all of them clearly getting on in years.

"'Bout time, Beasley was at negative fourteen!" grumbled one of them as he downed his remaining whisky.

"What were you playing?" John asked him.

"'Never Have I Ever'."

They put on their shoes and headed out the door, John letting them pass as he waited for the only person that wasn't downstairs.

Erica descended the curving staircase a minute later.

"Wow... you look... really nice," John said, not able to take his eyes off of her. The anxiety that had been twisting his insides all weekend since he'd heard the news report dissipated for an instant.

"Thanks," she smiled, faltering as she took a second glance at his strangely somber expression.

Mr. Daltuhn passed around glasses and popped open a bottle of champagne when their party was seated in the limo.

"Let's drink, everyone!" he poured for them all, then raised his glass. "To dissolve the awkwardness! *I'm* sitting in a limo with my daughter and assistant whom I think are dating but I'm not sure. You know how their generation doesn't give their relations 'labels' to keep their options open or avoid a potentially embarrassing situation where one liked the other more and thought they were going out but the other didn't!"

"My ex-wife is my ex-wife because of *this* guy!" one of the network executives slapped the back of the man next to him before they both cracked up.

"My tie's on too tight!" yelled another.

"To awkwardness!" everyone laughed and chinked glasses.

"Riding through the city in style, now that's what I'm talking about!" said one of the fifty-or-sixty-year-old network executives as they sped along.

"Hey! Shoffer! Could you drive a little slower? People don't have enough time to be jealous of us as we pass by!" yelled Beasley to the limo driver.

"Whassamatter, Parker, stick up your behind?" asked Beasley, turning to the only man besides John who hadn't cracked up.

"I'll stick it up *your* behind, Beasley!" yelled Parker, red in the face but not from embarrassment, rather his third glass of champagne.

"Hey! Look! People! I'm a successful network executive and who are youuu!" yelled another as he stood up and stuck his head out the sunroof.

"Sit down, Marshall! For all you know there could be a 'sploder out there!" yelled Mr. Daltuhn.

The chauffer closed the sunroof.

"Ah, late to my own party," Mr. Daltuhn said, pleased, as their limo pulled up to the towering hotel; he was already quite buzzed.

Everything was very dark except for nooks where bluish lights were artfully planted as if thrown carelessly into corners and odd spots. The bar glowed pale amber as young bartenders in dark blue cummerbunds rapidly poured drinks of all colors and mixes to Vandorn's elite, who sat elegantly in shimmering dresses and snazzy suits.

The network executives scurried off quickly, leaving John and Erica alone. They walked past people sitting around miniature glass tables laden with cups of espresso or martini glasses that refracted the light. Yet more people were strewn along the second floor balcony encircling the dance floor from above like a crown.

"Pricey party," muttered Erica as the two of them sat down at an atmospherically lit booth.

"Hey!" said a familiar voice above them. They looked up to see Luke bobbing toward them in spiffy attire, a drink in one hand and his free arm around a girl who looked delighted beyond words to be there.

"Sweet party, huh?" he beamed, joining them.

"How can these people carry on nonchalantly with everything that's happening right now?" Erica shook her head.

"They're too wrapped up in Lillian Holt's dramatic affairs to notice," said John darkly.

"Dude, that girl's such a slut. I have like no respect for women like that," said Luke. "Hey, look who's here!" he craned his head. Sajan Walker had walked in, looking his usual debonair self but not really noticing that fact as he whispered, lightly smiling, to the crimson-clad brunette on his arm. She mirrored his careless manner, not sparing a quarter thought for the space behind her.

"That's Caroline Ash, the Go GREEN model!" Jennifer exclaimed. "They're *so* cute together!"

"Dude, that guy gets the hottest chicks," said Luke.

"Ugh!" went Jennifer, looking him furiously in the face.

"Babe, you know what I mean. Come on, let's go talk to him," he grabbed Jennifer's wrist and dragged her along.

"What, are you two just gonna sit here?" he urged the motionless John and Erica. They reluctantly got up and followed.

Sajan stood in the center of a circle of network executives and prominent businessmen, Mr. Daltuhn included.

"...I've decided to delve into the holistic market," he drawled. "I've patented this," he held up a small-ish cylinder-ish item wrapped in green. John read the label:

Superproduct
with pomegranate, green tea, soy, and energy.

"My latest creation," said Sajan proudly.

"What is it?" asked John. Sajan looked startled, as if anyone should know.

"Why, it's Superproduct."

"Is it a food, or a chapstick, or – "

Sajan shook his head. "You're a little behind the times, my friend. It contains everything that's most marketable right now. And it's organic... obviously."

John turned the tube around and read: "'Made from organic and local-grown stuff'. What is 'local-grown' if you're marketing across the whole country – ?"

"Let me see that," Mr. Daltuhn grabbed the tube of Superproduct before John could finish. He closely examined the label, then took off the cap and sniffed.

"Açai," he ascertained. "It really *does* contain everything most marketable!"

"*And* we donate five percent of the profits from every tube sold to the Have-a-Hope-Foundation," Sajan said pointedly. Mr. Daltuhn's mouth dropped. Everyone suddenly gathered more closely around.

"Does it burn carbs?" asked NKOZ's Vice President of Marketing Strategies.

"While you sleep!" said Sajan.

"And is there a crash after the energy goes away?" asked the owner of Diletto's, one of Vandorn's most prominent restaurants.

"Nope," said Sajan smugly. "It's a smooth landing. *And*, you can buy separate Superproduct holding cases in a variety of eye-catching colors!"

"Ooh!" went every businessman in the vicinity. Like ravens they grabbed at Superproduct as it was snatched hand by hand, knocking Mr. Daltuhn and John out of the way.

Sajan stepped back from the crowd, watching them fight with a pleasant expression. He leaned toward Mr. Daltuhn.

"*Check. Mate*," he whispered.

Mr. Daltuhn was livid with fury. He stood rooted to the spot, gripping his champagne glass with a tight fist.

"This is just the beginning!" Sajan recommenced telling everyone. "Superproduct is the main accessory for my *next* big doll: Hipster Kimi Kool! When *that* gets out – let me tell *you*! – I'll *finally* build that gallery to house indigenous art from broad-nosed clans in Ubiqit, the proceeds of which go to building them schools, I've always dreamed of! My only concern is that the saltwater breeze might damage the works. My manor is by the ocean," he clarified. "It's got a gorgeous view, though, right, Daltuhn? He's seen pictures."

Mr. Daltuhn coughed. "Yes, the view is – gorgeous."

"Sajan, that's wonderful!" exclaimed every businessman and executive.

"Thank you, thank you, but really, we're not here to celebrate me. To Edmund," he raised his tone and chinked his glass to a response of relative silence. "Thanks to the success of his new show the yacht industry will never know better days!"

The room roared with laughter.

"To Edmund!" the executives mimicked and drank.

"Well put, Sajan. Listen, I *must* show the Senior Design Strategist your Superproduct," NKOZ's Vice President said immediately after swallowing.

"Certainly!" Sajan smiled as most of their crowd dissipated, leaving him and his date, Mr. Daltuhn, a few other executives, John, Erica, Luke, and Jennifer. Sajan noticed them seemingly for the first time.

"Erica!" he exclaimed, taking a step back, "you look just like your father. That dress particularly accents the fine bone structure I also find in him."

Mr. Daltuhn's expression looked confused, but also rather pleased.

"Uh..." Erica was not sure what to say.

"That is, you're lovely," Sajan touched her shoulder. Daggers shot out of Caroline Ash's back, gleaming in the swathing blue light.

"Not to worry, she's not dangerous!" Sajan assured as everyone jumped back.

"Dear, get us some drinks, would you? Kthanksbye," he mumbled to her, gently stroking her arm. She stalked off, giving Erica a scorn.

"Congratulations again, Daltuhn. Here's to an amazing recovery," they chinked glasses.

"Oh stop, it's just a twenty episode contract," Mr. Daltuhn happily drank, putting his empty glass on a tray and taking two more from a passing waiter in a velvet cummerbund, one of which he politely handed to Sajan.

"*Just*? Rumor was you were getting bought out soon."

"Well I can't take *all* the credit. It's John here's night, really. Whole thing was his idea!" said Mr. Daltuhn.

Sajan spun around. "John?" He looked at John like he never had before. In fact this was the first time John felt Sajan was looking *at* him, his materialized body, rather than past him.

"Oh yeah, he's been by my side through this whole slump. Great kid, too, I'm even okay with him dating my daughter... though I'll never tell him *that!*" Mr. Daltuhn cracked up, examining his second just-emptied champagne glass twirling between his fingers.

John did not know if Mr. Daltuhn was so drunk that his reality lines had blurred, or if he had forgotten that John was standing there.

"Yep, we had some *rough* weeks, let me tell *you*," he prodded Sajan's pectorals. "I was desperate enough to take on *any* forgettable musician, but John – John here was the anchor, said we had to hold out. And *then* he had that stroke of genius! I can't wait to see what else he's got up his sleeve!"

Sajan raised his eyebrows while the other network executives swarmed John with new interest.

"Looks like we've got a new golden boy in the business," one patted him on the back.

"He's only twenty-four, right? That's three years on you when you got your big break, Sajan," another nudged Sajan, laughing.

Sajan smirked. "Drummond, if *anyone* is capable of great feats I always knew it was John!" Sajan swung his arm around John's shoulder. "Looks like I'll have to show this youngin' the ropes. Don't worry, I'll be right behind you when the ladies start attacking," he grinned at him.

"To pick up seconds," another muttered and all three executives burst out laughing.

"Daltuhn, our main man!" Two more executive producers from other big networks arrived, both in expensive suits and wristwatches that garbed them in an exasperated manner such that they'd been worn a hundred times before to similar parties.

"Allen! Jefferson!" Mr. Daltuhn boomed.

"What a party!" Allen slapped Mr. Daltuhn across the back as he handed his champagne glass to John like he was a hat rack. "But the women! They're stiff as boards! I haven't gotten a single number all night," he complained.

"You animal, is that all you can think about!" Mr. Daltuhn erupted.

"You know Allen," Jefferson cut in, rolling his eyes.

"Oh, I know him, alright! New Year's party five years ago? Remember Rhonda? ... Or was it *Ronald!*" they all roared with laughter.

"We need more drinks if we're going down memory lane!" Jefferson said. "The second floor bar is *excellent!*"

"To the bar!" declared Allen, and their trio ambled off, recounting more stories of days gone by with their arms around each other.

Erica leaned in and whispered in John's ear: "I'm gonna make sure he gets there. Be right back."

John nodded and watched her go. Everyone else had dispersed. He stood alone with Sajan now.

"Well, John, how about that. Do you carry a journal around in case a sudden brilliant idea hits you?" Sajan chuckled.

"No."

"Oh," Sajan put the little black book he was taking out of his pocket back disappointedly. "So what was your inspiration? From one creator to another," he chuckled again.

"Well, to be honest... it was you."

"Really? I'm touched!" he looked it, holding his hand to his heart. "That's my real goal, not to make millions – like I've said over and over I don't care so much about the money – but to *inspire* people. And if I can serve as a beacon of hope to the next generation, then by Bob, it warms my heart."

John looked at him.

"You'll be getting a promotion any day now, I bet. No – he'll make you spokesperson! Yes, why wouldn't he? A young, fresh face. You'll skyrocket to fame faster than a comet," Sajan went on. "Daltuhn's network is bigger than ever, and with you spewing out three, four, seven more hit shows with your artistic genius – well he can afford *three* mansions in Bouclé.... We might be neighbors, is where I'm going with this."

"I don't think Bouclé is for me," said John.

"Oh, not you; Daltuhn. Hate to be a killjoy, John, but the big bucks don't lie in assistant positions," he leaned in and muttered. "Not that there's anything *wrong* with a five-figure salary. But if you ask me, Daltuhn's keeping you down on purpose – he doesn't want to lose a raw talent like you because he knows you could be great on your own – why, even start your own network to rival his if you wanted to. But I only tell you this as a friend."

"We're friends?"

"John, I consider you one of my closest!" Sajan looked hurt.

"We've seen each other four times."

"You're practically my best man."

"I don't know that I'm qualified to play that role based on how well I know you."

"*I feel exactly the same way!*" said Sajan emphatically. "That's why we need to hang out, so that when the time comes for you to be my best man, you'll be ready. Have you even been to my Vandorn loft yet? I have a loft in Vandorn," he explained.

"I don't think so," said John.

"Well come over tomorrow! We shouldn't be strangers if we're going to be best friends," he chuckled.

"Oh, gee, Sajan, I'd love to but I'm pretty sure Erica and I have plans."

"I was inviting her, too, duh. You guys are like one person; I'm saving you in my phone as 'Jerica'," he took out his Cranberry.

"We have different numbers."

"That's both your names. You can be 'Jerica 1'," he winked. "How's eight?"

"Um – let me talk it over with her first."

"Obviously," he rolled his eyes as he pocketed his Cranberry with style. "Well, I better not keep my lady waiting, she's looking a mite ticked," Sajan glanced into the distance. "She doesn't understand that guys sometimes need to bond with other guys – no girls," he shook his head. "You're lucky you have Erica, *she* seems grounded."

"Yeah, she keeps me sane."

"Ha! How often does a woman do *that*! Well I'll catch you later, try not to be too brilliant!" he slapped his back solidly and walked off.

John stood alone in the middle of the party. He wasn't sure what had just happened; had he made a friend, or an enemy, or both? He made a mental note to clear the matter with Milly when he got home as he headed to the upstairs bar to find Erica.

"I was just about to go back!" she ran into him as he stepped off the staircase. "Come on, let's walk around," she dragged his arm; John moved like an anchor.

"You okay?" she asked, peering into his face.

"What? Yeah."

"You've been quiet all night."

He shrugged. "I think I'm gonna check out the bar first. I'll catch up with you in a minute."

"Oh... okay. I'll be here," she watched him go.

Confused, she leaned against the balcony worriedly, watching the scene below without taking it in.

"Erica?"

She turned around again. Sajan was standing behind her, holding a glass of champagne.

"Are you alright?" his grin fell to a look of concern when it saw hers.

"I'm fine."

"Right," he returned a skeptical sort of smile, then after a pause: "Where's John?"

"He went to get a drink."

"Ah. So... charming shindig, huh," he commented, looking around at the crystal-encrusted walls.

"I guess," she mumbled.

"It almost seems like a waste, though, this meaningless glamour and pomp. It's like a candy wrapper that's empty inside, you know?" He looked back at her.

"No offense, but this is something I would peg you as enjoying," said Erica.

"That's just it! I know people expect me to enjoy this sort of thing, so I play along. But it's not really me."

Erica let the pause remain unfilled.

"What *is* really me? Honestly, I'd rather be sitting at home reading right now," Sajan leaned back against the railing next to her.

"Me too. I was in the middle of this great book before I came here."

"One of my life goals is to read every book I own. Shouldn't be too hard, right?, you'd think. Oh no. I have bookshelves and bookshelves sprawling over an entire wall, filled with volumes about everything from politics to travel to the occult."

Erica perked up.

"It's going to be a challenge to read the ones that don't interest me. Like the occult books – *those* I've read all of."

"Really?"

"Twice. I dabbled a bit, if truth be told, in my younger days. But even with my background knowledge some of the volumes were almost impossible to understand."

"I know, some of the symbology is so confusing!" she said.

"Oh, it's not the symbology," he laughed. "It's just that some of them are hundreds of years old!"

"Really?" her eyes popped.

"Yeah. The oldest I think is," he looked up, trying to remember, "three hundred? Three hundred fifty?"

"What is it?" asked Erica.

"An old religious manuscript, one of the ones that didn't make it into the Boble."

"Those are *impossible* to understand – the encryption," she shook her head.

"See, that's what I'm good with. I can read some for you tomorrow."

"What?"

"When you come over with John," Sajan said, thrown off. "We're hanging out tomorrow night at my place, I told him you should come... didn't he pass on the message?"

"No... maybe he forgot."

"That's probably it," Sajan nodded, but he looked perplexed all the same.

"Well, I guess I'll be there, then," said Erica, yet a skeptical note remained in her voice.

"Wonderful! I hate to cut our conversation short, considering I almost never get to touch this subject with people," he grinned, "but I don't want to be a bad date. Excuse me." But as he walked around

Erica he tripped, sending the contents of his champagne glass spilling over her leg and onto her satin shoe.

"Oh!" she exclaimed.

"Oh no! I'm so sorry, I'll replace them!"

"No, don't worry about it, it's just a shoe," said Erica as Sajan pulled off his shirt and swooped down to mop up the alcohol.

John returned from the bar just then, walking in on Erica leaning against the railing while a bare-chested Sajan wrapped one of her legs with the sleeve of his shirt, drawing stares.

"John!" Sajan's head shot up in alarm when he saw him. "It's not what it looks like!" he said so loudly everybody stopped to watch them.

"You mean you're not helping Erica clean up a champagne spill?" asked John.

"Wh – no, I am. I would never do anything – you know – I'm your friend."

"I trust you."

"I think you've got it all," said Erica to Sajan, looking down at the top of his head. Sajan stood up and pulled on his partially wet shirt, buttoning it carefully.

"So, John, you're joining us tomorrow night, then?" he turned around to face him. "Erica's been dying to get her hands on my collection of occult literature. It's enormous."

John cocked his head at Erica, who looked back at him with her mouth slightly open.

"Great! I'll see you both at eight, then." He disappeared.

They both shook their heads.

"Do you know what just happened?" John asked.

"No idea. How was the bar?" Erica asked John.

"Boring," he shrugged, joining her to look down at the dance floor filled with merry couples below, swaying like the tops of trees as a slow number began.

"John, I'm not blind. What's wrong?" Erica said after a minute.

"I'm just in shock over everything. I mean, not only did we go to a one-president system yesterday, but *nobody* seems to care! I haven't heard a single comment about Rutt tonight. I have heard about summer trends being bucked for fall, risky business ventures, and the wine selections of various upscale restaurants," said John.

"I think what it is, is it happened so fast that it seems surreal," Erica said thoughtfully.

"But it's *real*. And now with the Token Directory coming under government, they might do a system search – "

"Ooh," it dawned on Erica.

"I'm in more danger now than I've ever been in!" he said quietly, urgently.

"They never said anything about running a search, just about being on the lookout for suspicious activity! And you're not causing any. The token you wrote was so harmless, they'd probably gloss over it anyway," she consoled.

"No, it's not *what* I wrote – they have people who can filter lies, and if they catch that I lied they'll immediately get suspicious."

"So what are you going to do?"

John shrugged. "Live in constant fear that at any moment they'll pull out my file, come knocking on my door with an Identifier, and call me out?"

Erica's eyes popped. "That's it! John, why don't you go to an Identifier?" she said excitedly. "Find out what your token is!"

"Erica," he laughed, "you know there are like three registered in the country, and they're all government officials. Their identities are kept top secret."

"Well, maybe you could ask to see one," she started.

"And tell them that I don't know – "

"Tell them that you want to find out so you don't have to lie on government papers!"

"I already *did* lie on government papers. If they find out that's instant arrest. But more likely they'll throw me in a lab before I finish the sentence. Erica, *no one has ever not known what their token is before*," he impressed.

She sighed. "Have you ever considered going to a psychic?"

"What, like one of those with the seedy little shop in the middle of a tourist area?" asked John.

"They're unregistered Identifiers," she gave him a look.

"I don't really believe in that," he said skeptically. "Have you seen how many fortune telling shops there are? There can't be that many Identifiers, it's one of the rarest tokens."

"But *some* of them are real; they've predicted tons of cases of people with abstract tokens. How else are those people supposed to know what theirs are?" she defended.

"I'm not saying it's not possible, it's just, even if it is a real Identifier, having someone tell me isn't the same as really feeling and knowing it for myself. I wouldn't believe it."

"Then who *would* you believe?"

John chuckled. "Bob?"

It was very late and the party was winding down. John wasn't sure Mr. Daltuhn was even there anymore. He spotted Sajan downstairs, leaving with his arm around a blonde in a sequined mini dress, declaring the party unofficially dead.

***

He knocked on the door.

"Dude! You're famous!" said Hec, pulling him inside.

"Wha – ?"

He shoved today's newspaper into his face. There was a large piece titled <u>NKOZ's Big Gala</u> with pictures underneath.

"Look!" Hec pointed to one: Sajan Walker and Caroline Ash were standing arm in arm, the epitome of high society.

"Hot*tie*," said Hec.

In the background, John could just make out his own dim profile some ten feet behind Sajan, and Erica's arm, the rest of her behind Sajan's torso. Hec took the newspaper away.

"So, this is my new pad," he said, sprawling his arms.

"It's... small."

"Cozy."

John looked around. The living room contained one couch, a dingy table littered with empty beer cans and potato chip bags, and a medium-sized television that blared:

"...You see, Geoffrey, it is a symbol of chaos. The Great Wheel is not only longer than the Wheel of Consequence, but actually *propels* it up higher, distorting the balance," a middle-aged lady wearing a thick layer of makeup and tacky gold jewelry was saying as she held up a picture of the mysterious cross they'd first seen almost a month ago.

"So what you're saying, Rita, is that this symbol is potentially undermining every teaching in the Boble?" asked the wrinkled man interviewing her.

"Yes, *exactly*. It has the potential to totally destroy our faith in the delicate balance, and I personally fear that its proponents could be part of a – a, um, *bigger* unit, perhaps *connected* in some way to the LASS organization. It could be, I fear, a symbol representing a plan of mass evil."

"Rita Levinson, everybody," the host turned to the camera as a round of applause ensued.

"You're tuned into Bobnet, the channel devoted to the Truth of Bob. We'll be back to *Bobism Today* with Geoffrey Starmack after these commercial messages."

"...Have you let Bob into your life? Discover the wonder and joy of His Love with our brand new CD, *His Holy Sound* Volume 7!..."

Hec changed to the next channel up, which was playing reruns of *Milligan's Isthmus*.

"Sit down," he prompted John, doing so himself and laughing along with the laugh recording at a comic scene. "Grab some chips, they're in the box behind the couch."

"Actually, I didn't eat dinner yet," John said.

"Why didn't you say so!? Help yourself, buddy, kitchen's right around the corner. Grab me a beer while you're up?"

"Sure!" John called back from the kitchen.

He opened the fridge: it contained three bottles of beer and a package of hot dogs.

John handed Hec the beer and sat back down on the couch, his empty stomach grumbling.

"Ahh," went Hec as he took a gulp and set the bottle onto the table next to its many kin.

"Taking it easy before the workweek starts?" John asked.

"Oh, I'm taking off tomorrow. Mental health day," said Hec as he ate more chips.

"How are you spending it?"

He shrugged. "Dunno. Don't have any plans yet."

"What about skydiving? Marathon training? All those things you wanted to do, you've got a golden opportunity!" said John.

"Look, I had kind of a rough weekend, I think I just wanna relax tomorrow," said Hec.

"Alright. Wanna meet me at Mabel's later?" John asked.

"I dunno, might be kinda early," he said dubiously.

"Hec, that's six PM."

"My sleep schedule is very out of whack right now, dude," Hec informed. "I'll need at least a week to fix it."

"What about work?" asked John.

"Honestly, I think I might quit that job," Hec grimaced.

"Not fulfilling?" said John flatly.

"Not at all," Hec shook his head, missing the inflection.

"Well, before you start relaxing, wanna go to that foreign weapons exhibit at the museum for a bit?"

"Sure, gimme half an hour?" Hec glanced at his clock. "What!? Nine PM?" his head shot toward the window. "That can't be right."

"It's been nine PM since I got here. And probably for a while before then..." John mumbled.

At seven, he bid Hec goodbye and headed over to Erica's, from where they took a cab to Sajan's apartment in the nicest part of the city.

"Ah, welcome!" beamed a sharply dressed Sajan, leading them inside. They followed him into a luxurious sitting room whose walls were made of stone like an underground lair, except that his apartment was on the top floor. A wide archway hewn out of one side led to a small off-white room that opened to the balcony.

Sajan veered down a curving parquet hallway, calling out, "Make yourselves at home, I'll be out in a jiffy!" as he glanced back to catch John and Erica admire his abode with a satisfied look.

Erica started poking around the shelves. "Goldmine!" she exclaimed, pulling out an old, gray book from a corner.

"An occult manuscript?" asked John.

"Sajan's high school yearbook."

They scanned the sea of bland faces for that signature magnetic charm, but when their eyes snapped onto the name "Sajan Walker" they found an awkward black-haired boy with a wan look, no smile, instead a lopsided sneer like the shot had been snapped before he was ready. Framing his face were unsightly large glasses that reflected the flash, and he donned a button-up and tie like he did nowadays, but the confidence he carried them with was completely absent and in its place humiliation and the wish to be wearing a sports jersey.

They found him elsewhere only in the senior prom collage, where he stood alone behind a beaming couple, lanky and awkward.

They heard Sajan's steps approaching and hastily stuffed the yearbook back into its nook.

"I hope you're not too overwhelmed to see the rest?" he grinned as he set down the wine and glasses. He picked up a little remote, clicked it, and from the ceiling down came an enormous flat screen television.

"For when friends come over," he said, glancing back at them before clicking it once more into place. Then he led them down the hallway through his labyrinthine apartment, stopping last in front of the master bedroom. He knocked on the door. A girlish giggle issued from inside.

"Oh, Helga, my little love poodle! It's me-ee," Sajan cooed through the door.

"Just a meenute!" called a thickly accented female voice.

"She's a little shy around guests," Sajan explained as John and Erica tried to stifle their utter shock.

"Let's open that bottle!" he led them back, leaving John and Erica to wonder what femme fatale he had imported from overseas. In John's mind was a tall, hourglass silhouette whom light would reveal to be a deadly-gorgeous woman in a form-fitting red number, silky smooth hair falling over one eye and behind one shoulder that led to a lithe arm whose hand rested casually on the pronounced hip while it held a cigarette that it dropped to get squandered by a stiletto upon sight of a male guest, drawing attention away from that trifle with a seductive voice that began to lament how long it had been since they've had guests while the body's owner kept her eyes fixed on his as she blew out a final ring of smoke.

Sajan uncorked the red wine and poured a healthy measure into each glass as he talked animatedly of how much trouble he'd had picking out this loft, as he'd wanted something with a balcony view of both the city skyline *and* the water, and they were on different sides. Finally they'd hired someone to make the building rotate.

"...Just ninety degrees and you don't even feel it. You're sitting on the deck having a cappuccino with your sunset – " he smirked here at his own cleverness " – then you go inside for some massage therapy and when you come back out you're looking out over the heart of downtown Vandorn!"

"O therr you arre!" exclaimed a guttural voice behind them. John and Erica looked up, then dropped their gazes down: coming up the hallway was a short, plump blonde who looked older than Sajan, wrapped in a pink cocktail dress whose fluid satin skimmed over all her bumps and lumps like liquid sunlight giving love to every nook and fold. Her thick yellow curls with their fresh-out-of-rollers bounce messily brushed her puffy, flushed cheeks that almost buried her dark little eyes. With fat, pink-tipped fingers she adjusted the feathered boa hanging lopsided about her rippling neck as she rushed forward; a couple faux feathers floated to the parquet behind her.

"Darling, you didn't have to get all decked out!" Sajan jumped off the couch and ran to her, smiling. He took her hands in his. "John, Erica, this is my fiancé, Helga," he turned to them, then turned back to Helga and looked at her with love in his eyes. They rubbed noses, giggling, as Sajan stooped down and Helga stood on the tiptoes of her pink pumps to reach him, chunky legs extending maximally; she, the squishy pencil topper to his sleek fountain pen.

"Dearest, this is John Hallan and Erica Daltuhn. They work at NKOZ," he explained in the tenderest voice as he caressed her shoulder.

"A plessurr to meet you!" said Helga, shaking Erica's hand and then John's. Her accent didn't betray her country of origin, and John couldn't think of where it was in the custom to rub the palm repeatedly with one's thumb during a handshake, as Helga did when she took his hand in hers.

She sat down beside Sajan and promptly launched into the story of how they first met. Sajan chimed in with the occasional detail as he sat listening raptly, absorbed by every word rolling out of her lips as if he were beholding a Lauk. Helga, however, began taking frequent glances at John, and at first John thought he imagined her beady little eyes boring into his with a strange intensity, but as the night progressed he couldn't ignore the stomach flip he experienced every time her gaze snapped onto him and a smile curved over one corner of her mouth.

"Erica, are you alright? You seem a little fidgety," Sajan broke from their conversation much later.

"Not at all," said Erica, mildly surprised, waving her empty wine glass for further proof.

"I know what it is," Sajan ignored this. "You want to see my private library, don't you. Alright, I won't torture you any longer. Dear, would you mind taking Erica to the library?" he playfully pinched the fat on Helga's thigh.

"Of course," Helga answered in a purr. "Come," she commanded Erica. "We go to library for twenty – maybe five – minutes; then I show you my dresses...."

"Shall we?" said Sajan, gesturing to the balcony once the women were gone. John followed him out to a spectacular view of the city, hundreds of lights in a sea of dark.

"John, I'm in awe of you. *How* are you handling the pressure at NKOZ?" Sajan asked, sitting down in a chair and crossing one foot over the other on the railing.

"There isn't much to handle; I'm not that important there," said John, thrown off by this comment.

Sajan laughed. "John! You saved the network! Daltuhn can really spot the spark from a mile away."

"Spark? Oh no, he took me because I was desperate for a job and he could pay me change. I didn't even want to be in television. I was pre-med in college."

"So without any real desire or attempt on your part, Edmund Daltuhn took you straight into his inner circle."

"I suppose," this had never struck John before.

"Yet others who've spent months – years – exhausting themselves trying to get in are kept on the fringes."

John noticed that Sajan looked slightly maddened, as if he was unable to see something dangling so obviously in front of his nose.

"What is your secret? What is the source of your genius?" he asked.

"I'm not a genius!" John laughed.

"Oh, John, let's drop the pretenses; there's no need for false modesty, it's not like I'm trying to steal your other ideas for hit shows."

"I don't *have* other ideas for hit shows. There *is* no secret; Lil Holt – that was a fluke."

Sajan was silent for a long moment. "You're an interesting fellow, John Hallan," he then said. "None of this really impresses you," he waved his arms around his apartment.

"Not really," shrugged John.

"To know that for someone else everything I value is completely worthless," he shook his head with a joyless smile, "it really gives you perspective."

"*That's* true," said John.

"Someone once told me, 'something can only fall if you place it up high. If you want something to succeed, you have to place the same value on it as on everything else'," Sajan related, and paused.

"And yet," he picked up slowly again, "I've placed my career above everything else, and I've never been more successful!" he laughed. "So what's the deal? I could simply throw it away... and yet those words stick to me, and I don't know why."

"It'll probably be your downfall one day," said John.

"But see, I just can't see that! From where I'm standing I see only open skies. Who knows how far up you can go!"

"Maybe you're not looking at the right place. At the ground."

Sajan snorted. "You're a Debbie Downer. You can't imagine how exhilarating it feels to know no limits, to lose touch with the ground you thought you needed and fly, not knowing where you have to stop – maybe nowhere!"

"No, I can't imagine that. But I did know someone who felt the same, and I watched him follow that feeling to his death."

"You could use some lifting off from the ground, John Hallan. Otherwise you'll never know what life can be. I know you're probably thinking, what advice could an amoral, superficial phony give you about life – right? – but notice how far I've gone, and how far *you've* gone."

John was silent.

Sajan smirked. "You – you'll die and blow away like dust, leaving no trace. The world will be the same as if you never were on it – but I, I'll leave my mark."

An image of Kimi Kool flashed through John's mind.

"Typically, those who've left their mark on the world didn't set out with that as their aim," said John.

"I have a feeling," said Sajan slowly, "that we are never going to see eye to eye."

"Except on that one point," John nodded in agreement.

Soon the women returned, and Sajan seemed to lose all enthusiasm for having them over. He hastened finishing the wine and claimed he had an early morning.

They stood waiting for their cab in silence. Erica stared straight ahead, if John wasn't imagining things, rather tense.

"John, did Helga do some weird thing to your palm when you shook hands?" she asked.

"Yeah, she did the same to you?"

She nodded.

"I assumed that's the custom in her home country," he said.

But Erica was shaking her head. He could tell by the look she gave him that something was wrong.

"Remember I told you about psychics? The unregistered Identifiers?" she asked, her mouth a serious line.

"Yeah."

"That's how they read someone's token."

Silence fell between them. John recalled how Helga wouldn't take her eyes off of him, but kept looking at him with a strange, scrutinizing curiosity. And whatever it was she had found, by now Sajan knew, too.

***

Mr. Daltuhn sat in the break room with several younger members of his floor on Monday morning, enjoying one of the chintzy new Idea chairs they had just purchased.

"Mr. Daltuhn, are you seriously watching Bobnet?" Luke asked as he strolled in, looking condemningly at the television.

"What of it?"

"That's like the ultimate brainwash channel. This is what you wanna watch if you're staying informed," he changed the channel to NNC: Now! News Coverage.

Flashbulbs were going off everywhere around a tall figure entering a little uptown boutique; he glanced at them with mild surprise.

"...Sajan, do you truly believe that Bob was a figment of peoples' imaginations made up thousands of years ago to enslave the human race?" one reporter asked.

"Yes. That is one of the principles of Atheism," said Sajan. Muttering flared as camera clicks spiked.

"Sajan, your belief system has been around for a week and already has a million 'likes' on faceplace. What do you attribute to its popularity?..."

"That sly sonofabitch," Mr. Daltuhn growled.

"You just don't like him because he's a free thinker!" said Luke angrily.

Mr. Daltuhn laughed. "Boy, you are ignorant! This is all bullshit!" he laughed again.

"No it's not! It was *on his new blog*," Luke emphasized. "Which I bet you didn't even read before judging him."

"I have better things to do," said Mr. Daltuhn.

"*I* read it," said a young man in black-framed glasses. "Did you see the comments? People are *haters*. I mean, sure it's controversial, but he's allowed to say whatever he wants, it's a free country."

"Yeah," agreed the girl he'd been talking to. "And even if you completely disagree, it really makes you think, you know?"

"Exactly. Plus, ever notice how all the best ideas were hated at first?" Luke posed this interesting point.

"Yeah, maybe it'll force this country to pay attention to something a little more important than how many guys Lillian Holt hooked up with this weekend," said the guy in glasses, and all three of them laughed.

"Four," said Luke as John walked in and diverted their conversation, which had turned to how ridiculously big the ears on one of the four guys were it must've been his "gift".

"Hallan, I need to talk to you," Mr. Daltuhn caught up to him. He pulled him aside and said quietly, "Erica told me about Sajan's fiancée."

"Oh," was all John could say after a pause.

"This is a serious matter, Hallan. I know Sajan, and when he can get the upper hand he will. The Token Directory is going under government and looking out for suspicious cases. Sajan knows people in high places; all he has to do is say the word. Both you and the network are at risk."

"Are you firing me?" asked John, who, in a back corner of his mind, had been expecting this for a while.

"No. I'm sending you overseas to the Celestial Harmonies Retreat."

"Come again?"

"It's where people go for their spiritual needs, to get in touch with Bob," he looked like he was chewing a raw onion; Mr. Daltuhn took to spirituality like Milly took to popularity.

"Actors swear by it!" Mr. Daltuhn defended when John raised his eyebrows. "People come back transformed! Hallan, this is my last resort, you know I don't believe in this bullshit. I don't know what they do over there and I don't want to, but I'm hoping – praying – it opens you up to your token like nothing else has. Maybe you're blocked to Bob or whatever, maybe that's why you don't know – "

John was unable to believe what he was hearing.

"Don't look at me like I'm crazy, you can't fathom the strings I pulled to get you there, that place is damn near inaccessible! And not cheap either," he wagged a finger in John's face. "I've divided your assignments among the rest so that you'll be ready to leave by Thursday."

"Mr. Daltuhn, you can't send me away *now*! If Sajan makes a move I won't be able to do a thing from halfway across the world!"

"On the contrary, Hallan, this is the perfect time for you to go. He can't touch you over there, you'll be safe."

"Until I return to a mess!"

"Hallan, if you don't go then I *will* fire you! I need to protect the network. By the way, I told everybody you were going to a psychiatric hospital for a mental condition."

"*What?*"

"Well I had to tell them something for why I'm giving you a two week vacation! Did you want me to tell the truth?" Mr. Daltuhn countered.

"You couldn't have said I was visiting family? A relative died?"

"Look, I said the first thing that came to mind."

John stormed out and went to his office, where on cue he met Erica walking out.

"You told your father!?" he said without preamble.

"John – I was trying to help – I couldn't sit by and do nothing! My dad knows a lot of people, he can do more than we can."

"He's sending me halfway across the world!"

"What?"

"I'm leaving on Thursday to some idiotic spiritual retreat where instead of doing something useful, I'm going to be learning how to get in touch with Bob and my inner self! Your father has gone insane!"

"John, he has your best interests at heart. My dad does everything for the people he cares about, please trust him!" she pleaded.

"He didn't need to know this, Erica. I don't need more people making this a bigger mess than it already is." He walked angrily past her into their office.

"Oh, honey, don't feel bad. You were just trying to help," said Nancy-Beth from her desk.

"What happened?" a couple other nearby girls asked concernedly.

"It's John – he has a mental condition, and Erica told the boss, and now he's sending John away to get help," Nancy-Beth spoke discreetly. "Needless to say John's not too happy, he's still in the denial stage."

"What?" Erica looked at her confusedly.

"Don't worry, he'll come back better and realize what you did for him," one of the women consoled Erica.

"John doesn't have a mental condition," Erica shook her head.

The other woman put her hand on Erica's shoulder. "Honey, he doesn't need *you* to deny it, too."

Chapter 21: Spirituality

The bus pulled up to the stop and John got off. The empty dirt road stretching out to either side of the "Welcome to Celestial Harmonies" sign was quietly lit by the pounding sun. Before him lay a trail winding into the dense forest ahead, swallowed up by the darkness.

He commenced, justifying the trying trek by thinking this was how they cleansed one before immersion into spiritual work. After an hour he came upon a lone wooden cabin.

"Um... hello?" John asked when he walked hesitantly inside. His eyes roved around and landed on a man who blended in so perfectly with the background John had missed him the first time: he gave an aura of deepest reverie in the tranquility of his pose and the stillness of his shoulder-length gray hair falling serenely about his face.

The man opened his eyes.

"Ahh... welcome," he said, looking at John. "We have been expecting you...."

Ceramic beads woven into his braids chinked gently like tiny wind chimes as he got up, little fingers interlacing to play the music of the world.

"You are with us for the next two weeks?"

"Yes."

The man seemed to disapprove. "That is hardly enough time to generate your own energetic atmosphere. What you really need is a four-week immersion program. Might I interest you – ?"

"Sorry, my boss only paid for two," said John.

He followed the guide outside onto an ornate tile pathway garnished with semiprecious stones that glittered in the sparse rays of sunlight sneaking through the tree branches. His guide sprung lightly off the path and floated ahead, several feet above the ground. John followed him afoot.

They cut through a gently sloping mountainside into a valley that appeared like a bubbling hot spring of vibrancy: pagodas, water fountains, and meditative gardens flaunted color and texture like water spilling over a cup. It was almost too much to take in. The guide, however, led them off to the side toward a group of shady natural-brick buildings situated away from the spiritual hubbub.

"These are our dormitories," the guide explained. "Each one is named after one of the three celestial bodies that most heavily impact our humble planet. There is the Sun Wing, the Moon Wing, and the Star Wing."

"The sun is a star," said John.

"Here at Celestial Harmonies we see boundaries as artificial constructs, and believe that the first step to spiritual reawakening is to free oneself of such constructs."

Everywhere around the campus, people were flying like the guide, or transplanting statues from place to place with their minds to create more artful designs. One man was peacefully watering a garden with a stream of water that spouted from his index finger.

"We encourage the free expression of tokens; you won't find any restrictions on token practice here like you do in Vandorn. On the contrary, we believe that restriction itself is the source of those depraved manifestations restrictions try to prevent. Most people think that, given freedom, people will go crazy. In truth, there is nothing so calming to the soul as to be allowed complete freedom."

"I dunno. I've seen a lot of people go off the deep end in trying to embrace freedom back in Vandorn," John said.

"Ahh, well it is different in a setting so devoid of Bob's presence," his guide said.

"Have you ever been to Vandorn?"

"No. I know the archaic jungle that is the world. I see little reason to abandon my peace here for it. I have known many great spirits who, in their curiosity, left to cities like Vandorn and became corrupted, losing the knowledge and attainments they gained here and sinking into unsavory lifestyles."

"They weren't such great spirits then, were they," said John.

"I should think they were! I have personally seen many of them perform wonders, miracles!"

"Well sure, it's easy to be good in easy circumstances."

The guide looked at John. "The world is not kind to the growth of the soul," he said sagely.

"But isn't true spirituality independent of circumstance?"

The guide sighed. "Cities like Vandorn turn people into little more than animals in fine clothing. If we changed that structure, many of society's ills would be cured."

"So you're saying we should do away with big cities and house everyone in mountain retreats like this one?"

"It wouldn't do the world harm," remarked the guide.

John laughed. "That's impossible. Virtually every culture in our world's history has tended toward city life."

"And that is how we get massive spiritual voids, places where life is covered with grime so thick even Bob cannot reach the people."

"I thought Bob was everywhere?"

"No no no – I mean, yes, *in the abstract* – but there are forces that that pull one away from Bob, and these are devoid of His presence," the guide explained.

John gave him a quizzical look, never having come across this bit in his recent readings of the Boble.

They came full circle and entered the Star Wing, where John's guide left him to his room and soared off with a farewell wave.

He set his bag down beside the incense burner and had a look around, taking in the pale blue walls decorated with contemplative prints, the dozen votives scattered among the nightstand and shelves, and the yoga mat in the corner. It did lack a telephone, refrigerator, and electrical outlets.

John took out his copy of the Boble and set out. He settled on a bench under a shady flowering tree, and opened the book.

"...I already feel closer to Bob. Just this morning I came to a fork in the road and something – almost this intangible voice inside me – told me to go right, and it led me to this beautiful flowering shrub garden where I had a small revelation about my life's purpose," John heard a voice approaching. He looked up to see a man and woman roughly his age walking his way. It was the woman who had spoken.

"Is that the Boble?" she asked curiously, stopping before John.

"Yep."

"Being here will make you see that book in a totally new light," she said.

"Actually, I had a bit of a debate with my guide. *I* said that Bob is supposed to be everywhere, but he thought that Bob wasn't present in Vandorn because of some forces that pulled one away.... I couldn't remember reading that, but I dunno, maybe I skipped over it or something," John continued in search.

The guy peered at John's copy.

"Oh, you have the old version. They fixed all the mistranslations that have been around for centuries and it completely changes the meaning of some passages. Much more suited to today's sociopolitical climate," he nodded.

"I wonder which translation they used for the *Dumbass's Guide to the Boble*," John grinned at them; but their expressions were not sympathetic to his joke. They quickly walked on.

So they're not über-hip city youths. I picked the wrong stereotype to appeal to, John sighed. He retreated to his room for the rest of the evening.

"...Honestly, I feel like life in Artinia is meaningless. People only want to talk about the latest cars, the trendiest clothes, the football game they watched last night.... I came here in search of the deeper things in life," said a woman named Christy at their first lesson the next morning as the class sat around in a circle and introduced themselves and their reason for being here, or, as their mentor said, their reason for Being. "It's reassuring to find like-minded people."

"Oh, so you're looking to meet someone?"

"Yes," she nodded.

"Well I'm Bill," another started, "and I've been on this quest to find Bob my whole life, but no matter what I did I never felt closer to Him. I don't know *what* I'm looking for – maybe passion, maybe an intensely religious experience that'll bring a spark of joy into my dreary existence. I guess what I want is a permanent way to stay high."

Everyone nodded.

"Wait," people turned to John, "I understand wanting passion – but what does that have to do with Bob?"

"I – I mean – Bob is – "

"It's a legitimate desire, but you shouldn't confuse the chase for thrills with the search for Bob," John said.

There was a pause of silence.

"I think what Bill is saying is that he's in search of the deeper truth," another woman intervened. "Society places such high value on superficial things that life can seem empty."

"What about our society is so superficial?" asked John. Three people immediately erupted in talk.

"What – everything!"

"*Don't you watch T.V.?*"

"Look," John overrode them, "I know what you're saying: teen whores, headache-inducing reality drama, slanted news – but I don't think that's *superficial*. I don't think *anything* is superficial. Take Lillian Holt: she's detestable. She acts insincere, freeloads off her parents, shows the world as much of her body as your partner shows you – and for that she gets called superficial. But that's the two percent of her life we see. None of us know the path that led her to where she is, or what's going on inside. There was once a time in her life when she *didn't* act that way, when she was a little kid like we all were. Is it easier to relate to her when you realize you were both once in the same place? And don't you remember having your own dreams and ambitions, and how hard everything around you tried to push them down if they didn't accord with the world's expectations? Maybe she is who she is because those dreams she had are buried so deeply she feels she can't achieve them, is even ashamed for them and carries a dead weight around because no matter how much it's denied that part of us never dies? For us to sit here and judge her as if she is only what she seems on the surface speaks of *our* ignorance of the deeper truth, *our* superficiality. If something seems superficial, it's because *you don't understand it*. You may disagree with something, you may even abhor it – but nothing can be superficial, just as no plant springs up without a root in the ground."

Everyone stared at him.

"And I don't think liking poetry, mysticism, and religion makes you any 'deeper' than someone who likes cars, pop music, and shopping," John added.

"I personally feel that society urges us to abandon ourselves and chase empty dreams," said the next man. "Magazines following the sordid affairs of celebrities, the way we work for money instead of joy. That's why we come to places like this, where we can reconnect with our true selves through creative pursuits such as poetry and the appreciation of nature, outside of the standards imposed on us by society. My name is Stanley, by the way."

"What do you for a living, Stanley?" someone asked.

"Ah – I'm a freelance writer."

At the end of two hours, John walked outside and met a dazzling scene: dozens of people in the fields were unrestrainedly wielding their powers. One was playing with a vortex into a parallel reality through which odd creatures appeared onto the grass. Several people were flying. Another went around in a circle telling everybody their thoughts. The man standing next to John suddenly sprouted three more heads and started running around. The rest of the class followed suit.

John took out his Boble and sat down on a bench in the shade, reading again.

Suddenly half the world disappeared and became blank space, a sheet of untouched paper. Then it reappeared, upside down. Then John saw a squirrel run by that had been turned inside out.

"Come on, man, let loose!" yelled several people from class, running by him. "We have the freedom to let our tokens do whatever we want. Go crazy!"

"But I don't want to. I want to sit here and read the Boble. Don't I have the freedom to do that?" asked John.

They appeared thrown off.

"You *want* to be boring and everyday?"

John shrugged. "I guess so."

"Okay, but you're not going to be able to blog about your unbridled release from the repression of cloistered urban life when you return to Artinia."

"I don't feel repressed," John remarked. "Freedom means you *can* do something, not that you *have to*."

"What's wrong with that guy?" they asked each other.

"Maybe he needs counseling," one girl whispered, convinced that John was insane because he didn't want to go crazy

John soon got up and walked around. He met several more of his classmates by a fountain, talking about their class.

"It's like my soul has been fed and everything is more vivid," said one woman.

"Yes, I really feel myself moving along the spiritual path," nodded Stanley.

"It was a pretty easy for me compared to the meditation exercise I practice back at home, I hope they pick up the pace," said a man.

"So, how far along the spiritual path are you?" John asked, determined to turn his luck with his peers around.

"Me? Probably intermediate," he gave it thought. "I've been doing it for three years, so I've really built that solid spiritual base you need. But with the exercises my mentors know, I'm probably farther than where I should be for the time I've been studying. They don't teach those shortcuts here, unfortunately."

"Shortcuts?" John asked, not following.

"To accumulating energy," he explained. "The more energy you have stored, the higher you can go, so to speak, in one bout."

"But I thought spirituality was about giving away, not taking in. Giving away everything so you are left with nothing," John said.

They looked at him. He looked at them. There was silence.

For the rest of the week, John wandered the grounds alone when he was not in class. But even then as he was only partially there; he was too preoccupied with what might be going on in Vandorn. Thus, although life at Celestial Harmonies was peaceful, he could not enjoy it. Somehow his worries kept him so distracted he managed to miss the craze of "giving away" that had swept through the Retreat's students like wildfire as they raced up the spiritual staircase.

"I'm giving up the boat I spent the last five years saving up for," said one man at breakfast later that week.

"I've decided to give up rights to my poetry collection. I feel this is a significant step in my spiritual development, it's almost as if I'm giving up a part of my *soul*," said Stanley.

"*I've* given away my possessions in an abstract form: time," said a third.

"That's so profound!" gasped another.

"But that's not really giving away," said John, and the side conversations stopped. "What about the possessions you hold in your mind? Your 'spirituality'? Your 'goodness'? Giving away means giving away your notions about yourself. All the things you think you are, so that you are left with nothing."

The uncomfortable silence was dissipated by the arrival of their mentor, who came to share an announcement.

"Next week you will meet the Chief Guide of the Retreat. This is a very special event, as he rarely leaves his abode to venture into our realm."

Everyone turned to each other in awe.

"*I* know what his token is!" one woman whispered. "Every time he meets someone, he sees them as ideal, and every time he gets near them that ideal is shattered. He can't help but have hope no matter how many times it's broken. It's a gift and a curse."

"That is amazing! In spite of his constant suffering, what good he does for others. He is truly an inspiration," another woman nodded. "He must be *so* spiritually high."

"Duh, he's the head guru. He's practically *shrouded* in mystery," said a man.

"You're not excited, John?" one of their group asked him; John had been the only one to not respond to their mentor's announcement.

"No, I am. He seems like an interesting person, I just don't think he's *that* high up."

"How can you say that?" everyone wore faces of shock.

"Because he looks for happiness outside himself. He is trapped in enamor with his own token and thus dead to further development. How can such a person be the greatest spiritual guru in this world? He's great on his step, but it's not the ultimate. He can't go beyond the deluded belief that forms the crux of his inner world. But once you surpass that you realize how small your world was and how much more open space lies ahead, and within you, waiting to be explored."

He went for one of his usual walks, passing by landmarks that had become too familiar, stopping to direct an elderly couple who was new to the grounds.

"...Take this path down to the green pagoda, then make a right until you hit the outdoor incense court. Make a left there and the Sauna of Soul-Searching will be about five hundred feet up," he said. They thanked him and left. He sighed. Even exploring the grounds had gotten boring. Unable to stand it anymore, John headed for the exit and left the grounds to explore the outside world.

He felt a little rebellious as he imagined his classmates sitting around in a circle trying to bring sensation to their fingertips and toes. The bus took him to the nearest tavern, a dingy wooden building even more dilapidated than the Retreat's welcome cabin. He walked inside to a smattering of locals having drinks and watching an old, begrimed television set propped on a counter behind the bartender, who cleaned glasses.

All eyes turned onto him. Their glares did not look welcoming.

"You want phone?" the bartender asked in broken Artinian.

"No," John said simply, sitting down on a barstool.

He watched their T.V., where he couldn't understand a word the news anchors were saying. The customers shot each other looks; neither the bartender nor they knew what to make of this.

"I would want get away from that madhouse, too," the bartender muttered after a while.

"Yeah. I'll have a beer," John said.

"Ten dollars," the bartender slammed one onto the counter.

"For a beer?"

"He charged the other Artinians twenty," said one of the customers.

"And it wasn't even a beer," the bartender laughed. "Idiot Artinians. Come over here to 'help' us so you can call yourself 'better'. If you want to throw your money away, we take it," he laughed again.

"Don't worry, I'm not here to help you," said John, taking a swig from the bottle.

"What are you here for? To find Bob?" this time everyone in the bar laughed.

"At least I only have another week," John said darkly while they still chuckled.

"Better make it more. Don't want to be in Artinia now," said the bartender.

"Why not?"

"What you mean, 'why not'? Are you live under a rock?"

John still looked confused.

"Your country is going mad!" the bartender whispered dramatically, leaning in toward John's face.

"Oh, well yeah," John took another sip of beer. "I know things are going downhill, but it's all part of the natural progression."

"You are mad, too, then, if you think you can survive the storm."

"What storm?"

"The solar flare storm about to hit right over your country. It will be the biggest natural disaster in modern history! People all over the world are preparing, but Artinia will get hit the worst."

"There's no storm," John gave him a look, knowing how they liked to mess with foreigners.

"Haven't you noticed things get crazy lately? That's what happens before a solar storm. People go crazy. There is more fighting, more crime, lunacy, outbursts of mass hysteria."

John recalled the Pro-Choice and Pro-Life rallies.

"At the end everyone lose control of their tokens. There are wars, tsunamis, destruction, death. And you cannot stop it, only wait for it to pass."

John waited for the bartender to burst out laughing and shout "idiot Artinian!" like it was all a practical joke.

But he didn't. None of the men in the bar listening to his story laughed.

"I would've heard about it. There's been nothing on the news. Wouldn't they have known about this for a while?"

"The whole world has known! I prove it." The bartender reached under the counter and pulled out his laptop. With the aid of high-speed internet he pulled up several articles for John.

There it was; the whole world was getting ready for the cultimation of slowly building insanity.

It was all starting to make sense – the bomb threat, the June ninth attacks, the Go GREEN company. But why did the one place that should be most worried have not a word to say on the matter? Were they resigned to a mass wipeout, and decided to let the Artinian population enjoy its last days in bliss?

"You are in great danger. It is wise for you to stay here," said the bartender seriously.

"But I have friends and family in Artinia – I can't leave them."

"Bring them here."

"When is it supposed to hit?"

"A few week. Maybe a month. No one know the exact date."

For the rest of the week, John went to the tavern every day, where he played cards and drank beer (soon on the house for him). He could think of nothing but the impending solar storm and how he would get everyone out of Artinia. The bargoers had offered their houses, but there simply wasn't enough room for everyone John wanted to bring back. His time at Celestial Harmonies, where he did little more than eat and sleep, passed like a dream that wouldn't stick in his memory, and before he knew it he had flash forwarded to his final day in the mountainous sanctuary.

"John, teach us something!" he heard at breakfast that morning, where he had been vaguely aware of his class discussing how they would spiritually prepare themselves for meeting the Chief Guru that evening.

"What?" he looked up, startled to see every pair of eyes at the table turned onto him. "What do you want me to teach!?"

"Anything! Transmute your knowledge to our hungry souls!"

"I can't!" said John.

"But you can! You always bestow enlightenment."

"Teach us something *real*! Something we can *use*!"

John rolled his eyes. "That's impossible! You can't simply communicate knowledge. Take a man and a woman living together," everyone scooted in closer to hear him speak.

"They're having an argument. The man is convinced of his views. The woman, just as convinced of her own position, pretends to listen, but really she only half listens at best – as the man speaks she is already thinking of the strong reply she will give to counter his argument. Neither she nor he can stop believing in the rightness of their own position. To understand the man, the woman must stop believing in herself and assume that what he says is the truth, even though nothing could seem more absurd at that moment. Likewise the man must do the same with the woman's point of view. In life, no one can do this. No one can even try to listen to or understand another. Each person is so strongly convinced of his own view, and the worst thing is that it *feels* right to be convinced in this way! It feels absolutely right and true! And yet if one cannot throw oneself out of oneself, how can one ever make room for another? How can communication between two people be possible when we are like this? So don't you see how your question is pointless?" John asked. Before they could respond John hopped off his chair to venture to the tavern one last time.

"So did you find Bob?" the bartender joked.

"I didn't come here to find Bob," said John.

"Ah, then what did you come here to find?"

"...I don't even know."

"Did you find *that*?" the bartender chuckled.

"Nope."

"That is anticlimactic."

He ran back onto the grounds, panting. The sun had already set, leaving the dimmest red-plum glow on the horizon. Disappointingly, John knew that he had missed seeing the guru. He stopped running and stood there defeated, out of breath.

"I didn't expect you back so early," said a voice behind him. John turned around; it was an old man whom he had never seen before.

"I didn't expect you at all," John replied.

"You normally return much later. I've seen you come back almost every night.... I don't blame you for finding tavern life more exciting than spiritual work. Even *I* admit it does get a little dull when the well of epiphanies runs dry," he smirked.

"If it wasn't for the tavern I wouldn't know about the solar flare storm," John said.

"True," the old man nodded, which John realized meant he knew about it, too.

"I didn't mean to miss the guru. I wanted to see him to ask him about – something," John didn't want to share secrets with this stranger.

"You don't look like you are in a state to see any gurus," the man noted.

John sighed. "I haven't made much out of my stay here. I've been too preoccupied with figuring out what to do about my family and friends in Artinia."

"Bring them here," said the man simply.

"How? I don't have the money."

"You can stay here for free."

"How do you know they'll let me?" asked John.

He laughed. "It is my decision."

John doubled back. "Then wouldn't *you* be the – ?"

The man shrugged. "Titles belie judgment."

John looked at him.

"By the way, you won't find what you're looking for here," the man said.

"Are you able to see the future?" John asked.

"No, that is not my token," the man answered with a touch of curiosity.

"Then what is?" asked John.

"I can break apart every truth you know," he said simply.

John's eyes widened, as the man took one step closer....

Chapter 22: Queen Dee and the Masquerade

"So, I deleted my YourSpot," said Milly nonchalantly, swirling a baby carrot around in some dip.

No reaction.

"I deleted my YourSpot," she repeated.

"So?" asked Jean.

"So, aren't you in awe that I'm above a trend to the extent that I don't care about my popularity?" Milly asked.

"Please, that was cool, what, *one* months ago?" said Gretchen.

"Yeah, everyone already deleted their YourSpot," said Tai.

No sooner had Milly isolated herself in her room to brood on yet another failure that afternoon than her fortifications were barged through by Mrs. Hallan, who gently pushed open the door to find Milly lying on her bed staring out the window.

"Milly, what's wrong?" she asked her daughter softly.

"I just – I'm tired of being so naïve. It feels like everyone is cooler than me – "

"That's ridiculous! How can you think that?" Mrs. Hallan exclaimed, stroking her hair.

"Please just listen!" Milly cried, on the verge of tears. "At school – nobody notices me, I get pushed around everywhere, I feel so – so small... I wish I could make more of an impression!"

"Oh, honey. You *do* make an impression!"

"Not enough to win Queen of the Masquerade."

"Win *what*?"

Milly turned around to face her, sitting cross-legged on her bed. "Every fall there's a school dance, the Masquerade, and the students vote on a queen to be crowned."

"A popularity contest," said her mother.

"Basically, yeah."

"You want to make an impression by winning a popularity contest?" Mrs. Hallan asked, sympathy gone.

"See, I knew you wouldn't understand!"

"I *do*, I understand completely.... Well, why can't you win?"

"Because only the most popular girl wins. No one's gonna vote for me! They're all going to vote for Dee Allderbay, just like last year, just like always."

"Milly, if you think this Dee Allderbay has something in her that you don't – "

"Oh, not one of these speeches," Milly threw her head up.

"Go ahead, say I'm stupid," said Milly in defeatist tones when she caught sight of her mother's stern look. Mrs. Hallan merely sighed.

"You're not stupid, you just don't understand yet," she said at last.

"Understand what?" Milly asked moodily with a smidgen of curiosity.

"That Dee Allderbay being the most popular girl in school and winning Queen of the Masquerade doesn't attest to what kind of person she is inside."

How many times Milly had heard such commonly shared wisdom!

"She's just that kind of girl; she's used to everyone's jealousy and admiration of her," Mrs. Hallan continued.

"Well why can't *I* be that girl!" Milly whined.

Mrs. Hallan sighed. "Milly, what I think you need is some cheering up. Come on, let's go shopping."

"I don't want to go shopping."

"Not even to Hollister?"

All through the car ride, Milly stared out the window and remained purposefully sullen. She would not be cheered up. Even as they walked into Hollister (where Milly was praying not to run into anyone from school), she still tightened her face into stone any time the impulse to smile came over it.

"Ooh, this is nice! What do you think, Milly?" her mother asked, holding up a pink t-shirt with "HCO" on it from the clearance rack.

"Mom..." said Milly in a low voice as she walked by her, holding the clothes she was going to try on.

320

"Let me see what you picked out," her mother leaned over, rummaging through the small heap. "Goodness gracious!" she yelled. "Oh, no no no, Milly, this skirt is much too short!"

A couple of eighth graders sniggered as they walked by, one of whom happened to be wearing the very skirt Mrs. Hallan was protesting, in extra extra small.

"Let's go look at bras!" Milly heard the other eighth grader say to her friend in the skirt as they walked out. "My double A feels really tight."

"Yeah, mine too! I'm, like, popping out."

"Maybe they have those new bras on sale, you know, the ones that push everything up."

"Ooh! *Cleavage!*"

Mrs. Hallan put the skirt back on the rack. "Honestly, Milly, some of the things in this store, I had no idea..." she whispered. "Why don't you go try on what you have, and then we'll visit some other places...."

Milly left to the dressing room. *Why can't I have a cool mom?* she lamented. *Like one of those modern, edgy, smart-aleck moms they show in the most recent movies. The kind who've had a couple abortions, read* Cosmetology, *and occasionally cuss in a sharp, witty manner across the dinner table. The kind whom I can talk to about how her new boyfriend is so wrong for her and how she totally should've stayed with the last one. Why does my mom have to be the kind from movies they made twelve years ago: all calm and family-oriented and into baking pies! I'm never gonna have any good mom stories to share with the girls! Am I ever going to be able to tell my friends about the time when my mom was sixteen and ran away from home on a stolen bus she and her friends drove three hundred miles in order to protest unfair laws? No! Am I ever going to be able borrow my mom's favorite retro band shirt she bought at the beach thirty years ago that she still wears around the house when she's rockin' out to her favorite classics? No! Am I ever going to be able to bitch out some narrow-sighted doctor about what a stuck-up elitist priss he is when he snubs my mom, who, though she may not own a yacht, is way more open minded and accepting than his recently unpopular ass, for working at a nail salon? No, I am not!! I'm not even going to be able to do the simple things, like support my mom for dressing sexy at her age. And you know why? Because my mom doesn't dress sexy! She dresses like she's almost fifty! Granted she is almost fifty, but everyone knows that the coolest moms nowadays dress* at least *twenty years below what is appropriate for their age. I mean, why can't a smart, independent woman still want to look and feel attractive at midlife? It's so unfair....*

"Excuse me, this one's open," the lofty sixteen-year-old girl halfheartedly overseeing the dressing rooms said to Milly. Drawing out a key with her manicured hands, she walked Milly over to the empty stall and turned around without another word.

A bit sad from her musings, Milly gathered her parcels and made to go in, but did a double take. Right outside her stall there stood a mannequin whose narrower hips and smaller breasts showcased a complete ensemble of such utter cuteness that Milly could not help but marvel as she stood staring. From head to toe, the pink hat, maroon-and-pink faded Hollister t-shirt, faded torn ultra low-rise jeans and pink flip flops, all tied together with a chic belt and some funky jewelry that was both startling yet earthy, was so immaculately put together down to the last detail, was so reminiscent of Dee's perfectly harmonized outfits at school, that Milly immediately envisioned herself walking through the halls in an outfit like that, standing out from the crowd like a jewel. Such confidence did it inspire in her that her own imagination captured her heart and she eagerly believed it. And in that moment, Milly knew *exactly* what she needed to win Queen of the Masquerade: a makeover! A total makeover so extreme she would be unrecognizable!

Alive with the spirit of inspiration coursing through her veins, Milly threw all the plain, boring t-shirts and half-price jeans she'd picked out onto a bench that happened to be there and abandoned her place. A manic look in her eyes and a smile to match, she pushed her way through all the people she did not notice in her frenzied state and scavenged every shelf and rack in the unnecessarily dim store like a bloodthirsty pirate in search of rare treasure, starting with the most expensive and recent. She dart-like snatched a tank top here, grabbed skinny jeans there, and dove into a pile of new long t-shirts with the sublime agility of a savage lion among a buffet of bleeding deer, tearing artfully through the tender meat. Her hands swiped up the juiciest morsels guided by sharp eagle's eyes, leaving behind a wreckage of shreds and second-rate garments.

Returning to her former outpost laden with henleys, culottes, and things that had to be tied together to stay on, she grabbed the pink outfit that had been her muse off its mannequin, and dove into the dressing room.

Thirty minutes later she emerged. She was found by her mother at the accessories.

"Could you hold these for a minute?" Milly asked absently, handing over the enormous pile of clothes.

"You're trying all of these on?"

"No, I'm buying them."

Mrs. Hallan flipped over some of the price tags. "I can't pay for all of this!" she shouted in a ludicrous voice. "Have you even checked the sales rack?"

"Yeah, I didn't like anything," Milly dismissed as she admired the way a bracelet sat on her wrist.

"This belt would look *so* hot with the low-rise slim bootcut jeans, don't you think?"

With much effort Mrs. Hallan extracted the jeans in question and placed them up to Milly's body, so as to see how just how high they rose, or rather, didn't rise. What she realized was that, any way one sliced it, Milly would not be able to sit down in a chair in these jeans, even while wearing one of the Hollister long t-shirts.

They left the store twenty minutes later with three large Hollister bags depicting the torso or a male model on the front.

"Thank you, mom, thank you so much," Milly said for the fifth time.

"You're welcome Milly," said her mother flatly.

"I love you."

"Mhmm."

As soon as they got home, Milly ran up to her room with her parcels and tipped everything onto her bed, staring at the sizeable pile with glee. With these products, she would be transformed into a beauty unrecognizable; it would be so radical, so bold, that when she looked into the mirror upon its completion, she would find a girl capable of shocking everyone in her school with her fresh appeal. No one saw Milly for the rest of the night. They assumed she had gone to sleep shortly after. No one, not a soul save Milly herself caught a glimpse of the "new" her. *That* was to wait until morning....

***

Cue bad-ass music.

There goes Milly; she's walking to school; her heels are clicking; her leggings are black; her miniskirt is mini and her hair is straight; her makeup is done right and her face is perky; that lipgloss made them fuller and those lashes jump out; the mascara did the trick and the eyeshadow shimmers; just a subtle shimmer, to go with her sleek new top; it matches her miniskirt only too perfectly; the necklace and the bracelet tie it all together; just a hint of class but not over the top.

We skipped the part where she got off the bus, because it didn't fit it with her new image.

She's walking in the halls; she's commanding attention; oh my Bob look at her who is that girl?; her outfit is so cute!; ugh I am jealous; dude, I would bang her; hellllz* yeah!

It seemed everyone was paying attention to her! She felt so popular already, and all she had done was walk through the halls toward her locker.

Gasp! There he was! Marrik McFost, talking to some of his friends.

Milly tried not to look at him as she walked by, but she could feel every nerve tingling and was sure he could plainly see that she was determinedly not looking at him, as if the desire to glance over were spelled above her head.

For a brief flicker his gorgeous eyes met hers, glancing over her appearance. *He noticed her! Eeeek! Her plan was working!* Heart still hammering, she tried to cover up the smile of joy by letting her hair

*hellz; related: hellllz – not "hell" as we know it, but on this planet short for "hello," as in, to mark something as obvious. "hellz yeah"; "hello, of course!"

fall in front of her face; that golden moment was worth it all. As she reached her first class, she forced her smile into a straight line (she was sure it would be instantly obvious to everyone what she was smiling about), and only then entered.

"Oh my Bob, what happened to you?" Tai gasped.

"I gave myself a makeover."

"You look so cute! I *love* your outfit!"

"Thanks. It's from Hollister."

Their exclamations attracted the glances of the girls over on the other side of the room. Becky, Jen, and Stacy came up to see what all the fuss was about, and Milly's shocking new look jumped out at them like a cornered python.

"Aww, you look so adorable today, Milly!" Jen cooed.

"That skirt is *wicked* hot," said Becky. "Did you get it from Hollister?"

"Yeah." She couldn't help but smile as these three more popular girls admired the things she wore, making her feel included in their warm little group.

All day she received this kind of attention. Nor did people stop glancing at her in the halls, either. She was only disappointed that she didn't run into Marrik again, *or* Dee Allderbay. Maybe Dee was wearing the same flip flops or something as she was. Then she and Dee could start talking.

"I thought I should give myself a new look," Milly explained to her friends at lunch. "My mom took me shopping yesterday and I got a ton of new stuff."

"You couldn't have chosen a better time," remarked Tai. "Queen of the Masquerade nominations are in two days!"

"Oh, yeah!" Milly remembered.

"We should nominate you!" said Gretchen. "You're so pretty!"

"I'll vote for you," said Emma.

"Me too," agreed Jean.

"Aw, thanks guys, but even with all of your votes, I'll never win. Too many people are going to vote for someone like Dee Allderbay," said Milly dejectedly.

"It's worth a shot," Tai encouraged. "*Everyone* noticed you today! Just keep it up."

So she had secured a nomination. Behind the sigh of relief she breathed, Milly felt the strange satisfaction of success; all was going according to plan. Of course she would keep it up! They didn't know it, but she had her outfits planned out for the next three days.

Milly knew how this worked. Over her years of observing the machinations of the most popular girls in her school, she had come to recognize a pattern: Dee would come to school one day with a look engineered to attract attention. Stares and compliments flew at her like iron filings to a magnet as Milly watched in awe. But the day after that, Dee would dress plainly; there would be no diamond bracelet on that manicured hand. Occasionally, she'd even wear sweatpants. Oh don't get the wrong idea, she was still Dee Allderbay by all means; but her secret was to look fabulous only once in a while, not every day. However, Milly knew that for herself, such a tactic wouldn't work: in order to keep from fading into the background she had to send out the same shockwave every day.

That was why the next two days, Milly came to school in equally cute and stunning outfits and garnered the same influx of stares.

"Hey! Milly!" said a voice behind her during lunch that Thursday. Milly's head snapped around. It was Todd Baker from the table to their left.

"I heard you're nominated for Queen of the Masquerade," he said.

"I – I think my name's on there," said Milly in bemused response to this.

"No way, someone's running against Dee Allderbay?" asked Ryan from across that same table, overhearing Todd and Milly's conversation.

"Aww, you'd make such an adorable Queen," said Jen C.

"I put your name down!" said Stacy, who was sitting next to Jen C. and also overheard.

"Really? Thanks!" said Milly, genuinely bewildered.

"Awwww, look how happy she is," said Stacy.

"Good luck, Milly," said Todd, winking at her and then turning back around to his table.

Milly turned back to hers, smiling all over her face, but quickly stifling it: she didn't need to gain a rep as the girl who tried too hard to be popular; that would kill her chances of winning the popularity contest.

She knew she was making progress throughout the week because on Friday, Todd Baker talked to her again on their way to lunch.

"How's it going, Milly?"

"Good – I mean, it's cool."

"Cool," he nodded and went on.

She skipped into the lunch line, wondering how Queen of the Masquerade nominations were progressing, realizing through her daze that the people in front of her were wondering the same thing out loud.

"It's going to be even easier than last year," said a haughty female voice whose owner had her back to Milly.

"Like last year was hard, Delilah," said the voice of Dee Allderbay, who was standing in front of Milly buying a salad and some nonfat milk.

"There were, like, two other names, and both of them were random ugly girls someone put as a joke."

"Oh my Bob, you're *terrible!*" Delilah smiled.

"It's true."

"They're on there again, and there's some new girl – Molly Hillen?" Delilah said, reaching over Milly to pick up a yogurt she had overlooked.

"Who?" Dee asked.

"Some girl who got cute all of a sudden," said Delilah. "Jen or someone told me... or maybe it was Jen... anyway you've probably noticed her. She's got, like, brown hair."

"Uh, no. Whatever, it's probably just in Jen's little circle," said Dee dismissively.

"Yeah, they're just giving her their 'pity votes'," Delilah said, and they both laughed.

"Oh my Bob I wanna see if it did anything."

" We can check the stats at my house after school," said Delilah.

"Please, I can check them right now from my phone," said Dee as they walked back to their table.

As soon as she got home, Milly rushed upstairs and turned on her computer, not even bothering to throw down her backpack. It was the moment of truth. The stats loaded:

Dee Allderbay: 82%

Milly Hallan: 8%

Yutu Samke: 8%

"*What?*" Milly screamed. She fell to her bed, crestfallen. She thought it was a closer race; but it turned out there was no real competition.

All her illusions were shattered as her incredible week was suddenly thrown into a harsh new light. *Eight percent!* That was all her hard work had won her. She hadn't shocked the entire school; the news of her transformation had barely reached Dee Allderbay's ears! All the scraps she'd managed to glean in Stacy and Jen's coos and Todd Baker's few words – she was revolted by the fool she had been to attach so much importance to such trifles! It was probably less attention than what Dee was used to receiving every day! '*It's probably just in Jen's little circle.*' She'd been right! That's as far as her shockwave had reached, and even *they* thought her a joke. Yeah, some competition she was putting up. Yutu Samke, a faceless computer nerd, had tied Milly! And did Yutu Samke spend an inordinate amount of money on Hollister clothes, as Milly had? No! All she had to do was be Yutu Samke, and that alone got her *some* recognition. Without her clothes, Milly couldn't achieve even *that* marginal fame. *Pity votes*, she recalled bitterly. *Who was she kidding?!?* inside herself she screamed. Wave upon wave of self-disgust filled Milly as she realized the painful truth: she could wear all the glamorous threads she wanted, she could strut in spiky stilettos down the halls and she could put on an air of confidence – but it would never, ever be who she really was. She had to face the plain, cold fact: Milly wasn't a real Queen, and no matter how hard she tried, well that was just it – she would always have to *try*. Whereas Dee *was*. And that was why Dee Allderbay was meant to wear that crown, the one Milly so ardently coveted as a physical symbol of her worth and which Dee could throw away for all it mattered to her, which was exactly why she was going to win it! Forget those stupid outfits! They did her nothing!! All that had ever been within her power to do was refuse to write Dee's name on that stupid ballot and put her own down instead. But it had *never* been within her sphere to turn the school on its head. And even if she *did* somehow manage to make everyone believe in her sudden new royalty, there wasn't enough room for two Queens. Dee, rooted firmly in her post, would always have the advantage. And even *that* was just a fantasy, because the truth remained: Milly could never be a true Queen. Queens, official or unsaid, were born, not made.

In tears, Milly took all her new Hollister clothes and threw them onto her bed in hatred. What would she tell her mom now? Nothing – she didn't need words – she had just proven once more that she was a complete idiot. What a stupid, stupid idea it had been! She hated Hollister, and Dee Allderbay, and the Queen of the Masquerade contest, and everyone who happily put down their votes and looked forward to hearing the winner announced, and herself. Everything! Everything that came her way fell under the big blanket of anguish that covered her heart to make a little more bearable the sheer, undiluted humiliation she felt at having been so stupid!

Breaking, she let a piteous howl of despair escape the depths of her being and it transformed into a sob as she threw herself down and buried her face into the pillow. The gentle cloth muffled the cacophony of her bitter emotions, and continued to do so for an hour.

Milly slept soundly that night once she had exhausted her supply of tears. When she woke up on Saturday it was after noon. The house was quiet. Mr. and Mrs. Hallan had left long ago to run errands, and John had gone abroad a few days prior.

She felt somehow cleaner, refreshed. It took her a while to remember why she had stayed up half the night in tears; but it all came back as she did an internal "oh yeah...."

Dressing slowly, Milly bumbled about the house in her cat bathrobe and slippers, hair a mess and eyes still sore. She carried her bowl of cereal into the living room and set it on the coffee table, plopping herself onto the couch, turning on the T.V. to familiar scenes from one of her childhood classics. She settled in and began enjoying herself in this careless pursuit. *Maybe I'll ask my mom to take me to Hollister when she gets back so I can return some of those clothes and get money,* she thought idly.

The doorbell rang. It cut Milly out of her groggy thoughts.

"It's me!" came Tai's voice. Shocked, Milly opened the door and looked at her friend beneath scrunched eyebrows.

"I figured you'd be up by now," Tai said briskly as she stepped in. She turned to Milly and smiled. "You ready?"

"For what?"

"The perfect solution to your problem."

"What problem?" Milly looked confused.

329

Tai looked like water had been thrown onto her flame.

"You winning Queen of the Masquerade!" she said with all the air of "*duh, what else?!*"

Milly took a heavy sigh. "Tai, last night I realized – it was just a stupid idea," she shook her head. "I mean, I was just being a fool, you know?"

"But I don't get it, you've been set on this for the past week. You haven't talked about anything else since Monday. What suddenly happened?" Tai asked.

Milly sighed. "Tai, there are certain rules that govern society. We can't escape them. At the bottom of it, we are what we are, and we can't be anything else. I can't be Dee Allderbay, and she can't be me. Not that she'd want to be me, but that's beside the point. Everyone has their place. Dee Allderbay has hers, and in a word, it's Queen. I simply can't be in Dee's place because I already have my own. Everyone has to fill a quota," she finished, bestowing enlightenment unto her friend.

"So that's it, you're giving up?" Tai asked her, a thread of disgust running through her obvious disappointment.

"You don't get it, there's nothing to give up! I was under a delusion. There's no fighting the inevitable."

"I can't believe you," Tai shook her head.

"I thought you'd be happy that you won't have to listen to anymore complaints. Anyway, honestly I'm over it, I don't care anymore.... Besides, there's nothing I can do to improve my chances," Milly said.

"But there is!" exclaimed Tai, seizing the moment. "That's just what I came over here to tell you, I *know* how you can win!"

"How?" asked Milly, skeptical but a curious all the same.

"Kat!" she shouted. "Kat Staiten, my cousin. She's a *genius* when it comes to makeovers. I'm telling you, she works miracles. You know who she is, right?"

Of course Milly knew who she was; *everyone* knew who Kat Staiten was. Trampling through the halls in careless defiance of the dress code, she paid Dee and her posse complete indifference, for which they stared after her as she passed them in her cute pleated miniskirts, white thigh-high stockings, and studded black wrist cuffs, none from Hollister. She was the only other girl besides Dee to whom men ran at the snap of her fingers, holding her books, parting the doors, drooling after her scent while leaving their hearts bleeding at her feet; these useless things she gripped between her black painted nails and threw to the side as she continued along her stick-straight path like an iron bulldozer. Rumors abounded: she handcuffed the quarterback of the football team to her bed and tickled him with a feathered whip for three hours last year; she was sleeping with the Creative Writing teacher, Mr. Martin. Milly was too shocked at the idea that a teacher would ever have sex with a student, especially a married man who was – ew – middle aged, to believe the story at first, until she bore witness to a memorable scene one morning:

Milly was standing by her locker when Kat commenced her ritual plow through the hallway. All parted – nerds and jocks, girls and boys, teachers and janitors – watching her pass as she walked dead ahead, sword-straight black hair bundled in adorable pigtails today, eyes unblinking beneath their dark and heavy makeup. She stopped by the spot across Milly's locker where their Creative Writing teacher stood.

"Mr. Martin," she said sweetly, leaning against him in her crisp white button-down buttoned halfway down her chest, "could you give me an extension on that paper due this afternoon?"

"Kat! – Ms. Staiten – erm – you may – er – of course I could. I understand your – s-situation!" said Mr. Martin, his face turning red as he looked up and down the hallway. Kat smiled.

"Thanks babe!" she poked his nose and skipped off.

Did she just call her teacher *'babe'*? And that was when Milly began to have her suspicions.

"I know all about Kat Staiten," Milly said warily to Tai, jumping back into the present.

"Yeah, well, she's not exactly the pride of the family, but she was totally up for helping us out. She should be here any minute," said Tai.

"She's coming *here*?" Milly exclaimed.

"Yeah. Is that a problem?"

"No, it's just... well... I've never hung out with someone who wasn't – you know – a virgin," Milly confided.

"Oh, don't worry! It's totally almost like hanging out with normal people," consoled Tai.

"Okay, good."

Ten minutes later, the Hallans' doorbell rang again; Milly and Tai giggled from anticipatory excitement as they ran to answer it, but the face they saw made all laughter stop.

Kat Staiten walked in; she looked extraordinary, dangerous yet extraordinary, like she might have a dagger hidden somewhere down that corset.

"Milly," she looked into her eyes. It was not a question, even though they were speaking for the first time. She took her smooth long fingers and cupped Milly's face between them.

"So pure," she breathed, lips almost brushing the young one's neck. Milly was not sure how to react, never having been in this kind of situation before. She assumed it was just one of those experiences all teenagers went through and judged it best to go with the flow.

"Follow me," said Kat, and she led the way up to Milly's bedroom, which location she instinctively knew.

"What is our mission with this one?" Kat Staiten asked in a tone that demanded a concise response

"Can you help her win Queen of the Masquerade?" Tai asked.

"No problem. All she needs is some tweaking, and we'll turn her into the most popular girl in school."

"How much tweaking, exactly?" Milly asked, picturing heavy makeup and risqué clothing.

"Our aim is simple," said Kat. "We must turn you into a total nerd."

Milly reeled. "What? That doesn't make any sense!"

"Sit," Kat pointed to the chair by Milly's desk without commenting. Milly sat; Kat remained standing. Tai went off to the side and took a seat on the bed.

"So you want to win Queen of the Masquerade?" she asked Milly.

"It doesn't matter anyway, there's no helping me; I'm not cut out for it. I could never beat Dee Allderbay, especially at her own game. Dee doesn't even *have* to win Queen of the Masquerade, she's *already* a queen!... And I'm not," Milly hung her head.

"You're right, you're not a Queen and you will never be one. Good. I'm glad you noticed that. It's going to be the basis for our work on you," said Kat.

332

"I don't understand," Milly looked up, overcome with dejection; an outside source had just confirmed her worst dread, which she was hoping would on the other hand be denied. Kat was said to work miracles; Milly had expected her to turn her miraculously into a Queen.

"You have to work with what you've got," Kat said instead.

"I've got nothing," said Milly glumly.

"YES! Excellent! That's EXACTLY the attitude we need!" Kat screamed.

Milly jolted up, more bewildered than perhaps ever.

"Don't you see, don't you see," Kat continued in fervor, "you may not be a Queen, but you've got the *possibility* to be something else entirely."

"What?"

"An anti-Queen!"

"*HUH?*" went both Milly and Tai.

"What makes a Queen a Queen?" Kat asked them. They both looked at her, stumped.

"What makes a Queen a Queen is that she indulges her greatest vices more fully and shamelessly than the people around her. Look at Dee: she is never afraid to put other people down, never afraid to think that she is better than you, or I, or anyone in her vicinity, never afraid to throw men away once she's sucked them dry without thought for the consequences. You, Milly, do not have these vices. You do not have exaggerated, undue self-confidence; you cannot strut around like you own the ground you walk on; you cannot bear to be forward and domineering with men. You have *other* vices. Self-pity, low self-esteem, neediness, predisposition to depressed mood. Only you do not indulge them as fully as you could. When you claimed just now that you've 'got nothing,' you were indulging that vice we call self-pity. Believe it or not, this is very attractive to many people, and the more you immerse yourself in this mire, the more followers you will have. To put it in crude terms, just as Dee revels in believing she's the best, you revel in believing you're the worst. But don't you see, they're just two sides of the same coin! Don't you see the very essence, that underneath the surface you and Dee Allderbay are fundamentally polar opposite manifestations of one and the same thing: *an insatiable attention whore!*"

"No! I'm not an attention whore!" Milly exclaimed, offended that Kat would say such a thing.

"Embrace it, Milly. It's the only way you can command the kind of influence upon your peers as Dee does."

Tai interrupted. "Hold on, hold on. So you want to build Milly in the image of an emotional problemed loner type?"

"Something roughly like that."

"But those people already exist. They're called 'goths', and 'emos', and 'punks,' and they indulge all the vices you just mentioned," said Tai.

"Ah! I'm glad you pointed that out. Yes, Milly's going to turn out similarly, but with a twist!"

"What twist?" Milly asked, very curious and lost.

"Unique."

"What?" Milly and Tai were lost once more.

"That's going to be your key – that you're an individual, different from everyone else."

"But I'm scared of being different from everyone else!" said Milly.

"Don't worry, you're only going to say that you're different; in reality you'll still be following the most current trends. For example, I'm not going to make you wear a lumpy sweater that smells with orange velour pants that are too short for you – that would certainly constitute 'different'. You'll still be wearing trendy clothes; they just won't be from Hollister."

"There's trendy clothing that's not from Hollister?" Oh the new horizons.

"Oh, yes," nodded Kat. "Have you heard of *Abyss*?"

Milly shuddered.

"No denim miniskirts you can't sit down in," said Kat.

"I couldn't wear those, anyway, my mom would never let me, plus they're so uncomfortable, I don't know why Dee and they wear them."

"Because they have such low self-esteem that they have to reassure themselves of their worth by wearing revealing clothes that shame them to any sane person, but draw as much attention as possible to them," explained Kat. Milly couldn't help but note the obvious, that Kat herself was in a bustier and skin-tight leather pants Milly had not been able to take her eyes off of.

"But... look at you, no offense. You wear slutty clothes and you don't have low self-esteem," said Milly.

"Oh yes I do!" said Kat.

"It doesn't *seem* like it."

Kat scoffed. "I may be dumb enough to have low self-esteem, but I'm smart enough not to show it," she said.

"I know this may feel like walking on new ground, but I promise that once I get done with you, my dear, you will be feeling wholly at home in your new image," she said consolingly. "Now, the first thing I need you to do is sit up straight, take a deep breath, and throw everything you know about popularity and fitting in out of your head."

That simple, huh? Milly sat up and took a deep breath.

"Now let your mind go blank. You're not a loser, you're not unpopular; you don't know who you are."

Milly exhaled slowly and tried to throw every notion she had about high school – and she had many – out; but all that she saw were images flashing by of herself walking through the halls as Dee Allderbay would, bombarded by everyone's stares as she went on her way blithely, ignoring Marrik McFost as he trailed after her in adoration....

Milly gasped. *Oh my Bob*, she realized, *I am just like Dee Allderbay!*

"Oh no! It's true," Milly exclaimed out loud. "I crave attention just like Dee Allderbay does; the only difference is that I'm too shy to act on it!"

"Perfect," said Kat. "Now strip," she commanded. Into a tank top and some shorts. No Hollister.

Milly obeyed, and once she was plain, she, Kat, and Tai sat in a circle on her floor.

"Let me tell you first what you're *not* going to be," Kat stated to Milly. "You're not going to be popular, you're not going to be preppy, and you're not going to wear cute clothes from Hollister."

"But I'll get in trouble for breaking the dress code!"

"You hate the dress code!"

"I do?"

"Yes. You hate all rules. You don't follow anyone, except rock stars."

"So I idolize rock stars?" Milly tried to reiterate this new information.

"Yes; musicians, artists, and video game designers," said Kat.

"What kinds of video games do I like?"

"Death by Annihilation, World of Illusions I, II, and III, Star Kingdoms."

"What about the new Speed Crime Nightlife that just came out? That's the only one I know of," Milly offered lamely.

"No, you think the new version sucks and is just a cheap rip-off of Soul Hunters Arena. You're into old-school stuff, like Fumio and Blood Thrills. The classics. All unique people are into the classics."

"But I don't know how to play any of these video games! Shouldn't I at least know the basic plotlines and some of the characters if someone starts talking to me about a video game so I won't turn out to be a total poser?"

Kat pondered. "Yes, that does pose a problem. I don't suppose we have time to get you acquainted with video games... that would be a weighty undertaking and we don't want to overburden you."

"Maybe I could hate video games like I hate the dress code, and talk about how stupid and uncool they are?" Milly suggested.

Tai gasped.

"Never!" barked Kat. "You can never, EVER, say that video games are 'uncool'! Do you understand? Everyone will hate you forever, especially if you start ranting passionately about how they've brainwashed our generation and should be banned!"

"But I thought I was supposed to be bitter?" Milly was confused.

"You *are* bitter; you're bitter about society, and because of that, you seek absolution and escape through music and video games. Everyone loves video games, there's nothing cooler, except for a girl who plays them."

"But that's just what the losers and nerdy guys think," said Milly knowledgably.

"The dorks and nerds are going to be your best friends."

"But if I'm friends with all the most unpopular people, how am I going to get cool with Dee?"

"You're not. You hate Dee Allderbay. You hate *everyone* who walks around labeling people who don't conform to the majority as below them."

"What?! I can't *hate* Dee Allderbay!" Milly exclaimed in scandalized tones.

"Milly, this is the most important thing of all: you have to hate Dee Allderbay and everything she stands for."

"But why?"

"Because they are the 'pro' of society, and you have to be the 'con.' They are the positive, the light side, the clean, bright, picture-perfect paradigms of what society has for so long been publicly proponing as the image to strive for. *You*, on the other hand, are the negative, anti, against, the girl who hates everything they represent. You hate Dee Allderbay and her neat Hollister shirts with the button-down blazer on top and a string of pearls around her neck; you hate the mainstream music they listen to, the way they style their hair as seen on magazine covers, their perky excitement as they walk down the halls in their obnoxiously loud groups gossiping about so-and-so party they had which only they and other people they have deemed 'acceptable' attended; you can't stand how they participate in every spirit week event and hate that their enthusiasm over school spirit gains them favor with your teachers, pictures in the yearbook, and articles in the school newspaper that fail to cover the reality of what they are like as people; and during football games you stand alone in the crowd with your black t-shirt and jeans in stubborn refusal to wear the school colors like everyone around you as you boo when they win the big game! *You hate popularity!* Do you realize how popular that will make you?"

"No!"

"You'll see. Just trust me."

"But say I can't pull it off? I don't want random people to hate me, like – I dunno – Marrik McFost or someone – "

"Don't worry, I'll teach you how to show the popular kids that you think they're good-for-nothing shit the cool way. You're going to think that because you embody unpopular, counterculture trends that you're better than them, much like they think that because they embody accepted standards that they're better than you. You're going to be *known* for hating that crowd and for thinking that cute, popular guys like Marrik McFost are the most loathsome creatures on this planet."

"How?" Milly asked, suddenly ten pounds heavier with dread.

"First, you're going to bad-mouth the Popular People, and then Dee, to the Average Kids in your class. They gossip the most, so Dee Allderbay and her friends will get wind of what you're saying and, more importantly, who you are. As soon as they do, guys like Marrik McFost will start paying attention to you. First he will look at you – you are a source of bewilderment: why don't you idolize him? Then he will try to approach you. He will never show you his secret fascination, but it'll be there. *Only if you don't need him!* If you show him that you depend on his attention, your allure will lose its spell and he'll drop you like red-hot iron. Remember, people like Marrik McFost aren't interested in love or relationships; all they want is for everyone to adore them and support their deluded self-image of divinity, and the more you show him cold indifference, the more he will chase after you to get your approval. Now, when he approaches you, make sure that you avoid him, but simultaneously respond to everything he says so as to keep him hooked. He will start to think that you're mysterious. When you achieve this, you have reached the checkpoint. From there, you may slowly and cautiously proceed to hanging out, but let him initiate the whole thing. Act like he's slowly but reluctantly winning you over, as if you can't help but secretly fall for his charm even though you still think he's a complete asshole who's brainwashed by mainstream standards. If this continues, he will soon be yours. Do you know what happens when Marrik McFost is yours?"

"What?"

"You beat Dee Allderbay. Because an important person such as Marrik McFost is attracted to you, it will allow others to feel safe in leaving Dee Allderbay to join your side. Dee Allderbay will be furious. She will feel the gaping hole you left when you stole one of her prime sources of attention, which she is extremely dependent on by the way. She will hate you and try to turn as many people in school as she can against you, but this will only happen later in the game, when she starts to realize that she's no longer safe. Remember, it takes some shaking to convince Dee Allderbay that someone out there could be more popular than she."

"What do I do when that happens?"

Kat laughed. "Nothing. You will already have won Queen of the Masquerade."

"Are you sure?"

"If my calculations are correct, yes. Now, let's start with your personality makeover. First we need to make a list of your random offbeat hobbies."

"Why offbeat?" Milly asked.

"We're making you into an individualist, remember? You have to be quirky and unusual, otherwise you're a conformist. What do you think about painting?" Kat asked.

"It's, uh, fun," Milly offered.

"Painting is not fun, it's a *necessity!* For a tortured soul like you it is air!"

"But I don't paint!"

"I suppose we can demote you to sketching. Actually that will be better, you can carry your sketchbook around with you all the time. Just make sure to keep it out of your backpack and in your arms when you're walking down the halls."

"Okay. What do I sketch?"

"Angry things! Kittens exploding, babies guillotined, caricatures of your classmates being tortured en masse. Also – but rarely – sentimental things, such as trees and wild birds. Finally, you should have one sketch near the back of a desolate girl overcome with loneliness sitting in a corner. *Only one!*"

"Is that supposed to represent me?" Milly asked.

"Yes. Very good, you're catching on! Next, tell me what music you listen to?"

Milly went on to name several artists, including last season's winner of *Artinian Artist*, the popular boy band, Dream, and today's number one selling soloist, Aniqwa. Kat started shaking her head halfway through, which Milly took to signal disapproval of her musical taste.

Kat rummaged through her purse and pulled out some CDs, shoving them into Milly's lap. The latter surveyed them quizzically.

"'Mashéd Cabbages?' 'Angry Aardvark?' 'Devinah's Mother Eats Paste?'" Milly asked.

"Do you know any of these bands?" Kat inquired.

"No."

"Now you do. This is what you listen to, music no one else knows. I'm going to give you a guitar as well, and you had better learn how to play it. One of the most – I stress, *most* – important traits you must possess is the ability to play an instrument. Guitar is both easy and artistic, not to mention portable, so you can carry it around with you in case you feel sudden inspiration and need to walk out of class to write music."

"But what kind of artist should I be?" Milly wondered aloud. "Should I be edgy and full of angst so that my songs tell a coming-of-age story? Or should I be mellow and loose so that my music sends the message of enlightenment and a higher love? Free-flowing, low-cut monochrome dresses that are too big for my small frame for the purpose of embodying free-spiritedness would go well with the latter. Or would mismatched knee-high socks over my black leggings and a long striped tee be more appropriate?"

"Both," Kat moderated. "There's no harm in planting each foot in a different soil, it'll make you extra unique. Now turn on some of that music you like."

Milly popped one of the CDs she was holding into her stereo. Guitar blared as she, Tai, and Kat sat in a circle listening speechless for a few minutes. A few minutes was all Milly could manage; she turned the stereo off and massaged her aching forehead.

"I can't listen to that! Oh, I'm never going to understand how to be unique!" she pouted.

"Patience, Milly, patience! It's an acquired taste. Let us begin the physical aspect of your transformation now that we have sufficiently made over your mind. But first, a quick quiz to see if you have retained all that I taught you. You're at the mall and you walk by Barkerbrombie. Do you a) squeal delightfully because they are having a sale and run inside; b) walk by indifferently; or c) stop outside the store and make retching noises until enough Barkerbrombie-wearing people have given you weird looks because they are judgmental?"

"Um... C?" Milly said.

"Good!"

"Can I do this outside Hollister?" Milly asked. "After all, Hollister and Barkerbrombie are, like, the same thing."

"They most certainly are *not* the same thing! Too many people like Hollister, don't make fun of it; but don't wear their clothes, either. Feel free to make fun of Barkerbrombie, it won't directly offend anyone. In fact, a lot of people who shop at Hollister will find it funny and support you, as long as you don't call them out on the obvious, namely their wearing Hollister, which is almost exactly the same thing as the brand you're making fun of. Got that? I know it is a tricky nuance to grasp. Now, number two: that obnoxious jock in your math class who's really loud and who hangs out with Dee Allderbay's crowd thinking he's the shit starts doing a hilarious yet cruel impression of your teacher one day before class. What do you do? A) laugh along with the majority of the class, thus reaffirming the already disproportionately high and completely undeserved regard he is held in; b) not react; or c) snort and mumble a clever insult under your breath about what a buffoon he is that makes the people sitting around you chuckle darkly."

"C," Milly said with more confidence.

"Good girl! Last one: that offbeat kinda cute in his own way guy who doesn't follow the crowd and whom you heard practicing with his garage band down the street this weekend does a hilarious yet cruel impression of your teacher one day before class. Do you: a) hatefully tell him off for what an insensitive jerk he is in front of everyone and finish with a cheap shot at his scrawny frame; b) not react; or c) laugh along because he's got such a chill personality and has that witty sense of humor that belies his edgy yet underneath awkwardly sensitive character?"

"C again."

"Correct! I think you've picked it up. Now, onto your physical makeover," said Kat. "Take all the esteem you attach to the word 'prep' and transfer it over to the word 'nerd,' because at your core, that's what you're going to be. You're going to be aware of your nerdiness, and sometimes, when you need 'reality points,' you're going to say that deep down, underneath the exterior you present to the world, you're really just a nerd at heart."

"So I have to walk around looking like a nerd? With glasses, overalls, and the whole shebang?"

"No no no; much like with the 'unique' thing, you're going to *say* you're a nerd, but you're not actually going to be one."

Kat got up and strutted over to Milly's closet, throwing open the door. She rummaged through every knick knack, throwing random articles of clothing and accessories onto the floor.

Kat threw seven mismatched bracelets at her. "Arrange these in random order on your wrists like you didn't care enough to pay attention."

They did that together for the next ten minutes or so, and then moved on to painting Milly's nails lime green. While those dried, Kat took Milly's hair and put it up into a loose ponytail that looked like it had been falling out carelessly all day.

"For prop," Kat finished, handing Milly an old pocket watch on a metal chain. "Use it, not your cell phone, to check the time as you're walking down the halls," she instructed.

Kat took out her camera and snapped a few photos. "Look moody. Excellent. Now fold your arms against your chest and tilt your head down while keeping your eyes on the camera. Stop smiling! You only smile when you're taking a picture with a cute boy. And when you're with your friends, you make goofy faces because you're a nerd and they're the only ones around whom you can be the 'real you'."

"I'm going to email these to you. Use them as a base for how you must look every day," said Kat when they finished, putting away her camera and gathering her purse. "An assignment for the two of you," she said before she left. "Go to that music store at the mall where all the bad-ass punk kids hang out and get some more CDs by these same bands."

Milly and Tai looked at each other frightfully; they had always tried to avoid that store to the best of their ability; the people they saw walking around inside it as they went on their way to Forever Artinian looked threatening.

They walked through the mall that evening nerves a-flutter. At last they reached their destination. Music on no radio station Milly or Tai ever listened to blared inside the dark little store.

"Do you remember what any of the bands we're supposed to be looking for are called?" Milly mumbled quietly to Tai.

"No. Why are you whispering?" Tai mumbled back. There was a guy standing behind the check-out, sporting a band t-shirt and brightly colored hair that ended around his ears, which had a couple fangs in them. He momentarily stopped banging his head to the music coming from his headphones and looked up at his two new customers, gave a one-sided brief grin, and went right back to his previous occupation. A little nervous by that smirk of his, Milly self-consciously adjusted the hem of her black-and-white horizontally striped shirt, meanwhile noticing the black-haired heads of a couple, boy and girl, near the back of the store quietly poring over the long CD racks; the girl was wearing dark skinny jeans – something Milly didn't have – and a black tank top with a heavy metal chain that hung around her hips. Her bra straps were showing, and they were black.

"This band is frickin awesome, have you heard of them?" Milly heard the girl ask her companion while limply holding a CD in her skinny wrist.

"Yeah, like, five years ago when I went to their first show here," he answered in a low voice. "No one knew them back then, but I was always a fan. They're so chill, not like those mainstream bands everyone at school listens to." He threw back his bangs.

"Yeah," said the girl. "Hey, look at this album. It's so rare, Even Raven and Tobyas don't have it."

"They're *such* posers," scoffed the guy. "They don't even *like* The Sonic Cheetahs of Death."

"Maybe we should go, Tai," Milly whispered to her uncomfortably; just as she said this the boy glanced up in their direction, staring at her with his eye and making Milly became aware of how he and his girlfriend must look down on her for being such a prep.

"Yo, have you heard this song?" the guy said to Milly, holding out the CD his girlfriend had found, the Sonic Cheetahs of Death, and pointing to track one. Startled, Milly leaned in and read.

"Yeah!! I have!" it was that same song that she had played back at her house, Silly Juniper Trees Attacking a Bicycle.

"What did you think? Better than their new stuff?"

"Uh – oh yeah, the old stuff is always better. The new stuff is so poppy and commercial, you know?"

"Definitely," he nodded again. "So what else do you listen to?" he asked.

"I like Angry Aardvark, Devinah's Mother Eats Paste, you know.... Actually I was looking for them here, but – um – I doubt if this store carries them," she finished aloofly.

"Probably not," he responded in the same tone. "Well, I gotta go buy this, so, see ya," he waved to Milly and walked up to the register with the girl.

Milly and Tai didn't buy anything from the music store, but they didn't much care in light of Milly's successful interaction. They left in high spirits and went off to spend the rest of their night in search of skinny jeans and other accessories to prepare Milly for her grand re-entrance into the Peamount High melee....

***

Cue "Fuck Society" by Angry Aardvark.

Move out the way; here comes Milly; she doesn't give a fuck what the people think; she's her own person; she's an individual; look at her clever political tee.

Milly stomped down the halls in her new combat boots. She blew a giant bubble with her gum and popped it obnoxiously. People looked at her. She made no notice. They were such followers.

She's into classic rock; she's into indie; she'll tell you to your face that she thinks you're a douche; she's not popular; right, like she cares; she doesn't march to the beat of society's drum....

Whispers flew around her as Milly walked to Artinian History. But she wasn't paying them attention; she was thinking about how the song she was going to write for her guitar when she got home was going to go. It was going to be sick, true to the classic style but with an original twist. And she would just improvise the riff at the end –

BUMP.

She collided right into someone's muscular chest. She blamed it on the other person – even if that person was Marrik McFost! He was looking down at her, surprise in his blue-green eyes, half his books and binders on the floor jumbled in a pile with hers.

"Sorry," he said.

"Don't worry. You're nearsighted, I understand," she replied.

"I'm not nearsighted," he said confusedly.

344

"Sure you are, if you can't see anything farther than your ego.... On second thought, that's a pretty long distance."

He reeled from the cut.

"Do I know you?" he asked.

"Like, I'm only, like, the most popular girl in school, like," she twisted her hair around her finger sarcastically. He still looked confused.

"Never mind. No, I highly doubt that you know me. Anyway, you don't want to be seen in the presence of someone like me, so if you don't mind, we'll part ways now," said Milly in a cold voice.

"Don't you want your books?" Marrik asked her as she prepared to leave. He handed her several binders and a large textbook.

"Hmph," said Milly.

"And I think this is yours, too," continued Marrik. He held out a sketchbook, which had flipped open to a drawing when it fell on the floor. It was of a girl and boy flying through a vast universe of stars, only half finished. Milly's cheeks burned red as she glared at him with angry eyes. This jerk wasn't supposed to see something so personal!

She snatched the sketchbook from him. "Thanks." And then she walked off.

"Excellently played," whispered a cool voice in her ear.

"It was so hard!" Milly whined to Kat. "I can't believe I pulled that off! I wanted to *scream*! I mean, did you *see* that? He acknowledged me!!!"

Kat nodded. "You've been doing well. Keep it up. But don't act like it's a big deal, act like this is who you are and you don't know why everyone is so shocked by you."

"Right, right," said Milly as Kat disappeared behind her shoulder like a phantom.

It was a lot to remember, this whole 'unique' business, but Milly was proud of what she had accomplished on her first day. Or rather, she was comforted by Kat's approval. She trusted Kat, and even though she felt like she was walking blindly through the dark, she resolved to wait and see where this path led.

***

The student body looked cheery Thursday morning. Dee Allderbay and her girlfriends, for example, were wearing a lot of pink. Well actually, Dee was wearing *baby* pink with her dark jeans because it was more stylish than most other shades of pink, at least this season. Dee stood out more than her friends, too, because she wore a lime green belt with her baby pink tee, and, well, everyone knows that baby pink and lime green are totally like midnight blue and lemon yellow. She had considered wearing a black miniskirt with that same pink tee this morning instead, but on second thought she didn't like black. It was too... *dark* for the daytime. And it reminded her of sad thoughts, whatever those were. Plus, baby pink and black were kind of like... like orange and brown! Urgh!

"Hey, Dee!" said Delilah as Dee walked into History or Physics class.

"Hey, bitch," Dee responded, then glanced behind Delilah's head where Marrik McFost was sitting. "Is he sick?" she asked about Marrik. He was looking down at his desk without saying anything; in fact, he seemed not to have reacted to the sound of Dee's voice at all.

"I stretched too hard yesterday morning while I was doing yoga, and now my back is *killing* me," said Dee audibly as she took a seat next to Delilah.

"Aww, do you want a back rub?" Delilah offered.

"Yes, please." Delilah turned her chair around and began massaging Dee's shoulders.

"Ooh, that feels so good. You know how I like it," said Dee in a suggestive voice; she and Delilah giggled.

"Harder!" Dee moaned. "Ugh! Just stop, you don't do it right," she exclaimed after a minute. "I need a *man* to do it," she looked behind her to where Marrik was sitting in his chair, now chatting with some guys.

"Do you want me to try again?" Delilah offered after a minute.

"No, you're gonna be busy in the bathroom fixing that pimple on your chin instead of throwing yourself at my feet."

Delilah's mouth dropped open as she touched her face. She got up and left the classroom worriedly. Dee turned around in her seat and started paying attention to what Marrik and the guys were talking about.

"Yeah, she said she beat it in four hours!"

"No way, dude, I've been playing that game for a month and it still takes me at least six," said Marrik to the guy who'd just spoken.

"Yeah *snort*, I don't believe this chick either," said William, pushing his glasses up.

"Who are we talking about?" Dee asked in a curious tone, smiling.

"This girl, Milly Hallan," Marrik said, then turned back to William and Samuel.

"Oh okay, no one important," said Dee lightly. But apparently Marrik disagreed, for he ignored Dee and kept talking to William and Samuel about Milly. Dee didn't appreciate being ignored. She gave an audible huff and got up out of her seat to go sit with a couple of girls she sort of tolerated, accidentally knocking Marrik's head along her way.

"Hey Dee!" said Jen B.

"Stacy, I have a question," said Dee to Jen B's friend.

"Yeah?" Stacy wheeled around to her.

"Who is Milly Hallan?"

"You don't know?" Stacy asked in surprise. "She's this punkish girl who refuses to wear clothes from Hollister. She's gotten in trouble with the Enforcement Party like three times already."

"That's weird. Why doesn't she just follow the dress code?" Dee asked.

"She said something about how if they didn't stop trying to make her a clone in their herd of sheep she'd show up to school naked next week."

"That doesn't even make sense," Dee rolled her eyes. "OhmyBob! Is she the one who wore those hideous combat boots on Monday?" she burst out with realization.

"Yeah!"

"Ewww! She is *such* a freak!" Dee laughed so loudly the entire class heard her disgusted tones.

"Tell me about it," Stacy agreed.

"Isn't that the same belt she wore earlier this week?" Jen B. eyed the neon green chain screaming around Stacy's jeans.

"Oh, is it?" Stacy asked, looking down in surprise. Jen snort-laughed.

"Then why did *you* wear your hair in four braids yesterday?" Stacy shot back at Jen B.

Dee rolled her eyes....

"So what's the deal with her being 'punk'? Are, like, the geeks trying to find a way to be cool?" Dee asked.

"She's more artsy than punk," Jen B. said thoughtfully. "She's always got her sketchbook with her and she sits there and doodles in class."

"No way! She's definitely more of a rebel, she's *completely* ignoring the Role Enforcement Party," Stacy argued.

"Yeah, but she plays guitar, too. She was writing a song on the grass during lunch yesterday," said Jen.

"What, so she's a hippie, also?" said Dee aggravated.

"A little bit," nodded Stacy. "Although she's too angst-ridden to *really* be a hippie."

"She's an emo!" said Jen B.

"You guys have got it all wrong," came the voice of Marrik McFost, who shook his head as he stood by their clique with his backpack on. "It's not about falling into a commercially stimulated stereotype. It's about being yourself. She's totally indie," he explained.

"*What*?" Dee asked.

"That means she's not about labeling herself. She's against labels. She just wants to do her own thing. She doesn't dress mainstream, she doesn't like mainstream music or movies, she doesn't act like everyone else does, and she doesn't expect anyone to understand that."

"Seems like *you* understand her pretty well," said Dee coldly.

"I'm just explaining to you what her statement is. It's pretty obvious," said Marrik.

"She definitely does her own thing," Jen B. nodded. "Did you see on Tuesday, she wore five wristwatches on her arm and set them all to different times. Then she walked around school between classes and any time a teacher stopped her and told her to get to class, she'd point to one of her watches and say that it wasn't time for that class right now!"

348

"See? She does it her own way," Marrik affirmed.

"I don't think you can adjust time for your own way," Dee said scathingly, as if explaining a basic concept.

"You wouldn't get it, Dee," Marrik shook his head again, and then walked toward the door.

"Where are you going?" Dee asked, bewildered.

"Out."

"We have like twenty minutes left in class."

"We're not doing anything here anyway," he waved at the little cliques huddled around their desks chatting away while the teacher, Mr. Banks, sat behind his desk reading a newspaper and pretending like they didn't exist.

"I'd rather go do something useful."

"Like what?" she demanded.

"Like fix my car, play guitar, get lunch," he shrugged. "I've got a million things to do. Catch you later, Dee."

Dee stared after him, mouth open and insides sizzling with anger. Unless she was much mistaken, she had just been r-re-rejec – ugh!

***

Milly was totally psyched that it was Friday. She couldn't wait to get home and blast her new song on her guitar. It would totally piss off her snobby, iced-tea-drinking, proper-etiquette-displaying neighbors. But she had *school* first. *Lame.*

Throwing on some shorts over the band t-shirt she'd slept in, a few random black wrist cuffs found themselves on her arms, and she did some funky thing with her hair in all of a minute. Then she ran out of the house, black messenger back swinging wildly; one of the safety pins holding it together got caught on the tablecloth, making Milly curse out in anger.

"Damn you, vile implement!" she yanked it out and ran to catch the bus as it was pulling away before her house.

"Thanks, Mr. T," she said crisply as she climbed aboard, dropping some change into his empty coffee cup, even though of course a school bus offered free transportation.

Milly headed toward the back, scooted deep into a seat by the window, and put on her headphones, losing herself in one of her favorite songs. She walked with her head down through the halls, letting the world pass her by. It ended just as she walked into first period Writing Composition and she put her mp3 player away as she went over to sit with the guys.

"Hey, Milly, we're goin' over to Dustin's house after school today to play War Avengers. You in?" asked Tommy.

"*Hellz* yeah!" said Milly, putting her feet up on the desk and taking out her sketchbook.

"Dude, I played Spinners last night for like four hours, and I got to the dungeon level where you battle the Third Evil Chief!" said Sam.

"Aaw, nice, dude," said Martin.

"Are you kidding? Milly and I beat the whole game last night in three hours!" exclaimed Tommy.

"Are you serious?" Martin turned to Milly, who was buried behind the pad of paper, scribbling away.

"Damn straight; it was pretty sweet," she said without glancing up.

"What are you drawing?" asked Sam, leaning in to look over her shoulder. She shrugged.

"I dunno. Whatever I feel...."

"We're still on for the Arts Festival this Sunday, right? I told Mick and Angeline to just meet us there," Sam said.

"Frickin' yeah, should be awesome," said Milly in a happy tone of anticipation.

Mr. Ashleigh walked into the room just then. Milly popped her gum loudly.

Ahem, Mr. Ashleigh made a noise, passing by her desk. "You sure are lucky this isn't a foreign language class, otherwise I'd have to give you detention for chewing gum," he smiled.

"Aw, geez, Milly, looks like your plan failed. What does she have to do to get a detention with you?" asked Martin.

"Why would Milly want to get a detention with me?" asked Mr. Ashleigh.

"When else am I going to get the chance to torture you with my edgy analysis of the classics of literature?" she cracked out before one of the guys could respond.

"I know it's a crazy idea, but you could enlighten us during class. I'm sure your analyses are as fine and intricate as the doodles you're constantly working on under my nose."

Milly blushed. Mr. Ashleigh walked away toward his desk to get ready for class.

"You fagwhore!" Milly hissed at Martin. "What was that all about?"

"Just a reference to your little crush," he said. "Did you just call me a fagwhore? What is that, even?"

"Self-explanatory. And I do *not* have a crush on Assleigh," she snorted, lowering her shades over her eyes and immersing herself in her sketchbook again, just to prove that she totally didn't care what Mr. Ashleigh thought of her. He was such a goody-goody. The only instrument he could play was bass. And his college band *sucked*, from what Milly heard from the demo he gave her earlier this week. He was *so* not her type. And he totally needed to cut his ponytail. Or at least trim it, because that little curl at the end was bothering her....

"Sure, sure," said Martin.

The class lapsed into a discussion of the novel they were reading; Milly sat silently in her seat, head down, sketching as inconspicuously as she could to avoid being called on. She only glanced up when she caught Mr. Ashleigh surveying her, apparently confused as to why she was wearing sunglasses in his classroom.

That brief flicker between their eyes sent Milly into a mental tangent on the irony of sunglasses; funny how they were made to skew one's vision, and yet the darkness over the world they showed was more real than the false, sunny optimism society portrayed. Only through distorted lenses did one behold the actual truth... ooh, that was going into her sketchbook....

Milly was jolted from the scribbling of her quote by a nasally, high-pitched female voice.

"I think that, like, the main character was using color to portray herself. Like, even though she was a prostitute, she always wore something white, which lets the audience know that she's still, like, innocent on the inside."

"Very good, Jen," said Mr. Ashleigh. "Anyone care to argue that point?" and he looked straight at Milly, who was having a very hard time hiding her anger at the stupidity of that just-voiced comment. Suddenly, she decided to be bold. She raised her hand.

"Yes, Milly?" Mr. Ashleigh seemed genuinely surprised.

She lifted her shades and crossed her left foot over her right as she leaned back in her chair. "In context, that's totally wrong. What the author is really trying to show is the character's hypocrisy. See, he references that she wears white first, and *then* he makes her go fuck men for money – " everyone gasped a little – "which means that *she's* under the delusion that she's still innocent, but her actions totally contradict that notion."

"So you think she's blind to her own actions?" Mr. Ashleigh asked.

"Right on, Mr. A," she said, then slipped her shades back over her eyes as everyone continued to throw stares her way. Mr. Ashleigh raised his eyebrows.

"I'm impressed. That was a very pointed analysis."

Milly blushed. *Don't tell me you expected anything more from Miss Perfect Student Jen W. Like in her vacant cheerleading head she could come up with anything more insightful than a poorly reworded ChalkNotes analysis of chapter three.*

"Damn, Milly, you chewed Jen *out*," said Sam as he, Tommy, and Martin walked with her through the halls.

"One vacant cheerleader down, ten million more to go," she said dully.

They stopped by Milly's locker so that she could take out her math book. Milly threw down her backpack and leaned against her locker, arms crossed.

"What's wrong?" asked Tommy, catching the bitter expression on her face.

Milly shook her head. "They piss me off so much. All of them!"

"Nothing four hours of Soul Hunters Arena won't cure. Just pretend you're shooting all the popular kids at our school," said Tommy.

Milly smile-laughed and looked over sideways. "Nice, but it's not gonna help. Well maybe a little."

Just then, Marrik McFost passed by on his way to class. He glanced over at Milly, holding his gaze on her for a second or two very obviously, before it looked ridiculous to crane his head to that degree.

Milly scoffed. "Like him. All he is is empty good looks. There's nothing more to him, and yet every girl thinks he's ridiculously fabulous. Like he's Bob or something."

"Close, he's Marrik McFost," said Martin.

"See?! That's exactly what I mean! He didn't do anything noteworthy or original to garner such attention, and I'm not going to give it to him like a desperate puppy," she declared. "Plus, he's an arrogant jerk."

"So if he asked you out, you wouldn't say 'yes'?" asked Tommy.

"No!" She remained resolute in her declaration and refused any more questions about Marrik McFost, Mr. Ashleigh, or any other guy for the rest of the school day and all night as they played Soul Hunter's Arena and ate pizza at Tommy's house.

***

Marrik picked up his new guitar and held it awkwardly. He couldn't understand what had come over him, but he was inspired to learn how to play this instrument. He hadn't been able to put it down all weekend and now he wrestled with the urge to play it at this moment, so frightfully early in the morning that he was watching the sun rise up in the sky and his mother would kill him for waking her at this hour.

He put the guitar gingerly back in its case and dressed himself with care. *Music really gets into your soul,* he mused as he gelled his hair, looking at it from various angles in the mirror to make sure it looked good from all sides. *I wonder what it would be like, being a musician, writing songs for a living, living out on the road for months at a time,* he continued to ponder as he walked downstairs and stepped into his gleaming kitchen. *It'd be freedom, that's what it would be. Freedom from all this,* he looked disdainfully at the marble countertops. *Who needs all this crap?* he scowled, then went into the living room to turn on the A/C 'cause damn it was hot today!

After a leisurely breakfast, he grabbed his bag and keys, did one last mirror check, and headed out to his car. He turned on the radio and some popular song about a girl's recent break-up came on; here he paused, reflecting on how he'd heard this song so much in the past month it was giving him a headache. Then, struck by impulse, his hand tuned the radio to the indie station, which he'd never listened to, as hadn't any of his friends (in fact most of them didn't know of its existence). A much more low-key song was playing; the lyrics were about a guy's love for a girl he could never have, or they were about a bad fever that had kept him in all weekend – it could go either way. Another song came on after this, one with a two minute didgeridoo solo. The moment Marrik thought he could bear no more, this travesty ended and a third song came on. *Hey, I know this*, he perked up. He'd only recently heard its mellow tunes somewhere... at school... *oh, right, that girl Milly was humming it in the halls last Friday*, he remembered. He'd been walking behind her and had heard her humming the whole way. Marrik pulled into his usual spot and headed to the front doors, that last song still playing in his head....

...The safety pins on her black tank top were hot from being under the sunlight on the bus ride, Milly noticed, poking at one of them as she leaned against her locker, one leg bent up resting casually against it. It reminded her of fire. Fire was awesome!!! She would totally burn something after school. Maybe a yearbook. Or a school newspaper, or a cheerleader's pom pom, which would be even better because of the fumes it would release into the air and over her neighbors' backyard. Smiling to herself at the thought, suddenly an invisible, untouchable string jerked her head up. There, walking in her direction, was Marrik McFost, looking so clean and preppy and put-together that it hurt her eyes.

He passed right by her and gave a quarter of a nod and half a smile right in her direction. Milly inhaled sharply before she could stop herself.

"What, am I that much of a freak?" she called out to his retreating back after the moment passed and she was back in rhythm. Marrik's head turned, eyebrows raised a little, and he said, "No, I was just saying 'hi.' Am I allowed to do that?"

Milly snorted. "Hi!" she said and waved sarcastically.

"You don't have to be so bitter," he said.

"*You* don't have to immediately conclude I'm some emo goth freakshow... oh, I wear black and occasionally scowl, of course that makes me bitter!" she retorted. "But then again, it's you."

"What's *that* supposed to mean, 'it's me'?" he asked a little coldly.

"What that means," she looked directly at his face, "is that you, as a prime representative of the so-called 'popular' kids in our school, immediately judge others like me to be below you and as a consequence, instead of thinking that a depressed look on our faces might be spurred on by something in our lives actually being wrong, as you would consider with your friends, you assume that the source of our scowl is that we are simply 'bitter people.'"

"Well aren't you judging me, too, by labeling me as a 'popular kid' and assigning some pattern of thinking to me based on that label?" he posed.

"No, because by saying that I'm 'bitter' you have proved to me yourself that you do think that way. And, in all honesty, if you *had* to ask yourself, 'am I popular or unpopular here', which would you say?" Milly asked him.

"That's what I thought," said Milly when no answer came. She slammed her locker and walked off to class, leaving Marrik to stand there and stare after her.

"Did you see that?" one girl whispered to her friends as they stood by their lockers, having just witnessed the scene.

"Yeah! I heard yesterday afternoon she ruined all the Masquerade decorations in her art class by spray painting them black. Delilah was super pissed," said her friend.

"She's so badass. I love her whole I-don't-give-a-damn attitude."

"I know, I wish I was that brave."

"Milly's that girl with the guitar last week?"

"Yeah! I heard she's starting her own band! Their sound is supposed to be like Honus Chainmail's."

"Who's that?"

"This band she likes. You know them?"

"No."

"Me either!!"

Milly hadn't missed the bus, she simply decided that she was in a walking mood. Now she had a solid forty minutes to plan out her new song.

Tires slowed to a soft peddling at her side.

"Want a ride?"

It was Marrik McFost in his convertible. "No," she continued walking.

"Are you sure? You're going to miss the world premiere of the new Mashéd Cabbages video that starts in, oh, fifteen minutes," he said.

Milly stopped. Without a word she threw her bag angrily onto the floor of the passenger seat and got in the car.

"I'm surprised you know who the Mashéd Cabbages are," she said after two minutes of silence.

"Yeah, they're pretty good," he said.

"'Pretty good'? They're *legend!*" Milly snapped around.

"You'd know more about this stuff than I would," he shrugged.

"Left," said Milly four feet before the turn. Marrik calmly made a sharp left at her word.

"I'd probably be more knowledgeable of other bands if I played better myself," he said.

"You play at *all?*" Milly snorted.

"A bit. My dad used to be really good, played on his old Bender Flat. But he wouldn't let me use it, made me get my own guitar."

"A *Bender Flat?*"

"Limited edition. Numbered and signed."

"Man, if I could just *hold* one..." Milly said wistfully, lost in her daydreams. Marrik glanced over at her.

"Right," said Milly two feet before the next turn. With split-second reactions Marrik turned right.

"It's the white and beige one on the left," said Milly. A minute later he stopped in front of her house and she got out.

"Uh... thanks for the ride," she said awkwardly.

"No problem. Talk to you tomorrow," said Marrik.

"Only if you bring that guitar," said Milly. He smiled and reversed, leaving Milly at her doorstop, a bit confused. *Wasn't he supposed to be a jerk?* she thought as his car screeched away.

***

"Hey, Milly!"

"How's it goin', Mill?"

"Yo, Milly, let me be in your band!"

"Nice shoes, Milly, they're so retro!"

356

Milly's head twisted this way and that to catch everyone's greetings.

"Damn, Milly, you're so popular all of a sudden," said Tommy as he, she, Martin, Sam, and their other friends Dan and Dustin walked through the halls.

"Yeah, you could be the next Queen of the Masquerade."

"*Me*, Queen of the Masquerade! That's funny, Dan," she snorted.

"Why not?" Dan asked.

Milly let out a bark-like laugh. "Because I don't want to prance around in a pretty pink dress sold for two hundred more dollars that it's worth, wearing their plastic crown with rhinestones embedded in it that they bought at the dollar store the morning before the dance, posing for nice yearbook pictures with a bunch of people I hate! Nice big fake smile, everyone!" she forced a huge smile that showed all her teeth for a pretend camera in front of her face.

"It might be fun," Dan shrugged.

"Fun!?" she said. "What could be fun about playing into their game? I hate it! I hate all of them, how fake they are, how they impose their standards on the rest of the world as if it's law. It's not! Their self-declared and self-imposed hierarchy is as necessary as a sweater on a dog! Don't you see?" she had stopped walking now, and stood in the middle of the hallway with her arms out, "Either you become a follower running after their footsteps and in the long run never touching more than their shadow, or you oppose their sick standards and become ousted, alienated, excluded from the circle! A loner, a black sheep in their perfect pink society! And you know what the worst part of it is?!" people had stopped on their way to class to listen and stare as Milly kept ranting passionately in the middle of the hall, her arms flailing for emphasis. "The worst part of this whole sick charade is the perverse mantra they beat into everyone's head: if you are not one of them, then *you are not good enough*!!! You must *spend your life* trying to live up to *their* expectations. *Their* fucking inane standards! The only way you'll succeed is by giving yourself over and kissing ass! I don't know about the rest of you, but I'm sick of having my steps directed by Dee Allderbay and her crowd! Everyone wants to say it but no one has the balls, so I will: *I hate Dee Allderbay!* There! You know you all think it! But you go on playing their game, acting like they're a notch above you and somehow naturally bestowed with power you don't have. Well they're not! They're nothing more than pathetic teenagers with low self-esteem that they cover up with looks, superior attitudes, and inflated egos! The only difference between you and them is that they possess the gall and lack the shame to impose their way and convince you into their own belief system *that's been perturbed by their psychological issues!*" she shouted. "Well I don't want to beat them at their game; I *despise* their game!"

"Those are all great points," said Martin, blown over, "but I hear your name's already on the ballot."

"Are you shitting me?" said Milly.

"Nope. And you might be surprised to know that you're doing pretty well. As of lunch this afternoon it's your thirty-three to Dee's fifty-seven."

"I'll never catch up to her at this rate... good!" said Milly.

"But it'd be pretty cool if you won," said Martin, "'cause then you could prove that you *don't* have to be like them to prosper in society. Don't you think?"

"I – I guess – oh what does it matter, I don't even have a dress for that shit!"

What's happening?!? Dee thought wildly as she walked out of school that afternoon. No one looked at her, no one complimented her new haircut – she had gotten two inches trimmed off the bottom and none of her friends had a thing to say about it! This was absurd! Something wild had swept through the school, like a fever that plagued everyone. Except Dee. Only she remembered how things were supposed to be.

Milly Hallan. It was all she heard. Milly this, Milly that, did you see what Milly wore, did you hear what Milly did this weekend, did Milly let you look through her sketchbook yet? *What is so freaking special about this girl?? So she acts slightly different from the norm, big deal. I could wear five watches, too, only I don't waste my time on stupid shit.*

Flipping her hair behind her so that it shone gloriously in the sun, Dee caught up quickly with Marrik in the parking lot after school. Here was someone who could comfort her after this awful day.

"Hey, studmuffin! I haven't seen you in forever," she said brightly as he turned around, guitar slung over his back.

"Yeah, I've been busy," said Marrik.

"Too busy for me?" Dee made puppy dog eyes at him.

"Nah, never," he grinned back.

"Awesome! A bunch of us are going over to my place for lunch. Your ass had better be there!" she insisted cheerily, while Marrik opened his trunk and carefully laid his guitar in its black case.

"I can't, I'm hangin' out with Milly... we're gonna listen to some bands she likes."

Dee froze, smile and all. "You're hanging out with Milly?"

"Yeah. But maybe I'll swing by later," he said, then got into his car and drove off.

He picked up Milly from the front of the school and then drove to his house to show her, as promised, his dad's legendary Bender Flat guitar.

"Don't you think you should wear a Hollister shirt, at least for one day?" he asked her as they stepped into his large, clean house.

"Why?" she asked.

"Because you could really get in trouble with the P.R.E.P," he said, leading the way downstairs to his basement, where the guitar was kept.

"Like I care," responded Milly in aloof tones as they descended.

"They could keep you from going to the Masquerade."

"I'm not going to the Masquerade anyway."

"Why not?"

"'Cause it's a stupid school dance, that's why."

"But what if you win Queen?"

"You don't get it, do you? I don't *care* about this stupid high school Masquerade! It's a joke to me! I just can't wait until high school is over so I can run away from this place."

"But where would you run?" Marrik asked. He opened the door to a room and showed Milly inside. She stepped through slowly, surveying everything in it before proceeding cautiously amid its dusty knick-knacks.

"Anywhere but this shit hole," she replied darkly, seeing an old guitar case in the very center.

"I meant for college," he corrected, picking up that case and opening it with the utmost of care, as though it had become brittle over the years.

Milly shrugged. "I dunno if that's for me. I just wanna find what I love to do, and do it, you know?"

He nodded. "I do know. What do you love to do?"

Milly threw back her head and looked at the ceiling in thought. "So many things! Drawing, writing, designing – "

"Music," Marrik intervened, handing her the guitar.

"Music is my life. All sixteen-and-a-half years of it," she said, holding the guitar as gently as if it were, well, a Bender Flat guitar.

"I don't mean to insinuate that you're a bitter person, but I don't think I've ever seen you happier before," he grinned at her. Milly looked up at him, her concentration broken by his stare.

"I'm such a dork," she said, blushing, looking away. Marrik chuckled.

"No, really, I am. I'm the biggest nerd you'll ever meet."

"I think that's cute," Marrik said.

"Really? Someone as cool as you?" she tried hard to remain indifferent as she looked up at him. There were his eyes, so close to hers.

"I'm not that cool," he said.

The guitar was slipping from her fingers, its unscathed, smooth body heading straight for the rough stone floor. Marrik's eye caught the nearly imperceptible movement and in a flash he bent over and caught it.

"Phew," he said, holding it in his arms and getting up to put it back in its case. Milly got up, too, shaking nervously.

"I – I really should go. Do you mind giving me a ride home?" she asked.

"Are you sure you can't stay longer?"

"Yeah – I have a lot of sh-shit to do."

"Okay." He led them back upstairs.

"By the way," he said as she got out of his car and walked to her doorstep, "maybe you'll reconsider the Masquerade, 'cause I'm voting for you...."

***

Text from: Delilah.

OMB Dee! You: 37%, Milly: 62%

***

No one had seen Dee Allderbay all morning, but no one noticed that they hadn't seen her either. Little did they foresee the commotion that took place the next afternoon inside the cafeteria. Many of the school did not even witness it; they had joined Milly in eating outside to protest the school's underrepresentation of triangular tables (Milly figuring it was about time for her to lead a movement).

Dee slammed her tray down onto her usual table.

"Dee! You look cute today," said a friend. "That shade of pink looks nice on you."

"Oh, is that all you think there is to me? Cute clothes and the color pink?" Dee demanded.

"What?" her friends did not understand the nature of this question.

"You don't realize that I'm something more, do you!" said Dee.

"Uh, you're *Dee Allderbay*. Can you *be* more?" they looked around at each other, wondering if Dee perhaps had amnesia.

Her tray tipped over; her chair pushed roughly out; all of a sudden:

"None of you understand what it's like!" Dee Allderbay yelled before the entire cafeteria. "There's so much pressure on me to win this competition that it makes me forget who *I* really am! It's like all I do every day is play a role that this stupid society supports! Well I can't stand it anymore! Nobody in my life, not my teachers, not my boyfriends, not any of my supposed friends, cares about who I am inside! All you care about is image! Look at yourselves," she looked at everyone at her table in turn. "Are you really the people you pretend to be? Or do you feel pressured to conform to the role society expects from you? Have you ever spent a day just being yourself, not caring what the world thinks?" Everyone in the cafeteria had stopped talking to listen to Dee Allderbay yell. "I can't live like this anymore! All my life is an act! Maybe *you* all are okay with pretending every day that what you show is what you really want and what you really are – but not me! I'm through and I'm dropping *out* of Queen of the Masquerade!"

She grabbed her bag and stormed out of the cafeteria. Silence remained in her wake for the next five minutes, hovering in the air, untouched, too bizarre to sink in. Then hushed whispers erupted. Dee Allderbay was dropping out of Queen of the Masquerade? Had they really been so blind to her inner entrapment this whole time until this breaking point of revolt?

***

The gymnasium had been transformed into a place of glamour for Friday night. Milly bounced anxiously in her new dress. At last the time came to announce Queen of the Masquerade.

"Good evening, Peamount High!" Principal Warshburton shouted from the podium. She was answered by an ear-splitting "WOOOOOO!!!"

"It's time to announce this year's Queen of the Masquerade," she said. Milly was ever more jittery.

"This has been the most extraordinary, eventful, and unpredictable race in the school's history, and the results are unfathomable! Gaining an astonishing *ninety-four* percent of the votes – "

Milly gasped. She couldn't believe it.

"DEE ALLDERBAY!"

"WOOO!" went the crowd again as Dee ran past Milly onto the podium, holding up her fuchsia gown.

"Me!?" Dee cried into the microphone, grinning from ear to ear. "But I pulled my name out!"

Principal Warshburton stepped in. "Dee, although you took your name off the ballot, when the class heard your story of personal struggle, they decided to pull together and show you that we *do* know there's more to you. Here at Peamount we prize genuineness in

362

our students, and we want to show our support of you, the *real* you, by giving you the honor of being our Queen."

Everyone clapped. Marrik smiled at Dee from the front where he waited to grind with her.

"I can't believe this!" she put on the crown and made a kissy face for her first faceplace photo as the music started again. "Thank you all so much, I love every one of you!" she blew out kisses to the crowd. Everyone rushed into the middle of the dance floor to resume the most memorable night of Dee's high school career. Or rather, Dee rushed into the middle, and everyone followed.

Chapter 23: Revolution

John half-expected to be bombarded by policemen as soon as he stepped out of the terminal. But the space ahead of him was empty save for the people walking to and fro with luggage. He sighed with relief and walked on, past the many flat screen televisions lining the walkway and playing a Kimi Kool commercial: Kimi Kool's golden hoop earrings swung with each of her steps as she made her way through a dingy urban scene where she fit in perfectly, walking to a hip beat with her friends: Keona, Kiki, Miri, and Morena.

"What do you wanna do, Kimi Kool?" asked Keona, checking how good her behind looked in a store window they passed.

"Let's go shopping so that we can get some awesome clothes for the club tonight!" said Kimi.

"I know where they're having the greatest sales!" shouted Miri, whose curly brown hair had some cute berets in it.

Kimi Kool threw her arms around Keona and Miri and laughed, exclaiming "Awesome! I can't wait to save some of my parents' money!"

They were accosted just then by some boys – five boys to be exact – most of whom were wearing either wife beaters or button-down shirts, but all of whom were wearing the latest high-top sneakers.

Kiki went over to Mike as Morena high-fived Tyrone. Kimi Kool seemed to find her match in Esteban, from whom she turned, blushing, as she batted her eyelashes.

"I can't wait to practice my new dance moves tonight," she said, and Esteban looked intrigued.

"I can't wait either," he said with a one-sided grin.

"How short a skirt do you think I should wear?" Kimi Kool asked Miri, who was busy talking to Shmuel.

"It doesn't matter, baby; I'll be spinning you so fast it'll just be flying," Esteban said romantically, taking Kimi Kool's hand and drawing her to him via spin. They started dancing to the beat.

"I can't wait to shake my groove thang!" said Keona as she and Tyrese started dancing as well.

"Kimi Kool and Friendz! ...."

John looked numbly past the uncomfortable stares as he walked across the thirtieth floor the next morning. He went straight to the break room, where he found the newest edition of *enlightenment magazine* open on the table:

by *Kyla S.*

I walk out of my car and head toward the secluded café. It is a vegan place. Arms casually in the pockets of his slacks, he greets me with that mysterious grin, sealing my first impression of Mr. Sajan Walker –

"Welcome back," said a hesitant voice. John looked up to see Erica standing in the doorway.

"Hey," he said, leaving the page.

"So... did you – ?"

"No. But that's the least of my worries. Listen – " he moved close to her and dropped his voice to a whisper, "I found out some stuff while I was abroad. There's going to be a solar flare storm soon, the biggest one in modern history, and it's going to hit right over Artinia. We've got to get out of here, I can make arrangements for us to stay at the Retreat and you can bring whomever you want – "

"You want us to leave the *country*?" she stepped back.

"Artinia is a death trap. It's all over the news – just not our news," he muttered. "People go crazy and lose control of their tokens. There's no telling what'll happen – it could be destruction on a mass scale."

"John, that's crazy!" she shook her head, immediately regretting her choice of words. "I can't just up and leave!"

Luke walked in, followed by Sajan.

"Ah! John!" said Sajan, surprised. "Welcome back. I hope you're, er, feeling better," he chose his words with sensitivity.

"'Pparently not," snickered Luke. "A *deadly solar flare storm*? What did you eat over there?"

John recalled that Luke had supranormal hearing. He'd never worried about it because normally Luke thought him too boring to pay attention to; but with his mental illness he must've become much more interesting. He hadn't taken that into account.

"Come on, Luke, maybe John sees what the rest of us miss. It could be a gift. If could be his special gift," Sajan looked at John, who stared back at him fixedly. "Well, let's not dawdle, I'm ready for some coffee," said Sajan.

"Ooh yeah, I can't wait to try that new nonfat infusion tea everyone's been talking about. It's supposed to be *loaded* with antioxidants," said Luke as they walked out.

"He's just messing with you," said Erica immediately. "Don't let him get into your head."

But her assurances did little to assuage John. It was only driven out of his mind by the events at home, where he tried to convince his family, as he had Erica, of the danger they faced:

"It's the foreign food's gotten to his head, that's how they brainwash them, Merle! How much chocolate did you eat over there?" his father yelled at him.

"None!"

"*Two weeks* with those hippies! I thought you were a sensible adult! If you want to go back and dance around pentagrams then *go*, but leave *us out* of it!" and he stormed out, slamming the front door behind him.

"Let him calm down," said Mrs. Hallan. "You remember what happened when Mr. Pudgy called the police accusing him of that water main break."

"He caused a power outage across four blocks," said John.

"Exactly. Now sit down and watch the rest of *Artinian Artist* with us, there's the most adorable little gay boy with a powerhouse voice."

***

A month into the new school year, Dee Allderbay, now a senior and president of the student body again, carried out her first executive act by sending a newsletter to the student body, outlining important changes for the school year. Milly received her copy of the letter in the mail that Friday:

Dear classmates,

I am confident that you remember the letter I sent out to the student body last year discussing the social framework of our school. Recall the unanimous decision to continue to entrench our definition of popularity in such stable trends as striped polos, reality T.V. shows set in semi-tropical beaches, and intimate one-month long relationships. For a long time the official image of popularity grounded in those and other trends has served our school well, enabling it to run smoothly and without confusion in regard to the question: 'what is the norm?'

However, even as you read this, we find ourselves in the midst of a great transition. It is an exciting time for our society as we shift into new standards. They will first sweep our nation, then – because the leaders of every other country are under our influence – they will sweep the world.

You may or may not have noticed, but over the past few years we have been moving away from idolizing the classic, pristine, most-popular-girl-or-guy image to idolizing a nerdy, anti-classic-popularity, underdog image. Virtually every movie of the past decade has reinforced that the most popular person in school is 'bad' and unlikeable, while the average, unsuccessful, quirky-slacker-underdog is 'good'. This character 'defeats' the popular guy and gains his followers, in effect becoming the new most popular guy. He is always portrayed as quirkily rather than classically good looking, kind of messy but still trendy. This is the essence of the transition of standards that is taking place. Though it isn't complete yet, very soon it will be.

I propose that, in order to help our country move forward and set an example for other schools, we just skip the time it will naturally take for this new image to fully become the standard and embrace it now. We know how this will end, so why not get right to it? I am confident that you see the logic behind my proposal, and thereby I present to you the new base for the normal, accepted, and well-liked student of Peamount High:

The most important quality of the new popular persona is that he/she is 'real'. In order to be real, you have to say 'um' and 'like' a lot; if someone asks you a question and you jump right into an answer without first saying 'um', you will sound like a textbook and therefore too smart to be 'real'. To get the best example of how real people talk, watch reality television. Notice their (if male) drugged or (if female) constipated sugar-coated tone of voice, their excessive pauses, their repetitive statements, and their occasional bursts of wit amid a norm of purposely uncultured vocabulary.

'Real' people know themselves very well and are confident about what they know; they start many of their sentences with 'I'. Some sentences which 'real' people like to use are:

- "I like to do whatever I've been told not to do."

- "This is me, this is who I am."

- "I am a really outgoing person."

*Note: the basic structure of this type of sentence is the 'I am; this can be followed up with any manner of adjectives, although usually they are positive. Favorite positive adjectives include: 'unique', 'spontaneous', 'down-to-earth', and 'passionate'.

Negative adjectives real people like to use include 'promiscuous', 'problemed', 'complicated', and 'alone'. Often, when a negative adjective is used, the structure of the sentence changes from 'I am' to 'I can be'. The end result is a sentence such as: 'I can be a bitch', or 'I can be really promiscuous' *grin*.

Sentences which real people cannot say include:

- "I really like to follow the rules."

- "I'm not outgoing or spontaneous."

*Note: the ultimate poison to a real person's image is to negate any self-statement that includes a positive adjective or to replace the positive adjective with an antonym. For example, take this basic statement a real person would say: 'I am unique'. Somebody who negates this statement by saying 'I am not unique' or 'I am a follower' cannot possibly be real.

Whenever 'real' people are in front of the camera, they make goofy faces and then smile to show that they have a dorky side to them and are just average, normal people like you and I. By pretending to make fools of themselves, they are proving that they're not full of it and that they don't take themselves too seriously. However, they don't contort their faces into something grotesque, like a double chin, so as not to look plain ugly. Usually their silly face is their tongue sticking out and their eyes crossed. Followed, of course, with a dazzling smile (so as to redeem themselves and, by means of subtle body language, remind everyone that they are, indeed, attractive).

Real people like:
- Obscure musicians
- Hollister
- The idea of having lots of boyfriends/girlfriends in their lifetime.

Real people dislike:
- Fake people
- Barkerbrombie
- Traditional institutions that inhibit self-expression, against which they rebel

To be real you must cultivate several important habits:
- Find yourself. You cannot find yourself by being a 'good boy/good girl'. You must desire to rebel at least several times during your adolescence and experiment with food in order to expand your mind.

- Defend freedom. Go up to that quiet good girl and tell her to let go of her inhibitions and just be free. In order to help her be free, take her clubbing, make her argue with her parents about how overprotective they are, and get her drunk for the first time at a party. You have now liberated her spirit. Go tell other people what a good person you are for doing so.

- Take lots of photos of yourself making kissy faces (if girl) or shirtless (if guy). Post them online. Pretend to be modest when people say that you're hot. Pretend like you didn't expect that to happen after you put up photos of your abs or cleavage. Better yet, pretend like you put up those photos as a joke.

But the *most* important thing you need in order to be real is to be **yourself**. Be free. Be who you really are without holding back. So guys, rebel against the pressure with which your stupid parents constrict your freedom of self-expression, change into your new faded-graphic-tee, mess up your hair, grab your guitar, and go join your buddies at the corner store for a bar where you can talk about doing something unique with your life, like becoming a solo artist. And girls, get up, put on your foundation, put on your eyeliner, put on your mascara, put on your lipgloss, put on your cover-up, mousse your hair, throw on that thong, throw on that printed low-cut tank, layer it with a paper-thin henley, throw on that frayed denim mini, and go out to the club with your ho's where you can make fun of those popular girls who think they're so cool with their exclusive parties, and then follow your heart and hook up with that offbeat cutie holding the guitar. Remember to tell other people to just chill and be themselves, too.

Let us take this weekend to prepare so that come Monday we may officially embrace our new identity.

Whether or not Dee was aware that she had written her own death sentence with this letter remained to be seen. After all, she was that very classic-popular-girl whom everyone was now supposed to hate. What was she to do? It seemed that finally, the queen would be dethroned, by her own unconscious doing.

But during lunch that Monday, something happened that didn't go unnoticed by a single lunch table. Milly and her friends were sitting at their table as per usual, when Dee Allderbay walked into the vicinity, alone. She looked pretty much the same, but didn't have time to put in her contacts this morning because she was so tired from working for Peamount High all weekend, so she wore her glasses. Also she was a brunette now. A silent murmur filled the air as heads turned. What was she doing here? Dee Allderbay never walked through this neck of the woods. I mean, cafeteria. Heads turned back to the table where Dee usually sat with her very popular posse (who was now very unpopular). Apparently, she had dissociated herself from such company, of which she had once been the leader and paradigm.

As everyone stared, Dee walked closer to Milly's table. She simultaneously looked around and slowed to almost a pause, apparently deciding where to sit as she no longer cared about sitting with the popular people. She stood in the crossfire between Milly's table and the table to their left, who were looking at her in anticipation. Footing careful to the extreme to not act too soon, Dee's eyes scanned over Milly's table and then imperceptibly moved to its neighbor; her feet subtly followed as if she had planned this course all along rather than deciding in the moment. She took the place between Alex and Jen that had magically appeared.

A tsunami of awe rose up in their air: Dee Allderbay was sitting at their table!!! Their status had just been raised by, like, twenty points!

From that moment forth, confusion abounded. "Orange will be the new pink!" girls were saying. "So violet will be the new green!" they concluded in a panic.

Boys no longer knew if they should show up to school in a nice car or a crappy car. "If I steal my parents' sweet car, I'll be rebellious; but if I come to school in my parents' sweet car I'll be a privileged douchebag!"

Many opted to take the bus. Bus stops saw seniors standing around trying to look cool in their attempt to find the right way to go about the new changes.

Nobody knew what was mainstream anymore. They were supposed to be indie, but indie was the new mainstream, so did that make mainstream the new indie? It seemed anything went, for it was all passed off as conforming to the new norms, which required some degree of nonconformity to *any* norms.

The only person who found herself completely relaxed in this turmoil was Milly, who no longer had to stress about not having enough Hollister shirts.

"Um, excuse me, but you're not wearing Hollister," the P.R.E.P stopped her in the halls one day.

"I know. I'm rebelling," Milly said, and went merrily on her way.

If she wore a Hollister shirt, she was cool because according to the letter, real people liked Hollister and she needed to aspire to be real. But if she didn't wear Hollister, she was cool, too, because she was rebelling against a social institution that inhibited her freedom to express herself. So every day she wore whatever she wanted without a backthought. In fact, Milly found to her surprise that *everything* she did naturally fit into a frame of the new coolness. While her peers ran around in chaos, Milly strolled calmly through the tempest, never more at ease in life.

***

"Maybe it *was* just a joke. Maybe Sajan doesn't know anything, or doesn't care. You've made it through a whole week," said Erica the following Friday afternoon.

"Why didn't I throw him off the balcony when I had the chance?" John asked. He had been a wreck since the day he'd come back, unable to sit still for more than a minute.

"...Breaking News," said the report onscreen. "A riot ensued this morning when the Vandorn Police Force caught a group of masked men painting one the mysterious crosses. They dropped their cans of spray paint and ran as police approached. When they refused orders to stop the police opened fire. Five were killed and six more wounded, who now lie in the hospital and await questioning. 'This could be a sign of another terrorist attack,' spoke President Rutt, who has deployed every Vandorn police officer to conduct a city-wide search and given them permission to open fire...."

"And no one believes me that the world is going insane!" John yelled, temporarily distracted from his own problems.

A commotion of footsteps sounded outside. A trio of men in black suits, crew cuts, and sunglasses walked across the floor to scared stares from cubicled employees.

One spotted John as an assassin spots his target; he veered toward the break room and the other two turned and followed. John's stomach dropped and his throat went numb.

"John Hallan?" he said. "We're from the A.I.A. We need you to come with us. If you resist we will handcuff you."

John hesitantly stood up and let himself be seized roughly, catching a glimpse of Erica's blanched, horrified face before they marched him out the floor.

Like passing through an invisible gate, their car entered the dreary sea of oppressive gray buildings that spread endlessly out in all directions: it was the city within the city, the dense nucleus of constant rush and business, a place all avoided save for those who worked there; and *those* had become deadened to callousness to keep the impact at bay.

They parked in a dark underground garage and led John inside, taking him through granite hallways lined with obscurely closed doors. It was quiet, but it didn't feel empty, and John could sense activity behind them.

They stopped, opened one of the uniform doors, and pushed him into a metal chair in the middle of a small room with concrete gray walls. John saw several forms hidden in shadow against the wall and felt their eyes intensely on him.

"John Hallan," one of the agents who'd brought him began, "you've been taken into questioning for suspicious activity. We received a tip-off this morning that you provided false information on your Token Registration papers."

John looked from one agent to the other.

"Our informant is with us and he is prepared to speak," continued the agent.

From out of the shadows stepped forth Sajan Walker, casting his air of dark magic over the space as he came under visible light, his hair arranged attractively and the smirk in place on his handsome face. He and John locked eyes for a moment before Sajan turned somberly to the agents.

"Gentlemen," he began, "I have had my suspicions about John Hallan's nature for some time. I believe he is a threat to our country's, and the world's, safety."

Everyone looked at John, sitting in the chair in his button-down shirt and slacks, hands in his lap.

"Don't be deceived by the harmless image, there is more to him than meets the eye – or should I say, less."

The agents turned sharply to Sajan, looking confused.

"The reason John Hallan lied on his Token Registration," Sajan continued, "is that he does not possess a token." It was as if a lead ball fell through the roof. The agents turned to John and exclaimed, "*what?*" and "impossible!", staring at him as if he'd just transformed into a large bug. What John wouldn't give to have the ability to do just that.

"*My* source is with me," said Sajan, reaching back into the shadows and pulling out by the hand Helga, who rushed forward on short legs in a burgundy mink, her face so greedy with importance it left room for nothing else.

"A registered Identifier, she observed that John Hallan did not have a token when he was at our Vandorn penthouse one night," Sajan continued, handing over Helga's registration card. Meanwhile, Helga took the agent's hand and rubbed his palm with her thumb the same way she had to John.

"You can rearrange real-life places to look like the places you see in your dreams," she told him.

"So that's what it is!" muttered his partner.

"Well I'm not gonna do it at work," said the first.

"You cannot bury your token deep enough for me to miss; I can sense all," Helga said. "I have never seen anything like him before," she nodded to John. "I could find nothing on him."

"Mr. Hallan," the agent in charge turned to John, "do you deny that you have no identifiable token?"

John looked from face to face as they all stared back at him. He hung his head.

"... No."

"And you handed in Token Registration papers in August?"

"Yes."

"Lying on government papers is class A – lock him up," the agent ordered.

They handcuffed John and walked him down the hallway they'd come from. Back to the car they went, where a pair of forceful hands shoved John into the backseat; suddenly the pressure on his shoulders was gone. John turned around. The agent was zooming into the air, screaming as his arms and legs flailed pathetically.

"Get down!" screamed another agent as the flier reached the roof.

"Ahhhhhh!" his screams got fainter.

"What's going on?" shouted a third agent.

"He can't control himself," said the second.

"The solar flares," said John.

"What?" they turned to him.

"There's going to be a solar flare storm over Artinia soon. Apparently *very* soon," said John, watching the man like a balloon shrinking.

"What's the storm do?" one asked.

"Makes people go completely crazy," said John. He and the two agents looked at each other. Then all three burst out laughing.

"Oh, that's rich," said one of the agents, wiping tears from his eyes.

"Go on without me, I'll take care of this," he then said and abandoned their party to run back into the building.

People in the streets stopped to point and ogle at the man, whom John watched out the window. But his fate he never learned as they turned a corner and a building blocked him from sight.

By the time they threw him into his cell, the sky was ink blue beyond the barred window, and John's only thought was of how worried his mother must be. And Erica – his last memory of her face was a petrified mask.

Perhaps one of his five fellow inmates knew the policy on phone calls. Most of them were sprawled across the orange-red couches, watching T.V.

"...What an exciting episode, Candace," said Paul Fort as he recapped the latest episode of *Artinian Artist*. "Good to see some old favorites. Let's take a look:

'Put your hands together for last season's final four: Kyle Matthews, Cody Brown, Jamie Baker, and the winner... Ally Smith!!!'" Last year's final four walked onstage, waving, to maddening cheers from the audience.

"'They're here tonight to perform with our finalists. Give it up for *this* season's final four: Laniqua Stokes, Hachiri Yamamoto, Sky Blazer, and Rosalia Maria Sanchez Navarro!!!'" This year's final four walked on stage and joined their counterparts; then they all started singing.

"What're ya in here for?" one of the inmates from the couch, a large, beefy man in a wife beater lifting a weight with one arm as he watched the report, met John's eyes.

"Um... I lied on government papers," said John.

"Oh, shit, man!" he almost dropped the weight, staring at John in awe as though never seeing someone so bad-ass before.

"'...I just like chillin' with my guitar, ya know, doin' my own thing. I'm basically an average guy who at the same times doesn't like to follow the crowd, and that's where a lot of the inspiration for my music comes from'," Sky Blazer, sitting relaxed in a chair with khakis and an unbuttoned shirt, said during his interview.

"How can *this* be on the news?" John asked in disbelief as they took a break and went to a Kimi Kool commercial.

"...Neoliberal Kimi Kool! Comes with three mildly political t-shirts, seventeen bumper stickers for the Kimi Kool car, and 'Stop War!' poster!"

"Dude, it's *Artinian Artist!*" an inmate said. "It's our favorite show!"

"...Do you frequently blink? Are your eyes sometimes too watery, or too dry? Then you have Hyperblinking Eye Syndrome and you NEED this medication!"

The world has *really gone mad,* John thought, watching the commercial.

"Got that right," muttered an old man sitting in a distant corner, where he played internet checkers on one of the prison laptops.

"And we're back," said Paul Fort. "What a season of *Artist* it's been, make sure to tune into *Arist Now!* on the T.V. Directory channel for the full recap and the latest gossip, including rumors surrounding a romance between Sky Blazer and Rosalia Maria."

"Called it," muttered one of the inmates from the couch.

"Ooh! Not gonna go down too well with Hachiri," chuckled Candace Avery.

"Competition indeed," Paul smirked. "In other news, there have been reports of more gunfire between the Vandorn Police and the masked vandals. Police opened fire on a group of suspects and are tracking them as we speak. It has been reported that they are shooting at anyone showing suspicious behavior. The vandals, meanwhile, are armed and on the run. Citizens are urged to stay inside until the police put an end to the insanity."

"*What*!?" John jumped up with almost all the other inmates, who passed around looks of disbelief; only the inmate who had read John's thoughts didn't flinch.

"What's with him?" he asked the guy who was still holding the weight.

"He's deaf. Can't hear a thing, but he can read thoughts."

"So his world is the same as ours, but more honest?"

"Pretty much."

John couldn't believe what he was seeing on the news; from that standpoint he was safest in prison! He glanced out the window. *The solar storms*, he thought again, feeling an ominous weight sink in his chest and rest on his stomach. Something was at breaking point in the air, he could feel it.

"Shit's goin' down tonight," nodded the deaf inmate in agreement.

"...Received reports of several missing persons. We are unsure if they are connected with the vandal situation – "

"I think it's safe to assume they are," Paul chuckled.

"Oh – well – excuse me, Mr. Smart Anchor," Candace laughed sarcastically.

"Do they know how many are missing?" one of the inmates asked.

"They don't," Candace's head and torso leaned out of the television into their prison cell, each strand of her chemically damaged hair within reach of their fingers. They all jumped back and screamed.

"Holy shit!!"

Candace leaned back into the television, stark white and shocked. "Oh my – I don't – "

"What on earth was that!?" asked Paul Fort, looking at her like she was a freak.

"I've never done that – let's – let's move on."

The lights in the prison cell flickered on and off, as they did in the news studio.

"What was that?" Candace panicked.

"Ahh!" Paul Fort suddenly screamed, covering his ears.

"What is it, Paul!?"

"I heard a crash – it's somebody's jet on the other side of the city – crashed in a park," said Paul, holding his head with his face scrunched up in intense pain.

"Paul, I thought you could only *hear* things from far away?" said Candace.

"Yes but – this time I saw it, too," he said with a note of wonderment.

"Oh, Bob, this is – " Candace looked uncomfortably back at the camera.

"Yeah, I've never seen so many embarrassing glitches on the news, either," commented the deaf man from his corner.

"How did that man just read my thoughts from so far away?" asked Candace, affronted, giving the deaf man an angry look from the screen. "Wait," she seemed confused, "what is going – ?"

"Hang on, I'm picking up something else!" Paul Fort cut in. "Oh – oh my Bob! It's a bloody mess out there! The police and the vandals are in the midst of another gunfight! Bodies falling to the ground left and right – some of the vandals are escaping!" Then he opened his mouth and like a radio transmitted President Rutt's voice: "*Sergeant, I order you to round up every last one of them. Search the whole city. We must put an end to this evil.*'"

And then Paul Fort fainted.

"Go to commercial!" cried Candace as she dove to the floor to revive him.

Jake Crash came on from his neck to his waist, holding a shiny new laptop in front of his graphic t-shirt.

"...In between shows I can get online any time and check up on what my fans are saying on my blog, it's really cool," he elaborated as he flicked between faceplace and video editing programs using the touchpad.

John rapidly changed the channel to C-Span, where surely they would have more information on this massacre.

"...Hi! I'm Doctor Rosalie Beaumont and I'm here to tell you all about our amazing new product that's going to *change your life!*" said the thin blonde woman in a low-cut shirt, black miniskirt, and white lab coat. The magic weight-loss pill commercial explained for the fifth time the transformation your body would go through: "And not only does it remove all the fat from your waist, girls, but it widens your hips to give you that hourglass figure you've always wanted! It *builds bone mass!*"

John flipped to C-Span 2: "This shampoo is made from all-natural seaweed and minerals that won't damage your hair! Just look at our model, Bernette; see how her hair has that healthy shine but no grease! Bernette, it's been, what, three days since you washed your hair?" Bernette nodded.

"And no grease!" the narrator smiled at the audience.

He turned to C-Span 3: "*Look* at how clear her skin looks, you're not going to find this with any other product...."

"What is going on!?" John exclaimed; all seventy-two C-Span channels were playing the same five infomercials.

A terrible cacophony outside rocked their walls.

"What by Pat was that!?" yelled one inmate as they all rushed to the window. Smoke rose from a vehicle engulfed in flames far down the street. The fire hydrant it had crashed into spouted water as people gathered around to watch the burning and flooding.

It's starting, John thought with a feeling of almost heavy satisfaction as he watched the crowd of dozens dimly illuminated by street lamps, police sirens adding to the pile of noise several minutes later.

Suddenly all light, from the streetlamps and those in the prison, went out. Their world was plunged into darkness. The crowd's screams reached their window as if from a void.

"Don't worry, I've got it," said an inmate, and suddenly a pleasant blue light emanated from several spots down his back and arms.

By this lone source John saw that the city was pitch black for miles save for the light of the burning car and the two full moons, which lit the earth more brightly than ever before and, for the first time in a hundred years in these parts, were accompanied by a sprinkling of stars. It was this vision that John watched in awe as they stood with their noses pressed to the window.

Only the inmate who had first spoken to John wasn't with them; he sat in the cushioned hanging chair in the corner, muttering lowly as he scrutinized something in his hands.

Curious, John walked over to him. "What's up?" he asked as the man shook his head in frustration.

"My token won't work," he said. "See, if I cup my hands together I can see what other people are doing, mostly the ones I care 'bout," and he cupped his hands together to show John: a cloudy orb of white mist appeared nestled in his palms, rather like a fortune teller's glass one but with no defined surface. Vague images appeared momentarily in the haze, but none clear enough to discern.

"This way I can be with them all the time.... I just want to know that my little girl's okay," he said.

"Sorry, that's really unfortunate," said John, who wished he had that token right now, too. "I guess the solar flares make some people's *stop* working," he mused.

"Guess that's a good thing. I wouldn't wanna be around some people when theirs go berserk," said the inmate. "Like my cousin – he can make people bleed – cuts gashes without touching you if he wants."

"Let's hope his shuts down," said John.

The inmate laughed. "We're safe in here; these walls are like steel," he banged on them.

"Great," John said glumly, sitting down in the hanging chair beside his.

Something in the orb's white mass started to change; John leaned in closer, curious, and as he did some of the mist in the center cleared and faces appeared, blurry at first but becoming identifiable as the mist moved to the orb's edges and then disappeared altogether, leaving a clear image like a miniature movie.

"Who are these people?" asked the inmate in surprise, watching the tiny strangers in his hands; but they were no strangers to John: he was peering into his own kitchen, where two people sat in the dark, a single lit candle in the middle of the table.

"Those are my parents!" John exclaimed.

"You got the whole city, Stewart!" Mrs. Hallan yelled from inside the orb.

"It's not my Bobdamn fault! At least it didn't go the other way, or we'd all be blind by now!"

"Did you have to turn off the phones, too?" she snapped.

"I didn't mean to!" he huffed.

"For all we know he – he could've gotten into a freak accident!"

"Merle, if he was in a freak accident the police would've come around," he tried to calm her down.

"What police!? They're all running around the city looking for those – hooligans! Wasting their damn time on kids painting signs, this is ridiculous! He could be outside, too, he could get shot by one of those maniac cops!"

"Can you get anything on him?" Mr. Hallan said with forced calm.

"No. Not a single thing," Mrs. Hallan said in despair. "I have no clue where he is or if he's okay.... I can't even get a read on Milly upstairs!"

Mr. Hallan growled in annoyance and John knew what he was thinking: why couldn't it have been he who was shut down and Mrs. Hallan was who increased? It pained John to watch them and frustrated his core that he couldn't do a thing to let them know he was alright.

Suddenly a strangled cry pierced the scene in the orb, reaching them in the cell like a faint echo.

"Milly!" Mrs. Hallan yelled, jumping up.

Milly came ambling down the stairs, holding her face in her hands as she sobbed.

"Make it stop!" she cried while a circus of vibrant dark shapes whirled above her head.

"What's wrong!?"

"I don't know, I – ! Every horrible thing – !" but the rest was drowned out by sobs.

"Shhh," Mrs. Hallan said as she wrapped her in her arms while Milly continued to sob hysterically.

"Stewart, *do* something, turn the power back on!"

"I'm working on it!"

"Milly, calm down!" Mrs. Hallan ordered, leading her to the kitchen table.

"I – can't – !" Milly sobbed.

The scene faded out as the orb filled with mist, and then a new one quickly appeared. John saw Erica, struggling against arms that restrained her.

"Let me go! I have to go to the Directory!" she yelled, fighting.

"Erica, stop this madness, you're not going anywhere! It's dangerous outside!" yelled a woman standing off to the side, who resembled Erica physically and could only be her mother.

"I need to help John!" she continued, kicking and hitting a pair of arms that John soon saw belonged to an A.I.A agent.

"Ma'am, please talk some sense into her," he shouted over Erica's shrieks and fits.

"Erica, you can't help him!" her mother said.

"Yes I can! You don't understand! *Let me go!*"

"She's under government orders to remain in this house for the night," said the agent. "We have it on record that she is close to John Hallan, the man she's referring to. John Hallan is currently on the list of Artinia's Most Dangerous," he said. Erica's mother gasped.

"My daughter is dating a criminal!?"

"He's not a criminal!" screamed Erica. She punched her restrainer.

"Ow! Miss, if you don't calm down, I'll have to use force!" he said, getting a tighter grip on her; but not fast enough.

"Don't you hurt her!" yelled Erica's mother. But Erica had slipped out, spun around, and kicked the agent in the crotch. As he doubled over on the floor, moaning in pain, Erica ran out of her house.

"Erica!!" her mother yelled. The agent reached for his walkie talkie.

John jumped up. The orb disintegrated. He paced anxiously along the wall, staring out the window at the darkened city, which seemed to be getting louder, like someone had turned up the volume of its drone. He had to get out. He had to break out of this stupid prison and stop Erica. *How was her going to the Token Directory going to help him?* he wondered madly. He beat his fists fruitlessly against the brick wall.

"Tried that many times, man," his fellow inmate shook his head.

Never had he felt so helpless and incapable in all his life, to only watch the people he loved suffer for his sake and be unable to do a thing about it. He cursed his stupid token angrily, cursing himself for not trying harder to find it before – then he wouldn't be in this situation; he'd be at home, and Erica wouldn't be in danger for his sake. And maybe if he had a token he could make things explode, or walk through walls, or make windows disappear – *anything!* But his lack left him powerless in the world, a mere plaything able only to watch the destruction around him and do nothing to help.

Helicopters sounded overhead, flying from behind the prison toward the streets, illuminating patches with their searchlights. People were gathered outside; the fire was out but the hydrant was still pouring water and flooding the street.

"This shit's getting crazy; I ain't sitting here like a log. We gotta get out of here," said the man providing their light from their window to agreement from the others.

"If only you could use your token and blow up our wall," said another man to a third, the biggest inmate in their cell.

"Why can't he?" asked John, turning his head sharply to them.

"The guard's got him restrained; his token is to restrain people's tokens and he's got certain people with dangerous abilities under his lock," the man explained. "They hate 'sploders, takes a toll on the health to keep one down. But hey! I can still use mine!" he was suddenly possessed by an idea. "The power's out and that fan at the end of the vent tunnel should've stopped. I can climb through the vent and bust out through the wall!" Like a frog he hopped onto the wall and started climbing up, his hands and feet like tape on its surface.

"Almost there!" he said as he hung upside down from the ceiling, making his way toward the vent. Without notice he fell to the ground.

"Good thing this shag carpeting's here to cushion your fall," said the exploder inmate.

"Yeah, you wouldn't be saying that if you just fell! Damn it, it's stopped working!" said the climber angrily, trying to climb the wall again and failing like a fool. "There goes that!" He sat down on the couch.

"Wait! If your token stopped working, maybe the guard's did, too," John was struck with an idea.

"There woulda been an announcement, like 'security's been doubled' or some shit," he said shrewdly.

"No there wouldn't! They wouldn't say anything to make you think nothing's changed. Trust me!" said John. "Go ahead, try to make the wall explode!" he urged the big man.

"If I get caught..." he looked warily at him.

"We'll be gone by then. It's worth a try! Do you really want to stay here while the whole city's falling apart? What if they blow up this building or – or disappear it or *anything!*" said John. The full realization of the possibilities set off alarm bells in the others' heads.

"Alright, everyone, stand back!" commanded the light-shining man, dragging the deaf one with him as the other five stood against the back wall. The exploder stood ahead of them, concentrating for a minute while they waited anxiously; with a great groan he made an effort and blew a hole through their stone wall with a thundering blast. Rocks collapsed into rubble on the floor and a rough opening wide enough for any of them to fit through remained.

"Woohoo!" screamed the climber, jumping off the couch and running forth. The others followed behind him. John, last, glanced back, sure that the guards had heard the explosion. He clambered through the hole, jumped onto the grass, and ran with the others into the crowded streets.

Chapter 24: The Search Party Part 2

One fine day it happened; a boy he'd sent out returned to the old man.

"So, did you find any magic?" asked the old man, now older than ever. The younger man sighed deeply before replying.

"You started me on a journey that has carried me from one end of the world to the other. Through it I have accumulated a trove of material: I have money, knowledge, a wealth of memories and experiences. I have an understanding of how all things connect that is as clear as a spring pool. And I have peace of mind. After a lifetime of searching, I have every kind of treasure one could want... but none of it is magic."

"So you have not found any magic?" the old man asked again.

"No," the younger replied, hanging his head. "All I know is that from the day you told me about the magic land, my life has revolved around this magic I have never seen. Everything was lit up by the magic I *might* find in it... but always I found nothing but an empty shell. And now I feel that my life has been a waste for not finding the one thing I sought."

The old man burst out laughing.

"And that's not enough magic for you?" he asked. "Out of *absolutely nothing* I created your *entire world!*"

The young man looked up at him, stunned; but the old man continued to laugh.

"What did you think magic was made of? Gold?"

Chapter 25: The Apocalypse

John dared not look back. He was forming a plan to put as much distance between himself and the prison as possible as he ran onto the streets. He and his inmates split off immediately. He was alone.

All the noise was bringing disquiet to a city that had just settled down to slumber: instead, people gathered outside or stared from their apartment windows, the muted sounds of infomercials on every channel blaring behind them as they stood watching the police cars and fire truck gather around the still-flooding hydrant.

By now the streetlamps were flickering back on, and John watched them nervously; he'd be safer in the dark. He slowed to an ordinary but purposeful walk as he passed by the scene. One of the policemen there caught his eye and John's heart leapt in his throat. Surely the prison had notified the cops of an escape immediately and that was a glance of recognition that would lead to the dawn of realization shortly thereafter.

Paranoid, John ducked into the nearest corner store as casually as he could. It wasn't the best idea if the cop decided to venture inside for a low-fat fruit snack, like his kind often did, but it bought him the feeling of safety.

Inside it was empty save the clerk manning the checkout, who threw John a mere glance and turned his back to him again, staring up at the T.V. A blonde fitness trainer was explaining the benefits of a complicated workout machine.

John relaxed; he'd hide out here for a few minutes and then take the metro to the Token Directory. Surely he would beat Erica there, he was two stops away and she was on the other side of the city. A fresh stack of *The Currents* caught his eye. *What's short*, he thought as he picked one up and flipped past photos of celebrities and scientific breakthroughs. He stopped at *Tips For Life, The Current's* monthly self-help feature that delivered practical advice to its stressed urban readers for dealing with daily problems. Its most famous tips ranged from "using positive thinking to reframe any bad situation", to "organizing your life with lists". This month they offered a new approach:

Fuck It

Enough – you're not here to walk on eggshells. You're here to do what you want to do! So when you go to dinner with your friends but you can't sit next to that guy because his ex-girlfriend whom he's still awkwardly friends with will get upset because she was always kind of jealous of you but you can't sit next to the other guy because he kind of likes you and you don't want to give him the wrong impression so you have to artfully place every step perfectly – *Fuck it!* Sit where you want and let it blow up in their faces. You know they'll be shocked, you know they'll talk about it and analyze every move when you're not there, you *know* the dirty little underworld that thrives in your social group. Aren't you sick of all that bullshit by now after living for 20, 30, 40 years? Do you really want to wait until you're 60 when you inevitably realize how stupid all these worries are to finally live a peaceful life? Or do you just want to say 'Fuck It!' once and for all and enjoy your Bobdamn time!

Or how about this scenario: you're going on a date with someone you like but you don't know how they feel about you and you spend hours worrying over whether you're interesting enough, dreading meeting them, thinking nonstop of how awkward the night might get with those lapses in conversation that'll make them decide you're too boring, and maybe you two really *aren't* right for each other and you made it all up in your head, what's *wrong* with you why can't you have a normal relationship, and now you're in so deep you're standing before a whole hydra of complexes, insecurities, and fears. *Fuck* those thoughts! Don't *hear* them out; *take* them out!

You act nice to that person you hate; you consider other people's sensitivities; you bend around stupid rules like placing a band-aid around every hair so they won't feel a pinch. Scream it in their faces: 'THE WORLD DOES NOT CONFORM TO YOUR PARTICULARITIES! GROW ANOTHER BOBDAMN LAYER OF SKIN!'

All those stupid social nuances, all those little dilemmas that sap you dry, all the expectations around you you feel. Fuck it! Take a blow-torch to that social maze and make it a field!

No more morning breathing exercises to ready yourself for the day. No more spending hours trying to convince yourself that you're *not* upset, you're just a little annoyed, but actually it was a good experience to go through and it made you a better person.

Be prepared for other people trying to make you feel guilty when you remove the burdens they used as footrests and untie their selfish strings. They will say that you've become distant and closed off, that you're not yourself. The truth is, they can't stand that you've ignored their game. You know what you do then? You *Fuck It*. Because nobody who has your best interests truly at heart will drown you in a sea of eloquent trash.

Next month: *How to make people think you care about bullshit when really you don't.*

A sudden change in noise from the television distracted John from the magazine; the news had come back on.

"...An explosion by one of the convicts caused a breach in the downtown Vandorn Prison, resulting in the escape of six inmates. All of these men are currently at large. Sighting of any of them should be reported to Vandorn police *immediately*!..."

John got a shock to see his own face fill the screen, looking innocuously out at the primetime viewers. Heart hammering, he backed out of the store as quietly as he could. At the same time the clerk wheeled around, an expression of stupid shock on his face. But John had already rounded the corner.

He was on the lookout for every shadow, his mind sharpened by fear. But behind its pounding, a part of him couldn't help but notice that there was something strange about the city, as if an invisible poison was leaking out of the fissures of every crack in the road, from behind every cloud, out from the shadows of people watching from their windows.... Surely he wasn't alone in this perception.

He dodged into another narrow alleyway and knocked right into something hard. With a clang something fell to the ground; John saw a can roll out of sight.

"Shit!" exclaimed a voice. "*You* again?"

John looked up into a black-masked head atop a large, muscular body. It ripped off the mask.

"Akshansh!" exclaimed John with relief, recognizing the man in the dim light. "I've never been happier to see you!"

Three more masked men stepped out from the shadows, red bandanas around their necks. On the wall to his left John saw a giant cross exactly like one of the many that had cropped up around the city.

"*You* guys are behind this? The whole city thinks it's the symbol for some underground religious cult," he said.

Akshansh and his men looked confused. "It ain't no religious symbol. It's how we markin' our spots," Akshansh said.

"But you already know your spots," said John.

They hung their heads.

"We gotta leave our legacy. No tellin' how many of us's gon' be left after the police finish their killin' spree."

"So... you're marking your territory because the police are killing you... for marking your territory – ?"

Akshansh and his fellows stared back as if this was perfectly normal. John slowly backed away. They were inside of an infinite loop.

"Listen, can you take me to the metro station?" begged John. "I lied on government papers and now the police are after me, too. If they catch me – that's it."

To his surprise, Akshansh only chuckled darkly. "That aint nothin' to worry about. There's bigger things goin' on tonight," he said gravely; and his crew's expressions mirrored his fatal tone.

"I know, but after this – "

"You don't get it. There gonna *be* no 'after this'," Akshansh said, his eyes reflecting a sagely state. "This is it; the apocalypse is upon us," he kissed a Cross of Bob around his neck, and the other three did the same. "Can't ya feel it?"

John indeed felt the flares' strikes building momentum above them as they spoke, like gathering storm clouds about to release their rain; droplets were already falling. But the *end of the world*!?

Out of nowhere four new men materialized before them, blocking the way. Truly, only *one* of them had come out of literally nowhere; the other three were just crafty.

"We meet again," said Toki softly. "You always run into them before us," he said to John.

"Get away from him," Akshansh stepped between Toki and John. One of Toki's assailants restrained Akshansh with a clever grip.

"Marking your territory, I see?" Toki hissed. "Your little game has been getting all of us killed. We're here to settle the score... and when we do, you'll know once and for all who the true rulers of the Vandorn underground are."

"You fool... is that the only thing you can worry about tonight? Fine we'll settle the score, and you'll see who comes out lords of Vandorn's underworld," said Akshansh, preparing to fight.

"Not so fast," came a new voice down the alley. Everyone's heads turned. A man stepped out from the shadows, his red hair and freckles gleaming under the lamplight. Behind him were five other men; all had blue bandanas poking out of their pockets.

"Steven!" cried Toki and Akshansh together, both their voices mixtures of anger and alarm.

"Thought I'd told ya to scram," said Steven, twirling a gun around in a hand that led up to a muscular arm tattooed from wrist to shoulder as he and his gang walked forward.

"Thought I'd told you the same," growled Akshansh.

"The final battle for Lords of Vandorn, huh?"

"Yes, and I'm glad you could show up, makes our job easier," said Toki, looking at him with hatred.

Steven and his gang laughed. "It aint gonna go down like that, Tok." They advanced toward the others. "We're gonna settle this nonviolently," said Steven. His gang all threw their guns to the side.

"It's a trap!" yelled Toki.

"No. See? We're empty-handed," Steven and his men held up their empty hands. Reluctantly, Toki and Akshansh dropped their weapons.

"Sike!" yelled Steven and at once all of Steven's men's guns flew into the air and back to their owners; but before reaching their hands they curved in the air and shot toward something ninety degrees to their right, right past John's face, crashing into something metal with resounding clangs.

"Good work, Magnetic Magpie!" said a noble voice. Their heads spun the other way; a woman was holding a huge metal sheet with the guns bound firmly to it. The magnet turned out to be in place of a hand. Next to her stood a tall man in a mask and cape.

"And for good measure," he nodded to the woman, who swiftly attracted the guns and knives Toki and Akshansh's gangs had started scrambling for, sending them flying past John's face onto the metal sheet, where they, too, stuck, and then every piece of jagged debris littering the alleyway that the men frantically grabbed at to gain advantage in their fight, to feel rusty cans and bent poles slip through their fingers as they flew to the sheet, piling up – clack! clack! clack! – one on top of another, filling every square inch of space.

"There's no more room, Extraspecial Man!" cried Magnetic Magpie, looking at her full sheet frantically while the last metal bits zoomed toward her, finding their way into cracks.

"Let some of it go!" commanded her partner-in-saving.

"It won't let me," she sounded unpleasantly surprised by this news as Extraspecial Man tried to wrench away a rusty wrench that refused to budge.

"That is some magnetic field," he mumbled loudly. "It looks like this magnet is accepting no more applicants!"

All three gang leaders saw it at once, lying in the middle of the alleyway.

"The can! THE CAN!" cried Toki in a strangled voice as he and his men, Akshansh and *his* men, and Steven and his men all lunged at the only object left, the empty can of spray paint that had fallen out of Akshansh's hand when John had knocked into him. Their bodies crashed into each other at once and a terrific BOOM! rent the air as the can exploded upon contact, the heat searing John's face.

Where more than a dozen gang members stood a moment before remained hissing space. They were wiped out.

There was a moment of silence.

"It's his sign!" Magnetic Magpie gasped, holding her hand to her mouth.

Extraspecial Man and the other two with them gawked at the still-smoking spot on the ground.

"He must know we're onto him," said a younger boy fearfully.

"Come, there is no time to waste," said Extraspecial Man to his crew. "There is no need to thank us for our troubles, civilian," he turned to John.

"Who are you?" asked John, tearing his shocked eyes away to look at the four of them lined up before him, making out their facial features with difficulty by the lamplight shining behind them and by the costumes they all wore.

"Allow me to introduce myself," said the main one with grandeur, "I am Extraspecial Man, defender of the city against the forces of evil. And this is my crew – " he gestured to the others. "Magnetic Magpie – " the only girl, wrapped in what appeared to be forest green masking tape, and with glasses and a lackluster ponytail, nodded, wincing from the weight of an entire arsenal on her arm.

" – Squeak – " he gestured to the smallest boy, who looked nary above nineteen and was also in glasses, and who on cue opened his mouth to let out a few soap bubbles.

" – and Great Guy, with the extraordinary power to have impeccably neat handwriting whatever the situation. Unlined, tissue, sandpaper, you name it – he never fails." Great Guy smiled boastfully.

"So you guys are just... ordinary people running around in costumes?" John couldn't figure it.

"We have been blessed with superpowers and have devoted our lives to upholding the side of good in the world's endless war," said Extraspecial Man.

"But I thought the world was ending tonight."

"Not if we can help it," he said gravely. "But we're running out of time, he's moving as we speak."

"Who?"

"Explodio. A mad scientist bent on destroying the planet. Once an explosives expert for the A.I.A., he has turned to the side of evil and stays locked up in his lab, plotting the detonation of the human race. He has built an instrument that will magnify his explosive powers ten thousand times. If it works, the shockwaves will tear the planet in two. It needs be activated only by the light of both full moons, and tonight, as we know, is such a rare night. He plans to stand by the harbor in full view of the moons and launch the device in – " he looked at the watch on his wrist " – less than an hour."

"Won't he die, too?" asked John.

"Explodio is insane. We must stop him. He thinks he's thrown us off the track, but we've found out the location of his secret lair: in the underground of the Token Directory."

"So you're going to the Token Directory now?"

"Yes."

"Can I come with you? I've been trying to get there all night."

The foursome looked from one to the other.

"Very well, come along. But hurry! We're losing time!" said Extraspecial Man, and John joined the four of them in running out of the alleyway down the street. The bright lights threw the masked troupe into sharp relief, and John saw that Extraspecial Man, who was wearing a bright yellow onesie with a royal blue felt belt around his waist, looked to be in his forties; so said the straight brown hair poking at his forehead from a receding hairline.

"How are we getting to the Token Directory?" John asked as they jogged.

"The metro!" Extraspecial Man said, leading the way down the surprisingly deserted streets, his fabric-store cape whipping about him as he rounded corners.

John fell behind alongside Great Guy. He glanced at him; something about his face seemed oddly familiar.

"Hey! Didn't you go to Vandorn University a couple years ago?" John suddenly remembered where he knew him from.

"Uh – a true hero never reveals his mortal identity!" Great Guy kept jogging, averting John's eyes. Memories of playing Frisbee on the field with a bunch of guys from his dorm he'd barely known freshman year flooded John's mind; but Great Guy seemed keen to avoid them. John had wondered from time to time what his old college mates were getting up to now that they were out in the real world.

"So what is this, like a role-playing club or something? Is this your weekly meeting night?" John asked. Great Guy remained resolute but burned bright pink. John felt bad; he hadn't meant to hurt his feelings. He quickly changed the subject.

"So what's Extraspecial Man's token – I mean, his 'superpower'?"

"He can fly," said Great Guy in awe.

"Stop!" came Extraspecial Man's command from the front. They all stopped.

"Explodio might be trailing us. Let me check if the coast is clear." He shot into the air and landed on a high rooftop, his silhouette illuminated by the greater moon. He looked left, right, all around. Then he flew down.

"We can proceed."

Their coast was unnervingly clear. During their run they met only one person, standing outside a convenience store, who shot them a long, queer look. John thought that in retrospect he'd have been better off running to the metro alone than with this band of crazy people dressed in flamboyant costumes, one of whom had an entire arsenal of weapons attached to her arm, none of which were any use as they were permanently stuck there. Magnetic Magpie winced under their weight as she ran, resembling an ungainly mutant by lamplight.

They were almost at the metro station. The soft pounding of their feet stood out loudly against the silence, disrupted only by occasional low rumbles of the ground beneath their feet, throwing them off balance as it shook; never *too* turbulently; only once did Magnetic Magpie go tumbling to the asphalt.

"What is that?" asked Squeak nervously when the time between quakes began lessening to seconds.

"Explodio setting off celebratory explosives in his underground lair, no doubt," said Extraspecial Man. "No need to fear, team, we're almost there. Quick, we must catch the train before it closes for the night," they sped up. The entrance to the metro station lay within sight fifty feet ahead.

The place was peopled with dozens, but it was eerily quiet as if the noise had been muted. John got the feeling that something was creeping up behind him. The ground rumbled beneath their feet again.

Then he halted. There ahead was a cop, standing twenty feet to the left of the station, his back to John.

"What is wrong, civilian?" asked Extraspecial Man in a booming voice.

"Nothing, nothing, you go on ahead! I've got it from here!" John hissed.

"We never leave behind a fellow. Are you afraid? Let us ask this upholder of the law for help," and he swaggered over to the officer.

"Don't worry, the cops play along every week," Great Guy muttered in John's ear.

The police officer was busy with his walkie talkie, which was transmitting something: "*Come in, come in officers. Mission accomplished. I repeat, mission has been accomplished. There is no more evil; we killed it.*"

All of a sudden in one grand swoop, night turned to daytime and the city came into clear focus. Everyone screamed, pointing up at the bright blue sky where the midday sun blazed overhead among scattered puffy white clouds. The superheroes froze on spot and began yelling.

"No! Sunlight! We mustn't be revealed!"

"Crime doesn't happen in the daytime!"

Covering their faces, they screamed and scattered in the chaotic mass of people turning every which way, not knowing what was going on. Apparently the shift from dark to light threw everyone's destinations into question and potentially changed them to the opposite direction for a second.

John stood rooted to the spot as people knocked into him running past, terrified and screaming about the end of the world and how they'd known all along this day would come, why had they been so amoral recently and please, Bob, remember the time in my life before casual sex and recreational food consumption.

He dodged through outlets among bodies. He turned – and locked eyes with the officer. Recognition overcame the officer's face as shock paralyzed John's. Abandoning caution, John dashed for the metro. *For my assumption that in the midst of the apocalypse cops would put the catching of a convict in the backseat, I was wrong*, John thought as the cop chased after him, knocking people roughly aside. John was about to beat him to the escalator – when he crashed into an invisible barrier.

John tried moving forward. He could not. Something completely unseen and untouchable blocked him. Other people knocked into it, too, banging fruitlessly against whatever this nothingness was. They tried everything: blasting it, throwing flame onto it, imagining it away, softening it, boring psychical holes in it – to no avail. It transcended the immaterial.

John looked up at the daytime sky and saw birds crash into an unseen ceiling. They were in a bubble, he realized with a jolt. And he stood at its edge. He spun around to see crowds confusedly milling about in the unobstructed space behind him where the Vandorn Institute of Art's campus began.

A mere two feet from John stood the cop, so close yet infinitely far, his face pressed against nothingness and his teeth bared in anger; he was trapped in a completely separate bubble. Unfortunately, the entrance to the metro John needed was in that bubble. John checked his watch: 11:43 PM. The metro closed at 12. If he could get into that bubble somehow in the next ten minutes, he could still make it. But how? A thought hit him: perhaps their bubbles weren't completely separate – perhaps there was a point where they intersected. If he could find a hole or rip of some sort, he could slip into the next bubble and be on his way... even if he would have to follow the metro tracks by foot. *And get there by early morning*, he finished glumly. *No. Stop that kind of thinking. What would* The Current *suggest? 'Any situation is just how you look at it! Make a list of the positive aspects and keep it in your pocket so that any time you're feeling down, you can pull it out and remind yourself of all you have to be grateful for!'*

Abandoning his spot, John eased out of the thick crowd. He walked down a street lined with quaint thrift stores, the beginning of Vandorn's post-college town. Here was the habitation of twenty-somethings straight out of college trying to make it on their own in the biggest city in the world. Whether they were graduate students, struggling writers, struggling musicians, or – well there weren't many more options – they all had two things in common: they were poor, and their parents were rich.

People here were generally more approachable and agreeable, but currently this street was as chaotic as any other, with people up in arms over the sudden shift in celestial patterns and even laughing about it to be ironic. He tried to keep to the barrier while on his perimeter sweep, but it soon disappeared into a row of buildings and he had no choice but to part with it.

It's definitely been more than ten minutes, he thought. He checked his watch again: 11:43 PM. They were frozen in time.

John wandered deeper into the hipster parts of town, leaving behind the world he knew for a land where cafes were before him, cafes were behind him, and college students and graduates strolled the sunny sidewalks talking animatedly of the only thing anyone *could* talk of: the Orange Pro! The latest laptop from Orange, their favorite consumer electronics company, which had released its newest model last month. Unlike the Original Orange, which was a sunny, orange-yellow shade, the Orange Pro was more muted and subtle, like a rectangular pumpkin pie, perfect for fall semester, even for those who weren't returning to school.

Everyone had one. Except John. Even though it was good to be different from everyone else, it was not good to have a different laptop. That was ironic. But they loved irony.

A faint noise in the distance made him strain his ears – it was the sound of an acoustic guitar, getting clearer with each step until John saw sitting on the dirty pavement, leaning against a brick building, a form, his head bowed low like he was absorbed in his art.

"Jake Crash?" said John, recognizing the raw five o'clock shadow he'd barely seen since the summer. He'd completely forgotten about him.

"Hey, man," Jake Crash looked up at him. "You a fan?"

"Uh…" John faced a conundrum: he could tell Jake Crash that he didn't listen to much popular music and insult him for being a mainstream artist, or he could tell Jake Crash that he only listened to mainstream music and lose respect in his eyes at the cost of flattering him. Feeling he'd made enough enemies lately, he settled on the latter.

"Gotcha," Jake Crash nodded after half of his upper lip quaked in a small sneer.

"So, you… just hanging out?" John asked, looking around the cobbled street.

"These are my new digs, man," said Jake.

"This apartment building?"

"Naw, man, the world," he waved around. "Who needs shit like showers and television, I gave that up months ago. All you need is Life."

"Yeah, paying rent is overrated," John tried to stay in his good books.

"I been workin' on a new song, wanna hear?" asked Jake Crash, picking up his guitar.

"Sure."

"It's called 'Save Her: Reprise'."

He started strumming a chord.

> "Ooh, oh oh oooh, I wanna save her,
> Wanna save her from Pat's evil sway,
> Though I myself ingest twelve ounces of Crack every day.
> Ooh, oh, yeah I'm a hypocrite,

But that's okay 'cause everyone still thinks I'm the shit."

"That's it so far. What do you think?" he looked at John eagerly.

"Uh... needs some work, but it's not a bad start," John gave this non-answer as he started walking away, leaving Jake Crash sitting against the wall.

Media content sure has changed lately, he remarked to himself, walking on. People were passing him by on their bikes, enjoying the perfect weather. The sun overhead didn't move, nor did the clouds. No wind blew through.

Another strange difference he noticed was that tokens appeared to be null. Nowhere were people flying or emerging from solid walls, turning their skin bright purple or setting inflammable things on fire. He didn't know if they didn't want to, or if they couldn't – but either way, they didn't.

At last, many blocks down, John knocked into the barrier again. He frantically searched for a way out, but it proved fruitless and, dejected, he turned around and started walking back. *I'll never get out of here*, he thought hopelessly as he sat down on a bench he'd passed on his way there, wondering what kind of bubble Erica was stuck in. A man had been sitting on it earlier, reading a book. But the book now lay closed at his side in favor of a professional camera he was playing with.

"How far'd you get?" John asked him.

"Oh, I just finished. Couldn't put it down!" the man exclaimed happily, glancing up. "I totally recommend it if you have the time."

The book was over four hundred pages long. *That must've taken half a day!* John exclaimed to himself. But the hands on his watch had not budged a millimeter.

No one along their bustling street seemed troubled by events. Life soon returned to normal. Cafes reopened and started selling overpriced sandwiches again. All ties with the rest of the world had long been severed, but that didn't bother anyone. Day and day, bookstores and pubs were filled with lively chatter as everyone talked about the latest book they read, upcoming shows of their favorite bands, and how many miles they had last ridden on their bikes. John had no idea how much time had passed, or even if the concept of time made sense anymore. It could have been weeks – it could have been months – it could have been years! – all he knew was he had time to read every book he had ever wanted to read in his life.

John put down his thirtieth novel. He was tired of the same old stories. He needed coffee. It was a psychological thing; he'd read about it in a book he'd picked up from the "New and Quirky" section of that local bookstore. He walked into a pub where a television was blaring with some program:

"...Welcome to the Underground Knowledge Channel. Your source for secret knowledge known only to the initiated few that the government and other entities are trying to cover up from the public. We now broadcast nationally!... Brought to you by the Historic Network, which is sponsored by the Federal Media Agency. Go tell your friends."

Ugh. I don't even own one of those, John thought disdainfully, watching the television with a sneer since he couldn't enjoy it too much.

"Local brew?" the bartender asked.

"Uh, no, I need some coffee."

"This is a pub, son."

"I know, but I have this psychological thing...."

The bartender got him some coffee and John sat there, sipping it, people watching.

"Other than our confinement, this is a dream come true!" he heard one philosophy graduate student say to another at a nearby table.

"But aren't we *always* confined in some way? Before, it was the planet we couldn't escape. Confinement is just a question of scale, then, and our former freedom was an illusion."

"Well, they say nothing lasts forever, so in time our confinement will change."

"But since time doesn't exist, isn't *this* nothing? So by logical extension, it *will* last forever!"

"By Bob, you're right!"

"Fools," whispered a raspy voice to his right. John snapped around. A lady with eyes consuming one third of her face and a perfectly wedge-shaped nose that tapered to a point was sitting on the next stool over. "Talking of trifles when the Night of Destiny is upon us. Once all three Star Crystals are found existence will be obliterated from this planet forever."

"What are you talking about?" asked John.

400

"Don't you know the legend of the Star Crystals?"

He shook his head.

"Legend has it that long ago, an ancient magician from another planet harvested great cosmic power into an entity known as the Crystal Jewel. To keep the Crystal Jewel safe from theives, he divided it into three pieces, the Star Crystals, which he placed into mortals pure of heart who would never use its power for evil. But a dark sorceress has been hunting them, destroying countless innocent lives in the process. And she's already found two," she lowered her voice to a whisper and turned to John to stare him in the eyes. She had the biggest light glares he had ever seen. "Tonight she is destined to find the last Star Crystal. If she unites all three Star Crystals into the Crystal Jewel, she will wield the power of ultimate destruction."

"Can't anyone stop her?" John asked.

"It is rumored that a galactic warrior can also wield the Crystal Jewel. If it falls into *her* hands, the hands of Good, peace will be restored to the planet. But if it does not, we are doomed."

John walked out of the pub, wanting to get away from this freak as fast as possible. But as soon as he did he regretted it. This hag, who didn't even look like she belonged here in Hipsterville, was the only person he'd had a conversation with in he literally didn't know *how* long. All the other people were too wrapped up in their own spheres. Every café was a sea of lifted and lit Orange Pro monitors behind which the user sat in his virtual world, incapable of normal social interaction. Even their internet connection only spanned the two miles of their bubble. The past world was fast slipping into – well – the past, which was a strange notion for a place where time didn't exist! John lost himself in contemplating this paradox as he strolled along in his new skinny jeans he had bought on sale at the thrift shop two novels prior.

"Look at us, sitting at a café, commenting on this crisis of society," one twenty-something turned scrutiny onto himself outside of John's favorite café one moment, looking up and down the street in disdain.

"Typical. What else would twenty-somethings do in a crisis?" asked his friend.

"Provide commentary on the act of commentary in a crisis," answered the first.

"Our self-awareness has gone so far that we are aware of being self-aware," said his friend.

John had heard it all already. Every observation was repetitive. It was human interaction he craved, but an invisible wall separated him from the rest. *A bubble* inside *that mirrored the bubble* outside! John was in awe of himself.

He lost himself in the beginnings of a philosophical treatise regarding an overabundance of the mental stimulation humans sought resulting in a premature state of the very boredom they had tried to escape in the first place.

He would need someone famous to promote it. There was only one such person he really knew in Hipsterville, and he would have to do....

He saw Jake Crash standing outside a club, sort of in the midst of a crowd that was waiting to see a show.

"Hey, man!" Jake said brightly as John approached after throwing his empty iced cappuccino cup into the recycling bin. "You comin' to the show?"

"Who's playing?" asked John.

"Skitarra. They're so frickin' awesome."

"Oh, yeah, I've heard of them."

"Dude, you gotta meet 'em, they're so chill. Hey! Guys!"

"Jake, man, what's up, we're just gettin' ready to go on," said the one in a t-shirt about saving the planet, followed by his two bandmates as they approached them like it was no big deal.

"Who's opening for you?" asked Jake.

"Old Wave Crashes."

Jake nodded, "Sweet. They're one of my favorite new bands."

"Right on, man, they're so chill," said another one of the band members. "We played a charity event with them last spring, *and* taped a live recording of it!"

"Talk about helping two orphans with one donation!" said John.

"Right?" the rest agreed.

John didn't feel so alone in their world anymore, and less awkward just standing around now that he was just standing around with Jake Crash and his musician friends. They hung out with Skitarra and Old Wave Crashes for a while after the show.

"Hey, there're a couple other bands playing at a venue down the street," said someone from Skitarra. "We're huge fans of them, wanna check it out?"

"Sure," shrugged John and Jake Crash, and they all headed over.

So had John's life become; he went to show after show with Jake Crash and his friends, sometimes not Jake Crash, just his friends, as Jake Crash had an artistic or identity crisis and had to take a break from the world. Then they would hang out in the coffee shop and talk about the show for three cups. Then they would go to the next show.

John ran his hands down the front of his Devinah's Mother Eats Paste t-shirt out of need for something to do.

"Did you hear them at the end, that drum beat was sick!" Skitarra and Jake Crash were still talking about the last performance. "We played with them seven shows ago. I tell you, man, being up on stage with that in your ear, it's amazing."

"I thought it sounded kind of the same as the last band we saw," said John.

Everyone turned to him.

"Just saying," he shrugged.

"Dude, you're totally missing the nuances," said the lead singer of Skitarra.

"Yo, Jake, we're gonna go see this new band. It *just* formed. The drummer from Feverish Dream and the guitarist from Synonym Has No Synonym got together and formed Kohr. You comin'?" said Skitarra's drummer.

"Aw, yeah, dude. You comin', too, John?"

"Nah, I'll catch up with you guys in a couple shows. I think I might go read a book," he said with a bored sigh.

They parted ways. That little smidgen of boredom was starting to rear its ugly head more forcefully, and John decided to quench it by taking up a new language instead. He'd made decent headway into it when he was distracted by a nearby conversation between two show producers sitting at the next table over on the outdoor patio.

"What if we get old celebrities no one cares about anymore to live together and get wasted every night... three guaranteed seasons with top ratings!"

"No way. It's only going to last one season at most: any day half of those people are going to keel over and die at the rate they're going. We need another edge, something snappy, something we can poke fun at."

"There's those Flirtz dolls, you know, the ones that don't have noses – part of that 'everyone is equal' gimmick. We could make them real people. Picture this: four best friends enter high school, get broken apart by the bitchy popular girl, and discover the true meaning of friendship and their first loves at the ripe age of fourteen."

His partner was skeptical. "And what can we poke fun at there?"

The other thought a moment, then realized. "Nothing. Never mind. They're alright, they're doing everything perfectly."

John snapped out of conjugating the imperfect tense; had he heard right? Flirtz as real people, an acceptable concept? What was going on!? He felt like he'd been doused with cold water. Memories of a long-forgotten life came flooding back, along with the perfectly normal constricted sensation caused by wearing skinny jeans. He shook his head, feeling like he was waking up from a dream within a dream. *I have to get out of here*, he thought desperately. He dropped his book with disgust and changed back into his normal clothes, then he ran to the edge of the barrier where he'd first come from and threw himself desperately against the wall – but fell forward. He righted himself before hitting the ground. Surprised, he waved his hand through thin air again, and excitedly ran on, sprinting out of the intellectual lariat at last. The ground shook beneath his feet. He sprinted, feeling the tension in the air rise. He made it to the metro station and bolted down the escalator, checking his watch. It was still 11:43 PM; the trains should still be working.

One pulled up on schedule and he hopped inside, joining a dense crowd. After two stops he ran out and flew up the steps into the sunlight. The crowd was thick with professionals going about their day, rushing to nonexistent appointments, none confused but all lost.

A great rumble almost knocked him off balance, jolting many out of their dull stupor for a moment.

Suddenly the world flipped again. Daylight turned to night. Two large explosions happened nearby, their orange flames lighting pockets of darkness. Everyone screamed. John fought the crowds running back to the metro; only he was going the other way, his goal of reaching the Token Directory fresh in his mind.

Around him people flew high into the air, buildings crumbled, windows shattered, colors changed, lightning struck and rain fell, stones obtained the consistency of pudding, the air was all gone for a minute, causing the city to choke in silence until it gratefully returned. The ground shook almost permanently and harder. John dodged all the chaos, the light posts that came crashing to the ground, the tornadoes spinning along streets, the milliard of minute dangers that was wreaking havoc around them. Many people were just sitting on the ground, alone, holding their heads in their hands and moaning in anguish; others sobbed for no reason, others plain screamed, a few laughed maniacally. It was a perverse spectacle, the sacred hours of night exploding with action like an inverted parade.

John checked his watch: 4:37 AM. He saw the first signs of dawn in the far distance between several tall buildings. A few particles of dirty harbor water reached John's nose and filled him with encouragement as he made his mad dash under exploding streetlamps that rained glass over his head.

Out of his left corner he saw it: a giant purple shadow looming out from behind a building like a two-hundred foot long monster, creeping over the ground like an octopus over the ocean floor. Then he heard Bethesda's unearthly voice from far away cry, "Jo-ohn! I can feel you there! Where are you?"

He sprinted the other way, throwing his head back every now and then to check on the encroaching shadow. Many poor people were already hopelessly trapped in the fantasy world like flies in a net, dancing like puppets to classical music, strolling by lakes and rose gardens. The world moved as one toward John.

He cut through the city faster than ever. The shadow was gaining on him, ever growing – three hundred, three hundred fifty feet, consuming the city – nipping at his heels. He urged himself to run faster, but his physical strength was a well going dry. The edge of the shadow flirted with his heel – he made the fatal error of glancing back – and it just hooked the back of his sneaker as it went off the ground.

John was plunged into a magical world of scented flora and starlit romance, wearing a ruggedly unbuttoned ruffle-necked shirt that showcased his chest hair. His black pants were kept on by a thick leather belt and a heavy, golden Cross of Bob hung from a matching chain around his neck. Beautiful harp music was playing over the muted sounds of destruction and chaos outside their safe walls.

"John!" he saw Bethesda in the distance. Only her appearance remained unaltered by her fantasies. He glimpsed his reflection in one of the ponds and saw that his now dark, curly hair fell down his neck romantically.

"At last, we can be together forever!"

"No, Bethesda, I can't be with you, I – I have to leave," John pushed against the edges of the shadow, the metal cross clanking against his unbuttoned shirt-clasps.

"Oh, John, sweep me up in your arms so that we'll finally unite and remain embraced in bliss for all our days."

John resisted the force pulling him toward her. The more he did, the stronger it grew. *There* has *to be a weakness here*, he thought desperately. Invisible hands pulled him toward Bethesda's unfocused, glazed-over gaze. There was no fighting being dragged to the bottom of the sea! *Then I'll dive in headfirst*, he suddenly thought, and as if something in him snapped into place, John dropped the red rose in his hand with a swell of manly passion that made Bethesda gasp and charged forward like a bull.

"I love you, Bethesda, I always have," he grabbed her by the arms, putting his face inches from hers and looking straight into her eyes. "You're the one for me, you always have been and I just never had the guts to say it."

"Oh, John!" she threw her body onto his and kissed him full-on, holding her mouth on his for a long, passionate (to her) moment. Her world surged with light. They two were one bright orb sending its glowing rays out over everything.

Bethesda pulled back, her heart fulfilled. The surge dropped. Everything was perfect. *Now what?*

Her emotions retreated like entinels over the tightly woven threads of her dream whose dropped guard let the strands disintegrate like sugar in water. Everyone who'd been trapped was standing on clear ground again. The noise reared in John's ears like an ambulance coming from behind and he ran away from Bethesda, to the Token Directory. There it was, only slightly battered but still standing on the water's edge, which sparkled by the light of the full moons. He searched for Erica amid the dense crowds in the dark confusion.

And then he stopped in his tracks. There on the pier stood a crooked figure glowing metallic in the moonlight in his full-body suit as he played with an elaborate metal machine that had a pointed, ominous silhouette and was pointing up at the moons.

A familiar voice cut the night.

"Explodio!" cried Extraspecial Man, appearing on the far side with his crew. All four of them stood outlined against the night, Extraspecial Man's poorly-cut cape blowing in the wind. John was pleased to see that Magnetic Magpie had unburdened herself of the weapons.

Explodio looked up at him and let out an evil cackle. "You'll never stop me, Extraspecial Man!"

"*I* won't; but *we* will! Get him, Squeak!"

Squeak lunged forward, opening his mouth to let out a thick stream of soap bubbles that obscured Explodio's face and might've damaged his machine. The villain aimed with his eyes and blew up small craters in the ground at Squeak's feet, forcing the boy to run back for cover behind Extraspecial Man.

"Magnetic Magpie, go!"

Concentrating, the girl held out her magnet of a hand at Explodio's machine.

"It won't budge!" she cried.

"Ha!" Explodio cackled. "I've coated it with aluminum!"

He exploded the ground around the heroes again and they went tumbling like bowling pins.

Great Guy was the first to get up. He rushed over to him. "Time to *write you up!*" he menaced, clicking open a pen. He grabbed Explodio's arm, but the tip slipped off his skin.

"Agh!" yelled Great Guy, falling back. "My power, it's gone!" he lay on the ground, moaning.

"Man down!" cried Explodio triumphantly.

Extraspecial Man yelled, "You'll never get away with this, Explodio! We're going to save the world!"

"No you're not! *We* are!"

Everyone watching the spectacle's heads turned. The silhouettes of five teenage girls were outlined against the moonlight on the other side of the pier.

A different evil cackle pierced the air. There on the roof of the Token Directory sat a thin, corpse-like woman with long, blue hair, wearing a spidery black dress. Like a shadow she flitted to the ground and stood, illuminated, at the water's edge.

"Andruida!" cried the one named Serendipity. "Give up your evil plans or we'll be forced to stop you!"

Andruida laughed outrageously. "You!? You're but a fifteen-year-old girl!"

Serendipity took out a medallion, followed by the four girls behind her. "You leave us no choice!" she cried.

"What the – "

"Flower Loveheart Power!" all five said together. The world temporarily vanished to leave only the five girls enveloped in sparkles of varying colors, but it quickly returned.

"NO! It's the Rose Warrior!" screamed Andruida.

"That's right! I'm Rose Warrior, and these are my fellow Warriors!"

"Lily!"

"Violet!"

"Daisy!"

"Chrysanthemum!'"

"We are the defenders of good and truth, and we're here to stop you! Andruida, your hours of evil are numbered!"

Andruida laughed again."You're too late: I have all three Star Crystals, and tonight, when the Star of Wonders is directly overhead, I shall unite them and form the Crystal Jewel!! The most powerful entity in the world! And then the planet will be mine!!!! Ahahahahahaaaa!"

"What are you talking about, Andruida? You only have one Star Crystal!" said Rose Warrior, caught off her guard.

The corner of Andruida's mouth raised. "Ah, but that's where you're wrong, Rose Warrior!"

Andruida waved her hand and a burst of energy-power streamed across the air; a male figure appeared, limp, on the floor.

Rose Warrior gasped. "Andrew! NO!"

"Yes!!" Andruida waved her hand over his chest. He gave a grunt and a shining something burst out of it. It was the second Star Crystal.

"Nooooo!" Rose Warrior screamed, breaking free and running toward him, her long golden hair flying behind her and her great blue eyes sparkling with tears that streamed like diamonds across her cheeks. She fell on the unconscious boy, sobbing. "Oh, Andrew... Andrew...." The boy slowly turned his head and opened his eyes a tiny bit. His eyes met Rose Warrior's and they stared deeply, directly into them.

"Andrew, Andrew it's *me!*"

"Rose – Rose Warrior?" he whispered hoarsely. "Run, Rose Warrior... save yourself, it's too late for me...."

"No! I won't leave you, Andrew!"

"Serendipity..." he whispered weakly, his eyes closing, his head lolling to the side. He fell unconscious.

"*No!*"

Rose Warrior got up, shaking. *I must be strong,* she told herself.

"Your evil plan has failed, Andruida! You still only have two Star Crystals."

"That's what you think!" she snapped her fingers like a whip, and at once, Rose Warrior was bound by black rope.

"Mph! Ah!" the girl screamed as she struggled against the bonds.

"Rose Warrior!" the four Warriors shouted in unison.

"As you might remember, Rose Warrior, last season I obtained the Mystic Mirror, which gives me the power to absorb others' energy," Andruida continued, conjuring said Mystic Mirror, which she pointed at Rose Warrior. It sent a beam of black light into her chest and Rose Warrior wailed while the others watched in shock. Then it stopped and there stood plain, powerless Serendipity Slade, bound in black rope, head dropped.

"Serendipity!" they shouted.

Andruida walked up to her and reached into her chest with her bare arm – Serendipity screamed in agony – and pulled out the third Star Crystal.

"Oh my Bob! What an ironic twist of events!" Lily Warrior gasped.

"YOU MONSTER!!" shouted another of the girls, and she rushed forward at Andruida. The villainess blasted her back with dark energy, sending her skidding over concrete.

"Chrysanthemum Warrior!" they cried.

One by one Andruida directed the Mystic Mirror at each girl until they were all untransformed.

"Now the three Star Crystals are all mine!" she cackled while the girls lay weakened on the ground, watching in horror.

A shiny black van screeched to a halt on the street, making many of the bystanders scream and jump. A team of rocket scientists got out, three of them welding a heavy-looking object similar to Explodio's amplifying device.

"Hurry! Hurry!" one commanded.

"What's going on?" asked civilians.

"There's a meteor inside the planet's atmosphere and it's heading straight for Vandorn. Once it makes impact the city will vaporize instantaneously. The shock will generate tsunamis on the other side of the world. Every major city will be destroyed. Millions will die."

"What he's trying to say is, we're fucked," said the leader as he cut past him. He had that serious, life-worn look about him, like he had lived enough to be past the time where romance and competition took the forefront. He was wiser and readier to die, but he knew his fellows weren't; it was up to him to save millions of innocent lives that had everything to live for.

"Two minutes forty-five seconds," another crew member shouted from the front, where they were setting up their freeze-ray.

"If this doesn't work..." said the leader grimly.

"Rachel," said the young hero following in his footsteps, turning to the only girl on their team, "if we don't live through this, I just want you to know, I love you."

"Oh, Connor; I love you, too!" exclaimed Rachel. They kissed.

"Dammit! It's stuck! Connor, we need you!"

Connor dropped Rachel and rushed forward; Rachel stood watching him open mouthed, her lab coat billowing in the wind.

"Connor McFee, the world's fate is in your hands!"

"Call the president," said the leader somberly; "it's time to say our goodbyes."

"Twenty seconds!" screamed a rocket scientist.

The meteor was speeding forward. Explodio aimed his beam. Andruida drew the three Star Crystals together. Who would destroy the world?

John stood in front of the Token Directory, looking around. Erica was nowhere to be found.

A terrible noise above his head drowned out all other sound. John looked up into a blinding bright light as a strong gust of air blew back his hair. Something loud and whirring was in the sky right above him. It was the last thing he would see before the end of the world. He threw his head back; but fatigue overtook him like a soft club to the head, and he fainted.

Chapter 26: Parallel Universe Parody

All noise was gone. He was in a pure white space. He felt clean and alert, as if he had stepped out of a comfortably cool shower.

To his side was but a single man, tall, bald, in a suit, with a mean looking face and a rifle slung across his back.

"Welcome," he said to John.

"Who are you?"

"I am Bob."

"*The* Bob?"

"Yes."

John gawked disbelievingly.

"Where are we?" he asked.

"Nowhere. Or, if you prefer, everywhere.... You look disconcerted."

"Sorry, it's just... I pictured you looking differently. Like, a free-spirited woman, or a life-wise street rat. That's how you're depicted in movies," said John.

"I can take on any form," said Bob.

"Oh. So, what are we doing here?"

"You tell me."

John sputtered. *How was* he *supposed to know?*

"You're the one that found me in my usual abode," Bob read his mind. "You must have wanted something from me."

"I guess I came here to find out what my token is," it hit John, and he was suddenly filled with excitement like a swelling balloon.

"Why do you need to know what your token is?" asked Bob.

"Wh-what?" John faltered. "It's one's path in life, one's path to you!"

"Yet here you are with me, and you never knew what your token was. So why do you need to know now?"

John was baffled by this attitude.

"I guess I *could* tell you..." Bob mused. "But you'd probably be disappointed. So many of you people are."

"Trust me, I'd be happy with whatever I got. I'd even be happy with Milly's token."

"'*Even*'?" said Bob indignantly. "Milly's token is a remarkable gift! It allows her a means of direct communication with other people, a feat nigh impossible! Milly virtually alone does not have to suffer from secrecy and miscommunication."

"Well, sure, but having your innermost secrets constantly exposed to your peers can't be fun, especially for a sensitive high school girl," said John rationally.

"It is healthy to have one's ego periodically shattered. It keeps people from being wrapped up in their egos and what they think they are. It's a double gift. One that she'll someday be grateful for."

"I doubt it," said John skeptically.

"Trust me, she will," said Bob.

"Bob, I know Milly," John said.

"Better than I do?" Bob raised an eyebrow. John said nothing, but privately he thought, *yes*. Of course Bob could still hear him.

"Let's make a bet. If I'm right, I get to die a peaceful death. But if I'm wrong, then I have to live forever," John said, a sneaky smile creeping over one side of his face.

Bob smacked him across the head for his wiseass; it turned out that he was very solid.

"John, if you truly want to know what your token is you will have to give me a convincing enough reason to tell you," said Bob.

"Well it's obvious! I want to know my token so that I know how to be, what to *do* with my life! If I knew my token, I'd have direction, guidance, some sort of purpose."

"So you are waiting for your token to begin your real life?"

"Exactly!"

"You are misguided!" Bob crashed onto him. "Knowing your token will change *nothing*! You feel as if you are a gray blob and your token will give you color and bring you to life – it is not your lack of token but this very attitude which keeps you from living! You are waiting in vain, John! It will not be easier to do all you want to do, to be all you want to be, than it is right now. And really, the only thing you *can* be is – "

"*Yourself*, I know," John interjected. "But, Bob, I don't even know what that is! I mean, I see those quizzes in *Teengirl* magazine that go, 'Find out your deepest quality! Are you: a Leader? A Showman? A Perfectionist?' and they seem so stupid! Because I'm *not* 'real and down-to-earth, dishing out advice to my pals'; nor am I 'a one-girl party with incomparable zest for life'! I'm not anything! I can't say I'm 'realistic' or 'a dreamer' – one day I'm one, one day another, one day both at the same time and everything in between – but all those definitions fall off and in the center, underneath the swirling mass, what's left is... nothing. Emptiness."

"An emptiness you believe will be filled by your token."

"Yes!"

"*No!*" Bob pounded his fist. "John, John....You think that if I tell you what your token is, that will tell you who you are?"

"No...?"

"You said it yourself! You're not anything! You're not any *thing*! You are *not* your token! It doesn't define you. Don't you see what your mistake has been all along? *You've been searching for something that isn't missing!* The thing you seek is worthless to you. It will not fulfill you. Why do you chase it, then? Is it because you are afraid that what you see is all there is to you so you *hope* that you are something more? I think, deep down, you know that it is a meaningless chase, and your only fear is stopping. Because you do not want to admit that all you need is right here. It's a lie, John! Your whole 'search for yourself' is a way for you to keep up the excuse that 'if only you had this, you could do that' because if you *didn't* believe that you were waiting for something, then you would have no choice but to *act*, and you are afraid of that! You are missing nothing, John. You are whole and complete, only you don't want to see it!"

John was speechless. And he was blushing. Even when he was a little boy he hadn't feel like such a little boy.

"So there's nothing? No answer?" he asked.

"There's an answer, but it doesn't *matter*. You will still do the things you do, think what you think, react as you react."

"But I still want to resolve this conflict," John said.

"Must conflict be resolved? Your conflict is the biggest part of who you are. Why would you want to quench that?" asked Bob.

414

"Because it gives me no rest."

"But, John, that's life. You'll never have rest, until you die.... And even then you don't know," Bob added quickly.

John's eyes widened. "That's right! *You* know what happens after we die!" he exclaimed.

"Bobdammit."

"Can you tell me? Please? I don't care about my token anymore, I want to know this," said John.

"No! You'll find out eventually."

John sighed. "Fine. Can you at least tell me what my token is, then?"

"Alright, let's talk about your token."

John prepared himself.

"Your token is the ability to be free from your token," said Bob.

"That's it?" John said.

"Well... yes. I thought you said you'd be grateful no matter what."

"Yeah, but I meant I'd be grateful for the ability to leak slime out of my pores when frightened, or something like that. This – is essentially nothing. How is that going to help me in life?"

"What help do you need? You have proven tonight that you can handle yourself perfectly fine without a token."

"Yeah, I guess, but... it would've been cool to have some ability that I could explore and develop."

"Yes, but how many people can say they got to talk to Bob?"

"True," John conceded.

"And you're still here, so you could ask me some more questions...."

"Alright, then. How is one's token chosen? Is it chance, or is it predetermined?"

"It is neither," said Bob. "You choose it. At a level you cannot control, where choice and predetermination are one, it is your deepest desire."

"No way," John shook his head, thinking of Milly, whose energy went primarily to guarding her secrets from the rest of the world.

"Milly longs more than anything to share her reality. And she has her direct window to it," said Bob.

"But her greatest fear is that I'll steal her diary."

"Well, John, one side of the coin is never far from the other. Within each person is his own opposite, like the other side of the world that seems so foreign yet sits deep as a familiar memory one cannot feel because it is the perfect negative to one's picture. What fascinates one and terrifies one and what one doesn't understand yet embodies all at the same time. It is this mysterious force by which one chooses one's token, this force that shows us that towards and against are really the same direction. It is here we get to the essence of what a token *really* is."

"And what is that?" asked John.

"It is how you go around the world with your hand open and grab only your other hand. Throw out those images of golden stairs. The path of Bob leads you nowhere but *here*, to exactly where you are standing, but with the parallel universe parody you built in your mind dissolved. The path of Bob is to destroy yourself, your veils and your skewed mirrors and your baseless convictions which are the unnecessary causes of all your suffering. To destroy all that is extra to *you*."

"But then why did I choose to be free from my token?" John thought aloud. "Because... no matter what I pick, it wouldn't be what I *really* want. It would just be another game, and I don't want a game! No token could give me what I really want; what I want is nothing. I don't want one. I don't *need* one. It keeps you from seeing reality and I want to see the truth."

"Congratulations," Bob nodded approvingly. "You have conquered your token. You have attained bliss."

"Cool.... What do I do now?"

"You just... chill."

Bob and John sat there for what felt like a long time to John, not saying anything. John enjoyed a feeling of completeness and peace from a well-deserved rest after climbing what felt like a very long staircase.

"Come on, Bob, tell me some of the *big* secrets," John said from his conjured lounge chair, where he lay, one with himself. "What's the secret of life?"

Bob laughed next to him. "You really want to know?"

"No, no, Bob, I was just *pretending* to ask....Yes I want to know!"

"Very well. The big secret is: there are no secrets. There is nothing in this world – absolutely nothing – that is not the way you see it. The tree outside your house, the buildings in the city, the clouds in the sky – they don't lie to you! They are what they are. But your life is a constant search for 'something else' that you think is out there, that you are so *convinced* is out there because you cannot accept that *this is all there is*! You – all you people! – you see in others what you wish to see, not what they are – and what you wish is so often a misguided ideal that you *yourself* can't embody – and yet you expect someone *else* to exemplify that perfection! You judge, and judge, and judge! Trying forever to determine what is right, what is good, what is bad, just to make it easier to feel secure in your judgments! And then you search for this 'secret', this hidden treasure that you believe deep down holds the key to your paradise, to eternal bliss. You look for this 'golden key' in thrills, in places, in *other people* – and yet if you look inside yourself all you are is a mixed bag of random emotions and thoughts and a body dependent on food, sleep, comfort, attention, sex. You *yourself* don't contain this 'magical golden key' – so what makes you think someone else does when *all you people are the same*!?! Fueled by your expectations on a search for this magic mystic diamond that *isn't there!* There *are* no secrets, only ignorance! Is that enough *secrets* for you, John?"

"No, I have many more questions! For one, why is our world so crappy? Working all day every day at jobs we hate yet barely making enough to pay for a house, car, food, kids, saving up a little for three years to take off one week. What kind of life is that? And that's not even mentioning all the atrocities out there!"

"What do you want *me* to do?" asked Bob.

John was incredulous. "You're *Bob!* The Almighty! You can do whatever you want! You created this world! Can't you fix it?"

Bob laughed. And laughed. And laughed his head off. Literally, his head fell off; he quickly regrew a new one.

"Alright, John. The time has come, so listen closely: I'm about to give you an explanation to a most complex and labyrinthine mystery. Are you prepared to receive divine knowledge known only to the initiated few?"

John nodded eagerly, leaning forward to better hear the esoteric truths Bob was about to explain to him. Bob took a deep breath (for effect – Bob didn't need to breathe).

"BECAUSE *YOU* ARE SHITTY!!" he shouted. "Because you people are lazy! Because you people are stupid! Because no one on your planet *really* cares about making the world a better place; all you care about is feeding your egos! How can a world run by such creatures be anything other than what it is?"

"But what about all those movements everyone's involved in? Like the environmental one, that's really popular right now, thousands of people are in it!" said John.

"Lies, John, they're all lies deep down. They're only what they say they are on the surface, in their words; but behind it so few *really* care, or have so many dirty hidden motives that no one wants to admit are there; they seem so insignificant, even ludicrous, from the surface, but in reality they are the true determiners of outcomes. Nobody wants to admit that they are selfish, that they do all they do to satisfy their great hunger, their vanity. If you want the true test of a person, see how they react when they're asked to do not something they love, but something they detest and scorn or are embarrassed by. Then you'll see just how put-together they really are. Most likely you won't even get the chance to ask because they'll have run miles away before you even make the suggestion to them that they face some unpleasantness. The last thing one will do is step over oneself. Doing so shatters all organization one makes out of the world."

"Wouldn't people want to change if you showed them the truth?"

"I've tried, John, I've tried. There's no getting through to them. They can be surprisingly good at discerning others, but themselves – never! If you straight out tell them that they are selfish, lazy, liars none of whose manifestations are honest, they'll say that that is absurd. If you cite examples, they will get angry and retract their friendship. They're so afraid of confronting themselves that they almost don't feel this fear. Most will do anything to keep themselves from realizing what cockroaches they really are. You can only *show* them, sometimes. But when you do, they hate you. That's why so many of them hate me."

"I just don't understand; if that's true, then why do so many people devote themselves to making the world a better place?"

"Oh, John. No one wants to make the world a better place; they want *themselves* to make the world a better place. Often their preferred method to do this is to change others. One who wishes to 'fix' others is a danger to others. First and foremost people can make the world better by fixing themselves. But as it is, that is the *last* thing people want to do – it is the most difficult, the most unpleasant, what threatens to undo their certain view. So they continue to build their castles on foundations of sand. Continue to do surface-good atop dirty motives."

"There isn't *one* instance where someone can have even a partially pure and sincere motive? Not even that one tiny hope?" John asked.

"In the rare event that that does happen, still one may become so rigid and unwilling to adapt to the inevitable changes, may become so attached to the *form* his ideal takes, so convinced that his way is the right way and the only way, that he quickly goes off the track. It always takes effort to pause and consider instead of bulldozing carelessly ahead – this is just another form of laziness: mental laziness. What do you know about how much people love making effort?"

"Okay, okay. So no one really cares?"

"People care, but their care is like an electron that has been raised to an excited state – it lasts for a moment until they forget and get just as excited about their online shopping. Without an external stimulus to provide it the energy it needs to stay up the electron will fall back down to its ground state. Can you describe people's ground state?"

John shrugged.

"To forget. To succumb. To indulge. Above all, to feed. To feed one's ego the saccharine sweets it so craves. Let it hear its stories, let it smile at pleasant words, let it see only what it wants to see and feel its emotions, patch the little holes reality is constantly making in its rosy veil. For a moment one might feel something outside oneself, but soon the ego gets hungry and cries to be fed – you will feed it without even noticing, and what will be the food? None other than the initially noble aims you started out with, which have after three moments become corrupted and now serve only to prove to yourself the indubitable truth of your most important mantra: *I am better*. Every aim, every word, every thought, fantasy, and defense, is kept up for that belief, the belief of your self-importance. You *live* to prove to yourself that deepest-held belief. And yet the irony – no matter how many times you prove it, it is never enough. You must keep assuring yourself over and over; the ego is a demanding, expanding machine that burns its fuel faster the more you pour in – and the body lets it rule because the pain of a hungry ego no one can stand."

"But *why*? Why are we born with the tendency toward *this* side?" John asked.

"Because of the one great law that rules your planet: comfort is king," said Bob.

"Excuse me, but someone is dying. I must escort him to his new home. I will disguise myself as a cockroach. He will never recognize me. Would you like to watch?"

"Sure."

A middle-aged man walked alone along a path; in spite of all that had been his during his life, he was alone now, the way he had been born.

"Where am I going?" he thought-said. "Aha! I am dead. It stands logically that I must be going to a place of eternal bliss now."

He walked through a set of double doors and witnessed a large, large, seemingly endless room. People worked the lands, plowing fields; people went to business meetings in suits; people organized fraternities to include some and exclude others; excluded people became artists; lawyers had coffee; doctors smiled kindly at people who didn't manage to land as good jobs as they did; people talked constantly... on laptops and cellphones.

"Wait a minute... this doesn't look like paradise... this looks just like the world I left! What the Shugina is going on here?!" he demanded. "I expected eternal bliss!"

The voice of Bob spoke to him: "This *is* eternal bliss. Welcome to the afterlife; it's permanent!"

"Are you shitting me!? I devoted my life to making all the right choices so that I could spend eternity being the lazy asshole I've always wanted to be, *and you take that away from me!?*"

"Poor fool. There is no escape," said the voice of Bob as the man was absorbed into the afterlife world.

"So, John – any other questions?"

"Bob," he began slowly, "You know how the Boble talks about the constant battle between the Lauki and the Shugina in every situation? What *does* tip the scale? The nothing that determines everything? This is, like, the greatest mystery there is!"

Bob laughed. "What colors you see right then. If a butterfly passes you by at that moment. If a certain thought flashes across your mind."

"Is there such a thing as right and wrong?" John asked Bob.

"The only real divide is the one between your conscience and your ego. And see, here's the beauty of it: for every single person conscience is unique, and yet nothing binds two people together like their conscience. *That* is your 'good and evil', your 'right and wrong', your 'Bob and Pat'. And all it comes down to is your choice."

"Choice... but then... does our choice come from free will, or is it all preordained?"

"Oh no! We're not getting into that one!" he threw up his arms. "Don't fill your head with that crap. Just do what you truly feel you have to do, and you'll be okay no matter if it's a monkey behind your choice. And one more secret for you: it never gets easier to make the right choice. Just because you made it once, that doesn't guarantee you'll make it again. That's the one big mistake you people make – well, one of the many innumerable mistakes you people make – you do something once and you think you're past it. No! Again and again and again! It always takes effort to do the right thing, and as long as you're mortal, you'll always be caught in the middle; there's always a hook for everyone."

"That's hard, Bob."

"Oh, do forgive me, princess, I'm sure you'd be much better off with everyone around you powdering your precious feet and doing as *you* please! A lazy, weak, and utterly helpless tub of lard you'd be. You lot just need to be slapped sometimes, and realize that this struggle is the greatest gift you can be given, because it is the one thing that can propel you out of wasting your life in muck! And the tougher your struggle, the farther you'll get."

"But... some moments it's just so hard, and everything in you hates, well, everything in you! What then?"

"All you can really do then is live through it without doing damage to yourself and your life. That's one time when you *shouldn't* listen to that sadly misunderstood adage, 'follow your heart', because when you're angry and upset, your heart is full of enough crap to fertilize all of Artinia. You know what that phrase really means?"

"What? All I know is that girls *love* it."

"It means, do that one thing you're most afraid to do, the one that, when you ask yourself what the answer is, nine times out of ten it is the absurd one that makes you laugh or recoil and push it immediately away. It often seems like craziness, too rash, out of this world. But if you do not act on it you feel, whether dully or acutely, that you have stepped on your tail. It doesn't have to be anything big. It *can* be, but it can be a tiny thing as well. Therein is your conscience truly yours, and no one can tell you that it is wrong. I bet ninety percent of the people in your world would rather jump off a bridge than go admit their feelings to the person they like, or stick up to their friends, or jeopardize their standing in their social group to find out who their real friends are. The less you listen to that little thought that's so quiet and thin you aren't sure it's there, the more separate you become from yourself and the more alone, no matter how many drinking buddies you have."

"But I always think, how much longer?"

"How much longer? Until you don't *need* that struggle to keep you up where you belong. Until you can force *yourself* off your ass, out of your self-pity, and out of your little mental fantasies, you're going to be struggling every day, and you better love it. You don't even realize how much of the work gets done for you!"

"John, I believe it is time for you to go back to your world," said Bob. He conjured up a door. Knowing he couldn't refuse, John walked up to it.

"Bob, I have one more question," he said before he pushed it open. "Do you exist?"

"I don't exist; I *must* exist."

Chapter 27: The Snake Bites Its Tail

When John woke up, he was surprised to see thick, puffy clouds below him. His head was throbbing. Far out on the edge of the sea of clouds he saw the weak morning sun, just rising over a predominantly dusky sky.

His head was throbbing because he leaned it against a thick plastic window. He realized he was flying.

John shot up, looking around madly – and his eyes skipped past, then went back, and fell on Sajan Walker, standing on the opposite side calm as could be, his back against the window and a cup of tea in one hand. He took a sip, smiling as he saw John awake.

"Good morning!" he said jauntily.

John checked his watch. It was 5:45.

"What the – ? Where are we?"

"In a helicopter," answered Sajan in the simplistic voice of conversing with a small child. Gruff male laughter followed.

John spun around to see two army officers armed with automatics sitting in the front seats.

He got up and suddenly found a gun's barrel pointing at his face.

"Relax, Denber, let the boy stretch his legs," drawled Sajan, bobbing his teabag up and down.

The officer named Denber lowered his weapon, eyes still on John. John carefully walked to the large window by the door and looked down at the murky bay below, the Vandorn horizon so far away he couldn't make out individual buildings. It was a few moments before he realized it was getting farther.

"Where are we going?" he asked, confused.

"*You're* going to Shun Island," replied Sajan.

"The *detention center*!?" John looked up, shocked.

"John, John – did you forget? You're a wanted criminal."

A fist socked John sickeningly in the gut as he was awash with the reality of yesterday.

"What about the solar flares?" he remembered it like a distant dream.

"They're over. For the most part," Sajan qualified. "Some weak strikes are still to come, they forecast, but the worst is done with."

"But the city – is it destroyed? Are – are we the only survivors?"

Sajan and the officers laughed loudly together.

"The city's fine – well, not *fine*, several billion dollars worth of damage – but it held up," he said.

"What about the people? How many deaths?"

"Quite a few I daresay," Sajan said gravely. A rock fell into the pit of John's gut.

"Is Erica okay?" he asked quietly.

Sajan smiled, "Erica is safe and sound at home."

"And my family?"

"I don't know; I didn't check up on them."

John's anger bubbled under the unclear picture of the state of things his mind was trying to form.

"How did – ? The world was about to end – the meteor, Magnetic Magpie – what happened?" That was last thing he could remember, besides the crazy dream he'd just had.

Sajan burst out laughing again, nearly spilling his tea. "Those were all lunatics, John! Oh Bob, you didn't really believe the world was ending, did you?"

John's hazy memories were squashed embarrassingly back into an amorphous blob. He turned away and looked out the window. They were descending and he could see Shun Island not far ahead.

"Why am I being taken to Shun?"

"John, I already told you; you're the country's most dangerous criminal. Do you know what price there is on your head? *Was*, rather. While you were running around the city Rutt had the entire police force out looking for you. You're lucky it was so crowded last night, otherwise they would've found you much earlier."

"What do they want with me there?"

"*I* don't know," Sajan's eyes widened. "I'm curious as all Pat, though. You'll have to tell me about their sinister experiments next time we hang out. Assuming you get out, that is," he smirked. "Let's hope the powers that be smile upon you."

"I thought you didn't believe in all that," muttered John.

"Oh no I believe there is something greater than us, I just can't give it a name. 'Agnosticism', my new philosophy, it's on my blog, but that's neither here nor there."

Their helicopter made contact with solid ground.

"Ah! We're here!" said Sajan excitedly, setting down his cup. The officers each grabbed John under an arm and marched him forward.

"Sajan, this is insanity! It's not worth some petty rivalry!" John shouted, hardly believing it.

"Look, John, it's not my call. Perhaps they want to take a closer look at your anomaly," John heard the smirk in his voice.

"But I *have* a token! I know it now!"

Sajan ignored John's shouts and stepped onto Shun soil, satisfying a childhood curiosity. They had landed not on the island's edge, but somewhere in its labyrinthine interior. Mammoth concrete walls encased them on all sides.

"In Pat's Maze," said Denber.

"Excellent," replied Sajan.

"Sajan, you can't be serious," said John as the officers pushed him forward with their barrels in his back.

"Oh, I am. It was nice knowing you, John Hallan. You have truly been instrumental to my personal growth." He held out his arms for a hug.

"No? I won't beg for it," he turned around to board the copter when John didn't budge. The officers had already pulled the steps in.

"Wait up!" Sajan called angrily to them. "Or I'll have to report you for misconduct."

They closed the door.

"What do you think you're doing!?" he screeched. "Let me on!"

The rotor spun faster, the landing skids lost touch with the ground.

"Rutt's orders," Denber stuck his head out a window and smirked. Then he closed it. They heard faint laughter from inside as the helicopter took to the air, spraying them with wind. Sajan screamed in disbelief like a tortured prisoner as they watched it fly out of sight, its whirring getting fainter until it left them in silence.

He stopped, his chest heaving with heavy breathing, his hair in disarray. John stood a few feet behind him in silence. Sajan daren't meet his eyes.

"Those assholes are going to pay for their juvenile tricks," he said coldly, staring at the ground. He glanced at John and then quickly looked away. His cheeks burned red.

"Aren't there people here!" he asked demandingly, folding his arms and surveying their quiet surroundings, fighting to keep a quivering lower lip straight.

But they appeared completely alone. Only the impassable walls of concrete stretching ahead surrounded them on every side, shades darker than the bleak sky overhead.

"Looks like we'll have to venture to find out," said John as he started on the path branching left.

"How do you know it's this way?" Sajan caught up with him, a note of panic in his voice.

"I don't."

"Don't you want to figure it out?" he was incredulous.

"Well, if you lean against the wall and I stand on your shoulders I might be able to see over the wall and get a clearer view," John looked up thoughtfully.

"Are you crazy!? Didn't you hear? We're in Pat's Maze!" Sajan exclaimed. "The playpen of torture reserved for the most dangerous of the dangerous. The walls are really people who've been turned to slabs of stone, stupid people who tried their luck by touching one of them," Sajan looked fearfully at one.

John turned to him. "Are you serious," he said. "What's stupid is that rumor. They barely keep this place up anymore."

"That's what they *want* you to think."

John looked at the docile slabs of concrete.

"Fine, then you go right."

"Oh no, you're sticking with me," Sajan commanded. "I won't have a man's death on my conscience, even if he is a wanted criminal."

John ignored this comment as they walked ahead.

"Those idiots didn't even take us to the right spot," Sajan shook his head. "Your typical high-school jock, they all turn into losers when they grow up," he muttered.

John snorted.

"What?" said Sajan sharply.

"Nothing."

"No, *what*?"

"Talk of losers, who's the one who went out of his way to sack an inconsequential assistant and got himself stranded on Shun Island?"

"Inconsequential?" the corners of Sajan's mouth raised up. "Oh, if there is one thing I don't do, John Hallan, it is waste my time on inconsequential things. You were *quite* instrumental in your place."

"A straight shot to Daltuhn."

"Not Daltuhn – *you*. Daltuhn may be the big hand, but you were the finger that points to the spot where it strikes. Do you know how many people would kill for a pivotal position like yours?"

"Why do you care? You're *Sajan Walker*, you've got it all. Your life is that shiny golden wrapper everybody wants."

"I may have the wrapper, John Hallan, but I have none of the candy inside it," said Sajan. "And you, for whom mansions mean nothing, who ignores the affirmations of millions, have all the candy in the world."

John looked at him in surprise.

"For a long time I couldn't understand it," Sajan went on. "I thought you were just a loser who completely lacked ambition. But then the thought wormed its way into my mind that maybe *I'm* blind to something. At first I thought I was crazy, obviously. But it kept coming back to me, like an annoying little thorn scraping my side, and now I am beginning to see what you have that I do not."

"It's not that, Sajan; we're just different people. You value bright lights, comets in the sky – and take for granted the everpresent starlight, calling it darkness."

"We're not *so* different. In fact, I think we're more similar than either of us think. In a bizarre way, you and I are opposite halves of the same person, understanding nothing of each other yet striving for the pinnacle of the same mountain. And at the top we must cancel out until the one left becomes whole, knowing both sides of the world," a manic glint flashed across his eyes. "See, there is no 'right' or 'wrong' when it comes to who we are. Though we're looking at each other right now really you and I stand back to back, facing opposite sides of the world. And that makes us closer for each other than anyone else. I know that you, too, can sense what I am barely touching on," he spoke with electricity as he looked directly at John's eyes.

"...Do you want to *be* me?" John asked, taken aback. "Is this why you brought me over here, so you could dispose of me and step into my life?"

"I want to know what it is that is worth more than a collection of mansions, a crowd of admirers, a plethora of beautiful models at my call."

"Sajan, what about Helga?"

"What about her?"

"You love her!"

"Ha! What? *Love* her? She's a public embarrassment! Laughing at inappropriate times with that idiotic cackle – . How could I *love* someone so – she's a sweet girl, and she cares for me and listens to my stories, but... I couldn't *love* her."

"You don't choose that; it's whether you *let* yourself love her freely," said John.

"But how could I be with her? She doesn't belong in my world! What am I going to do, take her with me to parties when she wears that hideous cotton candy shade of pink with my arms barely around her waist? What are people going to say about me? A few steps down from a stream of models, don't you think?"

"*You* weren't always so suave," John snorted.

"It's not what you are, it's what you make of yourself that counts," said Sajan with a dilapidated grin.

"But you still are him, underneath all that affluence and learned grace. Only you squash him underfoot, pretending he's not you. If you want what's worth more than the treasures you spent your life acquiring that apparently do not satisfy you, you have to *be* that person you find so despicable, love him as you love the smooth, successful man you see in the mirror. Love who you are more than who you want to be."

Sajan laughed. "You're saying I have to love ugliness and awkwardness to be happy, is that it?"

"I'm saying a drop of poison corrupts a glass of wine."

Sajan eyed him with another lopsided expression. "You confuse me, John Hallan."

They continued walking along in silence, careful not to touch anything but the ground. John glanced at Sajan, who had mammoth stains beneath his armpits.

"I *knew* I should've stayed there and waited for those idiots to get back!" Sajan complained, picking a wedgie. "That's what I get for trying to be a good person."

John rolled his eyes, trying to strain his ears; he thought he heard a soft "shh".

"I think I hear the ocean," he said. "We just have to follow the sound."

They struggled to keep the soft, distant whisper from fading into silence as they walked. The sun was pounding ferociously down; though October, it was quite a hot day.

"Give it up, John Hallan! We've been wandering for hours," said Sajan tiredly.

"But it might be around the bend," said John.

Sajan ran ahead of him to see.

"There's nothing!" he called back when he got there. "There's nothing around the bend!"

"Then maybe that bend up there," John pointed far ahead again, catching up to him.

Sajan gave him a peeved look. "And then when we get there, the bend after that? Is that your whole plan? Walking around the bend forever?"

John didn't respond.

"Walk around the bend forever and you'll wind up right back where you started," Sajan said smartly.

John could head the water louder than ever. "The water's right here," he said, more to himself. He closed his eyes and was convinced he could take five paces forward and feel water wash up on his feet.

"Close your eyes," he told Sajan. Eyeing him suspiciously, Sajan closed his eyes for a brief second.

"I have to admit, that is a very convincing trick," he said. "Maybe that's how they lure people to touch the walls; they walk forward out

430

of desperation and... that's that. They probably have someone standing on the other side creating the illusion of the ocean."

John's eyes popped.

"Sajan!" he exclaimed. A memory came rushing forward, of the Shun Island worker he had seen while visiting the Token Directory, months ago. He had created mirages, such as an image of a pen that had looked indistinguishable from a real, solid object.

He looked around their surroundings ludicrously, realizing it. "*This maze* is an illusion! It's nothing but thin air!" he almost laughed. "We just have to walk forward."

"Are you insane? If you want to get swallowed up or mangled or whatever that's fine by me. Rest assured I won't lose sleep. But I'm staying right here," Sajan folded his arms.

"Fine. You'll see in a second," said John.

He turned around and walked through the empty space, finding himself staring at a lapping ocean, his feet in the sand. Smiling, he turned around.

"See? I told you. Walk through."

But there was no response.

"Sajan!" he barked through the image of the wall. Somewhat irritated at the silence, he made to walk back – but bumped into solid concrete.

"Sajan! I can't get back, but you can walk forward! They must have someone making it solid from my side so that one person can't relay the message to the others, like I'm trying to do to you now..." he realized it was fruitless. He gave up, resolving to go back for him once he returned to Vandorn.

He combed the shore until he came upon a quiet cove crowded with old, worn canoes, the relics of youthful adventures. John dug around for one that looked sturdy and whole, then for a paddle, managing to scrape decent models of both. Then he set out, rowing opposite the sunset. John was using strength he didn't have to keep going, as his body wished for nothing more than to pass out right there. Every few seconds his stomach grumbled piteously.

Soon the island was out of his sight and he was surrounded purely by the bay's murky waters, deep teal from the sky with a dancing overlay of glitter from the lowering sun. The sight filled him with peace, and despite the greater context of his situation, and his physical pain, he savored these silent, personal moments between only himself and the quiet world.

No thoughts came as he rowed. An hour later, he glimpsed the first buildings of the Vandorn skyline on the horizon and felt himself flooded with steely determination: his goal was within tangible reach. For another hour John rowed furiously until he finally docked, disembarking, climbing up the slimy pier and leaving the canoe to its fate. The city was empty and silent. Windows were broken, whole buildings abandoned, streets littered. This was normal for these parts, but here and there John saw parts of buildings crumbling like they'd taken a beating, lampposts bent or lying on the ground, fresh-looking craters in the roads.

He started walking.

***

Erica sat at her kitchen table, the evening news blaring monotonously in the background; tears leaked out of her eyes, averted from the sunset outside the window.

"...Eternal bliss! No more arguments! Never make effort again! It CAN happen! Sign up for LoveEquation.com today!" said the commercial.

Erica let out a sob. "I should've believed him, I could've helped him months ago and none of this would have happened! What if he's dead!?"

"He's not dead," her mother said, trying to talk her into comfort. "There, there," she patted her back as she cried. "Honey, no matter what, life goes on. It's only a boy. You're still so young!"

Erica threw her head down onto the table, sobbing quietly as her shoulders heaved. Her mother looked at her pityingly, not knowing what to say; she got up and ambled around to the stove top to make tea.

Erica lifted her head off of the table now, drying her eyes. Her sobs ceased and she sat there sniffling into a tissue.

"There you go," her mother said gently. "Honey, you'll be fine. I know it doesn't feel like it now, but trust me. Boys, they're like pieces of candy, and romance is nothing more than rummaging around in a bag and picking out one shiny wrapper after another. You lose one, and tomorrow you'll pull out another and be just as happy."

Erica looked up at her, staring.

"I know it's unpleasant to hear, but I think it's about time you came to terms with the reality of it, Erica," her mother said in a suddenly sterner voice. "You're an adult, and sooner or later you'll learn that relationships don't last forever."

"I already know that, mom," she said in a quiet voice. "I just hate feeling let down again."

"Well, I hate to say it but this time won't be the last time," her mother said. "Prepare for a long, hard road, my dear."

Erica's mouth dropped. "How can you be so harsh?"

Her mother chuckled into her disbelieving eyes. "Because I'm over two decades older than you."

"So, what, you're saying that I'm doomed to be alone for the rest of my life? That I can't go through everything with somebody else?"

"Erica, I know what you want. That pretty dream we all have when we're young. I was just like you when I was your age, looking for that something special that had to be out there somewhere; the diamond," she sighed. "But oh, honey – they're all just rhinestones!"

Erica's lip quivered at these words.

"I'm just trying to make you see that you haven't lost anything irreplaceable. What's so special about this boy? The way you talked about him he seemed just like an ordinary guy."

"He is just an ordinary guy," said Erica. "I just... wanted to get close to him."

"Honey, you'll get close with another," said her mother, putting her arm around her again. "The feeling is always the same." And then she added, rather wistfully, "That thrill..."

"But mom, when I'm with him... I don't feel like I'm by myself. Everything is a million times brighter. Everything becomes interesting – "

"Honey, you're chasing after moments," her mother smiled sadly. "If I wanted to count them I'd need the whole sky for all the moments I've had that led nowhere!"

"But life is *made* of moments! What else is there to go by?"

"Find someone who will give you a stable, secure life and let you pursue your own path. Someone who won't give your grandmother psychosis. It's a clinical approach, but it's the logical one."

"But I don't need a relationship for convenience's sake. I want connection, fulfillment. Isn't that obvious?" Erica asked incredulously.

"If you want fulfillment, find a hobby!"

"But nothing *gives* fulfillment if you don't have someone to share it with! I could travel the world but without someone to trade eyes, nothing would be new! And yet with the right person, your room becomes a universe of unknowns!"

"Erica, you need to come out of that dream world," her mother was shaking her head. "You underestimate reality. In a struggle pleasant memories do little to get you by."

"But it's not just memories, it's how you change. It's through another you see what you're otherwise blind to! Without this connection, life is flat; with it, whole new dimensions open up! The right kind of relationship expands you, it frees you from yourself and the bullshit you have built up in your head, your unquestioned notions of who you are and how life should be. Once you touch upon that you see the boundlessness there is and the limitations of all you do."

"Do you think you're the only person who has ever felt what you feel right now? You don't understand yet that people who once shared everything can stop understanding each other. People who at first were as convinced as you."

Erica shook her head. "But it was just so... pure," she said as more tears fell onto the table. Her mother looked at her sympathetically.

"Some things," she said softly, "no matter how pure or pretty they seem, just aren't meant to be, and nobody knows why."

Erica burst into sobs.

She cried for a long time. Outside the window the sun looked bloody as it cast long shadows over their battered world. After a while her heartache temporarily waned and her tears dried; she sat at her table slowly sobering, staring into her now cold mug.

"I know life goes on," she said wearily. "It's just trudging through these moments that's tough."

"Of course!" her mother's tone brightened. "You're a strong girl. There's no need to be down over a lousy boy."

"I know. I just thought – "

"Don't we all! I've met 'the one' a hundred times now!"

Erica chuckled very weakly. In the corner of her eye, the television caught her attention. Shock ran through her body as she focused in again to make sure she was really seeing what she thought she was: on the news was the very person she'd been thinking about, standing outside his house, wrapped in a blanket, with his family around him. As the camera zoomed in on his face, she saw that he looked cold, wet, and extremely weary, with his hair sopping all over his forehead and his eyes starting to close; he seemed to be explaining to the reporter just how he got that way.

Erica leapt from the table.

"I have to go, mom!" she cried.

"Erica – !" called her mom in surprise.

But Erica was already putting on her shoes and heading out the door.

Wanting some time to himself, John sat outside on his porch alone, looking down the quiet street of his neighborhood set against a cerulean sky. The reporters were gone at last and his family had gone inside, leaving him to his peace. Little golden lights in his house where his parents sat in the living room and Milly sat upstairs on her computer shone behind him; but he was looking into the lights of the streetlamps, illuminating patches in the dimness as they flickered on.

His mind was completely quiet. All he wanted was to stare at the outside world and think nothing.

To his left he saw a figure running along the sidewalk. As it got closer he realized it was Erica. She turned and ran up his walkway.

John automatically stood up.

"John! Oh, John!" she cried, flinging herself onto him and almost bowling him over, her words muffled by her head buried in his chest as she hugged him tightly. "You're alright!"

He hugged her back.

"I'm sorry," she started sobbing into his shirt.

"Sorry for what," he stroked her hair.

"I should've believed you about the storms, I shoud've – " her words were too muffled for him to make out any more. At last she looked up at him. "What happened to you?"

"It's a long story...."

They sat on his porch, watching twilight turn into night as John told her the whole tale.

"...It was so scary, I thought I'd never get out. I almost *became* one of them."

"But you were only a hipster... ironically... right?" asked Erica with concern.

"That's the thing – even *I* don't know if I was pretending or not!" said John.

"And you don't remember how you got off the pier either?" she asked.

"No, right as the world was about to end I blacked out," he was still in wonderment over it. "I had the weirdest dream – or I dunno what it was, I remember it perfectly – but I talked to Bob."

"So how is he?" Erica asked.

"Verbose," nodded John. "He told me my token.... It's to be free from my token," John held out an empty hand.

Erica's face came alight. "I knew you had one! I wanted to help you from the moment you told me you didn't know yours, but I believed you *did* have one!"

"Yeah, *how* were you going to help me?" John asked. Of all the details from the past two days, this was the one he had absolutely no clue about.

"I was going to give you my token. It's is to give my token away," Erica held out her own empty hand. "Some psychic told me when I was little."

The world seemed to pause with them as they stopped and stared at each other. From where they stood on the ledge where reality hangs forever suspended it all could have been a joke. And they sat there on John's porch, on the brink of laughter, just two tiny people on a tiny planet in an unimaginably vast universe.

Chapter 28: Status Quo

"Yeah... yeah... we've got them flying in next week, booked suites at the Paradise.... Five indie bands competing for musical dominion over a tropical island? This is as fresh as it can get," said John into the phone from where he sat on the sand, shades over his eyes, sipping on a strawberry daiquiri. A warm breeze blew through the palm trees and his hair.

"The president asked to be one of the judges for the finale."

Erica walked down along the sands, carrying a plate of sliced mango, wearing an easy t-shirt and a grass skirt that ruffled in the wind. She sat down cross-legged beside John and put the plate down between them, taking a slice, leaning back and sighing contentedly as she watched the waves roll in fifty feet ahead.

"... Absolutely we should give it to him," said John. Erica waved at the phone. "Erica says 'hi'," he told Mr. Daltuhn on the other line. "Yep... alright, then, we'll check in next week," he hung up.

A year had passed since the storm. Things were slowly returning to normal. The city was still being rebuilt, but they had made great progress; President Rutt had been killed in the storm and two new presidents had been promptly reelected, who found the Token Law unconstitutional and abolished it; in its stead, airline security had been tightened tenfold.

Other than that, not much had changed. Sajan had been collected from Shun Island and returned to Vandorn to release Back-to-School, College Grad, and World Peace Kimi Kool in the fall. Milly had started her last year of high school (w00t seniors!). And as for John, he couldn't complain. He and Erica had left the country months ago to pioneer the Lainii project Mr. Daltuhn had restarted with the network's surplus. There they'd lived for the past four months, watching the stars over the ocean every night. He didn't plan on staying in Lainii forever – maybe just for the year... or until he encountered the next metaphorical signpost.

By the way, I titled this "Chapter 28" because sometimes, when reading a book, the reader will go straight to the epilogue, especially if the middle gets boring and drags on. This is because he is impatient for closure and the epilogue is usually short and easy to read. This is no exception.

This is not, however, "Chapter 28"; it is the "Epilogue".

About the Author

The author is dead now. She was killed in an assault by a mob of readers who were offended by the contents of her book. Rest assured that her death was slow, painful, and well-deserved – and incredibly gory, images they wouldn't CGI into the latest horror movies. She was fully repaid for the mean, insensitive things she wrote. That should satisfy your righteous desire for revenge. Yep. It's pointless to go after her. Like I said, she's dead. Since you are a good and forgiving person, I know you will let her rest in peace.

www.ingramcontent.com/pod-product-compliance
Lightning Source LLC
Chambersburg PA
CBHW031028030726
47497CB00004B/1055